Take My Husb...

"Take one tantalizing premise (could the de...
ticket out, and would or could she ever reall...
up?) along with Meister's smartly sparkling w......g, and you've got a
page-turner with heart—and much-needed laughs."
> —Caroline Leavitt, *New York Times* bestselling author
> of *With or Without You*

"Laugh-out-loud funny and deadly serious, dark and light, it's got wild
cliffhangers, twisty twists and an unexpected but highly satisfying ending.
Do yourself a favor: READ THIS BOOK!"
> —David Henry Sterry, bestselling author of *Master of Ceremonies:*
> *A True Story of Love, Murder, Roller Skates and Chippendales*

"The perfect novel for anyone who's ever been annoyed by the sound of
their husband chewing. Laurel is the leading lady we need today."
> —Leslie Lehr, bestselling author of *A Boob's Life*

The Rooftop Party

"A wickedly entertaining rom-com/murder mystery from start to finish.
It promises to be a contender for beach read of the year."   —*Bookreporter*

"A fast and fun read with an engaging heroine and supporting cast..."
> —*Library Journal*

Love Sold Separately

"A great romp of a read."
> —Candace Bushnell, *New York Times* bestselling author
> of *Sex and the City*

"With plenty of red herrings and plot twists, this quick, breezy read is the
perfect late summer escapism."   *New York Journal of Books*

"A smart, dishy romp that serves up murder, romance and pages of fun."
> —*The Augusta Chronicle*

"A clever cocktail of mystery and laugh-out-loud humor with the perfect
twist of romance. Great fun guaranteed."
> —Tami Hoag, *New York Times* bestselling author of *The Boy*

Also by Ellen Meister

Love Sold Separately
The Rooftop Party
Dorothy Parker Drank Here
Farewell, Dorothy Parker
The Other Life
The Smart One
Secret Confessions of the Applewood PTA

TAKE MY HUSBAND

ELLEN MEISTER

mira

ISBN-13: 978-0-7783-0987-1

Take My Husband

Copyright © 2022 by Ellen Meister

For questions and comments about the quality of this book, please contact us
at CustomerService@Harlequin.com.

Mira
22 Adelaide St. West, 41st Floor
Toronto, Ontario M5H 4E3, Canada
BookClubbish.com

Printed in U.S.A.

For my long-suffering husband,
who has been sleeping with one eye open since I started writing this book.

TAKE MY HUSBAND

"If love is the answer, could you rephrase the question?"

—Lily Tomlin

1

Laurel Applebaum heard a familiar ringtone as she shuffled toward the lockers at Trader Joe's, tired and spent after a full day on her feet. Was that her phone? Her first instinct was to rush, but she stopped herself. It was probably her husband, Doug, with one of his inane emergencies, like running out of chocolate-covered almonds. God forbid he should go ten minutes without a snack.

The phone rang again, but still Laurel didn't pick up her pace. She could have—there was always a little reserve left in the tank—but she decided to indulge in her end-of-the-day crankiness, even though she might pay for it later, when Doug started whining about his deprivations. For now, for this one moment she had to herself, it felt like a miniature vacation.

Sometimes, Laurel told herself she should get a job where she could sit all day, like her sister-in-law, who answered phones in a doctor's office. Then Laurel would look at her co-worker Charlie Webb, who was more than twenty years her senior and the fastest cashier they had. Always smiling, he was beloved by staff and customers, and Laurel thought of him as a cross between Kris Kringle and the philosophical deathbed guy from *Tuesdays With Morrie*. He made her laugh. And want to be better.

By the time Laurel opened her locker, the ringing had stopped and started up again. She pulled her purse from its hook and fished out her phone. Sure enough, DOUG was on the caller ID.

"Hi," she said wearily, hoping she conveyed enough pathos with the single syllable to elicit some sympathy.

"Laurel Applebaum?" said a woman's voice.

A chill swept through her. Something was wrong.

"Yes?"

"I'm so glad I finally reached you. I'm calling from Plainview Hospital. Are you Douglas Applebaum's next of kin?"

"That's my husband," she said, her scalp prickling, her whole body suddenly alert. An instinctive chill had her in its grip. "Is he okay? What's wrong?"

"He was brought in by ambulance after a motor vehicle accident. We're still assessing his condition, but he's unconscious. Right now the doctors—"

"I'm not far," Laurel said. "I'll be there in ten minutes. Less." She dropped her phone into her purse and grabbed her jacket. Dear god, was this really happening? And why did it take a near tragedy for her to remember how much she loved him?

I have to do better, she thought, a lump taking shape in her throat. *I have to.*

"Is everything okay?" asked Charlie Webb. He had been standing close by, which wasn't unusual. Sweet as he was, the old guy was just this side of stalkerish when it came to Laurel.

She chalked it up to a harmless crush. To Charlie, Laurel was still in the blush of youth. But she understood that his age filtered her through a softening gauze. To most men, she was all but invisible—a fifty-two-year-old woman who maintained only the last vestiges of attractiveness. It had been at least ten years and as many pounds since anyone told her she resembled Diane Lane. Granted, she didn't make the effort she used to, but she simply couldn't see the point.

She looked into Charlie's kind face. "I don't think so," she said, her eyes watering. "Doug's been in an accident. They wouldn't have called me unless…" She searched his expression, hoping she didn't have to finish the sentence.

He nodded and took her by the shoulders. "You're going to be okay," he said slowly, "no matter what. You are here and you're fine. You only have one job right now, and that's to drive carefully. You understand?"

The cadence of his speech slowed her rocketing heart, but she was suddenly so overcome by his concern she couldn't speak. So she gave him a quick hug, and dashed out.

Laurel slammed the door of her twelve-year-old Altima, considering Charlie's advice as she pulled her seat belt across her torso. *Drive Carefully*, she thought, turning the words into initials. It was something she often did to settle herself, playing a game where she tried to think of famous people to match the letters. DC=*Don Cheadle, Dana Carvey, Diahann Carroll.*

Calmer, she realized Charlie was right—she didn't need to tear out of the lot. Reaching the hospital two minutes faster was not going to make a difference. Because realistically, she thought as the bulge in her throat swelled and tightened, Doug was probably already dead. She could almost feel it in her bones. He was gone, the life snuffed from his body. That was why she had been summoned. The hospital probably had a policy against giving next of kin the news over the phone.

Once she got there, she would be pulled into a private room by a doctor and a social worker. They would tell her they did everything they could, and ask if there was anyone they could call for her. She thought about her mother, elderly and detached, who would be no help at all. Then, of course, there was Doug's sister, Abby, who was just the opposite. She would want to push in and take over.

Laurel bristled at the thought as her salty tears began to dry on her face, contracting the skin on her cheeks. Abby. God, she was annoying. The woman had an answer for everything. And usually, it was wrong. Maybe Laurel wouldn't call her right away.

But no, Abby could be helpful if she stayed in her damned lane. Laurel would just have to be strong, assertive. She would give Abby a list of people to call. That would make her feel useful and important. Keep her out of Laurel's hair.

And then, well, Laurel would have to make the most difficult call of all—to her son, Evan, who lived on the West Coast and was expecting his first child. He'd want to fly to Long Island for the funeral, but what about his wife, Samara? She was having a difficult pregnancy and might not be allowed to fly. Maybe Evan wouldn't even feel comfortable leaving her.

It was painful to consider, and Laurel shook her head. She was making this too complicated. Of course they would both come to the funeral.

The thought of seeing them lightened her heart. She'd been depressed about not being able to fly out there for the birth of their child. Money was just so tight, with Doug still out of work. And he had insisted it was foolish for them to get any further in the hole on their credit cards. But now...now she'd be free to buy a ticket without getting into a fight about it. At least there was that. She would finally get her wish of being there for the birth of her first grandchild, to hell with credit card debt.

And then Laurel had a thought that made her gasp. She hadn't remembered it until this moment. Doug had a huge life insurance policy—$850,000. So much money! It would solve everything. She'd be able to pay off all the credit cards. She could sell the house, and move to a cute little apartment, all by herself, and live off the savings. *My place,* she would call it. The decor would be soft and cool, in shades of aquamarine and sand. She imagined getting up in the morning without thinking about making Doug breakfast, setting out his vitamins and medication, picking up his damp towels from the bathroom floor, washing the dishes he left in the sink, swiping his crumbs off the counter. There were always so many damned crumbs. But now, she might even get a little dog. Doug was allergic so she had never been able to, and the thought of it filled her.

Laurel stretched in the seat, thinking how lovely it would be to quit the long shifts at Trader Joe's and give her aching back a rest. And with no job, she would be able to stay home with a new puppy to train it.

And then there was her mother, who desperately wanted Laurel to spend more time with her. This could be just what their relationship needed. Laurel imagined her mother being so grateful for the extra attention she might even summon the courage to take a break from her vintage doll collection and leave the house. Laurel warmed at the thought, the tension in her throat easing.

And of course, that would be nothing compared to holding her first grandchild. How she loved newborns! Their impossibly tiny noses, their kernel-sized toes, the smell of heat rising off their velvety little heads. She imagined a baby girl with Evan's silky dark hair.

By the time she parked at the hospital, Laurel was trying to work out whether it made sense to get a dog right away, or if she should wait until after the birth of the baby, so she wouldn't need to worry about finding someone to care for it while she was in California.

She stopped the thought in its tracks. This wasn't about her, it was about Doug, and she needed to be sadder. He was her husband. They had been married for nearly thirty years. Laurel tried to picture the early days of their courtship, recalling when they first met. She had just landed her first real job, working in the marketing department of a trade magazine publisher, when one of the women in her office offered to fix her up with a friend of her husband's. "A solid citizen," the woman had said, and Laurel took it to mean he was someone she could trust.

The phrase stuck with her all these years because it had defined Doug from their very first meeting. He was an honest and decent man who had gone into his father's business. Eight years older than Laurel, he had a boyish face, unruly hair that charmed her, and an irresistibly corny sense of humor. Even on that first date, she didn't mind that he was overweight. It made her feel safe to be with someone who wasn't all that attractive to other women. Here was a man who would always be faithful. And also, he thought he was the luckiest guy in the world to be dating someone so very pretty. She was even flattered by his jealousy. It made her feel like a princess.

When he proposed six months later, Laurel was dizzy with joy. She was young—barely twenty-two—but she had always dreamed of being a wife. And she was being offered a sparkling emerald cut diamond solitaire ring by a man who wanted her so desperately he couldn't wait to make it official. She'd been so overcome she could barely choke out the word *yes*.

Laurel parked and pulled a tissue from her purse, well aware of what she was doing—digging into memories to feel appropriately sad. It worked. Her heart felt leaden as she slammed her car door and hurried to the emergency room entrance.

"I got a call about my husband, Douglas Applebaum," she said to the woman at the desk. "He was…in an accident." She arranged her face into a stoic expression so the receptionist would understand she was prepared for whatever bad news was about to unfold.

But the woman remained impassive as she tapped at her computer, asked for ID, and then printed out an adhesive name badge. "Observation unit 4B," she said, handing it to Laurel.

"What?" Laurel asked, confused. She had expected someone to come out and greet her.

The woman pointed a long nail embedded with a diamond chip. "Straight down that hall, all the way to the end. Make a right, show your badge to the security guard."

For a lingering moment, Laurel stood transfixed by the glamorous manicure, a covetous urge growing tight in her gut. She hid her raw, unmanicured hands behind her back as she recalled better days, when she would indulge in mani-pedis with her friend Monica, as they laughed and gossiped.

And then, just like that, the nostalgia was replaced with furious reproach. How could she possibly be so shallow? Especially now, when there was so much at stake.

Guilt brought her back to the present, where she tried to focus on the instructions she had just been given. Dazed, Laurel did as she was asked, going through door after door until she found herself in a room full of patients in reclining chairs, separated by curtains. Some were alone, others had a loved one sitting close by in a plastic seat, crowded into the tiny space. Medical professionals buzzed around the middle of the room, going from patient to patient. The air was too hot, and smelled like disinfectant.

Laurel followed the signs. 1B, 2B, 3B, and then she stood before 4B, where two nurses in lavender scrubs hovered over a patient, blocking her view. One was leaning across him, pulling off a Velcro blood pressure cuff, and the other adjusted a bag of clear liquid hanging on an IV pole. The patient said something to make both nurses laugh, and then they took a step back, as if sensing Laurel's presence.

And there he was, lounging in the reclining chair, a purple bruise across his forehead.

Laurel stopped and blinked, taking it in. The IV bag was connected to his arm by a thin tube. He wore the faded plaid shirt she'd been trying to get him to throw out, his belly hanging over his belt.

"Doug?" she asked, trying to make sense of the tableau before her. There was, she knew a term for what she was experiencing. Cognitive dissonance. Still, she couldn't understand what she was looking at. That is, until he spoke.

"Did you bring me a snack?"

2

Doug had been stupid. And lucky. He could have killed himself. He could have killed someone else. As it happened, he'd simply passed out at the wheel from low blood sugar as he was pulling away from the house, taking out a neighbor's garbage can and plowing right into their new fence. And it was all because he skipped lunch and was in the mood for a burrito from Chipotle.

And now, of course, Laurel and Doug would be on the hook for the two-thousand-dollar insurance deductible. At this rate, she would never get to California to see her grandbaby.

"The most expensive burrito I never ate," Doug said.

Laurel didn't laugh. There was nothing funny about all this. She knew she should have been relieved Doug was okay, but she couldn't shake her anger. And yes, disappointment. Everything would have been so much easier if he had just died.

She hoped she would feel different in the morning, but as they drove home from the hospital, Laurel seethed with resentment.

Doug, she could tell, was annoyed she hadn't laughed at his joke. And he had nothing else to say for himself except to complain that he was hungry as all they had given him was orange juice and an unappealing sandwich.

"One gray slice of turkey," he said, holding up a finger, "and it was dry as dust. No mayo, nothing."

"Doug," she began, her voice thick with annoyance as she tried to formulate a way to express her indignation.

"What," he snapped. "You can't muster a little sympathy? I was in an accident. I could have had a concussion. I could have *died*."

If only, she thought. But when she glanced at his face, pulled into a wounded pout, Laurel felt it all the way to her center. He was hurt, profoundly disappointed in the one person who was supposed to be there for him. And once again, Laurel swallowed her feelings. It was what she did. Her friend Monica had chided her for it countless times. *Speak up,* she always said. *What is so damned hard about that?*

But it *was* hard. Laurel could easily voice her displeasure when she was removed from a situation, but in face-to-face confrontations, the other person's feelings always took precedence. She couldn't help it. She felt others' pain more deeply than she felt her own.

You know what you are, girl? Monica had said. *You're a cipher.*

Laurel had to look it up in the dictionary. It meant *one having no influence or value; a nonentity*. She hated that, but she knew it was exactly how she behaved. And exactly why the thought of Doug's death had been so liberating.

She glanced at her husband and then back at the road, thinking about her friend Monica and, oddly, her co-worker Charlie Webb—people who cared about her, people who would encourage her to speak up for herself.

"I want to go to California," she blurted, before she could lose her nerve. She held tight to the steering wheel as she sat up straighter. A tear escaped as she thought about it. She wanted so desperately to hold that newborn close to her heart.

He looked at her, wretched and surprised. "You've got to be kidding."

Laurel rounded the corner toward their home and saw Doug's silver Camry half up on the curb in front of their neighbor's house, a section of fence under the front tires.

"And a dog," she said, sniffing. "I want a dog."

"A dog?" He sounded stricken. When she didn't respond he added, "I'm *allergic*." He pointed to his throat, as if it were proof.

"You're not *that* allergic." She pulled into the driveway and cut the engine.

"I really expected more from you," he said, angrily gathering the discharge papers they had given him at the hospital and rustling them into an uncooperative stack.

He seemed so surprised and dismayed by her outburst she felt like apologizing, but stopped herself. Doug stared down at the pages for a moment, unfocused, and then turned to her.

"Did you do a food shopping?" he asked. "That sandwich was so..."

Laurel gripped the steering wheel, her knuckles losing blood. *Food Shopping*, she thought. FS=*Frank Sinatra, Fred Savage, Franz Schubert*

"Laurel?" he prodded.

She sighed, suppressing her sorrow, releasing her resentment. And just like that, her own stomach rumbled in sympathy.

"I'll make you a steak," she said.

★ ★ ★

The next morning, before she left for work, Laurel smoothed out the discharge papers from the hospital and read them carefully. It was important for her to stay focused and keep busy so her mind wouldn't wander to what she would be doing right now if Doug had, in fact, been in a fatal crash. But it was no use. She had visions of herself on the phone with the funeral home while fielding calls from Evan as he searched online for quick flights home. In this other, better version of herself, she knew what she wanted and didn't let others influence her actions. She'd be firm with her sister-in-law, Abby, saying no, they wouldn't be using her half-senile rabbi for the services, even though he'd known Doug nearly all his life. She thought about the plain black dress in her closet that made her hips look so slim, and the smart black and gray blazer she'd bought nearly eight years ago when Doug's toy and novelty store was still solvent.

Laurel pictured taking her mother out to lunch, just the two of them, with hours to spend together. "Such a lovely place!" her mother would gush, delighted to be experiencing the world outside her home, grateful to the doting daughter who made it happen.

Focus, Laurel told herself, as she reread the hospital papers, making sure none of the instructions were contraindicated by Doug's normal medication routine. She laid out the weekly dispenser with his pills and vitamins, then circled the sentence that said he needed to make a follow-up appointment with his endocrinologist as soon as possible. And finally, Laurel called the insurance company about the car, making arrangements for it to be towed to a body shop.

Dressed in her blue Trader Joe's shirt, she grabbed her purse and her jacket, and turned to Doug, who was at the kitchen table, reading the newspaper and slurping at a bowl of store-brand Cheerios. Laurel fought the urge to ask him how he was feeling, because she knew he would go on and on about every ache and pain and how poorly he'd slept.

"The tow truck will be here within the hour," she said.

He didn't look up. "Uh-huh."

She waited a beat, hoping for eye contact, but he wasn't tearing himself away from whatever he was reading.

"Don't forget to call Dr. Marciano," she said.

"I won't." He slurped at his cereal again.

"And talk to the Patels. You need to apologize. Tell them we'll pay for the fence damage." She paused. Still nothing. "Oh, bring them that bottle of Riesling in the fridge," she added.

That got his attention. "I need to give them wine?" he asked over his newspaper.

"As a goodwill gesture," she said. "And take your meds. They're on the counter." She headed toward the door and paused. "Don't forget."

He went back to reading. "All right."

She stood there for a moment, her hand on the doorknob. But he was back in his article, even though he had the whole damned day to read the newspapers. Hell, he'd probably still be in that very spot when she got home. She touched her hair—sprinkled with gray since she hadn't colored it in so long—remembering when he used to like looking at her. Now, she could barely recall the way his eyes darkened with desire when she least expected it. She tried to tell herself she didn't mind. After all, she had gone through menopause early and her own libido was a relic, like something encased in amber that had once fluttered with exquisite life.

"I'll see you later," she said, and opened the door.

He glanced up at her. "Wait a minute."

She stopped and turned, hopeful.

"What about a loaner?" he asked.

A loaner? *That's* what he was concerned about? Laurel folded her arms. "It's not covered."

"What am I supposed to do without a car?"

"You have someplace to be?" she asked.

"I don't want to be stuck in the house."

Laurel rubbed her forehead, trying to massage away her frustration. "We're not paying for a rental car when we can't afford to fly to California."

"We also can't afford a solid gold toilet seat. Doesn't mean I can't—"

"Besides," she said, interrupting his lame joke, "you can't even drive until you're cleared by Dr. Marciano. So forget about it."

"And how am I supposed to get to the doctor?"

There wasn't one damned thing he could figure out on his own. Like a child. "Either work around my schedule or take an Uber."

"I don't know how to do that," he said.

When it came to technology, Doug acted as if the eight years between them was an entire generation. It frustrated her. There were plenty of sixty-year-old men who knew how to order an Uber.

"Yes you do," she said. "I put the app on your phone."

He went back to his newspaper. "Maybe I'll call Abby."

Just what she needed. Her sister-in-law getting neck-deep in their business. "I'll see you later," she said, pausing for a response. But he was lost in his newspaper. So she slipped out the door, and went to work.

3

At the store, Charlie rushed to Laurel in the back room before she began her shift. She had already punched in and was due on the register for her first hour.

"Everything okay?" he said.

Laurel bit back her shame and sighed, trying to keep her expression even. "It was just a minor accident. He's fine."

The older man studied her. "You look so troubled."

She struggled to speak, afraid if she said anything the dam might burst. So she just nodded and sniffed back tears.

Charlie took her hands in his cool papery fingers. "It's traumatic, I know."

Laurel nodded again, because what else could she do—tell him she was disappointed her husband didn't die? The man was a widower. He would think she was heartless.

She took in a juddering breath. "Thank you for understanding."

He searched her face, and she could feel his wintery blue eyes—set deep and small in his lined face—reading her. "Knock, knock," he said, and she smiled. Charlie had a knock-knock joke for every occasion, and was trying to cheer her up.

"Who's there?" she dutifully asked.

"Stopwatch."

"Stopwatch who?"

"Stopwatch you're doing and tell me what's bothering you," he said.

Laurel could barely muster a laugh before hanging her head to let out all the air in her lungs. "I'm awful," she whispered.

"No, honey. No you're not."

"I am. If you knew—"

"Let me guess," he said. "You were disappointed."

She felt a chill at the laser-sharp insight, and looked back at his eyes to be sure she'd heard right.

He clarified. "Disappointed he didn't die. Am I right?"

So he did understand. Laurel became aware that her cheeks were wet, and she wiped them with her fingertips. "I was actually looking forward to being...unburdened." She paused. "I'm a terrible person."

He waved away her remark. "How long have you been married?"

"It'll be thirty years in June."

"And in all that time, were you ever unfaithful to him?"

Laurel's hand flew to her chest. "God, no. Never."

"And you take care of him? Cook for him? Clean for him? Shop for him?"

"I do everything," she said, and it was true. Their marriage was such a throwback she often felt like a cross between Alice Kramden and Lucy Ricardo. Growing up, she had thought it was all she could ever want—the perfect marriage her parents never had.

"You're not a bad person, honey. You're an unhappy person."

This man. He really was so wise. And his understanding was gentle, kind, unburdening. "Thank you, Charlie." She hoped her tone conveyed the full weight of her gratitude.

He put a hand on her arm, and spoke in that careful way he had, looking deeply into her eyes. "You know, you don't have to take such good care of him."

He said it with such gravitas it hit Laurel right in her core. "What?" she said, surprised. But before he could respond, their manager, Tammy, walked into the room. She was a fair boss who seemed to like them both, but if they slacked off, that could change pretty quickly. Her appearance was intended as a tacit reminder it was time to get out front.

"Just think about it," he said, with a meaningful glance. Then he straightened his Trader Joe's crew member shirt and got to work.

You don't have to take such good care of him. Did he really mean what she thought he meant?

As she went on with her day—alternating between stocking the shelves, working the cash register, and helping customers find the turkey chili, the animal crackers, the barbecue sauce, the almond butter, the oat milk, the French brie, and the green tea ice cream—she kept replaying Charlie's words, going back and forth on her interpretation of them. One minute she was sure his message was to stop attending to Doug's health needs so he would die. And the next minute she thought, no, he couldn't possibly have meant that. He was simply telling her she was working too hard and didn't need to bear the whole burden.

By the end of the shift, Laurel felt dusty and worn, eager for a shower. Yet the thought of going home to see Doug still seated at the kitchen table, doing the crossword puzzle or sudoku, as if there wasn't anything in the house that needed his attention, made her stomach clench. She went to the back room where she caught up with Charlie.

"Do you have time to sit for a minute?" she asked, nodding toward the break room. "I think there's still coffee."

"Of course," he said. "But not here. Let's go to Starbucks."

She agreed, because it was only three storefronts away in the same strip mall. And this conversation would be better in private—away from their co-workers.

A blustery fall rain had started and Laurel didn't have an umbrella. But Charlie did, and he was gentleman enough to hold it over her as they scurried to Starbucks.

Once they settled into a table near the window with their steaming lattes, she said, "There's something I need to tell you." It was a confession, and she was ready to hear whatever he had to offer.

Charlie felt his hot cup with his fingertips and pushed it aside, clearly waiting for it to cool before taking a sip. "I'm listening," he said.

She cleared her throat. "Doug has a huge life insurance policy. It's one of the reasons I…" Laurel paused, searching for the right language.

"You don't have to explain that to me," he said.

"I do," she insisted. "It was one of the reasons I was so disappointed he didn't…you know. When I realized he wasn't…" She couldn't find the words, but pressed on. "Our finances are a mess, and I can't get him off his butt to look for work. For a few minutes yesterday, I thought all my problems were solved." Laurel paused, swallowed. "It felt good, Charlie."

There. She said it. Now, he would either offer comfort or a lesson on being a better, more compassionate person. Maybe he'd even compare Doug to his late wife, Marie, whom he had loved so dearly. Either way, she was ready to accept his judgment.

He nodded thoughtfully for several moments before responding. "Laurel, you've been a devoted wife for thirty years…"

Okay, she thought, here it comes, the lecture. He would tell her she needed to be more dedicated to her marriage and less concerned about money.

"And now, it's time to stop martyring yourself," he continued. "Doug is a grown man. If he values his life, let him take some responsibility for it. And if not, well…you'll get the freedom you've earned."

Earned? Laurel sat up straighter. He *had* been telling her to let Doug perish. "So all the things I do for him—" she said, "laying out his medicines, reminding him to go to the doctor…"

"Just don't do it anymore," he advised. "It's that simple."

"But he has serious health issues," she said, to be absolutely clear. "Diabetes, high blood pressure, high cholesterol, obesity. And if I don't remind him to take his medications…"

"Knock, knock," he said, his face serious.

"Who's there?"

"Everybody."

"Everybody who?" Laurel asked.

Charlie leaned in and said something so simple it shouldn't have registered as profound. And yet, at that moment, sitting in the corner of Starbucks as the heady scent of dark roast coffee swirled around her, and the wind pelted the window, sending a few yellow leaves sliding down the glass, she felt her world crack wide-open.

"Everybody dies, Laurel."

4

The next morning, Laurel asked Doug if he would consider laying out his own pills from now on, since she had so much to do every day and he so little. It was a rehearsed speech, clear and logical. She had gone through it in her mind several times so she wouldn't lose her resolve, imagining he would cheerfully agree. *Of course, babe,* he would say. *Of course I can take this one thing off your very full plate.* And then, well, he would either follow through or he wouldn't. And if he didn't, her fate could be entirely changed. It would be like a rebirth, and the thought of it sent pings of light down her vertebrae. It wasn't that she wanted him to die, but if it was meant to be, she would embrace it. Again, she imagined how it would feel to hold a soft warm bundle of newborn against her chest, the sweet-hot scent of love rising straight from the downy scalp.

But Doug just blinked at her, and his expression went from surprised to wounded. Betrayed, even.

"You know I'm job hunting," he said, his eyes tragic. "I check the listings every day."

Laurel sucked air as she searched for a route to get the conversation back on track, the way she had imagined it. But she had made a tactical error, mentioning his free time. Now, they were speeding headlong in another direction, with Doug's defensiveness at the wheel.

Focus, she told herself, and tried to regain her resolve, but it was no use. She felt his hurt in the deepest part of her heart, and just like that, her exquisite longing was gone, replaced by Doug's pitiful pain. She studied his face, pulled into a desperate pout verging on tears, and it undid her. This was her fault.

"Of course," she muttered.

"I thought you liked doing it for me." He paused, retreating into his pain, and she could tell it would be hard to pull him out of it. "I didn't know it was such a bother."

"It's not," she assured him, trying to salve his wound while searching for the joyful anticipation she'd felt just moments ago. But it eluded her, like vapor in a breeze. "I just thought... I thought you might want to get more involved with your health."

"It doesn't take you that long, does it?" His expression was soft and pleading. He needed more.

"No," she admitted, "it doesn't."

"You're so much better at that kind of thing than I am," he added. "So organized. I'd probably mess it up. And then what would happen?"

"I can only imagine," she said, intending to sound sympathetic, but it came out dreamy, even wishful. He cocked his head, confused, and she gave his arm an affectionate squeeze to end the conversation.

Later, Laurel watched as he opened the *Friday* compartment of his weekly pill organizer, which she dutifully filled every weekend, depositing his medications and vitamins into each tiny chamber. She noticed he paid no attention to what he was swallowing. He merely dumped the contents into his chubby palm, and tossed them into his mouth before swigging back an enormous gulp of water. His eyes were back on the newspaper before the slurry finished traveling down his gullet.

Laurel thought about his blood pressure medication, remembering the doctor's warning that it had to be taken every day. A few missed doses could be deadly. For a terrible moment, she thought about what would happen if she somehow forgot to include them. He wouldn't notice they were missing, wouldn't even notice any change in his health—at least, not until it was too late. High blood pressure, the doctor had said, was the silent killer. No warnings, no sickness. Just a sudden stroke. *He won't even suffer,* she mused, and the tingle in her spine returned. But she pushed it away. Such a terrible thought. Urging Doug to take responsibility for his own health was one thing—sabotaging him was something else entirely. It was... Laurel shook her head before the word materialized. She didn't want to think about it.

Picking up her phone, she gazed again at the ultrasound picture her daughter-in-law had sent—a hazy gray Rorschach of shadows she stared at until she was certain she saw the image of her first grandbaby. Her face felt wet, and Laurel realized she was crying. She glanced over at Doug to see if he noticed, but he had his head down, concentrating on the newspaper.

"What's on your agenda today?" she asked, hoping she could prompt him out of his self-pity and into thinking about job hunting. If he started pulling in some money—even at a lower level salary in retail like she had—it could mean the difference between affording the trip to California and missing that precious, once-in-a-lifetime chance to be there for the birth of her first grandchild. But Doug always insisted he couldn't take a job like hers, as his back was too weak to be on his feet all day. He wanted a job in retail *management*. It was, he had insisted, what he was qualified for. But almost every brick-and-mortar store was struggling, and there weren't many positions like that.

"I'm making a few calls," he said, without looking up.

"Did you ever hear back from Steve Schneider?" she pressed. He was an old friend of theirs who was a marketing VP at *Home Fair*, and had promised to keep his eyes open for Doug.

"Not yet." His voice was flat, as if he couldn't be torn away from what he was reading.

"Maybe you should nudge him today," she suggested.

"Maybe," he echoed, and gave a sharp shake at a crease in the newspaper, indicating the end of the conversation.

When Sunday morning arrived, Laurel pulled the tray of medications from the cabinet and opened all the little doors on the weekly dispenser. She lined up the prescription bottles and supplements, and began her weekend ritual. *Plink, plink, plink.* An assembly line of dropping the pills into their daily compartments. As she twisted open the cap on the Lopressor—his blood pressure medication—Doug shuffled into the kitchen, dragging his slippers across the floor, a sound that made the muscles in the back of her neck go taut. He said nothing, just grabbed the carafe from the coffee maker and poured himself a cup, using the mug she had set out on the counter for him. He turned and looked at the kitchen table, where she had placed a box of Joe's O's and a bowl for him.

"Where are the newspapers?" he asked.

"In the driveway," she said, annoyed. She was trying to be at peace with this marriage. Why did he always have to make it so hard?

"You didn't get them?" he asked.

She put the bottle of Lopressor on the counter so hard the

pills jumped and landed right back inside. "Does it look like I got them?"

"You don't have to get snippy," he said, and hovered by the kitchen table. It seemed like he was deciding whether to take the few steps toward the front door, and Laurel held her breath, her hand on the bottle of pills. Finally, he lowered himself into a seat at the table, and took a long sip of his coffee, too hurt by her sharp words to make eye contact. But after a moment, he looked back at her, concerned. "Sweetie, are you okay?"

And there it was. That decency. Her agitation evaporated. "Sorry I snapped at you," she said. "I just woke up."

"It's okay, babe," he said. "Take your time." He picked up the box of imitation Cheerios and poured it into his bowl. "Milk?"

Laurel put down the pill bottle, retrieved the low-fat milk from the refrigerator, and handed it to him. He gave her a grateful look. It seemed to say, *My darling, I will tolerate your minor failures because I love you that much.* And Laurel felt her heart go soft at his tender largesse. She was his whole world.

She went back to the counter, picked up the bottle of Lopressor, poured seven pills in her palm, and dropped them one by one into her husband's weekly organizer. *Plink, plink, plink.*

Later that afternoon, Laurel arrived at her mother's split-level house in Smithtown, a thirty-minute drive from her own split-level in Plainview. It was where Laurel had spent her childhood, and it had remained largely unchanged. Meanwhile, the middle-class neighborhood—which had been developed in the early sixties for young families who couldn't afford the leafier, closer-to-Manhattan real estate of Nassau County, Long Island—had been expanding and maturing.

Laurel took two bags of groceries from her trunk and

walked up the steps, where a package sat. It was a rectangu-
lar box, about two feet long, and she had a pretty good idea
what was inside—another doll. Her mother's collection had
never stopped growing.

She used her key to unlock the door, then picked up the
box and managed to carry it in along with the groceries.

"Mom?" she called, making her way up the half staircase
toward the kitchen landing. "It's me!"

"Down here!" her mother called, and Laurel understood
she was in the family room on the lower level, where her doll
collection now occupied most of the space. Laurel quickly
unpacked the groceries, cleaned a dingy glass her mother had
left in the sink, and made her way downstairs with the UPS
delivery.

It was a wood-paneled room where Laurel had spent most of
her childhood evenings, fighting with her older brother over
the TV remote, a new gadget that had kept them at odds. Usually, their mother was in the kitchen, ignoring their screaming fights as she cooked dinner or escaped to her bedroom to
rearrange the doll collection, which hadn't yet expanded beyond a single bookcase. One day, her father was home during a
particularly vicious fight between Laurel and Bruce, and insti-
tuted a half-hour rule, dictated by a sand timer he placed atop
the television. When the sand ran out, the timer got turned
over, and the remote passed from one sibling to another. It
was an ingenious solution—at least for Laurel, who learned
an important discipline. Delayed gratification.

Now, the old TV was gone, and the wood paneling was
barely visible behind the oversize shelving units filled with
collectible dolls—some on display, others protected inside
cardboard boxes. When Laurel was a child, her mother's collection was limited to antique dolls, with faces of bisque or
porcelain. But sometime in the eighties—when Joan's mar-

riage began to crumble—her hobby turned into an obsession, and she started collecting vintage midcentury dolls of molded plastic. That manic preoccupation slowly morphed into agoraphobia. More and more, the only place she felt safe was at home with her dolls.

Joan didn't look up when Laurel entered the room. She was bent over the old sofa—now moved several feet from the back wall to accommodate the broad industrial shelves that served as the warehouse section of the room. The catty-corner walls were the showcases for the collection, which never failed to make an impression. Even now, Laurel could appreciate the dense accumulation of dresses and faces and hairstyles and sizes. It was like a giant party frozen just as the celebration was about to begin.

A line of dolls was laid out on a sheet atop the sofa. Joan was bent over them with a feather duster flying in quick left-right motions. When she finished, she turned to Laurel and her expression changed from serious to delighted.

"Sweet Sue!" Joan cried with a gasp when she saw the box in Laurel's hand. "She's here!"

Laurel passed her the package. "Looks like you've been busy."

"You have no idea," Joan said, in a voice that implied it was all simply too much. She brought the box to her workstation—an old folding table in the center of the room. Then she picked up the Swiss Army knife resting in the corner and struggled to open the blade tucked tightly inside.

"I'll do it, Mom," Laurel said.

"What would I do without you?" Joan gushed, as she handed over the knife.

Laurel pulled out the blade and carefully sliced through the tape on the box, then she stood back to afford her mother the joy of opening it.

Joan—dainty and small, with a head that seemed too large for her narrow body—hovered over the box for a breathless moment. She was all bones and sharp angles beneath the blush-colored Juicy Couture tracksuit she'd had for over a decade. Her blond curls—overbleached and straw-like—had thinned over the years, and Laurel could see her pink scalp peeking through.

"Have you eaten anything today, Mom?" Laurel asked.

Joan ignored her question and extracted the doll from the box, holding it up for Laurel. It was a redheaded girl, with bow lips and a starchy party dress in pale peach with a dull ecru collar. She fluffed out the bottom of the skirt.

"Isn't she beautiful?" Joan sighed, as she adjusted the puffy sleeves.

"Very special," Laurel said, though in truth she thought the doll looked just like at least a dozen others in the collection.

Joan walked over to the shelf and made room between two other dolls. She stood back and assessed the display, then did some rearranging so that the new addition stood between a blonde in a green shift and a brunette in a chocolate polka-dot ensemble.

"Perfect!" Joan clapped.

"Why don't I make us lunch?" Laurel asked. "I'm starving."

Her mother dismissed the suggestion with a wave. "Oh, I'm not hungry. I had one of those Ensures."

"Come on," Laurel said, assuming her mother was humoring her with a white lie. "I bought bagels. And a nice tomato. I'll open a can of tuna."

Joan's doctor wanted her to gain weight, and Laurel spent a lot of energy trying to make that happen. But Joan was resistant. She mostly ignored the calorie-rich nutritional shakes Laurel left in her refrigerator, and could never seem to find the time to eat. Laurel was determined to tempt her with her favorite lunch.

"Go get everything ready," her mother said. "I'll be up in a few."

"Keep me company," Laurel implored.

"I have a lot to do." Joan swept her arm toward the sofa, where a line of dolls lay waiting for her attention.

"Let's have lunch and then I'll help you."

"You will not."

"I will," Laurel insisted.

"You don't care about my dolls."

It was true—she didn't. At least, not in the way her mother cared about them. Still, Laurel was grateful for the collection, glad her mother had something to keep her happy and fulfilled. The problem was that she still battled feelings of jealousy over these pieces of plastic and fabric. And sure, she knew that was a little pathetic. After all, her mother loved her fiercely—certainly more than she loved the dolls—but it was hard to compete with these tiny models of perfection.

"I care about *you*," Laurel said.

"You always pretend you want to spend time with me."

"I *do* want to spend time with you," she insisted. It was true, but there was always so much else to do. Guilt gnawed at her.

"But only on your schedule."

"I have work," Laurel said. "I have Doug."

"You know what would be lovely?" Joan said. "If we could go out to lunch together like other mothers and daughters."

It wasn't the first time this had come up. But for the past several years, Joan would only leave the house when it was imperative. And even that was getting harder. When she had a doctor's appointment, Laurel had to budget an extra hour or two into the day so she could get her mother out the door.

"I'd love that," Laurel said. "But, Mom, you never—"

"I know, I know," Joan interrupted. "But I think I could do it, if you would just be more *patient* with me. Maybe if you took time off from that silly job."

At that, Laurel felt a pang, recalling that moment in the car when she thought all her problems had been solved with a big pile of insurance money that would allow her to quit her job and have the leisure time she had always wanted.

"Mom," she said carefully, "if I didn't have... If I didn't have to work so much, would you really let me take you out?"

Joan picked up one of the dolls from the sofa, held it to her chest, and looked at Laurel, her eyes wet. "Oh, my baby," she said, squeezing the doll tighter, "it would complete me."

Laurel bit back her own tears, feeling like a lifetime of aching for her mother's approval was within reach. She approached and wrapped her in a hug, breathing in the familiar scent of hair spray and Chanel No. 5, registering only the minor discomfort of a Patti Playpal pressed between them.

5

Driving back from her mother's house, Laurel thought about her overburdened schedule. Though she visited every Sunday, it wasn't enough. Her mother craved more time and attention than Laurel could provide. Now, she thought about all the others she was also shortchanging. Her son and daughter-in-law. Her future grandchild. Even some anonymous pup currently trembling in an animal shelter. They all needed her, but she was forced to hold back because her husband sucked up all her free time. Laurel squeezed the steering wheel and wondered if ministering to Doug's myriad health needs was really the moral choice.

And of course, it wasn't just other people Laurel was neglecting, but herself. When Doug's store went bust, she'd been so quick to give up the manicures, the hair salon, the exercise classes, the dinners out with her friends. At the time, she felt almost noble in her sacrifices. A martyr. But now she felt a deep, gaping ache, as if the best part of her had been excised. And all that was left was Laurel the caretaker.

But what was the alternative when Doug refused to take responsibility for himself? She was simply stuck.

Laurel thought about that weekly pill dispenser and remembered the day she had forgotten to include Doug's vitamin D capsules. She revisited her speculation about his blood pressure medication, wondering what would happen if he went a full week without it. Certainly, he would have a dangerous spike. And possibly, a fatal stroke.

As she envisioned it, Laurel felt her pulse pounding at the sheer power she held, and wondered if this temptation might one day be too much for her to resist. The thought made her so nervous she almost didn't see the brake lights in front of her. She slammed her foot down, screeching to a stop with just inches to spare. Sweating and shaking, Laurel searched for a phrase to focus on so she could calm herself. She remembered her mother's words. *Complete Me.* CM. *Chuck Mangione. Chrissy Metz.*

Charles Manson.

At that, Laurel's skin went cold, and she understood she had to resist this...this depravity. She was no murderer. She was just a doting wife who was tired from three decades of service to her husband.

Then, on Tuesday morning, as Laurel was getting ready for work, her phone pinged with a calendar notification about Doug's checkup with his endocrinologist that afternoon. It was yet another way in which she managed his care. Doug couldn't be counted on to remember his own appointments, or write them down in a place he would see them. A few times, she had tried to show him how to use the calendar on his own phone, but he'd been so obtuse. "Everything looks so tiny," he had complained, squinting.

"Tap on it," she'd said.

"Hey, buddy," Doug said to his phone, tapping at it like it was someone's shoulder, "when's my doctor's appointment?"

She gave a small laugh, but inside, she was disappointed. He wasn't even trying. It was just easier to pretend he didn't understand and let her carry the burden.

Well, not this time. Doug could remember his own damned appointment. This was exactly what Charlie had meant by letting him take responsibility for himself. And if Doug missed his doctor visit and his health suffered as a result, that was his fault, not hers.

This, Laurel felt, was perfectly justified. It wasn't anything like omitting one of his life-saving medications. It was simply pushing him harder to be a normal, independent adult.

And so Laurel made the coffee, set out Doug's breakfast and his pill dispenser, retrieved the newspapers, and then kissed the top of his head as he read the letters to the editor in *Newsday*.

"I'm leaving," she said. "Do you need anything?"

"Could you bring home some Greek yogurt? And those mini croissants?"

The yogurt he liked was full-fat, and the croissants were made with just enough flour to hold the butter together. It was a cholesterol orgy. But instead of trying to cajole him into better choices, Laurel released the responsibility to him.

"Sure, sweetie," she said, "if that's what you want."

Laurel hesitated waiting to see if he had anything else to say. She wasn't even sure what she wanted from him. She only knew her heart felt porous, like it could absorb any little kindness it came in contact with. But he had made his request, and had nothing more to say. She had already disappeared from his consciousness, which was now filled with an editorial on local politics. She let out one soft breath, and slipped out the door.

As she went through her day, Laurel thought about what

she had done, neglecting to tell Doug about his doctor's appointment. There was, she knew, no reason to feel guilty. After all, a single missed doctor visit wouldn't be dangerous, especially since they would call the house to reschedule. On the other hand, Doug rarely answered the landline, and relied on her to check the voicemail. So if she didn't stay on top of it, there could be several missed appointments. And during that time, Doug might be getting sicker and sicker. Despite herself, she imagined him slipping into a diabetic coma early one morning after she left for work, with no one around to call for help. The fantasy was so vivid she almost expected him to be dead when she got home from work that day, and a coil of guilt returned to her gut.

But then she thought about the insurance money and the lovely apartment she had envisioned. She saw herself landing at LAX in time to be at the hospital for her grandchild's birth. Her sinuses filled with the memory of that newborn smell—a gentle mix of baby power, dryer-battered cotton, wet diaper and something else...something primal and organic her hormones still reacted to. She could imagine the flood of oxytocin as she connected with her only child's firstborn. This would be her reward for so many years of suffering. And then, when she got home, tired and sated with a suitcase full of dirty laundry and a trove of precious memories, she would make plans to visit an animal shelter, where she would rescue a funny-looking little dog who would love her with its whole heart.

The guilt transformed into something as light as hope, and when Laurel turned into her neighborhood, she had a vision of Doug laid out on the couch, with the television on. Only he wouldn't be watching it. He'd be in a coma. She would drop the package she'd brought home from Trader Joe's and call 911, but it would be too late.

By the time she rounded the corner of her block, Laurel had

convinced herself it was fated to happen now. But then she saw something that crushed her spirit—a silver Lexus with a vanity plate that said NAMST A. It belonged to Doug's infuriating sister, Abby, who assumed every driver on the Northern State Parkway needed to know how very evolved she was. Like she was the only woman on Long Island who took yoga classes.

When Laurel opened the front door, Abby's presence floated in a fine mist of lemon Pledge, and every corner of the living room looked pristine—cleaner than it had that morning—with fresh vacuum tracks in the carpeting and the furniture neatly squared. Even the silk ficus tree in the corner seemed to have been dusted. Laurel seethed. Abby knew it drove her crazy when she did this.

Why don't you just tell her not to clean your house? her friend Monica had said. But she didn't understand. Abby had a genius for passive-aggressive posturing. No matter how awful she was, it was couched in innocence. *Who me? Overstep my boundaries? I thought you wanted me to come in and reclean your entire house and imply that you were a slob. Well excuse me for being helpful!*

"Hello?" Laurel called.

"In here!" Doug yelled from the kitchen.

Laurel put her purse and keys on the table by the door and followed the sound of her husband's voice. He and Abby were seated at the table, which had two identical place settings consisting of a cup of steaming green tea and a baked puck of dried mulch atop a paper towel square. Laurel could never understand why anyone thought of rice cakes as food.

She took a quick glance around the room, which sparkled. The chrome faucet was nearly blinding in its silvery brilliance. She looked back at the siblings, who were considerably less dazzling. Abby was large, like Doug, with wavy salt-and-pepper hair she wore partially pulled back, allowing wispy tendrils to escape—an affectation that implied she was too evolved to be fussy with her hair. Her pale complexion, as always, was overmoisturized to the point of greasiness.

"This is a surprise," Laurel said to her sister-in-law, straining to sound chipper. She opened the refrigerator to put away the yogurt she had brought home, and noticed everything had been rearranged. She pointedly put the milk back in the spot where she liked it, then opened the freezer and angrily shoved in the frozen croissants.

Abby took a slow sip of her tea. "*Someone* had to take him to the doctor."

"Oh, was that today?" Laurel said, without turning around.

"You forgot?"

"I've been busy," Laurel said as calmly as she could. She turned and pulled at her Trader Joe's shirt to indicate what had been taking up so much of her time.

Abby gently put down her cup and brought her hands together, as if in prayer. "I'm not judging you."

"I didn't say you were."

"You don't have to get defensive. I understand how hard it can be to balance everything. You're not used to working full-time."

Laurel bristled at the insinuation that she'd had a cushy life of leisure. She had worked part-time at Doug's toy and novelty store throughout Evan's childhood, balancing work and parenthood, with virtually no help from her husband. Once Evan went away to college, she would have gladly worked full-time, but business was foundering at that point, and there wasn't much to do. Laurel wanted to get another job then— something full-time—but Doug insisted he needed her. It wasn't until the place went belly-up that she had an opportunity to look for a real job.

"We're managing just fine," Laurel said, and gave her sister-in-law a tight smile.

"I honor you for trying so hard," Abby said. "I'm just glad I was able to help. It was an important visit—the doctor increased his diabetes medication, and said if that doesn't work he might have to go on insulin. I don't know what would have happened if I wasn't available."

The two women locked eyes, and Abby's expression was arranged into such a beatific calm that Laurel wanted to smack her. And Abby damn well knew it. Neither of them spoke, and Laurel understood she was being dared to make a scene.

Doug broke the uncomfortable silence. "In a pinch I could have taken a car service," he said, trying to be helpful. "Laurel put a Goober app on my phone."

"*Uber,*" Abby corrected. She was three years older than her brother, but not as technologically challenged. "And that was very considerate of her, since she's so busy."

"She takes good care of me," Doug said.

In response, Abby scratched at a sticky spot on the kitchen table, then made a show of rubbing at it with a napkin.

But Doug, bless his heart, was sticking up for Laurel, trying to help. It softened her enough to arouse sweet melancholy about his likely demise. He was so loyal. She would miss that. Laurel gave him an affectionate hug from behind before going over to the stove to turn on the burner beneath the still-warm kettle.

"Anyone want more tea?" she asked.

Abby declined, insisting she had to go. "By the way," she said as she rose, "his car is going to be ready tomorrow."

"How do you know?"

"There was a voicemail when we got back from the doctor."

Laurel tried to hide her surprise. In her runaway fantasy, she had imagined Doug's continued obliviousness to their landline voicemail would result in future missed doctor visits.

"Great," Laurel said. "We'll pick it up in the morning."

"And we decided he should be checking the voicemail regularly," Abby announced, "since your schedule is so…hectic."

Laurel rubbed her forehead, frustrated. Her nosy sister-in-law had a knack for getting in her business. But there was nothing she could do but offer a forced smile. "Thanks, Abby," she said. "Thanks so much."

With a slight bow, Abby brought her hands together. "Namaste."

6

Laurel was in the break room pushing her wilted salad around with a fork, hunting for fresh pieces of lettuce, when she was distracted by a wonderful smell—like something from a fine Italian restaurant. She looked up to discover it was Charlie Webb, pulling a plate from the staff microwave. To her surprise, he put it on the table and slid it toward her.

"What is this?" she asked.

"Chicken marsala with a side of green beans. I made it last night."

Up close, the aroma was even better, and the sight of the neat little sliced mushrooms glistening in the brownish sauce made her mouth water. Had she ever mentioned to him that it was her favorite dish? She glanced up and he was beaming at her. Still, she was confused. "I don't want to eat your lunch, Charlie," she said, gently pushing away the plate.

"I made enough for two." He held up a second plate to show her, then put it in the microwave.

Her stomach growled in anticipation, and she was tempted to dig in immediately. But she couldn't do that to Charlie, who was so thoughtful. She put her fork down and waited for him to join her.

"Bon appétit!" he said as he sat.

They dug in simultaneously and the first bite did not disappoint. It was delicate and complex, the chicken as tender as rose petals. "You *made* this?" she asked, incredulous. He usually brought sandwiches for lunch, so she didn't know he could cook. It was a rare trait in a man of his generation.

"Pretty simple recipe," he said.

"You're being modest." She took another bite and dabbed at her mouth. "I had no idea you could do this."

"I had to learn," he said with a chuckle. "Marie, God bless her, could burn soup."

Laurel laughed appreciatively. There was even love in his reproach. "Did she know you didn't like her cooking?"

"Goodness, no. She would put a plate of dust-dry chicken in front of me and I'd go on and on that it was the best thing I ever ate."

She smiled at that. He was such a sweetheart.

"Problem was," he continued, "I convinced her that was how I liked it, so it was never going to get any better. I figured I'd have to take some cooking classes or starve to death."

"Well, I'm grateful," she said, hand to her heart in sincerity. "This is delicious. Marie was a lucky woman."

"I reminded her all the time!" he said with a laugh. But despite the joke, she could see him getting wistful.

"You must miss her," she said tenderly.

"Every day." He jabbed at a mushroom then looked back up at her. "You know, I never thought I'd be widowed and working at Trader Joe's at my age. I thought Marie and I would be in an RV, touring the country." He paused, coming back to the present. "But I have no regrets."

Laurel nodded, understanding his point. "She knew she was loved."

"Tell me what's going on in your house," he said, clearly wanting to change the subject.

Laurel shifted, uncomfortable. She didn't want to launch into her efforts to neglect her husband's health in the middle of this conversation about his love for Marie.

"It's...fine," she said. "Doug's sister took him to the doctor yesterday and his dosage was adjusted." She took another bite from her plate.

"Are you still doing all that caretaking?"

She looked up, marveling at his wisdom. "I asked him if he would take responsibility for his own medications, but he wouldn't."

Charlie chewed thoughtfully, his lips pulled closed. "So... you give him his pills every day?"

"It's not that big a deal," she said. "He has a weekly dispenser. I do it on Sundays." She avoided his eyes, worried he might intuit her terrible secret—that she had actually imagined omitting his lifesaving blood pressure medication.

"It's a big responsibility," he said.

She kept her eyes averted. "Too big," she whispered.

"Laurel," he pressed, "what's wrong?"

She shook her head, choking back guilt, and tried, unsuccessfully, to get a big gulp of air. Not here, she thought. Not now. *I am not going to cry.* But then she felt his hand on her wrist, and the gentle compassion broke her resolve. Tears spilled down her cheeks.

"Talk to me," he said.

She picked up a napkin and dabbed at her running mascara,

then glanced up at his lined face. Charlie's warm blue eyes were so tender, so nonjudgmental Laurel knew it was okay. She could unburden herself.

"He has high blood pressure," she whispered. "It's really dangerous. I mean, if he doesn't have his medication…"

A lump formed in her throat and she couldn't go on. For several long moments, Charlie said nothing. At last he leaned forward. "Laurel," he said softly, "did you withhold that medicine?"

"No!" she said quickly. "I didn't. I swear."

"So why are you—"

"Because I thought about it."

"Ah," he said, his expression turning soft. He gave her a tiny smile then, so warm and understanding she felt almost absolved.

"You don't think I'm awful?" she pleaded.

"Honey, you're the least awful person I know."

"But if I did this thing…"

"It wouldn't change my opinion," he said.

Laurel studied him as she took that in. He had, in essence, given her permission. They locked eyes for several long seconds, an understanding passing between them, as if they were both absorbing the enormity of that message. When he opened his mouth to speak, she wondered if he had changed his mind. Laurel braced herself, ready for him to walk it back.

But he simply put a forkful of food in his mouth, and chewed.

"You looked like you wanted to add something," she said.

Charlie shrugged. "Maybe just a little salt," he offered, and nodded at her plate. "How do you like the green beans?"

That night, Laurel locked the conversation away, as if it never happened. It was simply too overwhelming to dwell on.

Besides, she had been invited to her friend Monica's condo for dinner, and she was ready to unwind. So Laurel fixed Doug a quick supper, changed her clothes, and did her best to ignore his wounded look as she headed out the door. Her husband, she knew, would have preferred if she gave him one hundred percent of her time. But he was accustomed to her frequent visits with Monica, and couldn't think of a reasonable objection. So he had settled on looking hurt, and she had mastered the art of pretending she didn't notice.

"I hope sauvignon blanc is okay," Laurel said when she arrived at her friend's house. They hugged, and Laurel handed her a chilled bottle of wine.

"The only thing I like better than a bottle of sauvignon blanc," Monica began.

"Is two bottles of sauvignon blanc?" Laurel offered.

Monica gave her arm an appreciative squeeze. "C'mon, let's go find straws."

Laurel laughed and followed her through the elegantly decorated living room, which resembled a Realtor's impeccably staged model. The walls were painted a creamy French vanilla, and the pale yellow sofa always looked brand-new. Even the throw rug—a modern zigzag of cool blues—stayed pristine. Such was the life of a widow, Laurel mused. No one to clean up after, no one to dirty and stain and ruin the immaculate appointments. Everything had the clean, fresh scent of Febreze. Laurel ached for it.

As they approached the kitchen, she smelled something else—piquant and savory. Before she had a chance to ask what was cooking, she was distracted by the skitter of little dog paws. Monica's white bichon, Frida, pranced toward her and gave a tiny yip. Laurel adored the sweet pooch, considering her a friend. She scooped her up, kissed the top of her silky head.

"How's my sweet pea?" she cooed, scratching the dog's ears.

Monica opened a drawer, extracted a winged corkscrew, and went to work on the bottle. Laurel saw the source of the heavenly aroma—a large pan simmering on the stove.

"Need a hand?" she asked.

"Sit," Monica commanded. "You're on your feet enough."

Laurel didn't argue. She pulled out one of the kitchen chairs and sat, with Frida on her lap, as she watched her friend work. Monica was a little taller than Laurel, with shiny black hair, warm brown eyes, and slightly buck teeth, now encased in Invisalign braces. Though sixty-two, her skin was smooth and wrinkle-free, thanks to Botox and fillers. It was all part of the self-improvement regimen she began after the death of her husband almost three years ago.

"Smells good," Laurel said.

"Should," Monica replied, as she twisted the corkscrew, its arms rising up and up. "It's your favorite."

Laurel laughed. "Chicken marsala?"

"Arroz con pollo. What's so funny?"

"Nothing," she said, pausing to parse her words. "I'm just... happy. It's nice to be loved." It was true. Who cared about eating chicken twice in one day when it meant there were people in her life who cared enough to cook for her? Even before the first sip of wine, a warmth spread through her.

Monica pressed on the arms of the mechanism and the cork slid out with a soft pop. She poured two glasses and brought them to the table. Laurel returned Frida to the floor.

"Cheers," she said, holding up her glass.

"What are we toasting tonight?" Monica asked.

"Your boobs, of course." Laurel's friend had recently had a breast lift, and had been recuperating the past few weeks.

"I'll drink to *that!*" Monica tipped her glass against Laurel's and they drank.

"Tell me how you've been feeling," Laurel said.

"So much better."

"How do they look?"

"Like a twenty-year-old's! Point straight up at the moon. Want to see?"

"Yeah!" Laurel said, wondering if she would ever be able to afford such an indulgence. Of course, elective surgery required a fearlessness she didn't possess, but when she pictured herself as a widow, she imagined a bolder, braver Laurel. "I mean, if you don't mind."

"Hell, I have no one else to show them to." Monica stood and lifted her shirt and bra with one movement, revealing a perfectly symmetrical pair of breasts, so much prettier than Laurel's, with their pert, reddish nipples defying gravity. Laurel's own areolas were pale and oversize, drooping softly toward earth.

"Wow," Laurel said. "You could do porn with those."

"I'd settle for a decent guy with a taste for old broads and young tits." She pulled her bra and shirt back into place.

Over dinner, Monica said she had some news. Laurel swallowed a bite of the chicken—not as tender as Charlie's, but juicy and flavorful—and looked at her.

"I'm thinking about moving to Austin," she said.

"Texas?" Laurel tried to quell a wave of panic at the thought of losing her friend. What would she do without Monica? To settle herself, she went searching for initials. She landed on *Austin, Texas.* AT. *Alan Turing. Alex Trebek. Amy Tan.*

Calmer, Laurel realized it probably wouldn't happen. After all, Monica was always planning something life changing, and only occasionally followed through. It was like she spent every moment gathering ideas and throwing them at the wall. A few stuck, but mostly, they slithered to the floor and evaporated.

Still, she understood the pull of Austin. Monica's daughter, Daniela, lived there with her husband and two children. But her son, Dante, who was the same age as Evan, lived in Manhattan.

"You serious about this?" Laurel asked.

"I miss Dani. And the kids."

"What about Dante?"

"I never see him anyway, not since he moved in with Brittany. And they're spending Thanksgiving with *her* family."

Laurel was pierced by the sorrow in her friend's eyes, and quickly internalized the hurt and loneliness. Poor Monica. But Laurel knew how she could make this better. She put down her fork. "Then you're coming to my house for Thanksgiving," she said, tapping at her heart.

"Oh, sweetie, I don't know. I—"

"Please. I don't want to hear another word. You're going to come and pretend you love my turkey." Laurel knew her friend thought her tender bird was too salty—it was a standing joke between them.

Monica picked up her wine and held it toward Laurel, her mouth breaking into a grin, while her forehead stayed frozen. "Okay, then," she said, and they clinked glasses. "Here's to briny turkey."

They drank again, and the very real possibility of losing Monica formed a hard stone of worry in her gut. Surely she would come to her senses and realize there was so much more for her here...wouldn't she?

"Have you seriously thought this through?" Laurel asked. "About moving?"

"There's really nothing left for me in New York."

Laurel looked at her, surprised. Monica was involved in so many organizations, including a local Latino rights political group. "What about your church friends? And your book club? What about that campaign you work on? And tennis."

Monica shrugged. "My church friends are getting older and older. It's depressing. The book club fell apart. And I'm so burnt-out on politics."

"You love your Tuesday tennis, though," Laurel said.

"People in Austin play tennis, too."

"What about dating? I thought your profile was attracting all kinds of men."

Monica shook her head. "Just the wrong kinds."

"You have good friends," Laurel offered, hating how desperate she sounded. "Friends who love you."

Monica reached over and gave her wrist a squeeze. "I know. And I appreciate it. But most of my friends are married, like you. And the divorced ones don't understand what I'm going through. So it gets lonely, being by myself. If I could live closer to Daniela, maybe things would be better. At least I'd get to spend time with the grandkids."

"You think you'd feel differently if you had a close friend who was a widow?" Laurel blurted. She realized, then, that something inside her had shifted. It was so subtle she hadn't noticed it happening. But the truth was, she was thinking of her widowhood as inevitable. Not an *if*, but a *when*.

Monica took a bite of her chicken and wiped her mouth as she swallowed. "What am I supposed to do—wait around for my friends' husbands to drop dead?"

If you don't mind, Laurel thought. But she gave her friend a polite smile. Then they finished dinner, cleared up, and took the rest of the wine to the living room, where they lowered themselves into the butter-yellow sofa, prompting a puff of scent to encircle them. Laurel breathed it in, filling her lungs. It smelled like more than fabric freshener. It smelled like her future. It smelled like hope.

7

"We have news!" Evan said, excited.

Laurel adjusted the laptop screen so she and Doug could get a better view. They were at the kitchen table, having a video chat with Evan and Samara in California.

"Twins?" Doug asked.

Laurel swatted his knee, annoyed he was stealing their thunder with a stupid question. Of course it wasn't twins—they would have heard two heartbeats weeks ago. He could be such a dolt sometimes.

The call, Laurel presumed, was about the baby's gender, though she hoped it was a different kind of news. She crossed her fingers under the table and made a wish that Evan got offered a terrific job in New York, and that they were moving back.

She closed her eyes for a moment to punctuate the wish, and when she opened them, Laurel was struck by how happy they looked, sitting together on the leather love seat in their Los Angeles living room. It filled her, their joy. But it also made her ache for their company. She would have given anything for just one quick hug of her son, to smell his hair again, and search for that hot primal scent she remembered from the first moment he'd been lowered into her arms.

Samara laughed. "Not twins," she said. "But we got the results of the amnio."

"Everything checked out fine," Evan beamed. "And now we know the gender."

"I bet it's a girl or a boy," Doug joked. "What do I win?"

Laurel wanted to shush him, but she just leaned forward, holding her breath.

Evan and Samara looked at each other, then mouthed it together in an obviously rehearsed cadence. "It's a...girl!"

"A girl!" Laurel cried, and warm tears spilled down her face. A granddaughter, just as she had imagined. Knowing the baby's gender made it that much more real, and she struggled to take in a staccato breath, fighting against sobs as she imagined the soft, swaddled bundle in her arms.

"Congratulations," Doug said.

Laurel reached for a paper napkin from the table and wiped her eyes, then blew her running nose. Despite her efforts, she emitted a small wail.

Evan laughed gently. "I knew you'd be a mess, Mom."

She had to grab another napkin because she had turned into a human faucet. When she was able to catch her breath she said, "I'm going to find a way to be there for the birth, I promise."

"Laurel," Doug said, his voice heavy with reproach.

She shook him off. "Come hell or high water," she said into the webcam, catching a glimpse of her own mascara-streaked face, "I'm going to be there."

Doug put his arm around her. "We'll talk about it," he said through a tight smile.

Laurel ignored him. "Mark my words," she said to the young couple, then pried her husband's fingers from her shoulder.

That night, as Laurel brushed her teeth, Doug knocked on the bathroom door.

"Don't you think we should discuss this?"

She finished with her back molars, bent over the sink, and spit. "There's nothing to discuss." Talking through the bathroom door gave her courage, as she didn't have to look into his eyes, which had a way of liquefying her resolve, no matter how solid it felt.

"Laurel, you're not being reasonable."

"This is important to me."

"I understand," he said. "But they're probably coming to New York in the fall, so you'll see the baby then."

Laurel lowered her head toward the faucet and washed her face, ignoring him. Didn't he understand how much a baby changed in six months?

"Sweetie?" he called.

"It's not the same thing," she said into the towel as she patted her face dry.

"What?"

"I said it's not the same thing!" Raising her voice was liberating. Damn him and his thick head. Damn him for always thinking what he wanted was a *need*, and what she wanted was a *luxury*.

"Open the door."

Laurel decided to let him stew. She took her time applying eye serum and inspecting her reflection. She ran a brush through her hair, hating how the gray strands crimped, refusing to be tamed.

"Do you know how much two round trip tickets to California cost?" he said.

Oh, for god's sake, she thought. Laurel sighed and opened the door to face him. "Who said anything about *two*?"

"Huh?" He looked genuinely confused.

"I can go to California by myself," she said. "I'm the one who wants to be there for the birth, so—"

"You would go without me?" He looked hurt. But also, utterly bewildered, as if she were speaking another language.

"Of course I would go without you. I'm not a *child*."

"And you'd leave me here?"

Do you expect me to put you in a kennel? she wanted to say. But Laurel just pushed past him to her night table, and pumped lotion into her palm.

"We can't afford one ticket, either," he said to her back. "And now we have the bill from the body shop."

Whose fault is *that*, she thought, working the lotion into her hands.

"Laurel, look at me."

She wouldn't. She wanted to stay in this place of fury, and knew that facing him would drag her right into his pain.

He said something inaudible that started with "I wish you…" and trailed off.

Frustrated, she turned around. "What!" she demanded.

"I said I wish you understood how hard this is for me."

"For *you*?"

She wanted to fly into a rage then, but he took her by the shoulders and gazed into her eyes. "Don't you understand?"

His voice was pleading, but she didn't want to yield. Not this time. "All I *do* is understand."

"I don't think you do," he insisted. "I don't think you understand what a failure I feel like for losing the business, and how much it hurts me when you act like this. It's salt in the wound, Laurel." He paused, his eyes going moist. "*Salt* in the *wound.*"

His agony was so profound, his neediness so overwhelming, she felt it to her core. And just like that, his pain overwrote her own. Her fury—right there in front of her only seconds ago—was like a deleted file. His sadness was hers, and she could do nothing but throw her arms around him to offer comfort. As Laurel rested her head on his chest and listened to the stubborn beat of his heart she thought, *Oh, Doug, why do you have to make it so hard to hurt your feelings, and so easy to want to kill you?*

8

On Sunday morning, when Laurel heard Doug start to stir, she cracked two eggs into a bowl and gave them a vigorous whisk. The bacon was already cooked—a little rubbery, the way he liked it—but still resting in its own shiny fat inside the cooling pan.

"Wow," he said, a short while later when he shuffled into the room and saw the table laid out with a plate of creamy scrambled eggs and glistening bacon, two mini croissants nestled on the corner of the dish. A steaming cup of coffee sat to the side, along with a small glass of chilled, no-pulp orange juice. The Sunday papers were piled in the middle of the table. To the left of his plate, Doug's weekly pill dispenser waited patiently for his attention. Barely looking at it, he opened the Sunday compartment and spilled the contents into his palm.

"It's like I'm at the Four Seasons, Laurel," he said, before throwing the pills into his mouth. She watched carefully as he took a big gulp of orange juice and gave his head a shake to encourage the slurry down his throat.

Satisfied, Laurel quickly turned from him and went to work cleaning the pans in the sink, enjoying the simplicity of the task, pleased with how well her dish soap cut through the grease. It was just as they promised in the commercials.

As she worked, Laurel considered how easy it had been to omit Doug's blood pressure medicine from his organizer. It was almost incomprehensible that she had waited this long. Such a simple solution to her problems! And look how happy he was. Laurel watched him shoveling eggs into his mouth while he read the Sunday *Times*. He put down his fork and took a sip of coffee, engrossed in his reading. This, she thought, was a win-win. There would be no more deprivations for either of them. Doug chomped on a croissant, then shoved the rest of it into his mouth as a shower of crumbs fell onto his lap.

With a contented sigh, Laurel finished the dishes and snapped off her gloves. "Salt?" she offered, holding the shaker toward him.

"Thanks, babe!" he chirped, and sprinkled it over what was left of his eggs.

"How's the breakfast?"

He picked up a slice of bacon with his fingers and took a bite. "Perfect," he said as he chewed. "You haven't made real bacon in so long."

"It was on sale, so..." She trailed off with a shrug.

Doug gave her an appreciative chuckle. "I guess once in a while won't kill me, right?"

Laurel considered the two packages of thick-cut bacon in the refrigerator, and imagined cooking it all at once, the fat liquefying before it congealed again. She would never dream of subjecting the sink's drainpipes to that mess. Smiling, she looked back at Doug.

"I'm glad you're happy," she said, then kissed the top of his head, gave his shoulder a pat, and went into the bedroom to get ready for her day.

Driving to her mother's house with groceries in the trunk, Laurel imagined a day in the not-too-distant future when they could have regular lunches at favorite local restaurants, like Ben's Deli or the diner, or even that nouvelle Mediterranean bistro in Woodbury. She pictured running into some of the women she knew from the PTA—the fancy ones who played tennis nearby. Surprised and happy to see her after so long, they'd stop at her table to chat—just for a moment to catch up on their kids and other gossip—and her mother would be so delighted.

Of course, Laurel understood that getting Joan out of the house for these lunches would require Herculean effort. But after the first few times it would get easier. Eventually, her mother's anxiety would dissolve like a packet of Splenda sprinkled into hot coffee.

Laurel pulled into the driveway of the Smithtown split-level and popped open her trunk. There were a lot of groceries today—her mother had emailed a surprisingly long list—and Laurel struggled to carry all four bags at once. She was about to put them down on the porch to hunt for her key when the front door swung open.

"Let me help you!" Joan sang, her voice rising happily.

Laurel clocked her mother's good mood as she passed her the lightest bag. Then she followed her into the kitchen, where they went to work unpacking the groceries.

"This wasn't your usual list, Mom," Laurel observed as she pulled items out of the bags. "Trail mix? Brioche buns? Two pounds of ground sirloin?" She assumed this had something to do with her mother's high spirits, but she couldn't quite figure it out.

Joan giggled, delighted. She grabbed a bottle of ketchup and put it in the pantry. "I'm having *friends* over tonight!" She emphasized the word *friends*, as if Laurel might otherwise think it was some kind of elaborate tea party for her dolls.

Laurel considered this news as her mother grabbed a bottle of Formula 409 and bent to fit it under the sink with the other cleansers.

"Your mah-jongg ladies?" Laurel asked. It had been a long time since her mother had seen her friends. At first, the women tried to be accommodating of Joan's growing anxieties about leaving the house, but eventually they lost patience.

"Excuse me, dear?" Joan said as she straightened.

Laurel studied the food, perplexed. "Are you making them hamburgers?"

"From ground sirloin. It's superior to ground chuck."

"Your mah-jongg ladies?"

"No!" She laughed at the silliness of the suggestion. "Not my mah-jongg ladies. Eleanor and Bob."

"Who?" Laurel asked, aware that her mother often forgot to fill in details.

"They're my friends."

"How come I never heard of them?"

"They're doll people," Joan explained. "Well, she is. I met her in one of my groups."

Laurel studied her mother, concerned. She knew Joan was on Facebook, and that she spent a lot of time chatting with fellow doll collectors in specialized groups, but had never anticipated an in-person meeting. "You met them online?" she pressed.

"They live in…one of those fancy towns out east. Sag Harbor, I think. But Eleanor doesn't mind driving."

"Are you sure these people are okay?" Laurel asked.

"They're very popular in the doll community."

"Still, I'm not sure—"

"Laurel," Joan interrupted, "this is an *honor*. A feather in my cap. A few people will be green with envy, I assure you."

Her mother seemed so excited, her spirit so delicately animated, that Laurel didn't want to risk piercing her bubble. She just needed a little more information to be sure it was safe.

"Did they invite themselves or did you—"

"There was a big get-together at their place a few weeks ago. And I, you know, I had to miss it. I felt awful—there were all these lovely pictures posted online. Everyone was dressed so nicely, and they posed with their *dolls*. And with Bob!" She brought her hands together in delight, as if Bob from Sag Harbor was some sort of celebrity.

"I'm sorry you couldn't be there."

Joan nodded. "They understood how badly I felt, so they agreed to come here for a little dinner party." She paused to take her daughter's hand. "It's a *feather* in my *cap*," she repeated, as if she were dumbfounded that Laurel couldn't understand how momentous this was.

"I'm glad for you, Mom," she said.

"I'm thinking of using the Lenox, although with hamburgers, perhaps that's a bit much. What do you think?"

"I don't think they'll care much about the dishes," Laurel said, trying to be at peace with the idea that her mother would be entertaining these strangers in her home.

"I suppose not." Joan studied the hamburger meat and pressed a finger into the plastic film, as if she needed to feel the squish to be sure it wasn't frozen. She put it in the refrigerator.

Laurel, meanwhile, considered this strange development in her mother's isolated life. "What are they like?" she asked.

Joan paused to think. "I think Eleanor comes from money. In any case, she's a very knowledgeable woman."

"And Bob?"

"He's…colorful," Joan said, and tittered into her hand.

"What does that mean?" Laurel pressed.

Joan waved away the question. "Never mind. It's going to be a delight to entertain them."

Laurel shook her head, and assumed the couple had to be oddballs. But she told herself it was likely they were *benign* oddballs. "I guess they really love dolls," she offered.

Joan put a hand to her heart. "I can't wait to show them my collection!"

When she got home, Laurel wasn't surprised to see Doug still sitting at the table reading the newspaper. But she noted that his breakfast plate was nowhere in sight, which meant he had actually risen, rinsed it, and put it in the dishwasher. Clearly, he was grateful for the bacon and eggs.

"How's your mother?" he asked, glancing up.

"Happy," she said pointedly, still wondering if she should be more concerned about this strange little dinner party.

"That's excellent."

"I don't know. She's having people over for dinner—friends she met online."

He went back to his article. "Good for her."

"You think?"

He folded his paper and looked at her. "Why wouldn't it be?"

Laurel sat at the table opposite him. "Their names are Eleanor and Bob," she offered, as if saying the names aloud might offer some insight into their character.

"Well, then, lock them up."

Laurel tsked. "I'm just saying. Why would these strangers want to have dinner with my *mother*?"

"Maybe they like her."

"I suppose. She met them in one of those Facebook groups for doll collectors."

"So there you go," he said, and went back to his newspaper, signaling the end of the conversation.

Laurel knew he was probably right. This dinner was a good thing for her mother. Still, she texted Monica for the extra assurance, explaining about Eleanor and Bob from Sag Harbor.

Her friend texted back: Hmm.

Laurel replied: You think I should be worried?

A minute later, her phone rang. That was Monica's modus operandi. When things got complicated she called. But there was no hello, no preamble.

"It might be perfectly innocent," she said. "But the internet. You never know who these people are. And your mom is…"

"Vulnerable?" Laurel offered.

"And naive," Monica said. "It can't hurt to be a little cautious here. But I have an idea."

9

It felt like a caper. After an early dinner with Doug, Laurel drove by Monica's condo to pick her up. They made a quick stop for a cheesecake—Monica's idea—and Laurel insisted on the pretty one with raspberries on top, which she knew her mother would like. Then Monica called Joan from the parking lot, which had been carefully discussed as the best way to approach her. They both knew Joan would be so delighted to hear from Monica she'd welcome the extra guests. Laurel had bet her mother would use the words *the more the merrier*.

The call was on speaker, and Joan answered with her Hollywood *helloo*—throaty and stretched.

"Joan, it's Monica Robbins. How are you?" She sounded upbeat and assertive, like a talk show host.

"My goodness!" Joan said with a gasp. "What an unexpected delight!"

"I'm here in the car with Laurel. I hope she tells you I ask about you all the time."

"And it means so much to me! How have you been? And the kids? What's that handsome little troublemaker up to?"

Laurel was pretty sure her mother was remembering the time Dante grabbed a plateful of brownies and tried to hide them in his shirt. The kid had been only six, but to Joan, the incident was legendary.

"You know, I'd be happy to give you all the good gossip in person," Monica said. "Laurel and I just picked up a cheesecake and were going to take it back to my house, but I thought, 'Let's bring it to Joan's!' Laurel said you have people over, but I just knew you wouldn't mind a little extra company for dessert. You were always so gracious." She shot a glance at Laurel, who gave her a thumbs-up.

"Of course!" Joan said, sounding excited. "It would be my pleasure."

"You promise it's not too much?" Monica pressed.

"The more the merrier!" Joan chirped.

Laurel and Monica shared a look—amused but tender, as Joan was so guileless—and moments later they were on their way.

"I hope these people are genuine," Monica said. "Your poor mother deserves some friends."

"How will we know?" Laurel asked as she steered onto the Northern State Parkway. "Maybe we'll all be conned."

"Trust me, I can spot a scammer a mile away."

Laurel pressed her on what a grifter would look like in the collectible doll community.

"Not sure about Eleanor," Monica said. "But for Bob I'm picturing a young John Cusack." She paused to look swoony. "Then again, I'm often picturing a young John Cusack."

Half an hour later, they arrived at Joan's house and Laurel let them in with her key.

"Mom?" she called. "We're here!"

"In the kitchen!" Joan sang, and Laurel understood her mother hadn't wanted to entertain in the dining room when she was expecting only two people.

They made their way up the short staircase to the first landing, where they could see straight through the living room to the right side of the kitchen table. Joan was fussing with something at the counter—probably the coffee maker. Laurel could make out the back of Eleanor's head, which was hard to miss, as she was a large woman—tall and broad shouldered. She could hear Bob's voice, but couldn't see him.

"Behave yourself," he said, and Eleanor ignored him as she pontificated on something to do with molded plastic doll heads.

"Behave yourself," he repeated.

"Oh, shush," Eleanor said.

So they're one of those couples, Laurel thought, as she followed Monica toward the kitchen. She and Doug had always found it uncomfortable to be around bickerers. Still, she was relieved they seemed like an ordinary married couple, and not a team of grifters.

While Laurel paused, making sure she didn't tip the box with the cheesecake, Monica burst into the kitchen, filled with enthusiasm. "Joan!" she gushed. "You look wonderful."

"Oh, nonsense," she responded, as they hugged. "But look at you! You don't age."

"I'll tell my plastic surgeon you said so," Monica joked, then turned to the couple. "So nice to meet you. I'm Laurel's friend Monica and...oh, Jesus!" Her hand flew to her chest in alarm. "Oh, fuck. Why didn't you warn me?"

Laurel paused, wondering what on earth Monica had just

seen. She studied her friend's face for a moment, watching the blood drain from her complexion. Laurel rushed into the kitchen to see what was going on.

She put the cheesecake on the counter, and looked from her mother to Monica to the couple.

"Behave yourself!" screeched Bob, and it took a moment for Laurel's brain to register what she was staring at. There was Eleanor—a powerful-looking older woman with red hair and sun-damaged skin—and her cantankerous partner. But he wasn't a man, he was a beast. Huge. Feathered. Multicolored.

A parrot.

"This is Bob?" Laurel said when she caught her breath.

"And this is Eleanor," Joan responded, turning to her. "May I introduce my daughter, Laurel, and her friend—"

"Mom," Laurel interrupted, "you didn't tell me Bob was a bird."

"I did say he was colorful!" Joan smiled, pleased with herself.

"Excuse me for assuming the couple you were having over were both human."

"Bob doesn't like the word *bird*," Eleanor interjected.

"I'm sorry?" Laurel said, not sure she heard right.

"He prefers macaw. Though parrot will do."

"He's a very clever fellow," Joan offered.

Laurel turned to Monica. "Help me out here."

"Joan," Monica said, "it is a little…unexpected."

"Hi, baby. You're pretty," Bob said.

"You're not so bad yourself, cookie," Monica shot back.

Laurel shook her head. "You know he doesn't actually understand what he's saying, right?"

"Actually," Eleanor said, "you'd be surprised. Bob is highly intelligent. He has a limited number of phrases, but he uses them quite appropriately."

Laurel took a moment to study the strange couple. Eleanor wore her hair up in a messy bun with a bright blue ribbon that matched Bob's wings. The bird—or rather, the macaw—sat on a makeshift perch attached to a collapsible black tripod.

"Do you always take him with you?" Laurel asked.

"He doesn't like to be alone."

"Copy that," Monica said.

"I love you," said Bob.

Eleanor gently stroked his head. "I love you, too, baby."

"Just to be clear," Laurel said to her, "you take the bird everywhere?"

"Where I go, Bob goes."

"Isn't that a little…limiting?" Laurel asked.

"He's worth it," Eleanor said, and leaned toward Bob, who touched her lips with his beak.

"They have such a warm relationship," Joan explained.

"I don't know what I'd do without him," Eleanor said.

Monica nodded, agreeing. "It's hard being alone."

Laurel stared at her, surprised her friend was encouraging this. She looked back at Eleanor. "Does a bird really keep you from feeling lonely?"

"Of course!" Eleanor said. "He's my best friend."

Laurel shook her head, unable to stop herself from stating the obvious. "He's a parrot."

Monica leaned toward Bob. "Don't mind Laurel. She's just jealous because you didn't tell her she's pretty."

"'How *you* doin'?'" Bob said, in a familiar voice.

"What was *that*?" Laurel asked.

"It's from *Friends*," Eleanor explained. "He watches TV with me a lot. *Friends* and *Schitt's Creek* are his favorites."

"Oh my god, David!" said Bob, sounding like the sister from *Schitt's Creek*, and Laurel supposed he had, in some way, understood what Eleanor had said.

"Isn't that impressive?" Joan gushed. "Sometimes I think I should get a parrot. It would be so lovely to have company all the time."

"You would really consider getting a bird?" Laurel asked, before realizing she had inadvertently used the *B* word.

"It's hard being alone," Joan explained.

Monica nodded. "Tell me about it."

Laurel looked from her friend to her mother to Eleanor, who was cooing to the parrot, and thought about her life with Doug. She wished she could explain to them that there was a lot to be said for being alone, that companionship had its downsides, too. That sometimes you were stuck with someone who was needy and demanding. Someone who didn't appreciate you. Someone who sucked the joy from your life and got in the way of your hopes and dreams.

"I don't think I would mind being alone," she said.

Her mother cut into the cheesecake, put a slice on a plate and handed it to her. "Sweetheart," she said, "I don't think you understand the first thing about loneliness."

10

When Laurel awoke the next morning, she kept her eyes shut, imagining an empty space in the bed next to her. She dug deep, trying to tap into the loneliness her mother had mentioned the night before, but couldn't feel it. The idea of having the whole bed to herself was dreamy, luxurious. She imagined getting up and having no one to answer to, and it felt nothing like loneliness. It felt like freedom.

She opened her eyes and glanced at the mountainous shape of her husband next to her. Resentment simmered as she thought of all she needed to do that day. Before even leaving for work, she had to throw in a load of laundry, give the bathtub a quick clean, respond to that email from their health insurance company. Also, she had to figure out what to do about the yard. The night before there had been a voicemail from the kid who mowed their lawn. He said he broke his arm and wouldn't be able to come, and if she couldn't find someone to fill in, he would ask around to see if any of his friends were interested.

Doug yawned aggressively. It was a message, reminding her it was morning—time for her to get up and let him have the bed to himself for an hour or so. Then, he'd spend the whole day doing nothing. Normally, she would tamp down her irritation and get on with her day, telling herself that when you loved someone you put up with their shortcomings. But today, she thought back to that feeling she had in the car when she believed she had a glorious, wide-open future as a widow, and her anger pushed right through.

"You up?" she said.

He was. The yawn had been a giveaway. Besides, she knew his breathing well enough to tell. But he hesitated before answering, probably considering whether he could get away with pretending to be asleep. She wondered how long it had been since he wanted her to stay in bed with him…or since she cared.

"Sort of," he finally said.

"I need you to do the laundry."

"The *laundry*?" he sounded confused, as if she had just asked him to put on a blindfold, take the car apart, and then put it back together.

"I have a lot to do today," she said.

"You hate the way I do the laundry. Last time I put your bra in the dryer and you were furious."

"So don't put my bras in the dryer," she said, realizing the last time she asked him to do the laundry was over ten years ago, when she had gallbladder surgery. "It's not rocket science."

Another long sigh from his side of the bed, and she could tell he was searching for a better excuse. "You really want me to do the laundry?"

That was her cue to back down, but she wasn't having it.

"Why do you think I asked you?" she said, her tone even harsher than she had intended.

"Okay, okay. I'll do it. Sheesh."

She sat up, swung her legs over the side of the bed, and thought about the lawn. It might, she realized, be a golden opportunity. Her pulse quickened.

"And you need to mow the lawn," she blurted, before she could lose her nerve. Laurel imagined him overheated and sweating, struggling to push the old Toro around the yard.

"Are you kidding?"

"Cody broke his arm."

"How'd he do that?" Doug asked, as if it might change the outcome.

"I have no idea." She was exasperated, and wanted to get the conversation back on track. "But you'll probably have to buy gas."

"Can't we hire someone?"

"Like who? The kids are all away at college. And you know how much the professional guys charge."

"What about my back?" he whined.

"The exercise will do you good."

His expression turned earnest. "You think so?"

She didn't. She thought it was a dangerous exertion that could spike his blood pressure—it was the only reason she had suggested it. But now, hearing the guileless tone in his voice, Laurel swallowed against a rock of guilt stuck in her gullet. She pictured him behind the mower, his face turning as red as the fist-size tomatoes the Patels grew every summer. She could imagine him keeling over in the garden like Don Corleone, humbled and pathetic in death. Laurel shuddered at the imagined thud of his body hitting the earth. She couldn't look at him.

"Maybe not," she choked out. "I'll… I'll call Cody and see if—"

"You know what?" he said, sitting up. "I'll give it a try. It might feel good to work up a sweat."

"I don't know, Doug," she said. "If your back is acting up…"

He thumped his chest. "Me strong like bull," he said with a laugh. "Don't worry. I'll be fine."

She looked at his face, sincere and trusting, and could think of nothing to do but offer a weak smile. Then she went into the bathroom and quietly threw up.

Driving to work later, Laurel struggled to find a set of initials to calm her down. With the term *blood pressure* replaying in her mind again and again, she settled on BP. *Brad Pitt. Billy Porter. Busy Philips. Beatrix Potter. Bonnie Franklin. Benjamin Franklin. Betty Friedan. Bobby Fischer.*

Finally, she was composed enough to put on her game face and get to work, confident no one could see her distress. But later, Charlie waylaid her as she restocked yogurt.

"What's the matter?" he asked. "You look terrible."

Laurel touched her throat, self-conscious. "I thought I was hiding it."

"It's in your eyes," he said. "Talk to me."

She glanced around. There were customers within ten feet of them. "Not here," she whispered. "After work."

"Dinner?" he asked.

Laurel shook her head, straightening the yogurt containers. She pulled out a maple vanilla that was mixed in with the strawberry. "Doug will be expecting me."

"Blame it on me," he said. "Tell him old Charlie had a problem and needed your help."

Laurel hesitated, considering it. Doug, she knew, would

be angry she'd had dinner with another man, even if it was someone as benign as "old Charlie."

"We'll make it fast," he promised. When she didn't answer right away he added, "We can go to that Zippy's burger place."

At that, she perked up. There was nothing date-like about two mature adults stopping for a bite at a burger joint. And she would be able to bring home takeout for Doug, which would mitigate any jealous rumblings. Plus, it had been forever since she'd had a burger.

For the first time that day, Laurel smiled.

It was early for dinner, so the place wasn't even half full. Laurel and Charlie were able to grab a quiet booth where they could talk. The waitress took their order, and soon delivered their burgers in paper-lined baskets, French fries standing like pencils in neat tin cups.

Laurel grabbed a fry and dipped it in a little white ramekin of ketchup. It was so indulgent she took a moment to savor it. "I'm glad we came here," she said, and wondered how it would feel to have a bite with friends whenever she wanted, without worrying about Doug.

"Me, too." He smiled at her with eyes that said she could never disappoint him. It was the unconditional love she had always craved from her parents, and it gave her the courage to speak.

"I did it," she said softly. "That thing with his pills."

"Meaning?" he asked, his head cocked.

Laurel fought a moment of panic. Surely he knew what she was talking about. Hadn't he given his tacit permission for her to do this? Her phone buzzed and she ignored it, assuming it was Doug responding to her text about why she would be home late. No doubt, he was pissy and resentful.

Laurel took a fortifying breath and leaned toward Charlie.

"I laid out his medication for the whole week," she said, "but I left out his blood pressure pills."

He nodded serenely, and Laurel exhaled. She hadn't shocked him.

"You're not feeling guilty, are you?" he asked.

"I didn't at first, but now…" Laurel trailed off as she thought about her scheme to get him to mow the lawn and have a stroke.

"What changed?" he asked.

"It's him. He trusts me. In a million years he'd never suspect I'd do such a thing."

"He trusts you because you're a good person."

"Am I, though? What kind of person tries to kill her—"

"Nonsense," he said. "You haven't done anything that aggressive. You're just not going overboard with the kind of care you gave him for far too long."

"Today I told him to mow the lawn."

"So?"

"So, I knew it would be too much for him. With his weight and his high blood pressure. Because without those pills…"

He waved off her comment. "Lots of husbands mow the lawn."

"Not Doug. At least, not for a long time."

"Did you threaten him?"

"Threaten him?"

"Did you pull out a gun and force him to do it?"

She knew it was a rhetorical question so she didn't respond. She just shook her head and straightened her basket of food.

"Laurel," he said, "you have to understand that you're not asking him to do anything millions of husbands don't do every day. If he's not up to the task, that's *his* fault, not yours. And if he pushes himself too hard? That's on him, too. Let him take some responsibility. It's not fair that you've had to shoulder all this for so many years."

She couldn't argue. After all, she tried to let Doug off the hook for doing the lawn. He was the one who insisted he wanted to do it.

"You have a way of making me feel so much better about everything," she said, looking into his Kris Kringle eyes. He launched into a knock-knock joke then, and she played along, asking, "Who's there?"

"Dishes."

"Dishes who?"

"Dishes what I'm here for," he said.

Laurel laughed and he joined in, before turning serious again. "The point is," he said, "you just have to keep reminding yourself you deserve happiness."

"It's easy to forget."

He picked up her chin with his knuckle. "I wish you could see yourself through my eyes, Laurel—beautiful, smart, compassionate. Your husband should have you on a pedestal, making sure you feel happy and loved. *That's* what you deserve."

She nodded, letting his words sink in. It had been like that at the beginning of her marriage. The change happened so slowly she didn't notice it. They fell into traditional roles, and at first it was like playing house. That filled her, as she had yearned to be like the wives on old TV shows—her model for perfection. Instead, she wound up with a marriage that was a lot like her parents', with a husband who was largely checked out. It was everything she had striven to avoid, and here she was, settling for it, as if it were her lot in life. Charlie was right. She deserved better.

Laurel picked up her low-calorie turkey burger, suddenly regretting her choice. She had really wanted the big beefy Zippitydo Burger, which had blue cheese and bacon. But she had determined it was too indulgent, and had gone with what seemed the nobler choice. But now, she imagined sinking her teeth into the decadent selection, her mouth filled with tanginess, smoke, and the sweetness of ketchup, while juice seeped through the bun and trickled down her hand and wrist.

She bit into the turkey burger, which was heavily peppered to make up for the lack of fat. As compromises go, it wasn't bad, but she coveted that juicy burger with layers of flavor. And while Laurel understood that no one got everything they wanted, she'd had decades of deprivations. Now, at last, wasn't it her turn to bite into something better?

11

When she got home, Doug was on the couch watching TV. Laurel stood at the door to the den, holding the take-out container. He didn't look up, didn't say hello.

"I got you a burger," she said, noticing he was freshly showered and dressed in the new pink polo shirt she had bought on sale at Kohl's.

In response, he picked up the remote and turned up the volume on CNN, freezing her out.

"What the hell, Doug?"

He ignored her, folding his arms.

"Don't be a child," she called, raising her voice to be heard.

He snapped off the television and slammed the remote onto the couch. "I did the laundry, I mowed the lawn, and you went out to dinner with *Charlie*?" He drew out the name as if it dripped with absurdity.

"What's the big deal?" she said.

"Did you run into Adam Sandler while you were there? Maybe you can go on a date with him next."

Now, he was drudging up ancient jealousies. And it was ridiculous. Back when they were dating, Laurel had gone out for drinks with a friend from the office, and a guy hit on her, saying she was the prettiest girl in the bar—a fairly run-of-the-mill pickup line. After she blew him off, her friend gushed, "Do you know who that was?" She didn't. So her friend explained he was a new cast member on *Saturday Night Live*. Later, after Adam Sandler went on to become a big star, there were moments when Laurel wondered what might have been. But it had been years since she thought about it, and the memory was so faded it was as if it had happened to someone else.

She remembered Doug's reaction to the whole thing more than the incident itself. It was the early days of their courtship, and she hadn't understood the depth of his jealousy, so she told him about it, expecting him to laugh. When he exploded with rage and hurt, she'd been shocked, and made a mental note to never share that kind of thing with him again. But it was time for him to get over it.

"Adam was busy tonight," she said. "But I'm thinking of running off with Jon Lovitz."

Doug wasn't amused. "Did you really think I'd be okay with my wife going on a date with another man?"

"Oh, for god's sake. It wasn't a *date*."

"Maybe not to *you*."

"Trust me, we're just friends. He's a sweet old guy who was having some personal problems."

"But he's single, right?"

"He's a seventy-five-year-old widower. And he's not on the make. Besides, look at me." She pulled at her Trader Joe's shirt. "I'm not exactly dressed for a hot night out, am I?"

He snorted. "How could you possibly be so naive?"

"How could you possibly be so paranoid?" she countered. Doug folded his arms and pouted. "I'm not cool with this."

"Well, get over it."

"Can you honestly look me in the eye and tell me he isn't attracted to you?"

Laurel let out an exasperated breath, because it wasn't relevant. Sure, Charlie had a little crush on her. But it was harmless. And meaningless. He respected her, and would never cross any boundaries.

"So what if he is?" she said.

Doug rose from the couch. "I knew it! I knew it!"

"Oh, come on! He's a little old man. I'm not having an affair with him."

"Not *yet*."

She tsked. "Doug. You're being ridiculous."

"Promise me you won't go out with him again."

"No."

"Laurel—"

"I promise I won't sleep with him, Doug. But he's my friend. And what you're asking isn't fair."

"Do you know how much this hurts me?" he asked.

Laurel wasn't going to entertain his crazy jealousy for one more second. "Do you want this or not?" she asked, holding the take=out container toward him.

He glanced covetously at the Styrofoam box. "What is it?" he asked.

"Mushroom Swiss burger, medium rare."

It was his favorite and his eyes went soft. He took the container and sat back down on the couch. The fight was over, his passion redirected. He might continue pouting for a while, but that would pass once his belly was full.

"Could you get me something to drink?" he asked, opening the box.

Laurel went into the kitchen and got him a cold Diet Coke. Then she showered and went to bed, feeling strangely pleased. It took her a few minutes to understand why she was suddenly happier. It was her starved ego, feeling sated. For the first time in years, she felt desired. And that was all she needed. Doug's jealousy—together with Charlie's flattery and the memory of being a desirable young woman—awakened her libido. *I remember you,* she thought, and despite how tired she was, Laurel's hand moved instinctively between her legs. Still, the pull of sleep was too powerful, and she began to drift off. There, in that strange space between conscious and unconscious, she discovered a song. What was it? She listened, as the distant chords of an acoustic guitar strummed just for her. Then a funny man's voice began to sing, forming the words with baby-like pronunciation. *That's not very romantic,* she thought, until she realized what it was. "The Chanukah Song."

Adam Sandler.

12

The next day, Laurel wore more makeup than she had in years. She assessed her face and decided she didn't look half bad. If it weren't for the salt-and-pepper hair, she could pass for a younger woman. Midforties, perhaps? Laurel smiled at her reflection and decided she still had the cheekbones of the pretty girl who had attracted Adam Sandler. Maybe next week she would do her hair color and get rid of the gray.

At work, people seemed friendlier toward her, more eager for connection. At first, she assumed it was the eyeliner, and was amazed what a little makeup could do. But then she wondered if it was her attitude rather than her face. She was exuding more confidence, and people were reacting to it. That made her even bolder, creating a glorious cycle of positive feedback.

In the afternoon, she was on the cash register, smiling more than usual. She gave an especially bright grin to the regular customer who had secretly been nicknamed Marcello by the women at Trader Joe's. They didn't know his actual name, but he looked romantically Italian, with a pretty face and hair as dark as black olives. He always wore shirts so crisp and clean they seemed brand-new. Normally, Laurel was shy around him, intimidated by his slick good looks, but today she felt inspired.

"Find everything you need?" she asked, wondering if he noticed just a hint of flirtation in her eyes. Probably not, she figured. He was the kind of guy who drew so much attention from women he grew oblivious to it. To him, she was likely just another middle-aged woman on the brink of making a fool of herself.

But he looked right into her face as if really seeing her. "What a beautiful smile," he said, showing his own white teeth.

Laurel thanked him, feeling such a rise in warmth she knew she was blushing. Damn it. She had tried so hard to keep her voice cheerful but even, as if she got compliments from devastatingly handsome men all the time.

As she finished scanning his groceries, he kept stealing glances at her, and it took all Laurel's concentration to pretend she didn't notice. But when he paid, swiping his credit card, she let her guard down and looked him straight in the eyes. He held her gaze, and an electrical charge passed between them.

It lasted only an instant before his eyes went to her name badge. "See you later, Laurel," he said. One final smirk—flirty and heated—and he was gone.

It took a moment for her to recover. And as Laurel turned to get back to work, she noticed that Suze, the cashier next to her, was staring, her mouth opened in a delighted grin. When she caught Laurel's eye she mouthed, *Marcello!*

Soon, word got out among the women at Trader Joe's, and

they began teasing Laurel about it—a good-natured game. They asked when she and Marcello where planning to run off together, and begged her to send them a postcard from her villa in Tuscany. It became a favorite pastime that rose to near-fever pitch the next time the handsome customer came into the store, even though Laurel wasn't on the cash register and had only seen him from a distance.

Later that day, when Laurel and Charlie were having coffee in Starbucks—which they now did at least twice a week—he asked what the women had been going on about.

She shrugged it off. "Some of the girls thought it was funny that a handsome customer got a little flirty with me."

"One of the regulars?" he asked.

She nodded. "I don't know his real name, but you've seen him. Sort of average height, maybe shorter. Very slick-looking, with shiny black hair. Wears a gold chain. He had on a purple shirt today."

"Always buys the cold-brew coffee?"

"That's the guy."

"Alan," Charlie said.

"His name is *Alan*?" Laurel was incredulous. It seemed so...banal.

"He's a bartender."

Laurel laughed. "The girls are going to be so crushed. They imagined him with a name like Marcello, and more like an Italian wine sommelier than someone who pours Budweiser."

"You're not disappointed, are you?"

"Me? Of course not." She meant it. The guy was good-looking, but she had no designs on him. Even when she was young and single, Laurel didn't go for head turners. She needed to be appreciated, to feel like the prettier one in the relationship. Guys with vanity and smoldering good looks had no focus. Their gaze was always off in the distance, looking for someone better.

Doug, on the other hand, was a teddy bear, adorable to her from the start. And in the beginning, she was everything to him—the air he breathed, the sun in the morning sky, the stars he wished on. It made her feel safe. It made her feel wanted. And that, she learned early on, was at the very core of her libido. Feeling desired lit her ablaze.

But it had been so long since anyone felt that way about her, she almost convinced herself her libido had shriveled and died. And if it weren't for the steamy romances she read, maybe it would have. Now, she wondered if she might one day get a chance to be a sexual being again, and the thought brought a rush of heat to her face. She just needed someone to fan the embers before it was too late.

"Not your type, right?"

His insight never ceased to impress her. "Right," she affirmed. "But how did you know?"

"Easy. You're not a frivolous woman. You're a person of depth and substance."

She drank that in along with her latte, wondering if he was right about that particular perception. She knew she wasn't shallow, like some of the other women from her town who could, quite literally, have a two-hour conversation about manicures and handbags. But she never thought of herself as particularly deep—just a person with solid values.

"You give me too much credit," she said.

Charlie shook his head. "You don't give yourself enough."

Laurel didn't think she could argue the point without sounding like she was fishing for compliments, so she changed the subject. "You're the one with depth."

He bowed his head in thanks.

"I mean it," she continued. "You always see right to the core of things. I don't even know how you do it."

"When you spend so much time alone, you get to do a lot of thinking."

She tried to read his serious expression, which seemed tinged with sadness. "Do you get lonely?" she asked. Laurel knew he missed Marie, and wondered if he felt the kind of loneliness that Monica, Eleanor, and her mother had tried to convey.

"Of course," he said, "but it's not that bad. Not when I have friends like you to talk to."

"My mother thinks I don't understand loneliness."

"That's a blessing," he said.

Again, she tried to imagine what it would feel like to live alone, and she just didn't think she was the kind of person who would be too troubled by it. She'd have friends, and a dog. And maybe she would even date. The thought of it quickened her pulse, but she turned her attention back to Charlie.

"Do you think about getting out there?" she asked. "About dating?"

He chuckled. "I never was much of a playboy."

"I don't mean playing the field. I mean finding someone special. I know you still love Marie, but maybe there's another woman out there for you. In fact, I'm sure there is. You just have to…find her."

"I don't want you to worry yourself about me, Laurel. I'm fine."

She thought about how hard Monica had tried to meet someone on a dating site, and knew it wasn't the right environment for Charlie. Then she had another thought, and it seemed so obvious she couldn't believe she hadn't thought of it before. Monica was single. Charlie was single. They were both good, kind people with love to give. So…why not?

But of course, she knew why not. Monica was a young sixty-two. Attractive. Vibrant. And Charlie? Well, maybe he wasn't an old seventy-five in spirit, but he looked closer to eighty, and she wasn't sure Monica would find him appealing. At least, not until she got to know him. Then, something might really click between them. And even if they didn't have a romantic connection, at least they could be companions.

Plus, maybe a good friend like Charlie would be enough incentive to give Monica second thoughts about moving.

But how to get them together? Laurel was pretty sure Monica would balk at such a setup. She might even be insulted that Laurel would think Charlie was a suitable match. If they got to know each other, though, it just might work.

"You okay?" Charlie asked.

Laurel nodded, the perfect idea crystalizing. "Can I ask you something?"

"Anything," he said.

"What are you doing for Thanksgiving?"

"I don't know yet. Sometimes I go to my friend Pete's..."

"Come to my house!" she said.

"You're inviting me for Thanksgiving?"

"I'm a pretty good cook, I promise."

He laughed. "I wasn't worried about your cooking. I just don't want to impose on your family time."

"Oh, please," she said, waving away his concern. "I'd love to have you. We'll be a nice little party. My friend Monica will be there. My brother and his wife. My mom. You'll get to meet the whole clan!"

"Laurel," he said, "I would be honored." Then he picked up her hand and gave the back of it a gallant kiss.

It was only then that she remembered the fight she had with Doug about her friendship with Charlie, and hoped she hadn't made a terrible mistake.

13

Despite Abby's instructions, Doug rarely checked the voice-mail on their landline. So Laurel was the one who heard the message confirming his annual physical. She should have anticipated it, but she'd been too distracted by her hopes and dreams. Now, she felt a jolt of panic, because there was no doubt the examination would uncover the change in his medication. At the very least, there would be concern about the spike in his blood pressure.

Plus, the doctor would be alarmed to learn about the stress on his system caused by all his recent exertions. These strenuous activities started after that first day he mowed the lawn. Doug began noticing all the issues that needed attention, so he did a thorough cleaning of the yard, and then tackled the project of painting the garage floor, which required moving everything out into the driveway, and then back in again after the job was done. Laurel hoped he would take the opportunity to throw away at least half of it, as the garage was Doug's repository for all the junk he didn't want to lug down to the basement—half-filled paint cans, rusty tools, an old folding table, rolled-up carpet remnants, a broken AC unit, and even an ancient and rickety wooden ladder they had inherited from the previous homeowners. Laurel doubted it could even hold Doug's weight.

But no, after the floor was dry, he started dragging everything back inside. Laurel had watched from the front door as his face got redder and redder, and anticipated the worst. Despite herself, she made him take a break and hydrate. Old habits, she realized, might die even harder than middle-aged husbands.

Today, as she finished her shower and toweled off, Laurel pictured Doug sitting on the exam table in a paper gown as the concerned doctor pulled off his blood pressure cuff.

Have you been taking your medication, Mr. Applebaum? he would ask.

Of course, Doug would answer.

Are you sure you haven't missed any doses?

Then the two of them would fit the pieces together and Laurel would be grilled.

But no, she decided. It wouldn't play out like that. Doug would insist he hadn't missed a dose, and his doctor would believe him. It was just his deteriorating health, combined with too much physical activity. And no one could blame Laurel for that…could they?

In any case, she wasn't going to remind him about the exam. Not when she was feeling so close to having everything she wanted. Laurel thought about the young mother she had seen in Trader Joe's the previous day, wearing a newborn baby strapped to her chest. When the mother gently hovered her hand over the baby's tiny head, instinctively protecting the soft spot from a dangerous world, she felt an ache in her aging womb. How she needed to hold her grandbaby!

It was time to get ready for work. Laurel stood in front of the mirror and put on the new makeup she had bought, including something called age-defying foundation. It had been a few years since she'd worn foundation at all, and Laurel was so delighted with the transformation she doubted her own perception. Could she really look that much better? She went into the kitchen where Doug was eating breakfast and waited a beat to see if he noticed her. Nothing. She said goodbye and went to the store.

She was almost finished with her day when an infant in a stroller caught her eye. She always noticed the babies, but this one was particularly beautiful, with large black eyes, thick curly lashes, and full cheeks, perfect for kissing.

"She's beautiful," Laurel said to the man behind the stroller.

"*He,*" the man corrected with a chuckle.

Laurel's hand fluttered to her chest. "I'm so sorry!"

"Don't worry about it," he said. "My daughter insists on dressing him in gender-neutral colors. That's the thing now, I guess."

At that, Laurel realized he wasn't a young dad, but a grandfather, around the same age as Doug.

"Is he your first grandchild?" she asked.

He nodded, and she thought his eyes went misty. "Greatest thing that ever happened to me."

Laurel felt that right in the center of her heart. "I'm expecting my first in the spring," she said, her own tear ducts kicking into gear.

"You hardly look old enough to be a grandmother."

His voice was deep and gentle, and Laurel took a step back to see his face. Was he flirting with her? He was a large man, with the same body type as her husband, but more fit. That's where the similarities ended, though. This man was Black, with a shaved head and a single earring. He had neat, symmetrical features and a carefully sculpted beard peppered with gray. The effect was…cool. There was no other word for it. Here was a man who hadn't waddled into middle age, content to ride it out on the sofa. Laurel recalled just last year, when she tried to get Doug to go to a rock concert at Forest Hills Stadium with her, and he couldn't see how it was worth the trouble, even though the tickets were half-price and it was one of his favorite bands. This man would think it was worth the trouble.

Plus, he seemed to be checking her out. The makeup, she thought. She hadn't been wrong about the transformation.

"Must be the Trader Joe's uniform," she joked.

"That's definitely it," he said. "Couldn't possibly be your resemblance to a young Diane Lane."

Laurel swallowed hard. How many years had it been since anyone compared her to the beautiful actress? Self-conscious, she laughed. Because what else could she do?

"What's the baby's name?" she asked.

"Isaac."

"Hello, Isaac," she cooed, grabbing his little foot. It earned her a wide grin and a view of two perfect little teeth. She pegged him at about eight or nine months—the happy age. The age where you find them standing in their crib, smiling at the sight of you.

"And I'm Luke," the man said.

"Laurel," she responded, pointing to herself.

"Luke and Laurel," he said. "Weren't they on some soap opera?"

"General Hospital," she said. "But it's Luke and *Laura*."

"I guess I'm not up on my soap operas."

She laughed again. "Clearly. Because it's been going on for at least a million years."

"Now that I'm retired, maybe I'll have a chance to catch up. At least, when I'm not looking after Isaac."

She felt a pang of envy. "It's so special that you get to spend time with him."

"I just moved here from Jersey for the honor."

"I wish I could do that for my grandbaby," she said, nearly choking at the thought. She let little Isaac wrap his chubby fist around her finger. "But my son and his wife live in California."

They were in the cereal aisle, and her manager, Tammy, rounded the corner. Laurel glanced up, and Luke seemed to register her concern about being caught chatting too long with a customer. It could be a fine needle to thread. Tammy liked when they were friendly with shoppers, but not *too* friendly. Laurel extracted her finger from the baby's fist.

"Can you tell me where to find the oatmeal?" he said, with a surreptitious wink.

It melted her, making her feel like they shared some special bond. This was the kind of man she could develop a crush on, given even the tiniest opportunity.

"Oh, right behind you, sir."

He laughed. "I wonder how I missed it when I have such good eyesight."

He gave Laurel a playful smirk, letting her know what he meant. But with Tammy standing right there, she couldn't respond to the flattery.

"Can I help you with anything else?" she asked.

The baby began to fuss, and Luke picked him up out of the stroller and held him close, patting his back.

"I'll let you get back to work," he said.

As Laurel walked away, glancing at this elegant and gentle

giant of a man tenderly soothing his grandchild, two longings collided like rain clouds, and she fought to keep the storm under control.

The next day, Laurel returned from work to see her sister-in-law's car, with its NAMST A license plate, parked in front of the house again. She wondered if it meant Doug remembered about his physical and took Abby along with him. He had his car back, so there was no reason for it, unless he decided this was his new normal—having his sister at his side for his doctor visits. After all, she was the expert on *everything*.

Laurel stayed in her car, bracing herself for an assault. She could imagine Abby haranguing her for Doug's high blood pressure. And what if she checked his weekly pill dispenser and found the medication missing? Sweating, Laurel tried to practice a surprised expression. *What do you mean the medication isn't in there? I put it in myself, I'm sure of it.*

Could she really pull it off? Would Abby believe it had been an accident?

Unable to calm herself, Laurel searched for initials, settling on *NAMST A*. NA. But all she could think of was *Not Applicable.*

Still wrestling with the knot in her gut, she slammed her car door and went into the house. It was, of course, freshly cleaned, but before Laurel could work herself into a froth, she heard laughter coming from the kitchen. It was Doug and Abby, sharing a joke. She couldn't imagine why they would be in such a good mood.

"I'm home!" she called.

"We're in here!" Doug yelled back, his voice cheerful.

When Laurel reached the doorway to the kitchen, she saw Doug sitting at the table with a cup of tea in front of him, and Abby at the sink, cleaning the faucet with a fresh sponge.

"Abby," Laurel said, annoyed, "I asked you not to—"

"Doug had such a good checkup today!" Abby interrupted, her voice bright.

"He did?"

"I'm down twelve pounds!" Doug said, grinning.

"Twelve pounds?"

Abby put down the sponge. "And his blood pressure was one-forty over eighty."

"Lowest it's been in years," Doug added.

Laurel was so surprised she could barely speak. "Wow. I... uh..."

"Dr. Hayworth said it's all the exercise I've been getting lately, taking care of the yard and everything."

"Oh, I didn't realize..."

"Me, neither," Doug said. "I guess I never really believed it would make such a big difference."

"I'm so proud of my baby brother," Abby gushed.

"I'm... I'm proud of you, too," Laurel said, reeling. Instead of Doug's health declining, he was better than ever. At this rate, he could live to a hundred. She lowered herself into a chair, distraught.

"Are you okay, babe?" he asked.

"Just tired."

"Maybe *you* should mow the lawn!" he joked.

"I *work* all day," she muttered, humorlessly.

"He was just kidding," Abby said, going back to work on the faucet.

"Can you put down the sponge please, Abby?" Laurel begged. "I really don't need help with the housework."

"Oh, I don't mind."

But I *do*, Laurel thought.

"Hey, guess what?" Doug said. "Abby and Gavin aren't going to Connecticut for Thanksgiving this year."

"Jessica and Brandon are going to *Hawaii*," Abby said, referring to her daughter and son-in-law. "Can you imagine traveling all that way to spend just a few days there?" It was her version of a humble brag. She was always going on about the young couple's affluence.

"Uh-huh," Laurel said, her brain still too foggy with the news of her husband's good health to follow the trajectory of the conversation.

"So they're free to come here for Thanksgiving!" Doug announced.

"If it's not an imposition, of course," Abby said, bringing her hands together and bowing.

Doug laughed. "Of course not. We'd love to have you."

"What?" Laurel said, trying to catch up.

"Abby and Gavin are joining us for Thanksgiving," Doug explained. "Isn't that great?"

"Great," she echoed, realizing she never told Doug that she had invited Charlie. This, she realized, might be the perfect opportunity. He was in such a happy mood. And anyway, he would never boil over into a jealous rage in front of his sister. "Seems our guest list keeps growing," Laurel began, but before she could finish her thought, a phone buzzed.

It was Abby's. "Gavin is wondering where I am," she said as she looked at the screen. "I'd better get moving." She gave the faucet one last polish with a dry dishcloth, and left.

Laurel sat there for several minutes, trying to gather enough strength to go into the bedroom and change.

"Dr. Hayworth told me I need to keep up the exercise over the winter," Doug said. "So I'm thinking about rejoining the tennis club."

Her head whipped toward him. It had been one of the first expenses they gave up when the store was in trouble. "What?"

"I know it's a lot of money, but you can't put a price on health. Right?"

She stood. "Doug! You are *not* joining the tennis club."

"Why are you getting so excited?"

"California!" she shrieked. "Our *grandchild*!"

He stared, confused. "You sound like a crazy person."

"For god's sake, I work my ass off every day and you sit around doing nothing and think you'll get to spend the winter playing tennis?"

He looked shocked at her outburst. She felt pretty shocked, too.

"You're being so unfair," he said.

"Me?" She was furious.

"I'm trying to find work!" he said. "I even called Steve Schneider yesterday."

"You made a phone call? Hallelujah. Let's take a *third* mortgage out on the house."

Doug's eyes went dark with rage. "I can't believe you're throwing that in my face."

When things got bad at the store, Doug had taken a second mortgage on the house to keep it afloat. Laurel had tried to talk him out of it, but he was insistent. So now here they were—with massive debt and only her tiny salary coming in.

"And *I* can't believe you think it's okay to join a tennis club when you don't have a job."

"What are you saying? That money is more important than my health?"

"Maybe I am," she spat.

Doug's mouth fell open, and his eyes went from angry to hurt, as the full force of her betrayal seemed to hit him like a club to the gut.

Laurel felt it deep in her own belly. It overwhelmed her. "I... I didn't mean that," she said.

"Yes you did."

"Doug, I'm just stressed about money. About not getting to see the baby. You don't seem to understand how much that means to me." She was always so busy feeling his pain, she didn't try to get him to feel hers. But maybe now he would get it.

"Of course I understand," he said.

"I don't think you do."

"Don't turn this around, Laurel. This isn't about you. My health is at stake and you don't seem to care."

She rose and walked to the kitchen doorway.

"Don't you have anything to say?" he asked.

She turned to face him, caught between his pain and her own fury. Just this once, she wanted her anger to win. Laurel closed her eyes and begged it to surface and explode. It was only fair, after all. He wasn't the only one who had feelings. But her flame had extinguished. There was simply nothing left.

But then something happened. Behind the darkness of her eyelids, Laurel saw a flicker of images playing out like a slideshow. The grayish sonogram of her grandchild's profile. The young mother in Trader Joe's who delicately protected her newborn baby's fontanel. The chubby fist of baby Isaac wrapping around her finger. When Laurel opened her eyes, tears were spilling down her face.

On seeing this, Doug's expression softened, his head tilted in gratitude. Clearly, he had misinterpreted the reason for her tears. He bit his lip, assuming she was weeping in sympathy to his pain.

"Laurel—" he began.

She held up her hand to stop him. "I invited Charlie Webb to our Thanksgiving dinner."

He blinked in surprise. "You did *what*?"

She turned and walked toward the bedroom.

"Laurel!" he called after her, his voice rising in anger. "Laurel!"

14

When it was clear the subject was not open for discussion, Doug went into the den and turned on CNN, blasting it at full volume to annoy her.

Laurel ignored him as she made dinner, splashing teriyaki sauce onto a piece of salmon and measuring out white rice in a saucepan. As she hunted in the freezer for a package of green beans, she considered telling Doug the real reason she had invited Charlie to Thanksgiving—so she could introduce him to Monica. That, she knew, would calm him down. But right now, she wanted to let him stew. He deserved it for his nonsense about joining a tennis club.

When everything was ready, she wiped her hands on a dish towel and went into the den.

"Dinner is ready if you can tear yourself away from Wolf Blitzer."

He trudged into the kitchen as if he were doing her a favor, and they ate in silence. After he scarfed down the salmon she had put on his plate, he helped himself to seconds and scarfed that down, too. Sated, he burped into his napkin and put down his fork.

"You really just had to throw it in my face, didn't you?"

"Throw *what* in your face?" she asked.

"Laurel the beautiful. Laurel the hottie. Laurel who has guys tripping all over themselves to get to her."

"Jesus, Doug."

"What? You're going to tell me I'm wrong?"

She leaned forward and enunciated carefully. "You're. Wrong."

"Ha!"

"First of all, I'm a fifty-two-year-old woman. To most men, that makes me invisible."

"Not to Charlie, I'll bet."

She shook her head, exasperated. "Would you like to know why I invited him?"

Doug folded his arms and turned his head from her.

"I invited Charlie because I want him to meet Monica. They're both widowed and lonely and I thought they might hit it off."

He looked back at her, staring for two long beats as he studied her expression. "For real?" he said.

"For real."

"Why didn't you tell me?"

"Because you were being such a jerk."

His expression softened. "You really want to fix them up?"

"I didn't think Monica would agree to a date, so I'm being... sneaky. I thought maybe if they got to know each other..."

She could see the wheels turning as he reassessed the whole situation. "So you really didn't do it to piss me off?"

Laurel shook her head. "Stop it, already."

She knew better than to expect an apology. It wasn't in his DNA. But now that he was appropriately chagrined, she knew she could circle back to his other foolishness.

"You know," she said, "we really can't afford that tennis membership."

He sighed and pushed his plate away. "Maybe I'll just take up jogging."

"Smart decision," she said, and he gave an appreciative nod. Then he sat with her while she finished her dinner, waiting patiently until he could get back to the TV.

Over the next several days, Laurel dragged her feet, feeling weighted and sad. With Doug getting into better shape, nothing would change. Their finances would continue to get more strained as their savings depleted, and her dreams of seeing her grandchild disappeared completely.

She trudged through her days at work, and very nearly canceled her coffee date with Charlie, but he was insistent.

"I hate to see you like this," he said, when they were settled at their usual table in Starbucks. "What's wrong?"

"Everything's backfired," she said. "Doug is getting healthier. All that yard work and everything. He's lost weight, and now he wants to take up jogging."

Charlie took a sip of his coffee and leaned back. "Oh, honey, don't worry about it," he said, smiling gently.

"That's easy to say, but I'm—"

"Laurel," he interrupted. "It's almost November. The grass is going into winter hibernation, and Doug will, too."

"I know there won't be any yard work," she said. "But the jogging..."

"Trust me, there won't be any jogging, either. Not when the temperature gets below forty."

"I don't know," she said, "I see people running in the winter."

"Those are fitness enthusiasts. Not fat sixty-year-old men who lost weight because they got off the couch for the first time in years. Trust me, he'll go back to his old ways the minute the cold weather sets in."

"You seem so confident."

He nodded. "Be patient, Laurel."

15

It was one of the last temperate days of the season, so Laurel and Monica decided to spend their Saturday afternoon at Jones Beach, traversing the full length of the boardwalk, their arms pumping. The breeze-cleansed air smelled fresh and briny, and the sun glinting off the ocean lifted Laurel's heart.

"Beautiful," she said to her friend, "isn't it?"

"I love the light here," Monica agreed.

Laurel tilted her face toward the sun, warmed by the response, and breathed in the perfumed beach air. She knew that later in the day she would find a ghost scent of this moment still tucked deep in her sinuses. "You won't get this in Austin."

"But I'll get the Colorado River," Monica said. "And it's pretty spectacular."

It wasn't the reaction she had hoped for. They power walked in silence for several minutes, fists moving to keep their heart rates up.

"You're really serious about this?" Laurel asked.

"I'm going down there next week to scope out apartments, possibly a condo."

Laurel glanced out at the ocean, and felt herself ebbing and flowing along with the whitecaps. She wanted her friend to be happy, but ached at the thought of losing her.

"I didn't realize this was happening so fast," Laurel said. The wind whipped a strand of hair into her face and she pushed it away.

"Doesn't feel fast to me," Monica said. "I've been thinking about it a long time. My big issue will be finding a place that takes dogs."

A dog. Yet another joy Doug had quashed. She pictured herself with Monica's life—a clean, beautiful condo, a soft pet to keep her company, the freedom to do as she pleased. Laurel envisioned herself enjoying a glass of wine on the terrace, hugging the little white bichon frise close to her chest.

"Hard to imagine anyone would have an issue with Frida," she said, as they found themselves behind a slow-moving gaggle of elderly people in matching white sweatshirts that said *The Silver Singers Choir.* The two friends scurried to the left around the group and resumed their pace.

"Any chance you can take her while I'm gone next week?" Monica asked. "I hate to put her in a kennel."

"I'd love to but Doug—" Laurel began, and stopped herself. No, she thought. Not this time. To hell with him and his allergies. Bringing Frida home for a week would be the pure joy she deserved. And if Doug suffered, too bad. He could live on antihistamines.

"Yes," she blurted. "Yes! Absolutely."

In the back of her mind, another thought took hold—an allergic reaction severe enough to cause anaphylactic shock. She knew that without an EpiPen, it could mean a quick death. And while she understood it was an unlikely reaction to a dander allergy, is was still possible. She pushed the thought from her mind, and listened to Monica's detailed instructions about Frida's care and feeding, pushing in with appropriate questions. All the while, the idea stayed somewhere in the background, like the sound of lapping waves, buoying her.

"I can't believe you agreed to this," Doug said the following week, after Monica dropped off Frida, along with a crate, leash, bowls, toys, and wee-wee pads.

"I knew you wouldn't mind," Laurel said. "She's such a lovely dog. So sweet." She held the animal toward Doug, who backed off, as if she were toxic.

"Of course I mind! I'm allergic to dogs."

"If it gets bad, you can take a Benadryl," she said.

"I don't want to take a Benadryl," he whined. "It makes me sluggish."

Life makes you sluggish, she wanted to say, but bit her tongue. "Just hold her for a minute. She'll win you over."

"She's very cute," Doug admitted. "That's not the issue."

Laurel put Frida down, and she trotted over to Doug, nosing at his pants leg. "Hey there," he said to the dog, clearly charmed. "I wish I wasn't allergic to you." He took one finger and gently scratched at her head, then went to the kitchen sink and washed his hands.

The next morning, Laurel took Frida for a long, happy walk before work. The air felt crisp, and she wore a thick cotton hoodie to keep herself comfortable. By the time she got home, Doug was seated at the table, having his breakfast.

"Do you know where the Benadryl is?" he asked as she unclipped the leash.

"Do you need it?"

"I might."

"I think it's in our bathroom," Laurel said, pretty sure the blister-packed capsules were old enough to be expired. "But don't take it unless you really need it. Maybe you won't be that allergic."

"Remember how sick I got at the McBrides'?" he asked, referring to a couple who had invited them over for an anniversary party.

"But they had cats," she said.

"It was like I had the flu. I was miserable."

"I know. I'm just saying. Don't expect the worst."

He picked up a tissue and blew his nose, as if to let her know she should spend the day thinking about his suffering. When she didn't say anything, he asked, "You know what would make me feel better?"

She folded her arms, prepared for an outrageous request. "What?"

"That cookie butter ice cream they have." He gave her a pathetic look, and she understood. He didn't want a lecture on fat and calories. Not now, when he was feeling so needy. What he didn't understand was that she was done with that, willing to get him whatever indulgent treats his gluttonous heart desired.

"You got it," she said.

"Really?" He looked as if he couldn't believe his good fortune.

"For being a good sport about the dog," she said.

He picked up another tissue and blew his nose melodramatically.

"Is that your way of asking me to get two quarts?" she said.

"Not at all!" he protested, shaking his head, as if offended she would think he was trying to manipulate her. "But, Laurel?" He opened his eyes wide in innocence.

"Yes?"

"Hot fudge would be nice."

★ ★ ★

His bit of drama with the tissue worked, as Laurel spent the next several hours thinking about his suffering. As she unpacked boxes, stocked shelves, worked the cash register, and helped customers find items from one end of the store to the other, she pictured Doug running through that box of tissues as he got sicker and sicker. Eventually, he would pad his way to the bathroom and find the Benadryl. She wondered if he would check the expiration date, or just swallow the capsule and expect the best.

In the middle of stocking the Trader Joe's animal crackers, she stopped herself for a reality check. Of course, he wasn't going to die of anaphylaxis. The expired capsules would do enough to alleviate his symptoms. And if not, he'd be smart enough to step outside, or call an ambulance if he were really in trouble.

"Hello, Laurel," a voice said.

She turned and there stood Luke the grandpa, with little Isaac seated in the front of his shopping cart, kicking his feet. As he pushed the wagon toward her, Laurel thought she noticed a limp, and wondered if he'd had it last time, or if it was a recent injury. Perhaps it was the reason for his early retirement. She wondered, now, what he had done for a living.

"Hello again," she said, glad she had reapplied her lipstick after lunch. He was even handsomer than she remembered, and the baby looked delighted to be riding in the cart.

"I hope you won't get tired of us," he said. "My daughter decided I'm the designated Trader Joe's shopper." He held up a list.

"How does Isaac feel about that?" she asked.

Luke gave her a wide grin. "I think he likes all the pretty ladies."

She smiled back, wondering if he flirted like that with everyone. "What do you guys need today? Anything I can help you with?"

"How are those animal crackers?" he asked.

"Delicious, but not for little guys like this. Choking hazard," she explained.

He gave a delighted, musical laugh.

"What's so funny?" she said.

"They're for *me*!"

She laughed along with him. "You like animal crackers?"

"What's not to like?"

I was thinking the same thing, she mused, admiring his bright eyes. The baby kicked off one of his socks and Laurel bent to pick it up.

"I got it," he said, and they came so close the moment felt intimate—like something from one of her romance novels. She backed up and watched as he put the sock back on the baby's meaty foot, warmed to know they would be regular customers. She made a mental note to dye the gray from her hair before next Tuesday.

Laurel finished up her day and punched out. Then she went to the freezer section to find the ice cream Doug requested. They had run out of the cookie butter flavor, and she wondered if she should get him the Golden Caramel Swirl or maybe the Coffee Bean Blast. She pulled out her cell phone and called, but he didn't pick up. That wasn't unusual for Doug, who often left his phone in the bedroom when he was home. So she called the landline, and he didn't answer that, either. Laurel's scalp prickled. She knew he didn't have any appointments that day, and at this hour, he was usually on the couch watching TV. And if he did go out, he'd have his cell phone. She tried it again, but it rang and rang.

Laurel's mouth went dry. Could this really be it? Would she arrive home to find him lifeless on the floor, dead from anaphylactic shock? Laurel searched her heart for grief, but came up empty. All she could find was Luke, the handsome grandfather with the deep syrupy voice.

She pictured them on a date in the future. It was summer-time, and they were sitting at an outdoor café table as the sun set over the horizon. He'd look like a god in a linen shirt, his eyes shiny with wonder at how pretty she was in her new yellow dress, her shiny brown hair fluttering in the breeze. She would tuck it behind her ear, then pull out her cell phone to show him pictures of her granddaughter.

Heady with anticipation, she belted herself into her Altima and drove home, thinking about what lay ahead before her new life could begin. If Doug was, in fact, unconscious, she would need to summon the paramedics, conveying her shock and grief when they broke the news he had died. Then she would phone relatives to explain what had happened.

Abby, no doubt, would blame her. *You brought a dog into the house? How could you!*

But Laurel would explain that Doug had agreed, promising he would take antihistamines if he felt ill. Abby would never fully forgive her, and they would grow distant.

Laurel imagined her widowed life, and understood Abby's animosity would fade from her consciousness, as they would go years without seeing one another. Even if Evan and Samara went on to have several children, their special events would be in California, and it was unlikely Abby would make the trip.

As she put her key in the front door, Laurel understood that Doug's funeral might be the last time she would have to see Abby. Never again would she come home to see that stupid Lexus parked in front of the house.

"I'm home!" she called, as she walked through the front door. On one hand it felt like she was acting out a play, pre-tending she didn't know she was the only living person in the house. On the other, she knew it was silly to assume he had a fatal allergic reaction just because he hadn't answered the phone. Frida skittered to the top of the stairs and yipped twice.

"*Someone* is happy to see me," Laurel said, feeling like she was playing pretend.

Then came a line that wasn't in the script. "We're *both* happy to see you."

"Doug!" she said, her heart sinking in disappointment.

"Why do you look so surprised?"

"I was...worried," she said. "Are you okay?"

"Why wouldn't I be?"

"I tried calling," she said. "You didn't pick up. I thought—"

"That must have been when we were out for a walk."

"You took her for a walk?"

"All the way to the park and guess what? I spoke to a lady there who told me what breed Frida is."

"A bichon frise," Laurel said.

"You knew?"

"Of course."

"But do you know what's special about this breed?" he asked, a delighted smile on his face.

"They're very friendly. And awfully cute."

"Not just that," he said, stooping to pick up the dog. "They're *hypoallergenic*." He rubbed his cheek against her head. "See? No sneezing! No reaction at all!"

"Hypoallergenic?" Laurel repeated.

"Isn't that doggone great?" he joked.

Laurel dropped her keys on the table by the door. "Yeah," she said. "Woof."

16

By the next weekend, Frida was back with Monica, the weather turned colder, and Laurel discovered Charlie had been right. Doug's resolution to get in shape had blown away with the autumn leaves. He'd stopped jogging, and was spending more and more time on the couch, snacking on cookies and chips.

Keeping her promise to herself, Laurel went to a beauty supply store to purchase hair coloring. In her old life—when Doug's store was solvent and life relatively normal—she'd had it done in a salon. But it was a pricey indulgence, and she was sure she could do it herself. The saleswoman went through several options with her, and they spent time deciding which shade would be best. Laurel chose Iced Golden Brown, because the woman on the box looked sultry yet ebullient, her hair impossibly shiny. So much promise in one little package. Laurel couldn't help picturing herself with such luxuriant tresses, catching the overhead light in Trader Joe's in resplendent glory the moment Luke walked into the store. She brought the package to the counter, where she inserted her credit card.

"Could you try again?" the saleswoman asked. "It didn't go through."

Laurel pulled out her card and tried again, but it was denied. This made no sense. Sure she carried a high balance, but she knew she was well under the limit, and had paid her bill on time.

"Do you have another card you can use?" the saleswoman asked.

"I'll just pay cash," Laurel said, annoyed that there was now one more thing on her to-do list—straightening out this error.

When she got back in her car, Laurel tossed the package on the seat next to her and called the credit card company, hoping it would be a quick fix. After answering a series of security questions, the representative—who identified himself as Hank—explained that the card was over its limit.

"That's not possible," Laurel said.

"There was a charge made yesterday for $3700 at the South Woods Country Club. Can you verify that?"

"The South Woods Country Club?" Laurel repeated, trying to process the information.

"Yes, ma'am."

A bitter chill seized her. The tennis club. That son-of-a-bitch. That selfish, sneaky cheat! He had gone ahead and purchased a membership without telling her. After they had already decided it was too expensive. Laurel thought about all the times she had been tempted to book herself a flight to California, despite Doug's objections, but wouldn't dare cross that line.

She steadied her breathing, and understood just what was

going on here. Doug had counted on her acquiescence. He knew she would be angry, but also knew she'd back down once he pouted and tantrumed and displayed his pain in its full spectrum.

Not. This. Time.

"Never mind," she said to the credit card representative, and disconnected the call. She sped home in a fury, only to find Doug dressed in a jogging suit, rummaging through the hall closet.

"What are you looking for?" she said through her teeth, though she had a pretty good idea. He was hunting for his racket.

"Oh, I, uh…"

"You *bastard*," she muttered.

"What?"

"You joined the tennis club?" Her voice, she knew, sounded hysterical. "The goddamned tennis club? When I can't afford to go to the hair salon? Or to see my *grandbaby*?"

"Hold on, Laurel," he said, looking frightened. He wasn't used to seeing her like this. In the whole thirty years of their marriage, she had exploded like this maybe two or three times.

"You liar!" she seethed. "You sneaky, selfish—"

"I was going to tell you."

"When? When were you going to tell me?"

Doug blinked, literally petrified. It took a minute for him to find his voice. He swallowed. "Today. I got a doubles game lined up this afternoon."

"Oh, no you don't. Because you are going to call the club and cancel that membership for a full refund."

"Laurel, babe. You don't understand. I tried jogging. It was too *cold*. And I've been overeating again. This was my only option."

"If you don't cancel that membership, God help you."

"Please, sweetheart," he said. "This is important to—"

"You think I'm going to back down? Seriously, Doug? We discussed this!"

"I didn't think you'd be this upset."

Of course he didn't. Because she always looked the other way, like the time he signed a lease on a Jeep, after they had jointly decided it was too expensive. She had been livid, but when he launched into his explanation of why he needed it for business and how he might be able to write off part of it, she backed down, swallowing her anger, keeping the peace.

Now, he looked shaken and perplexed, as if he couldn't imagine who had just swooped in and replaced his wife with this angry she-devil.

She stormed into the kitchen and grabbed the landline handset. "Call them," she said, holding it toward him. "Right now."

"Don't you want me to be happy? And fit?"

No, she thought, *I want you to drop dead and let me enjoy the rest of my life!*

At that, something in her broke. Because it was true. She wanted him dead. There was no more pretending this was a desire she could compress like clay, kneading it for stress relief. Doug had to go.

Laurel bent at the waist and began to sob, straining against juddering breaths to get air in her lungs. She wept for her unhappy life. For being stupid enough to burden herself with such a selfish man. For her own weakness in allowing him to tread on her for thirty years.

That part, at least, was over right now. Laurel was done acquiescing. At last, she was ready to draw the one weapon she had kept holstered all these years. It was a threat so pointed, so deadly, she had never dared utter it.

He took a step back, as if sensing something dangerous was

happening. And he was right. In three decades of marriage, she had never threatened to leave him, never once used the word *divorce*. Because she knew he was too emotionally fragile to handle it. That one threat would destroy him.

Now, though, she was ready to deploy. It was, of course, a tactical distraction. Because divorce would ruin everything, leaving them both penniless.

When she pulled her hands from her wet face and looked into his eyes, she could tell he felt the change in her, even as he didn't understand exactly what it meant.

"Okay," he said, taking the phone from her. "I'll make the call."

Laurel simply nodded. Then she locked herself in the bathroom, and sat on the closed toilet until her pulse steadied. It didn't take long. She picked up the package of L'Oreal Preference and followed the instructions for transforming her dull, gray-streaked hair to Iced Golden Brown. When it was dry, she looked in the mirror, comparing herself to the woman on the box. The hair color matched, only she didn't feel sultry and ebullient. She felt invincible.

Along with the gray, Laurel rinsed out the last of her sympathy for Doug, deciding she would redouble her efforts to free herself of him and collect his insurance money. She deserved nothing less.

Later, her hair softly touchable and delicately perfumed, she lay on the bed, lost in a romance novel set in World War II. As she became the heated, pulsating heroine of the French Resistance, Doug appeared at the door.

"It's done," he announced. "They're processing a refund."

Laurel had been so connected to the novel's swarthy, rock-hard love interest, she couldn't even look at him. "Okay," she said coldly, and went back to her book.

"I'm thinking of cleaning out the basement," he said.

Laurel understood he was trying to make amends, as if that was all it would take to fix her broken life. She was ready to tell him she didn't care, but when she recalled the strain on his system as he pulled all those heavy objects from the garage, she said, "Fine."

As Doug turned to leave, she had another thought and stopped him. "Wait a minute," she said, picturing the rotting wooden ladder leaning against the garage wall.

"Yes?" he asked, looking as if he hoped she would tell him not to bother.

"Clean the gutters, instead."

"The gutters?"

"They're all clogged with leaves. We're getting flooded by the back door when it rains."

"Um…it's a big job," he said, stalling to give her time to back down.

"And?"

"It's very high."

She let out a breath as she picked up her book. "You didn't throw away that ladder, did you?"

"No, I, uh… I put it back in the garage."

"Good," she said, and went back to reading.

She was deep in her book—past the glow of the first heated kiss—when she heard the garage door opening and the ladder being scraped out. But soon after that she fell into a deep sleep, worn-out from the high emotions of the day. Losing her temper had taken so much out of her.

She awoke to the sound of someone yelling. A familiar female voice. It took Laurel a moment to get her bearings and recall that it was the middle of the day and she had been napping.

The voice was screaming, "Doug! Are you crazy!"

It was Abby. Laurel bolted up in bed, trying to make sense

of what was happening. She rushed to the window and opened it. There was her sister-in-law, standing in the street by her Lexus as she looked up at the house, her arms akimbo.

"What's going on?" Laurel called.

Abby was livid. "You let him do this? He'll break his neck!"

At that, Laurel realized Doug was still perched on the ladder, cleaning out the gutter. She stuck her head out the window to see him holding on to the roof with one gloved hand, and pulling leaves out with the other as he dropped fistfuls of clumps to the earth. She glanced from him to the ground where they landed, assessing the likelihood of a large man surviving that fall. And that's when she saw it. The ladder. It wasn't the rickety old wooden relic, but a shiny new contraption of reinforced aluminum.

"Where did you get that ladder?" Laurel called to him.

"The Patels loaned it to me. Did you know that wooden one is completely rotted through?"

"What are you two going on about?" Abby shrieked. "He needs to get down this minute! Do you have any idea how dangerous that is for a man his size?"

"I'm almost done," Doug called.

Abby folded her arms. "Laurel, what is *wrong* with you? Don't you know he could kill himself?"

"Back off," Doug said to his sister. "I'm fine."

Abby watched as Doug dropped another chunk of muck, and her face contorted in disgust. "Do you know how much bird poop is in there? You'll get yourself *sick*."

"I'm wearing gloves," he called, letting go of the roof to show her.

Abby's hand flew to her heart in terror. "You make him get down this minute!" she screamed at Laurel. "This is crazy! You're both insane! I should have you committed."

"Mind your own business," Laurel said.

"This *is* my business! He's my brother."

"Go home, Abby," Laurel said. "I promise I'll call you if he falls."

"That's not funny!" Like an angry cartoon character, she stamped her foot, shook her fists, shrieked in fury.

"Namaste!" Laurel called cheerfully. Then she slammed the window shut so hard the house shook.

"Whoa," Doug yelled, and Laurel paused, waiting for a crash. But all she heard was silence, followed by the sound of a car door slamming and a silver Lexus driving away.

17

Later, Abby texted to say she wasn't *mad*, just *concerned*, as if Laurel owed her an apology, but she was magnanimous enough to let it go.

Laurel knew she was expected to express appreciation for this largesse, but caught herself, and simply texted back: Me too.

For several minutes, Laurel's message app indicated that Abby was typing a response. She took so long Laurel figured she was having a hard time expressing herself. Or perhaps it was the opposite and she was going on and on and on. But when the text finally came through, it was just an emoji of praying hands. And that was it. The fight was over.

Doug, too, was eager to make peace with Laurel. After finishing with the gutters and returning the ladder to the Patels, he wrapped her in a bear hug. He was sweaty, and smelled of damp leaves and sodden earth. But it had been so long since

Laurel had physical contact that her body welcomed the warm embrace, despite her heart. In fact, the steamy scenes in the romance novel were still fresh enough for Laurel to feel a familiar twinge between her legs. She rested there a moment, letting herself enjoy it, then she gave his chest a pat and broke free.

"You need a shower," she said.

"Oh, look at your hair!" Joan said the next day, when Laurel showed up with her groceries.

"Do you like it?" She shook her shiny locks to let them grab the reflection of the kitchen's light fixture.

"You look like a teenager again."

Laurel laughed. She knew the hair color took a few years off, but not decades. She reached into a grocery bag. "Speaking of teenagers," she said, extracting packages of chips and crackers, "are you having a party?"

"Just Eleanor and Bob. They're coming here later to help me sort through some things."

"What kind of things?" Laurel asked, ignoring the implication that Bob might play any part in the favor.

Her mother looked delighted that she'd asked. "You've heard of Mariquita Perez, right?"

"Enlighten me."

Joan's eyes went wide in surprise. "You never heard of her? She was the most famous doll in Spain."

"She's only famous to collectors, Mom, but I take your word for it."

Joan put a hand to her heart. "I've been wanting one for years. A mint condition 1948 Mariquita just came on the market." She bit back tears thinking about it, and needed a moment to collect herself. "But she's very pricey, so I want to sell a few things. They're going to help me decide. Isn't that just wonderful? I'm so blessed."

"Wonderful," Laurel agreed. "But to be clear, *she's* going to help you decide. He's a bird."

"Macaw," Joan corrected.

"Point is, he's not a person."

"That doesn't matter to me," Joan said. "I like spending time with them."

Her, Laurel thought. But this time she let it go, telling herself it was harmless. Her mother's world was so small.

"And Eleanor is so knowledgeable about dolls," Joan continued. "She knows more than *anyone.* I'm very fortunate to have such terrific friends."

"Well, I'm glad you have company you enjoy." Laurel pulled a six-pack of chocolate-flavored Ensure from the bag.

"I'm so happy to hear you say that," Joan said, biting her lip, "because I have a little confession to make."

"Confession?" Laurel put the nutritional supplement in the refrigerator, shut the door, and turned to her mother.

"I invited them to your Thanksgiving dinner." Joan's wing-like shoulders hunched, as if braced for rejection.

Laurel stared at her for a moment then lowered herself into a chair. "You invited Eleanor for Thanksgiving?" she asked, to be sure she heard right. A headache began to form behind her eyebrows.

"Eleanor *and Bob,*" Joan corrected. "She wouldn't come without him."

Laurel was fine with her mother entertaining the strange couple in her own home. But this was different. She tried to picture the Thanksgiving dinner, with everyone seated boy-girl, boy-parrot around the turkey. "It might be a little awkward, Mom."

"Oh, please don't say no! They have nowhere to go. She has only one sister and they're estranged. Because of Bob. It's so heartbreaking."

"Maybe they should patch things up."

Joan's eyes turned sad. "Her sister won't let Bob in the house. She says birds are *dirty*. Can you imagine how that hurts Eleanor's feelings?"

"I suppose," Laurel said, not sure the sister was wrong. Who wanted a huge macaw flapping around their living room?

"Please," her mother begged. "You know how hard it is for me to get out of the house. If I have Eleanor and Bob with me, I think I can do it. I'll be calmer."

That was pretty persuasive. After all, Laurel was already worried about how much time it would take to coax her mother out the door and into the car, inch by terrified inch. If Eleanor—okay, Eleanor and Bob—could whisk her out of the house, that was half Laurel's day. Then again, she had to consider her other guests. She wasn't worried about Monica, who had already met the strange couple. But what would Charlie think? Or her brother, Bruce? He was blustery and conservative—the kind of guy who could go off on the issue of trans rights, as if his whole life revolved around some weird obsession with public restrooms. And if he got that worked up about affording rights to fellow human beings, how would he feel about a companion who was an actual nonperson? And then there was Abby. She had the same attitude about birds as Eleanor's sister. It was sure to create some drama.

But maybe, Laurel thought, the drama would work in her favor, and distract Doug from his lingering jealousy over Charlie. Laurel exhaled, her headache dissipating.

"You know what?" she said, taking her mother's hand. "It sounds delightful."

Over the next two weeks, Laurel began preparing for Thanksgiving, which included several trips to different markets to find just what she needed. Each time, she came home with more of Doug's favorite treats, including Mallomars, hot Cheetos, thick-cut bacon, corn muffins, Peanut M&Ms, soda, ice cream sandwiches, Entenmann's pound cake, Pop-Tarts, Pillsbury Cinnamon Rolls, Frosted Flakes, and potato chips. Doug believed it was an effort to make up for her intractability on the issue of the tennis club, and missed the irony of replacing exercise with pound-packing snacks. He was so grateful he occasionally grabbed her for a surprise hug.

One day, as she did the dishes after dinner, Doug sat at the table eating a brownie over a napkin, managing to get crumbs all over the table as well as the floor.

"Mmm," he said, lost in the delight. "Heavenly."

As she took the last plate from the table and passed him on the way to the sink, he grabbed her around the hips for a hug. Laurel had to hold her gloved hands above her head to avoid getting him wet. He was growing friskier by the day, and she wasn't sure how she felt about it.

The next morning, as she was getting ready for work, Doug sat on the edge of the bed watching her.

"Did you do something different with your hair?" he asked.

"You're just noticing?"

"You look gorgeous," he said, and his eyes got that animal look—the one she hadn't seen in so long. He reached out and grabbed her hand, trying to pull her next to him.

"Doug, I have to get into the shower. I'll be late for work."

"Mind if I join you?"

"At work?" she asked, confused.

"In the shower." He raised his eyebrows suggestively, which she found ridiculous.

His attentions felt neither flattering nor seductive, despite how much she yearned to have sex again. Her body ached for it. Just...not with Doug. If she acquiesced, she'd be doing it for him, not for herself. And she was done with that. She thought about Luke, the Trader Joe's customer with the smart eyes, the mysterious limp, and the syrupy voice, feeling a rush of heat.

"Well?" he said, tugging on her hand.

She pulled away. "Oh, for god's sake, Doug."

Laurel locked herself in the bathroom and wondered why her husband was suddenly so amorous. It had been at least three years since he made an overture. At first, she had been insulted, certain he didn't find her attractive anymore. Eventually, though, she came to accept it, as her own libido withered like a neglected houseplant.

As she considered what had changed for Doug, Laurel wondered if it was her new attitude—the raw sexuality of personal empowerment. But no. It was clear he was so wrapped up in himself he barely noticed her. The real answer was less complicated. It was the blood pressure medication. It had left him virtually impotent. Now that he was off those pills, his libido had bounced back with a force. In truth, it had absolutely nothing to do with her.

While showering, Laurel imagined another man's eyes on her. A man who found her beautiful and could appreciate every single thing about her. A man who would be in the store that very day.

18

Laurel was making an unintentional racket, restocking crinkly, crunchy plastic bags of pasta, when she heard a deep voice behind her cutting through the noise.

"We've got to keep meeting like this."

It was Luke. She straightened and offered him a smile, wondering if he would notice she had dyed her hair. Probably not, she decided. But she felt pretty and confident—a lot like her younger self. She had even lost a couple of pounds over the past few weeks, and knew it made a difference.

"You guys match today," she said, noticing that grandfather and grandson were both in orange shirts. Luke had a broad, appealing chest and smelled of spicy aftershave.

"He wears it better," Luke said, giving the baby's leg a squeeze.

"I think you make a winning team." She laughed, hoping it sounded more playful than flirty.

"Would you root for us?" he asked.

Now *that* was flirty. "Go, orange!" she said.

"Hear that, Isaac?" he said to his grandson. "Prettiest lady in Trader Joe's is our cheerleader."

Laurel felt the heat rise in her face. But as pleased as she was, she knew she needed to reel this in, as there were other customers around, and possibly a crew member, as she had seen a blue shirt pass by on her periphery. She gave him a quick and secret smile, with a nod of her head toward the other shoppers. "You need help finding anything today?"

He nodded back, showing he understood. "Found all we need," he said, pointedly. Then he smiled, and it was so beautiful, so warm, it felt like a precious gift. Something to hold close and treasure.

Laurel remembered the early days of her relationship with Doug, when he never missed a chance to pay her a compliment. It had made her feel so loved and appreciated. And while she understood that no relationship could sustain that level of intensity over thirty years, she also knew that other husbands still thought of their wives romantically. Her brother, for instance, showed appreciation for his wife with gestures large and small. A diamond necklace for their anniversary. A surprise night out to celebrate a good day at work. A bouquet of roses for no reason at all. He even built her a studio in the garage when she started sculpting again. Lucky Rhonda. Laurel hadn't been a romantic object for Doug in years. She was his caretaker. A benevolent and doting mother figure.

Luke, she could tell, was not that kind of man. He had pride. He was self-sufficient. If a woman was lucky enough to be in a relationship with him, she would always feel cherished.

But of course, she barely knew him. He was single—that much was obvious. She assumed he was divorced, like so many people her age. And he didn't project fresh pain, so she figured it had happened long ago.

Isaac kicked off his sock again, and Laurel laughed. "I think that's his new game."

"Nope," Luke said as he positioned his bad leg and he stooped to pick it up, "it's you. You knock his socks off."

She laughed, only slightly embarrassed. It was a dad joke—corny and obvious—but it pleased her.

"I'm flattered," she said, straight to Isaac.

"Must be the hair," Luke said. "He likes what you did with it."

Laurel touched her head, deeply delighted, but hoping he didn't suspect the truth—that she had done it for him. "Thank you," she said. "I'd let it go for too long."

He rubbed his gray-flecked beard and winked. "I hope you have nothing against salt-and-pepper."

She blushed, wondering if he was pushing the metaphor to see how she felt about the two of them together, as a mixed-race couple. But no, that would be too forward...wouldn't it? She wore a wedding ring, after all. This flirtation was just his charm and nothing more. She couldn't let her imagination keep running wild.

"It's like the orange shirt," she said. "You wear it well."

Another customer sidled up, waiting for Laurel's attention. Luke clocked it with a glance.

"I'll let you go," he said, and then walked off, his back straight, his limp as elegant as a dance step.

By the end of the day, Laurel was still cheerful from her encounter with Luke, and eager for her Starbucks chat with Charlie. It was their first tête-à-tête since the credit card incident, and she wanted to get his take on it.

"How are things at home?" he started out, as she brought

the coffees to the table. At her insistence, they took turns treating one another. Charlie had balked at first—he was so old-fashioned he thought there was something ungallant about letting a woman pay. But she insisted she wouldn't be comfortable if he always footed the bill. And besides, it was just coffee. And so he relented.

She took her seat and started the story from the moment she discovered the credit card was denied, watching Charlie's expression as she spoke. He was appalled that Doug had made such a duplicitous and selfish decision, clucking over all she had to put up with.

"I hope he at least noticed your hair," Charlie interjected. "And told you how beautiful you look."

"Thank you," she said, and considered telling him about Doug's renewed interest in the bedroom, but decided it would be inappropriate. Charlie was game to talk about anything, it seemed, but she didn't want these chats to turn sexual. Self-conscious, she touched her neck, and went on with the story.

When she got to the part about sending Doug out to clean the gutters on a broken ladder, he leaned forward, a concerned expression deepening the crease in his brow. It felt like judgment, and she got defensive.

"I know it was terrible," she said. "But by that point I felt so justified."

He waved away her concern. "I agree with that part," he said. "It was absolutely justified. You deserve so much more than what this man is giving you."

"But you're frowning."

"Because I'm worried about you, honey. You have to be more careful."

Laurel tried to sip her coffee, but it was too hot to drink. "What do you mean?"

"Look," he said, speaking softly, "if something happens to

Doug and it seems in any way suspicious, you're going to be scrutinized. So your public behavior has to be irreproachable."

"Have I done something wrong?" she asked.

"That customer—the big guy in the orange shirt."

She laughed. "Luke? He's a sweetheart. A grandfather."

"But you were flirting with him, Laurel."

She felt her face grow hot. "No," she protested. "I wasn't."

"I'm telling you how it looks, for your own sake. I overheard some of the conversation. He was coming on to you pretty hard, and you weren't discouraging him."

She shook her head vehemently. "You misinterpreted."

"He said you knocked his socks off."

"That was just a joke," she insisted, dismissing his observation. Luke may have been a little flirty—okay, a lot flirty—but he wasn't hitting on her. She wondered if Charlie's own feelings for her were skewing his perceptions this time.

Charlie leaned forward. "If I misinterpreted, I'm sorry. It's possible I'm a little overprotective of you."

"And I appreciate that," she said with a gentle smile.

"But here's the thing," he went on. "I might not know what his intentions were, but I know how it looked. And if that's the impression *I* got, then others would feel the same. And you need to stay squeaky-clean right now."

"You really think I need to worry about being suspected of Doug's…of whatever might happen to him?" She felt a prickling at the back of her scalp and struggled to take a deep breath. She'd been so sure she hadn't done anything that could get her in trouble. After all, she wasn't being that aggressive. She had simply stopped protecting him from himself. There was nothing illegal about that. He was a grown man.

Then she paused for a moment to consider the ladder. If he had been foolish enough to climb that decrepit old relic, would anyone have faulted her? She could imagine Abby saying, *Couldn't you see how rotted that thing was?* To which she would respond, Couldn't *he?*

Still, the thought made her nervous, and she pulled at a cuticle as she searched for a set of initials to calm herself. *Couldn't He. CH. Chrissie Hynde. Charlton Heston. Chris Hemsworth.*

"Are you okay?" Charlie asked.

"I'm fine."

"No you're not."

She nodded. It didn't pay to try to hide anything from this perceptive man. He could see right through her. "It's hard not to be nervous about all this."

"I didn't mean to scare you," he said. "You don't need to fret. I promise."

"How could I not?"

"Just be careful and you'll be okay."

"What do you think I should do? About Luke, I mean. He's a customer. I can't be rude to him."

Charlie studied her face, as serious as a doctor examining a patient, and she looked away, embarrassed.

"You like him," he said. It wasn't a question. It was an observation that sounded like an accusation, and it made her feel as if she'd done something wrong.

"He's…you know, charming." When he looked dubious she added, "And good-looking. But I don't have any…"

Charlie shook his head and wagged a finger. "This is very dangerous, Laurel. You *cannot* pursue this. Not now."

"But if he comes into the store…"

"Try to avoid him if you can. And if you can't, just make it quick and formal. Give him the message that flirting isn't welcome."

Laurel knew he was right, but wasn't sure she could follow his advice. Her few minutes with Luke every Tuesday were the highlight of her week—the only thing she really looked forward to. But she just nodded at Charlie, and took a sip of her too-hot coffee.

19

On Thanksgiving morning, Laurel's to-do list was formidable. But since she didn't have to pick up her mother and spend hours gently coaxing her into the car, it felt like half her day was free. She would even have time for a video chat with Evan and Samara, and that put her in a good mood. Besides, this was the part of the wife job she still loved. Cooking, organizing, entertaining. Putting together a memorable feast and dazzling her guests.

Laurel checked and rechecked her list. The turkey was stuffed and in the oven, the table was set, the place cards laid out—including one for Bob. A pile of green beans was cleaned, trimmed, and ready to cook. Salad ingredients were set up on the counter in a row. Her cranberry sauce, which she mixed with chopped walnuts, was prepped and in the fridge. The white potatoes were boiling—she'd have them mashed ahead of time and then heat them up when the guests arrived. She'd be making a roast beef, too, as she liked to offer a variety for this special dinner. That meant two different gravies. There was white wine chilling, and soda for those who wanted it. Monica was bringing a sweet potato casserole as well as fried plantains, which Laurel loved. Bruce and Rhonda were bringing a couple bottles of Beaujolais nouveau. Charlie had promised homemade roasted harvest vegetables, and she didn't know what Eleanor might bring, other than Bob and Joan. Laurel still needed to vacuum the den and give the powder room one last wipe down.

Doug appeared in the doorway and surveyed the hectic scene, which—to the untrained eye—looked like the aftermath of an enemy attack on a catering kitchen, but Laurel had it all under control.

"How many people are we having?" he asked.

"Eleven," she said, "but only ten who eat turkey."

He tilted his head, confused. "We have a vegetarian among us?"

"I guess you could say that."

She hadn't yet told Doug the truth about Bob, because she didn't want him tipping off Abby. The thought of her sister-in-law's shock at the oversize bird was just too delicious to spoil, especially since it would distract Doug from overreacting to Charlie. But it was probably safe to let the parrot out of the bag now.

"Bob eats a very special diet," she began, searching for a way to explain the situation. "Mostly plants and seeds."

Doug rolled his eyes. "I have no patience for these vegans," he said. "Anyway, more for me, right?" He rubbed his belly.

Laurel decided to let it go, realizing it would be amusing to witness his reaction in real time. "I'm pretty sure you'll find enough to eat," she joked.

He closed his eyes and sniffed. "I'm already looking forward to the leftovers."

She picked up a head of romaine lettuce and began breaking it into a colander. "I still have a lot to do."

"Need a hand?" he asked, reflexively.

"I'm fine," she said, also reflexively. But then she paused. Laurel was on a mission to stop martyring herself, and she was entitled to some help, damn it. "On second thought, yes. The den needs to be vacuumed."

"You want me to get the vacuum from the closet?"

She laughed.

"What's so funny?" he asked.

"I guess I wasn't specific enough. I want you to get it from the closet, plug it in, turn it on, and move it back and forth over the carpeting."

"Seriously?"

Laurel couldn't blame him for being so confused. For nearly thirty years she'd been treating him as if he couldn't possibly be competent enough to help with housework, and he had no way of knowing she had changed the rules.

"I'm a little busy here." She swept her arm to indicate all that was going on in the kitchen.

"Okay," he said, standing straighter. "I'll take care of it. Don't worry."

"And make sure the throw pillows are arranged."

"Arranged?"

Laurel sighed. Hadn't he ever noticed that she arranged the throw pillows every day? "Just...use your judgment."

As she went back to work, Laurel listened for the sound of the vacuum. Nothing. After an hour of tearing, slicing, mashing, stirring, washing, wiping, and prepping—without even a moment's break—she went to investigate. There was Doug, on the couch, fast asleep. The vacuum was standing upright in the center of the room, plugged in. Apparently, he had decided to take a break before actually turning it on. Laurel weighed her options. Wake him? Do the vacuuming herself and expect him to feel guilty? Realistically, she knew the latter never worked. All it did was fuel her resentment, she already had enough of that for this lifetime and the next.

She switched on the vacuum and left the room, imagining Doug awakening to think the machine had magically turned itself on.

Remarkably, it took a good ten minutes for the noise to rouse him, but eventually Laurel heard the sound of the vacuum cleaner moving back and forth across the carpet. She was buoyed, proud of herself for pushing him.

Two hours later the doorbell rang, and Laurel wiped her hands on a dish towel, eager to greet her first guest. It was Monica, arriving in time to put her sweet potato casserole in the oven, and help get everything ready.

"You don't kid around, girl," Monica said, surveying the kitchen. She helped carry hors d'oeuvres out to the living room, and Doug began digging into the stuffed mushrooms before the tray landed on the table.

"Don't you ever feed this boy?" she said to Laurel.

Charlie arrived next, with his aromatic root vegetables. Laurel introduced him to Monica and Doug, and asked the guests to make themselves comfortable. But before she went back to prepping, she lingered by the kitchen doorway to be sure Doug was on good behavior.

"The vegetables smell delicious," Monica said to Charlie.

"My not-so-secret ingredient is garlic," he said. "Always a crowd-pleaser."

"I'm lucky I never had to learn to cook," Doug interjected. "My wife—she's the cook here." He gave a self-deprecating laugh. "You can probably tell she's pretty good at it!"

Laurel steadied herself. Doug wasn't being charming—he was marking his territory. He'd probably find a way to refer to Laurel as "my wife" as many times as possible in the conversation with Charlie.

But at least he was being amiable. He even offered them beverages. So Laurel got back to prepping, wondering if she should come up with an excuse to get him into the kitchen so her friends could get to know one another. She thought about it as she worked, but ultimately let it go, knowing it might seem too contrived. Besides, Doug was holding court—regaling them with old stories about funny encounters with customers in his store—and she didn't want to upset the delicate balance of their conversation. She hurried through the rest of her to-do list.

Next, Doug's sister, Abby, and her husband, Gavin, arrived, bearing an unwelcome and unneeded green bean casserole, which Laurel accepted graciously. The guests exchanged lively banter in the living room as the conversation turned to horror stories of Long Island traffic. Laurel darted in and out of the kitchen, finishing up.

As she waited for the others to arrive, Laurel kept an eye on the clock. Her brother, Bruce, and his wife, Rhonda, could be counted on to make a late entrance, so she wasn't concerned about them when another half hour had passed. It was her mother she worried about. She imagined that Eleanor wasn't having an easy time getting Joan out of the house.

Laurel knew her mother would have a wonderful time once she overcame her fears and joined the party. Despite her agoraphobia, she enjoyed being around people. Also, she'd be so impressed by the work that had gone into this perfect meal. The very thought of that filled Laurel with pride.

At last, the doorbell rang, and she rushed to answer it, anticipating her mother's face, brightened with a smile and doll-red lipstick. But it was Bruce and Rhonda.

"Didn't you get Mom?" Bruce asked, shoving the wine bottles at Laurel. He shrugged off his coat, then made a show of helping Rhonda out of her fur.

"A friend is picking her up."

"What friend?" Bruce said, laying the coats over Laurel's arm despite her full hands. His voice implied it was an absurd explanation.

At that, Laurel heard a car door slam. "I think that's them," she said, relief washing over her like a breeze. Monica helpfully took the wine and the coats from her arms, and Laurel rushed to the front door, swinging it open.

Her mother was coming up the steps, carrying a small tray in one hand and a doll in the other. Immediately, Laurel sensed how Eleanor had coaxed her into the car. *Bring a doll,* she must have said, and Laurel was glad she had entrusted this job to her. Eleanor understood Joan in ways Laurel couldn't.

Glancing toward the Range Rover wedged into the back end of the driveway, Laurel saw Eleanor pull the tripod perch from the back seat.

"Come on, Bob," she said, and the bird flew from the vehicle, flapping its bright blue and yellow wings. Eleanor ducked as it soared past her toward the mature oak tree in the front yard, where it landed on a high branch.

"Not now, honey!" Eleanor called to him. "We have to go inside."

"'How *you* doin'?'" said Bob, in the voice of Joey from *Friends*.

"I mean it!" she said. "Come down."

"'We were on a break,'" said the parrot.

"No, Bob," Eleanor insisted.

"Do you need a hand?" Laurel called.

"They'll be fine," Joan said as she came through the front door. "This happens all the time." She handed Laurel a tray of brownies, announcing that she baked them from scratch.

Laurel gave her a hug, ignoring the continuing drama outside. "They smell delicious, Mom."

Everyone greeted Joan warmly, including Charlie, who was meeting her for the first time. Joan seemed giddy with excitement, and Laurel understood. Her world was so small that having a new person in her orbit was like a cosmic event.

Joan turned back to Laurel. "I also brought you this," she said, holding up the other gift. It was an antique baby doll, with a whitish porcelain face, pouty pink lips, blond ringlets, and a pale blue bonnet.

"For me?" Laurel said, confused. Her mother never gave her dolls.

"I'd been meaning to give her to you for a long time," Joan said. "So when Eleanor suggested I bring a doll, I knew it was the right time."

"The right time?" Laurel echoed, trying to understand why her mother wanted her to have this particular doll.

"Look at her face," Joan insisted.

Laurel studied the full cheeks and blue eyes, wondering what she was supposed to be noticing.

"Don't you recognize her?" Joan asked.

"Should I?"

"This is your namesake. This is the Baby Lorelei doll!"

"I thought I was named after Grandma Lillian," Laurel said. She had never heard she was named after a doll.

"Well, a little of both," Joan admitted, with a laugh. "I thought I told you."

"You never did."

"I guess I kept putting it off. That was your father's fault. His family could be so prickly, I had to be careful."

So she was named after a doll. Laurel knew she would need a little time to process this. Meanwhile, her mother looked so overjoyed to be bestowing this gift that Laurel accepted it with as much delight as she could muster.

"Thank you, Mom," she said, holding it to her chest. "I'll treasure her."

Joan took a seat in the living room next to Charlie, and Laurel passed the doll around for everyone to see. As the antique went from one guest to another, they heard the bickering outside continue, as the front door was still open.

"Bob, you're being rude!" Eleanor called. "Get down here this minute."

"Get down from *where*?" Laurel's brother asked.

"He's in the tree," Joan explained.

"Her husband climbed a tree?" Abby asked.

"Oh, he's not her husband," Joan said.

"They're just good friends," Monica interjected, offering Laurel a wink.

Abby tsked, annoyed. "I don't understand what is going on here."

At that, the massive, multicolored bird flew in the front door and circled the living room, flapping its broad wings. Abby shrieked and scrambled under the coffee table. "We're under attack!"

Eleanor appeared at the door. "Come on, Bob," she said calmly, as she set up the tripod. "You're scaring everyone."

Bob swooped toward her and landed on the perch. "'Disgruntled pelican!'" he squawked.

Abby poked her head out from under the table. "What the hell?" she asked.

"Oh, it's a line from *Schitt's Creek*," Eleanor explained. "He's a big fan."

Abby crawled carefully out from her shelter. "What is it doing here? Why did you bring a bird with you?"

"Macaw," Eleanor corrected.

"What?"

"Macaw," Eleanor repeated. "It's a type of parrot."

"It's okay, Abby," Laurel said. "They're my guests."

"You knew about this?"

"They're friends of my mother's," she explained.

"Hi, baby. You're pretty," Bob said to Laurel.

"This is insane," Abby said. She turned to Doug. "How could you allow this?"

"Don't blame me," he said. "All I knew was that Bob is a vegetarian."

Abby folded her arms. "I hope you don't intend to let that filthy thing in the dining room while we eat," she said. "Birds carry all kinds of diseases."

"He's very clean," Eleanor assured her.

"Am I the only one here who thinks this is clinically insane?" Abby asked the group, her eyes wild with rage. She turned to Laurel. "Don't you care at all about your home? Your guests? I think you've lost your damned mind!"

"Hey, watch it," Monica said, coming to Laurel's defense.

"Watch it?" Abby shrieked. "Watch it? You want me to watch it, when Laurel pulls a stunt like this?"

"I think we all need to bring this down a notch," Charlie said.

"I think Abby needs a drink," Bruce corrected. "And I could use one, too."

"Pour one for me while you're at it," added Abby's husband, Gavin.

Dutifully, Doug went to the liquor cabinet. Abby demurred, as did some of the other guests, but Bruce and Gavin eagerly accepted his offer of Chivas Regal. He poured one for himself, as well, which concerned Laurel. She liked her guests to stick to wine on Thanksgiving, especially since Doug wasn't used to drinking, and could be an inappropriate drunk.

"I bet that thing set you back a pretty penny," Bruce said to Eleanor. "How much do they go for?"

"They're expensive to buy and expensive to keep," Eleanor explained. "You have to be really dedicated before you get involved with a macaw." She kissed the top of Bob's head.

Abby grimaced. "What do you mean 'involved with'?"

"One doesn't really *own* a macaw. They're very independent." Abby snorted.

"Here's what I don't understand," Doug said to Eleanor. "Why do you take him out with you?" He paused to take a big sip of his scotch, and wiped his mouth with the back of his hand. "Most people leave their pets at home."

"Like I said," Eleanor explained, "I don't really think of him as a pet. And he hates being left home alone."

"I love you," Bob said.

"I love you, too, baby," Eleanor responded, and leaned in for a peck on the lips from Bob's black beak.

Abby looked like she wanted to vomit, and her husband put a comforting arm around her.

Laurel's brother, Bruce, gave a world-weary sigh. "Liberals," he said, shaking his head. "I always knew it would come to something like this."

"Hey, what is that supposed to mean?" Eleanor said, looking angry.

Laurel felt a tightness in her chest. The last thing she wanted was a political screaming match. "I think we should sit down for dinner now," she said.

The subject of Bob the macaw continued to dominate the conversation over dinner. It was hard to ignore with him sitting right there on his makeshift perch, between Eleanor and Rhonda. Bruce kept trying to steer the conversation in a political direction, baiting anyone who dared to disagree with him.

It was Charlie who changed the topic of conversation. "If I may," he said, raising his wineglass. "I'm grateful for a lot this year, but today I'm grateful to our hosts, and especially to Laurel, for making this sumptuous feast."

Laurel thanked him, and everyone raised their glass to toast her meal. She noticed that Doug—who had brought the bottle of Chivas to the table—had poured himself another for the toast. How many had he already downed? Laurel lost count, and this was trouble. At her urging, he rarely drank. And when he did, it wasn't pretty.

"That was kind of you, Charlie," Joan said. "What a lovely man you are."

Laurel put down her wineglass. Was her mother flirting? She glanced at Monica, who was busy with her meal, paying no attention to either of them.

Abby, who still looked tightly wound, seemed to be trying to get into the spirit. "We should all say what we're grateful for," she announced. "Why don't you start, Laurel?"

For once, Laurel appreciated her sister-in-law's bossiness. She knew just what she wanted to say.

"I'm grateful to be surrounded by so many people I love, and just delighted we could be joined by our new friends—" she paused to raise her glass toward Eleanor and Bob "—as well as old friends who are joining us for Thanksgiving for the first time. Charlie and Monica, you're two of the biggest-hearted people I know, and I am so grateful for your friendship."

There, now they had something in common, and were made aware of each other's specialness. Perhaps it would bring them together. But instead of registering Charlie's presence, Monica toasted Laurel.

"Love you, girl," she said, raising her glass.

"I love you," Bob chimed in. "You're pretty."

Everyone laughed except for Doug, who glared at the bird as if he were a rival. Laurel was pretty sure she was the only one who noticed it. She placed a gentle hand on his arm, trying to coax him to put down the drink, but he shook her off and took another gulp.

Joan added, "I'm grateful for these delicious roasted vegetables Charlie made. He's quite a cook!"

"Bob is wonderful, Charlie is wonderful, everybody is wonderful," Doug slurred, oozing sarcasm, and Laurel felt a rumble of panic. He was getting himself worked up.

Gavin said, "I'm grateful for my healthy kids, and for my beautiful wife, Abby—a rare bird if ever there was one!"

Doug laughed. "Nice going, Gavin. I bet you're gettin' some tonight!"

"Not appropriate, sweetheart," Laurel said sharply.

He stood up at the head of the table, and had to hold on to keep from swaying. "I'll tell you what's not appropriate."

"Stop it, Doug."

"Why don't you say what you're thankful for," Abby suggested to him.

"What do I have to be thankful for?" he demanded. "I'm not gettin' any."

"I think you've had enough to drink there, champ," Bruce said, from the other end of the table.

Laurel tried to grab Doug's glass, but he held it up beyond her grasp. "To my beautiful wife, who has no time for her husband, but still has men falling at her feet."

"That's not true, sweetie," Laurel said, trying to calm him. "Let's sit down and finish our meal."

"Oh, it's true," he said. "You know it's true. You go to work all dolled up to see some guy who has the hots for you. And you pretend you don't even notice."

"You told him about Luke?" Charlie asked, his brow tight in confusion.

Horrified, Laurel gasped.

"Who the fuck is Luke?" Doug bellowed.

"'Who the fuck is Luke?'" Bob repeated. No one laughed.

"I'm sorry," Charlie said to Laurel. "I thought that's who he was talking about."

"I'm talking about you, you little weasel. You think I don't know you want to get in my wife's pants?"

Laurel sank. What a disaster! She covered her face, and began to weep.

"I'm a gentleman, sir," Charlie pronounced. "Which is more than I can say for you."

Doug leaned over the table toward him. "I could crush you."

"Okay," Bruce said, as he walked around the table toward Doug. "That's enough for you." He took Doug's glass. "Let's get you settled down for a little nap."

"I'm not tired."

"Sure you are," Bruce said, putting his arm around Doug and leading him from the table.

"Where are we going?"

"Take him to the den," Laurel instructed her brother.

"We're just going to let you rest for a bit."

Bruce and Doug disappeared down the stairs leading to the den, and Laurel turned to Charlie. "I'm so sorry," she said. "He's a different person when he's drunk."

She looked around the room. Most of the guests avoided her eyes, embarrassed for her, but Abby glared, as if Doug's drinking were her fault.

Laurel glanced toward Charlie, whose eyes were so soft

with sympathy she felt it right in the center of her throat. "I'm sorry, too, Laurel," he said.

"I love you," Bob said.

"Not now, honey," Eleanor said to him.

"Doesn't that bird ever shut up?" Abby asked.

"Shut up," said Bob.

"You shut up," Abby countered.

"You shut up," the parrot repeated.

Laurel poured herself another glass of wine. It was going to be a long night.

20

For the rest of the evening, the guests tried to be extra cheerful to make up for Doug's awful behavior, complimenting Laurel's cooking and keeping the conversation sunny and light. As if nothing had happened. As if Doug had simply gone to take out the trash and would be back any minute.

Bob, it seemed, was the only one willing to acknowledge the earlier scene, as he kept repeating the new phrase he had picked up. "'Who the fuck is Luke?'" he said every few minutes.

To Laurel, it was clear the other guests were eager to leave, despite their politeness. Abby and Gavin had barely put their forks into dessert when they announced it was time to go, and Laurel surmised that her sister-in-law was overwhelmed by Doug's behavior, and even a little embarrassed by her own, especially since Bob kept reminding her. And of course, their departure gave everyone else permission to go. Bruce whispered in Laurel's ear that if she needed anything she should call him. Eleanor took Joan home, Bob perched on her shoulder as they left. Monica and Charlie stayed behind to help her clean up, but Laurel shooed them out, saying she was tired. It wasn't a lie, as all she wanted to do was get in bed and pretend this day never happened.

Still, she had work the next day, and couldn't deal with the thought of a lingering mess. So she worked for a couple of hours after they left, making sure the house was spotless before finally getting into bed for her well-earned sleep.

Doug was still passed out on the couch, which was just as well. She was in no mood for his drunken snoring and grunting. She didn't even want to hear him breathe.

Realistically, she knew he would come to bed by midnight or so. He always did when he fell asleep on the couch. And he would probably wake her, stomping into the room and heaving into the bed like he'd been dropped from the ceiling.

Despite her anger and resentment, Laurel fell into a fast, hard sleep. It had been an exhausting day.

When she woke up parched in the thick of the night, Laurel was surprised Doug had managed to get into bed without waking her. She leaned toward her night table for her water glass and took a long, welcome gulp as she glanced at the clock. Three fifty a.m. She fell back into her pillow and rolled over. In her bleariness, she was confused by what she saw in the blue-black darkness—an expanse as flat as a still lake. Her bed was empty. Doug had never come upstairs.

She rolled back over and looked at the clock again to be sure she hadn't made a mistake. But no. It was deep into the dead of night, and he still hadn't come up. Tired, Laurel let her leaden eyelids close, drifting into a scenario so welcome it cleansed her anxieties and surrounded her with light. Doug, she understood, could not possibly have slept so many straight hours on that couch. That could only mean one thing. All that alcohol must have been too much for his unhealthy system and his heart simply stopped. How nice, she thought. He passed peacefully in his sleep. The night grew heavier, and her thoughts fell away.

Hours later, she awoke confused and groggy from a dream where she had been introduced to Luke's family. She was holding a baby—Isaac at first, then he morphed into her granddaughter. A great gulp of love entered Laurel's being. Overwhelmed, she cried with joy. Suddenly, she saw that Evan and Samara were there, too, and everyone was exultant, jubilant.

As consciousness took a slow hold, Laurel tried to recall what cheerful thing had erased her fury over the Thanksgiving dinner. Then she remembered. Doug had never come to bed. This day, this glorious day, might well be the one she had been waiting for. The dream that had wrapped her in bliss could literally come true. She rolled over, ready to welcome that flat expanse of her bed, anticipating what she would need to do first. Only instead of a still lake, she saw a mountain range—a bulky mass draped in a beige down comforter and pulsing with life.

Damn.

Despondent, it took Laurel several minutes to find the energy to get out of bed and pad down to the kitchen for coffee. When she got there, she discovered why it took Doug so many hours to get into bed. He had awoken during the night and attacked the leftovers, leaving dirty dishes and cutlery in the sink, as if moving these things from the table to the basin constituted cleaning up. Crumpled napkins and balled-up aluminum foil stayed behind.

By the time she was showered and dressed for work, Doug

was at the table, slurping at a bowl of strawberry-flavored cereal as he stared at an article in the *New York Times*.

"Well?" she demanded, standing in the doorway.

"Well, what?" he said, not looking up.

She went into the room and stood in front of him. "Don't you have anything to say about last night?"

"Don't you?"

She clucked, disgusted. "I wasn't the one who got drunk and ruined the dinner."

"And I wasn't the one with a secret boyfriend named Luke." His eyes were cold and dark.

"You've got to be kidding." She had assumed he was too drunk to remember that. But no. He had sunk his teeth into it so deeply he couldn't let go.

"I guess you thought Charlie would keep your precious secret. Too bad for you the little man has a big mouth." His face was pulled into such an ugly sneer Laurel could barely look at him.

"For god's sake. Charlie doesn't know what he's talking about."

"Who's Luke, then?"

Ten times the man you are, she thought, looking at her husband in his undershirt, a drop of pinkish milk pooled at the corner of his mouth. *He smells good, and dresses well, and probably never denied his wife something as important as being there for the birth of her grandchild.*

"Just a customer. I've spoken to him for a total of three minutes."

"Bullshit."

"I'm not having this conversation," she said. "You're insane." Laurel grabbed her purse and headed for the door.

"What about your new hair color, Laurel!" he yelled. "Did you do that for Luke?"

"I sure as hell didn't do it for you!" she called, and slammed the door.

★ ★ ★

Laurel was halfway to work when she realized she had screwed up her schedule. It was the day after Thanksgiving, and she wasn't due at the store for another hour. Just as well, she thought, as she needed the time to cool off. Her only regret was that she hadn't brought a book along. It would have been a great escape to sit in her car and get lost in a romance novel.

She parked her car in one of the employee spaces and texted Monica, asking if she was up. As she waited for a response, Laurel put down the phone and turned up the radio. Abba's "Waterloo" was playing, and Laurel went for it, her mood struggling to shift gears as she sang along. She was approaching the crescendo when she heard a tapping on the passenger side window.

She looked over, and there was Charlie.

"You all right?" he shouted over the music.

Laurel switched off the radio and rolled down her window. "Just killing time," she said. "I'm early."

He leaned his elbows on the window ledge. "Everything okay at home?"

"Not even close to okay."

"Give me two minutes," he said, and dashed off. She knew where he was going—to Starbucks to get them coffee. And she would bet he even texted Tammy to say he'd be a little late for work. Her guardian angel.

When he returned with the coffees, he pointed to the passenger door and she unlocked it.

"I've been worried about you," he said as he slid inside. He handed her a paper cup in a sleeve.

"Thank you," she said with a nod. "You're a good friend."

He gave her a poignant look. "So are you."

Her heart felt weary and she shook her head. "I should have warned you," she said, "about Doug's jealousy. I'm sorry. You didn't deserve what he said to you."

He waved it away. "No, I'm sorry about how things worked out. And after you did such a wonderful job with that dinner."

Laurel thought about all her plans for the night. All the cooking and cleaning and prepping. All her dreams of impressing her guests, only to spend hours enduring their false cheer.

"It was a disaster," she said, though there had been one bright spot. Her mother. She had seemed genuinely delighted by the evening. But that was the thing about being cooped up. It could feel so good to simply get out of the house.

"And I shouldn't have mentioned Luke." Charlie put his hand to his heart. "I just thought—"

"Never mind," she said. "You did nothing wrong."

"I hate to see you like this," he said. "You look so sad."

"He was awful, wasn't he?" An image of him at the head of the table, glaring at Charlie, formed a lump in her throat. "I'm so ashamed."

"It's not a reflection on you! Good lord. Please don't think that."

She rubbed her forehead. "He was still at it this morning with the jealous accusations."

Charlie laid a sympathetic hand on her shoulder. "I honestly didn't know it was that bad. You've endured so much."

"Do you think I should leave him? I just... I don't know how much more I can take."

"Oh, don't do that, honey. You need patience. I know it's tough, but you don't want to put yourself in a situation where you'll spend the rest of your life struggling. You deserve so much more."

"But nothing I've tried has worked. This could go on and on."

Charlie considered that for a few moments as he sipped his coffee. "I saw the shape he's in—sweating, overweight. I'm confident this winter could be his last, but you have to be a little more aggressive."

"What more can I do?"

"Indulge *all* his gluttony. The more you feed him, the more he'll eat—that man has no self-control. Let him gorge on fat and sugar. And don't ask him to do any more work around the house. When he's sedentary, his heart will weaken. Then, when the first big snowfall hits, hand him a shovel. It's a widow-maker, Laurel. Ask any ER doctor."

"You seem so sure."

"Just optimistic."

Laurel shook her head. "I don't know. It still feels like such a long shot."

"Tell you what," Charlie said. "I'll keep my thinking cap on, and if I can come up with anything else, I'll let you know. In the meantime, try to be patient. This is going to happen, Laurel. You're going to get everything you wish for. Keep that in your heart, and carry it with you."

Laurel thought about her dream with Luke and the babies. For now, it would have to sustain her.

21

Inspired by her conversation with Charlie, Laurel began bringing even more junk food into the house, and she cooked the most indulgent dinners she could think of, including deep-fried chicken cutlets with homemade mayo-based dipping sauce, baked ziti with sausage and extra cheese, garlicky chicken with sherry cream sauce, and fettucine alfredo. Doug didn't seem to notice that she barely touched these meals, or even that she had lost a few pounds. He was too busy sopping up the remains on his plate with a piece of bread. For Laurel, it was an unexpected pleasure to watch him enjoy her cooking so much. Despite herself, she tingled with pride at her culinary talents. Plus, the whole issue of Luke was forgiven and forgotten.

One evening, while she was finishing the dinner dishes and Doug was in the den watching CNN, she got a message from Evan and Samara, asking if she had a few minutes for a video chat. This was unusual timing for a call from them, and she assumed it was important. Laurel hoped it was something happy, like a promotion for Evan. He worked as a junior account executive in a midsize advertising agency, and she knew he had been going after a big client. It was his white whale, and reeling it in would mean a huge raise. Laurel dried her hands and opened her laptop.

As usual, the two of them were sitting together on their love seat. Today, they looked tired as they waited for her. Samara had a hand on her belly.

"Is everything okay?" Laurel asked, studying their faces, but their expressions were inscrutable.

"Everything is fine," Evan said. "Both of us, the baby..."

Laurel exhaled. "Thank God."

"It's my mom," Samara said. "She had an accident yesterday in that ice storm."

Laurel gasped, covering her mouth. She knew Samara's parents lived in New Jersey, and that they'd been hit hard by a storm that barely grazed Long Island. She leaned forward.

"She'll be okay," Samara went on. "But it's going to be a long road."

"What happened?" Laurel asked. Poor Samara looked like she was trying to put a stolid face on a shaky foundation.

"It was a freak thing," she said. "Mom was stepping out of the house and her one leg lost traction, while the other stayed put." She shuddered. "I won't go into details, but she had major surgery on her leg and there are pins and well, it's going to be at least six months of rehab. Maybe more."

"Oh, sweetie," Laurel said. "I'm so sorry."

Samara reached for a tissue and blew her nose. "The good news is that they're confident she'll be able to walk again. And she's being so brave about the whole thing. But obviously, she won't be able to make it out here in March."

Laurel held her breath, getting a pretty good idea of where this was going. Natalie had been planning to fly out there the minute Samara went into labor, and then stay with them for two weeks to help out, like a baby nurse. Laurel had been jealous they had asked Natalie and not her, but she understood that a girl wanted her mother. Her own visit, she had assumed, would be as a guest, staying at a nearby hotel and getting limited time with the young family. But now, everything was different, and she felt herself growing excited despite Natalie's terrible circumstance.

"She must be so disappointed," Laurel said. "And you, too."

Evan cleared his throat. "We were wondering," he began. "I mean, I know it's a lot to ask because you have work and everything, but do you think you might be able to come out here for a week when the baby is born? It would mean so much to us."

"If you can't, we understand," Samara said. "I know it'll be expensive because you won't be able to buy a ticket until I go into labor, and those last-minute flights are crazy."

"Of course I will!" Laurel said. "Are you kidding? I would move heaven and earth to be there." It was as if her post-Thanksgiving dream was coming true. She wouldn't just be visiting, she'd be needed. Laurel could imagine reaching into the bassinet for the tiny bundle, and holding her close. Maybe she would even get to give her a bottle. And if not, that was fine, too. Laurel would be thrilled to change her, bathe her, hand her over to her mama for feeding. And for the rest of her life, she would have that one perfect week, and the knowledge that she had been the one to care for the newborn in those first precious days. Their bond would be permanent, immutable.

"Do you need to pass it by Dad?" Evan asked.

"Absolutely not," Laurel said.

"Are you sure?"

"He won't mind," she lied.

Laurel heard Doug's heavy footsteps coming up the stairs toward the kitchen. "Is that the kids?" he called.

"Hey, Dad," Evan said, when Doug came into view.

"They were just telling me Natalie was in an accident."

"Is she okay?" Doug asked, pulling out the chair next to Laurel.

"It's going to be a long road, Dad," Samara said, and recapped the details for him.

Doug clucked. "Poor Natalie. Let us know if there's anything we can—"

"Actually," Evan interrupted, "Mom said she would come out here when the baby was born to help us out."

Doug turned to her. "You told them you'd fly out there?"

"They need me."

He avoided her eyes and looked into the computer. "Your mother and I have to talk about this."

"Not really," Laurel said through her teeth.

"I'm not having this conversation in front of them," he murmured.

Laurel folded her arms. "We're not having this conversation, period."

"We didn't want to start a fight between you two," Samara said.

"Don't worry about it, sweetheart," Laurel said. "I'll be there, come hell or high water."

Doug pushed back his chair with a dramatic scrape against the kitchen floor and stood. "I can't do this," he announced, and left the room.

"Uh-oh," Evan said. "I think we got you in trouble with Dad."

Laurel put on her brightest smile. "Don't give it another thought. I'll handle him."

After getting off the call, Laurel considered ignoring Doug and letting the argument fester. After all, if everything went according to plan, he'd be gone by March, and she'd be making the trip as a brave new widow. And if he wasn't? Well, she'd go anyway. But right now, she needed to stand up for herself. And he needed to learn he couldn't rule by tantrum. She had rights in this marriage, too.

Laurel went into the den and stood in front of the TV.

"I'm watching that," Doug said, moving his head to see around her.

She folded her arms. "We need to talk." When he ignored her, Laurel turned and hit the power button, forcing the room into silence. They glared at each other.

"I think I made my position clear," Doug said.

"Fine, I'm going anyway."

"Seriously? You're going to have a bag packed and jump on the first available flight to Los Angeles the minute she goes to the hospital? That will be even more expensive than your original plan. And *that* was too expensive."

"I don't care," Laurel said.

"Where are you going to find the money? We can't even afford a gardener!"

"I'll put it on the credit card. Just like you did with the tennis club."

"That was for my health!" he shouted. "And I got a refund. So it's a *moot point*." He pronounced the last two words as if he'd landed the final blow in the argument.

"They need me!"

"*I* need you!"

"Is that what this is about?"

Doug looked into her eyes and then down at the floor. She waited, and when he looked back up, the rage was gone, replaced by fear. He rubbed at his eyes, as if trying to force back tears. "I couldn't believe it when you said you would be fine going without me. You were so casual about it, like it was nothing."

"You're a grown man," Laurel said, fighting to keep his despair from crawling up inside her. "You can live without me for a week."

"I can't." His eyes were scared and pleading. A tear escaped.

Her indignation was softening. Damn him. "Doug," she said, trying to hold on, "it'll be okay. I'll pack the freezer with leftovers. You can just nuke them."

"This isn't just about food."

"What, then?"

"You're so nonchalant about leaving me."

"Yes, because it's a week. I'm not running off to Rio with Tony the mailman." She immediately regretted the reference. Tony the mailman was built like Dwayne Johnson.

"Why do you say that kind of thing to me? Don't you realize how it hurts?"

"You're being too sensitive. I'm not running off with anyone."

"But you *could.*"

"So could you," she said, trying to sound conciliatory.

"Oh, come on, Laurel." He gestured toward his oversize torso. "Me?"

"The point is, I'm not going anywhere. I mean, other than California. For one week, to help our child with his firstborn. You've got to be able to understand that. Even if it makes you sad, you can deal with it. I know you can."

She approached him, and he put out his arms, embracing her lower half in a hug.

"I'm so afraid of losing you," he said, weeping into her hip. She patted his head. "You're not losing me."

"I'd die if you left me," he whimpered, pulling her tighter.

Uncomfortable, Laurel glanced at the doorway, wondering how to wriggle from his grasp without hurting his feelings. "Till death do us part," she assured him, with a pat on the back. And finally, he released her.

22

It was a crisply sunny morning, and Laurel thought Monica's condo development—with its primly matched buildings, neatly curved streets, and sculpted evergreens—looked particularly appealing. The two women marched side by side, with Frida scampering along at their heels. Laurel only wished the tiny dog could trot a little faster, as she was eager to burn calories and get her heart rate up. It had been so long since she had the luxury of a gym membership.

Lately, Laurel had been thinking about letting Monica in on her plans to expedite Doug's demise, as it was hard to keep such a big secret from her best friend, and she thought Monica might understand. But Laurel knew she had to tread carefully, because it was a lot to burden her friend with. And if it seemed like Monica couldn't handle the news, she'd hold back. Laurel led into the conversation by rehashing the Thanksgiving fiasco.

"Honestly, it wasn't as bad as you think," Monica said, when Laurel complained that the humiliation of that day hadn't abated for her.

"You're being polite."

Monica feigned indignation. "Moi? Polite?"

Laurel laughed. *"Diplomatic,"* she revised. "Is that better?"

"Borderline," her friend said. "Point is, he was just drunk. And it's not like he called you a whore."

"You've got a low bar for acceptable behavior."

Monica raised a finger to correct her. "Acceptable *male* behavior."

Laurel sighed. "I felt terrible for Charlie. He's such a sweetheart, a real gentleman. He didn't deserve Doug's abuse." She shot a look at her friend, hoping for an opening—any kind of reaction that might indicate she would consider dating him—but Monica merely clucked in sympathy.

"Poor old geezer," she said.

Old geezer, Laurel thought. So much for a love match.

They walked on in silence for a few minutes while Laurel thought about Monica's late husband, Andrew, who was nothing like Charlie. He was a quiet, awkward guy—a corporate accountant who Laurel thought might have been on the autistic spectrum. So she had been shocked when Monica told her he was having an affair with a woman from his office. And even more shocked when Monica decided to forgive him. Then, when Andrew died from pancreatic cancer a few years later, it was as if Monica had been robbed of a second chance with him, and her grief focused on the unfairness of it all. Laurel had been heartbroken for her friend, unable to offer any solace except to agree that yes, it was terribly, terribly unfair.

Once the worst of her grief had passed, though, Monica began taking little shots at Andrew. And bit by bit, her resentment grew. It seemed like she was furious at him for dying. Then, every terrible man she met online became the personification of Andrew's worst qualities.

"If you're so cynical about men," Laurel said, "why do you bother with dating sites?"

"I'm only cynical on the outside. Inside, I'm a hopeless romantic. Or maybe I just don't want to be alone."

"I think I would like being alone," Laurel mused.

"Trust me, it gets old fast."

Laurel dug her hands deep into her coat pockets to warm them. "But I put up with so much shit," she said, hoping her friend would prompt her to elaborate, and then agree that life with such a man was untenable.

Instead, she said, "Be careful what you wish for, because the alternative is worse."

Laurel studied her friend's face. Was she saying she had wished Andrew dead? This could be her chance to open the conversation.

While she thought about a response, Frida yanked on the leash, excitedly following a scent as if discovering something that would change the course of her life. Then she squatted to pee.

"I'm not sure what I wish for," Laurel said.

Monica looked from the dog to her friend. "Are you thinking of leaving him?" Her expression was serious, concerned.

Laurel sighed and watched her breath vaporize into the ether. "I don't know." She paused. "Maybe. Sometimes I wish—"

"He'd never cheat on you, Laurel. There's a lot to be said for that."

The wind blew Laurel's hair across her face and she tucked it behind her ears "That can't be all there is," she said, turning up her collar.

"I don't know if I've ever seen a guy so madly in love with his wife after thirty years. You should count your blessings."

At that, Laurel knew she couldn't tell Monica her plans. At least not now. Frida finished her business and strained at the leash. The threesome walked on.

"That's not love," Laurel said, "it's desperation. He's like a needy child...or a dog."

"Not like a dog, sweetie. Frida has never accused me of fucking someone I work with."

"So you're admitting the jealousy was ugly."

"Of course it was. But in a way, kind of sweet."

"You wouldn't feel that way if you had to live with him," Laurel insisted. "It's suffocating."

"Andrew never felt that way about me. Not for one single minute. He had no...*passion*. Not even for what's-her-name. That was just convenience. But Doug thinks the sun rises and sets on you. You're his whole world."

"I wish I wasn't," Laurel mumbled.

"All I'm saying is, don't rush into anything. I know a lot of divorced women who regretted their decision." Monica looked up the block and Laurel followed her gaze. A woman in a silver down jacket and high-heeled boots was walking toward them. She had an excited schnauzer on a leash.

"Oh, shit," Monica said. "Do you know who that is?"

Laurel squinted. "Roxanne Cardinali? Does she live here?" They both knew her from when the boys were small. She had been at the center of a major PTA scandal, finagling her way into being a co-president, then accusing the other president of favoritism in committee assignments. It caused such an uproar she'd been able to push the other woman out and take over.

"Moved in after her divorce," Monica said.

Laurel nodded. She knew this condo development was like Divorce Gardens—the place upper-middle-class Long Islanders moved to once their marriages dissolved and their homes were sold. "I'd heard she was cheating with Lisa McElmon's husband."

"Now, she's seeing her cosmetic surgeon and I'll bet a hundred dollars she brings him up within five minutes."

"Not taking that bet," Laurel whispered as Roxanne approached them.

"Laurel Applebaum?" she gasped. "Oh my god! How long has it been? Look at you! You look marvelous."

"So do you, Roxanne," Laurel said, moving in for an air kiss. She pulled back and studied the woman's face—a marvel of modern technology and expensive makeup. The dog, she noticed, was wearing some kind of Burberry coat.

"Well, I'd better. I'm seeing a plastic surgeon!"

Laurel felt a complicit nudge in her side as Monica and Roxanne exchanged greetings.

"Good for you," Laurel said. "I'm sure he's a great guy."

"Did I hear you're working at Trader Joe's?" Roxanne asked, pity in her eyes, and Laurel knew it was just the kind of gossip this woman needed to make her feel superior.

"I love it there," Laurel said.

"I admire that," Roxanne said, putting her hand to her heart to prove her earnestness. "I really do!"

Monica jumped in. "Would you believe Laurel and Doug are coming up on their thirtieth anniversary? I've never seen a couple so romantic after all those years. He *adores* her. We should all be so lucky."

"Stephen always says, 'Be careful what you wish for.'"

There was that phrase again, and Laurel wondered if it was a familiar refrain at the condo's social gatherings.

"Who's Stephen?" Monica asked, goading her. She gave Laurel another surreptitious nudge.

"My boyfriend. I was just reading this article in *News-*

day—you must have seen it. About Danny and Tricia Wein-
stein? Happiest couple you could imagine. All this money,
two perfect kids. He was an anesthesiologist. Gorgeous, fit,
the whole nine yards. And Tricia was like a size zero, even
after having kids. I knew her from years ago because she was
a fashion buyer and Stephen knew Danny because they were
colleagues."

"What happened?" Laurel asked, trying to follow the con-
voluted story.

"He *died!* Out of nowhere. Can you imagine? He probably
gets exposed to diseases every day at work, but he gets this
weird virus in his own basement."

"He got a virus in his basement?" Laurel tried to sound
nonchalant, but her interest was piqued. She needed more
information on this.

"I can't believe you didn't see the article. He got something
called…hantavirus. Stephen says it's very rare."

"How did he get it in his basement?" Laurel kept her tone
light, as if this were just idle gossip. But she felt herself growing as excited as Frida chasing after that scent.

"Tricia was visiting her mom with the kids, and Danny—
he's such a sweetie, or *was*—he decides to clean out the basement and—" Roxanne stopped talking abruptly and looked
at Monica. "Oh my god. Should I not be talking about this
kind of thing in front of you? I'm such a clod!" She smacked
her head, as if she just remembered she was in the company
of a widow.

"Don't worry about it," Monica said.

"Finish what you were saying," Laurel prodded.

Roxanne looked plaintively at Monica. "You sure?"

Laurel held her breath, because she needed to hear the end
of the story, and she sensed Monica was about to cut the conversation short. But before her friend could say anything, the

dogs began to sniff and circle one another, and their leashes entangled. The women had to go through a complicated choreographic maneuver to separate the leads.

"I guess I won't bore you with the rest," Roxanne said.

"I'm not bored," Laurel insisted.

Roxanne glanced at Monica for permission and it seemed to take forever for her to respond. She stooped to pull a stick from Frida's mouth, then tossed it off and shook the dog's saliva from her hand.

"It's fine," she finally said, with a wave of largesse. "Go on."

Roxanne smiled, and though the rest of her face remained still, Laurel could tell she felt triumphant, delighted she could share her insider gossip.

"Okay, so, Danny and Tricia had this gorgeous old house and everything. Only there's mice in the basement, and apparently when you breathe in mouse poop you can get this hantavirus. It gets in your lungs and it's *over*. I can't believe you didn't read the story. Stephen said they might make a movie about it."

"It was in yesterday's paper?" Laurel asked, picturing the stack of newspapers in her garage. She hoped Doug had been lazy about taking the recyclables out to the curb.

"Yesterday or the day before. Whatever. Point is, everybody thought Tricia was the luckiest girl in the world and now look at her. Two little kids and a dead husband."

"Tragic," Laurel offered.

"Oh! The *worst*. Stephen was beside himself."

At that, Frida was finished with the schnauzer and began to strain on the leash again.

"You girls go," Roxanne said. "I have a manicure appointment anyway. Stephen is taking me to the city tonight. It was great to see you, Laurel. Maybe I'll stop into Trader Joe's!" She gave a laugh, as if she'd made a joke, and then she was gone.

★ ★ ★

That evening, Laurel combed through the newspapers in the garage, frustrated that the article wasn't in yesterday's *Newsday*, nor the day before's. Roxanne Cardinali, she realized, sensed the passage of time about as well as her schnauzer. But Laurel was determined, and kept digging. For once, she was grateful Doug had neglected to take out the recyclables, because after going back several more days, there it was: *Hantavirus Kills 38-Year-Old Bridgehampton Man*. She read through it twice right there in the dimly lit garage, trying to glean every possible bit of information, because she didn't want to risk Googling *hantavirus*, and leave any kind of a trail on her hard drive. She closed her eyes and pictured the whole thing playing out. Doug spending hours in the basement, breathing toxic fumes. It would be followed by a mild illness that escalated quickly. Before the doctors could even figure out what was wrong, Doug would be on a ventilator, unconscious. And then, after sitting by his bedside day after day and finally going home for some rest, Laurel's phone would ring in the middle of the night with the news: he was gone.

Laurel ripped the article from the paper, folded it into a careful square, and stuck it in her pocket. Then she neatly restacked the newspapers, went into the house, and made Doug a dinner of chicken paprikash with noodles and lots and lots of sour cream.

23

At work that Tuesday, Laurel couldn't stop thinking about the hantavirus article she had slipped into her purse. She thought about it as she unpacked and restocked the ice cream, as she worked the cash register, as she cleaned out the fresh vegetables. She even thought about it as she was facing and straightening the spice shelves and happened to glimpse Luke walking into the store. A trill of excitement shivered through her. What a life she could have! It was all so close, if only this plan could work.

Despite herself, she warmed as he approached. Laurel didn't forget that Charlie had warned her to keep her distance, for appearances' sake, but her resolve evaporated as she breathed in his sweet and spicy cologne. And the way he smiled at her made Laurel feel twenty-two again.

Isaac was happy, too, kicking his chubby legs at the sight of her.

"I think he had a growth spurt," she said. "He looks so big." It seemed he got cuter every time she saw him, and today he looked as huggable as memory foam. She wished she could pull him from the cart and give him a squeeze. It would be fun to play grandma to this beautiful baby, with his sparkly eyes.

"The pediatrician says this fella's off the charts."

"Watch out," she said. "He'll be bigger than his grandpa soon."

Charlie appeared at the end of the aisle and shot her a warning look. But Laurel didn't see what could possibly be suspect about cooing over a baby. It was all utterly benign. Still, her plans for the basement were so aggressive Laurel knew she had to proceed with extreme caution. Complacency could be her downfall. She took a deep breath and forced herself to switch modes.

"Can I help you find anything today?" she asked Luke.

He looked taken aback by her change in demeanor. He recovered quickly, though, and offered a chuckle. "I think by now I have the layout of the store memorized! But thanks."

She felt a pang as he limped away, sensing there were some hurt feelings. Next time, she decided, she would be friendlier, to make up for it. To hell with Charlie's warning.

A short while later, as she was restocking the dairy case, Laurel felt a presence behind her. Certain it was Luke, she whirled around, offering her flirtiest smile as she tossed her hair back. But she found herself face-to-face with the exotically handsome customer she had known as Marcello, but who was actually a bartender named Alan.

"Hey, I remember you," he said. "The lady with the beautiful smile." He looked at her name badge. "Nice to see you again, Laurel."

She felt self-conscious, as his voice carried across the store, and two of the cashiers glanced up to watch the encounter.

She knew how it looked—like she had welcomed his attention with a beaming grin. But even as she took a step back and re-arranged her expression, she saw that a customer near the exit had been watching, too. It was Luke. They locked eyes for a moment, and then he turned, straightened, and walked out.

Now, she'd definitely hurt his feelings. Laurel sensed it in a specific part of her gut. Immediately, she decided Charlie had been wrong. She could be as friendly as she wanted to-ward Luke, and no one would make a connection to what-ever might befall Doug.

She tamped down the part of her that feared Luke wouldn't come back. Of course he would. And she would smile so brightly he would know it had all been a misunderstanding. And he would also know that one day, she would be available. And maybe then, the two of them could discover some fated love they'd both been hungry for their whole lives.

Laurel held that thought close to her heart as she sat across from Charlie at Starbucks a few hours later, hoping the article in her purse would be the ticket to her dreams. She pulled it out, unfolded it, and pushed it across the table.

"What's this?" Charlie asked.

"Read it," she said, and he slid a pair of glasses from his jacket pocket.

She sipped her coffee as his eyes moved down the page. At last, he took off his readers and spread his hand over the article. "This," he said to Laurel, his eyes lit with determination as he tapped on the page "This could be exactly what you need."

She shifted, a tremor of nervous excitement running through her. "I know."

"I mean it," he said, as if she'd disagreed.

Laurel leaned forward, keeping her voice low. "It's perfect. I wouldn't even have to ride him about cleaning out the basement. He's been wanting to do it for weeks. It would just take the tiniest nudge." She paused. "There's only one problem."

"You don't have mice?" he guessed.

Laurel nodded. "I just need to figure out where I can buy enough to breed and do the trick. A specialty pet store, I guess?" She shuddered. "They creep me out, but I think I could do it."

"No," he said. "You can't. That would leave a dangerous trail. Leave it to me."

"Oh no, Charlie. I don't want to involve you. It's too much." In truth, she craved his help, but thought it was unfair to ask.

He waved off her concern. "Listen, next week I'm driving up to Rochester to visit my brother. I'll buy some mice up there. It'll be untraceable from Long Island—completely anonymous."

"Are you sure? And where would you even get them?"

Charlie looked pensive as he considered this. "I once knew a guy who fed live mice to his pet snake. I think it's kind of black market, but I can work it out."

"That sounds so criminal!" Even as she said it, Laurel understood the irony of worrying about the purchase of black market mice, when they were plotting something far more nefarious.

"It's fine," he assured her.

Laurel pictured driving all the way home from Rochester with a box full of mice in the car. The thought of it made the flesh on the back of her neck go cold.

"You sure you want to do this?"

"It's not a problem. Your job will be to get him out of the house."

Laurel thought for a minute. "Monday morning," she said. "He has an early appointment with his podiatrist."

Charlie crumpled the newspaper article into a ball, wedged

it into a half-filled paper cup on the next table, and began a knock-knock joke.

"Who's there?" she asked.

"Allah."

"Allah who?"

"Allah be there when you need me."

24

That weekend, Laurel was hoping for a distraction so she could stop obsessing about her plans for Monday. Luckily, Monica mentioned she needed to stop at Randee's Childrenswear to return something she had bought for her grandson, Mateo. The place was a veritable Long Island institution—a department store for children's clothes, including a huge layette section for baby items—and Laurel jumped at the chance to come along. She had been dying to finger tiny outfits for her future granddaughter, and this was a perfect opportunity. She wouldn't buy anything, because she considered it bad luck to bring home baby items before the birth, but she could shop and dream, perhaps even have some selections set aside for her.

From the moment she and Monica stepped inside the door, Laurel felt her oxytocin skyrocket. Babies! They were everywhere. In strollers, on hips, in carriers. Laurel even got a kick out of the toddler smacking every item of clothing he passed by, his frazzled mother too focused on her mission to even notice. Not that Laurel romanticized those sleepless nights and bleary days. She remembered how hard it was, even with only one child. But there was so much wonder and rapture to balance it out. She recalled Evan's graduation ceremony from preschool. The children were all lined up, singing for the parents, and Evan was the most earnest of all, standing like a soldier, his head back as he sang louder than everyone else, putting his whole throat, body, and soul into it, sending a ripple of delighted titters through the crowd. An elderly woman on Laurel's right—presumably someone's grandmother—had grabbed her arm. "What a joy he is!" she said, tears in her eyes. Laurel wept, too, looking back at her son, treasuring the moment.

A grandchild, she knew, would be a chance to live it all again, but without the sleepless nights and endless worrying. Life didn't deliver better gifts.

Laurel glanced toward the toddler boys department, channeling the sweetest nostalgia, just as a young mother with a delicate newborn strapped to her body passed within inches of her. Laurel wanted to lean in and sniff, but she knew how crazy that would seem, so she kept her baby obsession to herself. Soon enough, she would be holding her very own grandchild, and all would be well.

Monica laughed, noticing Laurel's expression. "Girl," she said, "there are two kinds of grandmas—obnoxious and more obnoxious. I think we both know which kind you're going to be."

Laurel couldn't disagree. "I'll be stopping random strangers on the street to show them pictures."

Monica went off to the returns desk, and Laurel walked the store's center aisle, surveying the merchandise. When Evan was born, baby clothes were binary. Blue for boys, pink for girls. Garments in yellow, pale green, and white only occasionally broke up the monotony. But you never crossed that pink-blue boundary, and Laurel had pined for the girl's section of the store, mildly envious of women with daughters who got to pick out pretty things with flowers and ribbons.

Now, of course, that was starting to change. Young parents were mindful of the inherent sexism in projecting gender biases onto newborns. Laurel understood this and agreed with it, and yet... She'd spent a lifetime pining for pink, and hoped Evan and Samara would afford her the indulgence of selecting just a few girlie things.

The impossibly adorable baby booties rack seemed to call out to her, and Laurel stopped to examine the miniature footwear, even as several strollers pushed by. But then, one caught her eye, and Laurel did a double take. She knew that baby. It took an extra second, but the synapses connected—it was Isaac! Laurel looked up, and the person behind the stroller wasn't Luke, but an attractive young Black woman in hospital scrubs. She surmised it was Isaac's mother—Luke's daughter. She was tall, like her father, and pretty enough to be a model, but she had clearly chosen another career path. It struck Laurel that she still had no idea what Luke had done for a living before his retirement.

Laurel smiled at Isaac, and then at the mother, wondering if she should introduce herself. But what would she say? *Hi, you don't know me, but I work at Trader Joe's and have this inappropriate flirtation going on with your father.* No. Best to just keep her mouth shut.

Laurel continued wandering the store, but never stopped clocking the young mother's whereabouts. After several minutes, she saw the twosome in line at the checkout, where they had caught up with a third member of their party, presumably the dad. Unable to resist, Laurel fell in behind them to eavesdrop. She couldn't make out what they were saying, but the line was slow, and after a while Isaac started to fuss. His father picked him up out of the stroller and patted his back. Now, Laurel was able to hear the exchange, as the couple raised their voices to be heard over the baby's cries.

"Should I take him outside?" the young father asked.

"Go on to Celia's. I'll meet you there."

Laurel surmised they were talking about Celia's Café, a casual organic eatery on the corner of the strip mall.

"Should I text your dad?"

"He's probably already there," she said, waving him away.

Without another word, the man walked off, carrying Isaac in his arms, leaving the mother with the stroller and a pile of baby clothes. Laurel felt proud of herself for staying put instead of chasing after him like a love-starved middle schooler. She wanted to, of course. She wanted to run into the café and apologize to Luke for what he thought he saw at Trader Joe's on Tuesday, and tell him exactly how she felt about him— schoolgirl crush and all. Alan the smarmy bartender meant nothing to her.

Instead, she met up with Monica, and left the store. When her friend asked if she wanted to stop for a bite to eat, Laurel didn't even suggest Celia's. She was, after all, a mature woman. A married woman. Still, she stored away the information that Luke was having lunch at a specific local restaurant on a Saturday afternoon. And as a creature of habit—as well as someone dedicated to eating wholesome food—it was entirely possible he was there every week.

"I'm here!" Laurel called, as she let herself into her mother's house the next day. She walked up the short flight of stairs to the kitchen landing, set the bags of groceries on the table, and began to unpack. The room looked freshly cleaned, as if her mother had just finished polishing the surfaces and squaring the counter items. Of course, she could have done it yesterday or the day before. Since she lived alone, the house never had a chance to get dirty.

Laurel considered what it would be like to clean her house and go out for the day, only to come home and find it exactly as she had left it. The very idea made her shoulders relax. She could imagine coming home and kicking off her shoes on a spotless carpet, letting her bare toes sink into it. With nothing pressing her to clean and straighten, she could pour herself a crisp glass of white wine and relax in a perfectly pristine living room.

Laurel heard her mother coming up from the den and was struck by the clipped sound of the footsteps, realizing they were hard-soled shoes, not sneakers. At almost the same time, the scent of Chanel No. 5 wafted into the kitchen. Laurel glanced up to see her mother in the doorway, dressed for company in black slacks and an ombré sweater set that began as a rich coral at the bottom and lightened to pale peach at the top. Perhaps that was why the kitchen was so neat.

"Look at you!" Laurel said, pleased to see her mother dressed for a social encounter more formal than reorganizing her doll collection. "Are you expecting someone?"

"Oh," Joan said, looking down at her own sweater as if she'd forgotten she was dressed up. "Do you like this? I got it from QVC. It was on sale."

"It's lovely. I didn't know you were having company." Her mother hadn't requested any special groceries, so Laurel was surprised.

"Not company," she said, "but I'm thinking about…" Joan put her thumbnail to her teeth and tapped nervously.

Almost instantly, Laurel clocked her mother's anxiety and understood. "You're thinking about going *out*?" She practically laughed with joy. This was progress!

"Yes, if I can." Joan tried to offer a brave smile, and Laurel could see how hard it was for her.

"That's so great, Mom. Where did you want to go?"

Joan held her face in her hands. "I don't know if I can do this."

"Tell me what you wanted to do," Laurel said, hoping to keep her mother focused on whatever had excited her, rather than slip into the deep groove of her anxiety.

"There's a doll and teddy bear show at the Melville Marriott," she said. "Some of my friends from the doll club are going to be there. And the exhibitors! There's so much to see."

"Let's do it!" Laurel said.

"You...you want to?" Joan asked.

Laurel had to choke back tears. This was momentous. And she knew exactly what had spurred the change. It was that crazy Thanksgiving at her house. Despite everything, Joan had enjoyed getting out, and had gained confidence from making it through a fraught evening without faltering.

"Of course I want to go!" she said, speeding up her grocery unpacking. "I can't think of anything more fun than spending that kind of time with you."

Joan clasped her hands in front of her heart as if protecting herself. "You think I can do this?"

Laurel recalled the image of her mother happily walking up the steps to her front door, clutching the Baby Lorelei doll, and knew what she had to do. "Of course you can!" she said, and held out an empty tote bag. "Put a couple of dolls in here—the ones you want to show your club friends. I'll just finish putting away the groceries, and then we'll leave. How does that sound?"

Joan clapped her hands in glee. "I can't believe we're really doing this!"

Minutes later, they were ready, only Joan hesitated at the front door. "Are you sure this is a good idea?" she asked.

Laurel understood how desperately her mother wanted to go on this outing, and just needed a little push. Instructing her to be brave, she knew, would do nothing except fuel her anxiety. So Laurel said, "Tell me which dolls you decided to bring."

As Joan began to talk, Laurel put a hand on her elbow and guided her right out the door and into the car. She was still yammering about Sweet Sue and Nancy Ann and Mariquita Perez when Laurel backed out of the driveway and steered them toward freedom.

To Laurel, the grand ballroom at the Marriott looked like her mother's den on steroids. There were dolls and stuffed animals everywhere—laid out on tables, propped up on shelves, standing on boxes, dangling from hooks. Bright exhibitor displays lined the walls of the room. The interior space had aisles created by rows of narrow tables dressed in pleated black drapes. Few of the attendees had empty hands. Some, like Joan, held tote bags, while others clutched dolls to their chests.

Laurel looked at her mother's face, which was lit with joy. Her eyes scanned the room, taking it all in.

"Happy?" Laurel asked.

Joan nodded, unable to speak, as her eyes brimmed with tears.

The two women took a step inside the chilly ballroom toward the exhibit closest to the door, and Laurel understood that her mother would want to spend time at each and every display. This was fine with her. She would not be rushing home to Doug that day. He would be upset, of course. But she would deal with the repercussions of that later. For now, she was focused on the life she would have one day soon. A life that would afford her time to do what she wanted, like spend a day with her mother.

Before Joan even finished examining the first display, she looked up to discover she was standing next to a woman she knew from her online meetings with the doll club. Laurel watched the drama unfold as the two women squealed in delight.

"Beverly!" Joan exclaimed, and they fell into each other's arms like long-lost family.

Joan introduced Laurel, and then Beverly introduced Emma, the eerily lifelike but not very pretty newborn doll she cradled.

"She looks so real," Laurel said.

Beverly was thrilled to meet a doll neophyte, and explained to Laurel that these infants were called "Reborns."

Reborn, Laurel thought, looking at her mother, who was now chatting so breezily with two women holding plush stuffed animals it was as if her anxieties had vanished.

She took a deep breath and thought about the ambitious plan she would be putting into action the next morning. If it worked, maybe she could be reborn, too.

25

Laurel awoke early the next day to make Doug an egg and bacon sandwich on the flaky Pillsbury biscuits he liked. For good measure, she added American cheese—the deluxe kind that melted into creamy satin. He dug in with relish, making small purring noises as he ate, and she hoped he would finish quickly.

Standing at the sink, Laurel fussed with the dishes as she kept an anxious eye on the clock, eager for him to leave for his doctor's appointment. She had to make sure he got out of the house in time for Charlie to come over and release the mice before they were due at work. The timing had to be precise. Laurel glanced over as Doug sipped his coffee and read the newspaper. If he reached for a pencil to do the sudoku, she knew she'd be in trouble.

"What time is your appointment?" she asked, as if she'd

forgotten. In truth, she wanted him to look at the clock and feel some urgency.

"Nine twenty," he said, wiping his mouth with a napkin. He didn't check the time, made no effort to rush.

Laurel waited a beat, hoping he would make a move. Nothing.

"When do you have to leave?" she asked, her voice as light as a feather.

At that, he glanced up at the microwave's digital display. "Pretty soon."

Now, she thought. You should go *now.*

He shoved the last of his breakfast biscuit into his mouth, polished it off with another sip of coffee, and wiped his mouth again. Laurel crossed her arms over her Trader Joe's shirt and tapped her foot, trying to transmit her impatience. He didn't seem to notice, but at last he got up and went into the bathroom. She was cleaning up after him in the kitchen, pretending to be engrossed in her task, when he said goodbye and headed out the door.

Laurel counted to three, and then rushed to the window, watching as his car drove off and rounded the corner. This was it. She was really doing it. Taking a deep breath, she grabbed her phone and texted Charlie the code they had worked out: *Knock-knock.*

The next fifteen minutes were excruciating. Laurel wiped down the kitchen counters, cleaned the table, paced. At last, there was an actual knock-knock on her front door.

"Thank you for doing this," she said, when she swung it open.

Charlie, also dressed for work in his Trader Joe's shirt, held two brown paper bags, which bulged and skittered. She had expected a shoebox or a small carton, and this made it so much more real. The mice moved and scratched inside the bags, trying to get out. Laurel shivered, and for a terrible moment considered pulling the plug on the whole operation. Could she really go through with making her basement a breeding ground for rodents? How long before they made their way to the main level?

"You're very welcome," he said, bowing his head.

Laurel touched her throat. "Are we sure this is really a good idea?"

Charlie looked almost hurt as he cocked his head. "You're not having second thoughts, are you?"

Now, she felt guilty. He had driven all the way home from Rochester with these frantic creatures in his car. And he'd done it for her.

"I guess not," she said. "It's just… I wasn't expecting them to be so active." She rubbed her arms against a chill. "How many are there?"

"An even dozen. Half male, half female. And I'm assured at least one of them is already pregnant."

Laurel fought a wave of nausea, shuddering at the thought of the critters reproducing in her basement. She felt an unpleasant tingling in her scalp. *You can do this,* she told herself, taking a big gulp of air for courage.

"Okay," she said, and led Charlie down to the den, where the door to the basement was located.

"You stay here," he said, and she almost laughed. Laurel had no intention of accompanying him down those steps and watching the mice scamper into the dark corners of her basement. In fact, she didn't even want to know what they looked like. This way, she might be able to block it out.

Laurel stayed at the top of the stairs as she heard him moving around, and assumed he was looking for a strategic place to release the tiny beasts. A few minutes later, he walked back up the steps, crumpling the brown paper sacks.

"Do you know you have a ten-pound bag of wild bird feed down there?" he asked.

She pictured it on the shelf next to the box of old plates she had tried to unload at a garage sale. "We used to have a feeder in the backyard, but it broke."

"What a feast for mice," he said. "They'll be the fattest, happiest rodents in Nassau County. If all goes well, you'll never even have to feed them."

Laurel's queasy stomach roiled. "Feed them?" She had never anticipated such a thing. "I... I thought they found their own food."

"Well, sure. But you don't want them coming upstairs to look for it."

She covered her face with her fingers. It was all too much.

He pulled her hands away and made her look in his steadying eyes. "You'll be fine, honey."

"But, Charlie—"

"They'll feast on that food for months. The job will be done before they get a hankering to leave that cozy basement. Then you'll just hire an exterminator."

She took another fortifying breath, trusting him. And in any case, it was done. In six weeks or so, the basement would be teeming with the well-fed creatures and their droppings, creating the same toxic environment that had infected that man in Bridgehampton. She promised herself that once it was all over she would find a humane exterminator to clean up the mess and set the mice free in a field someplace.

"Let me throw those out," Laurel said, gesturing toward the wadded bags.

Charlie shook her off. "Just to be safe, I'll toss them in a dumpster."

"Is that really necessary?"

"Probably not, but why take a chance?"

She was so grateful for his assistance, his caution, his capable hands. It relaxed her. "Charlie..." she began, eager to express the full extent of her appreciation.

"Let's stick with the plan," he said gently. "We can talk later."

Laurel nodded. They were on a schedule, as they both had to get to work. Also, the sooner Charlie got out of the house, the safer they would be. She led him up the stairs to the front door and paused.

"I hope I can repay you for this one day," she said. "You may have changed the course of my whole life." She got choked up, and he moved in for a paternal hug.

"You deserve happiness," he said into her ear as he cupped the back of her head. Laurel nodded, sniffing back tears. She *did* deserve happiness. She'd been struggling for so long. And now, everything might change. In that single moment, she envisioned all of it—the week with Evan, Samara and the newborn...a bright, pristine apartment with contemporary throw rugs...a little dog to love and treasure...time with her mother at last...and maybe even a romance that would make her feel like a girl again.

She heard something then that confused her. It was the sound of a key in the front door. What the hell? Charlie was still holding tight, but she pushed him away. At that moment, the door swung open, and there was Doug. She watched his shocked expression as he looked from Laurel to Charlie and back to Laurel. Her mouth went dry.

"What the hell is going on here?" Doug demanded. His eyes were dark and filled with fury. Laurel saw the blood rise in his face, turning it so red with rage he looked like a stroke about to happen. Or maybe a heart attack. Laurel could almost hear the thud of his body hitting the ground. What would she do then? Call 911? How would she explain what happened?

"Um, I…" she said, trying to get her bearings. "Oh, he just stopped by to—"

"I should fucking kill you!" he bellowed at Charlie. His whole body tensed and Laurel feared he might actually swing a punch. It was terrifying, as he had almost a hundred pounds on the older man.

"Wait, stop," she said. "It's nothing. Honestly. What are you doing home anyway?"

"I forgot my insurance card," he seethed. "What are *you* doing?"

"We were…just going to grab a cup of coffee before work." It was the only thing she could think of that came even close to being plausible.

"You think I'm an idiot, Laurel?"

"You need to calm down, son," Charlie said, his voice slow and steady.

"Don't 'son' me, you old fucker. The two of you have guilt written all over your faces."

Charlie was steady as a brick. "Look," he said, "we just found out our hours got shifted today, so I told Laurel I would pick her up and we could stop at Starbucks before work."

He sounded so natural Laurel almost believed him, but Doug wasn't having it. "You really expect me to buy that?"

"It's the truth!" Laurel insisted.

Doug held open the front door. "You'd better go, man."

"He's right," Laurel said gently, her eyes landing on the balled-up paper bags he still held. "You should leave."

He looked at her. "Are you okay?"

"It's fine," she said. "He would never hurt me." She knew she spoke the truth. Doug might deck Charlie, but he'd never lay a hand on her.

"You sure?"

Laurel glanced again at the crumpled wad, and hoped Doug

hadn't noticed, because she had no idea how she would explain it.

"Absolutely," she insisted. "Go." They locked eyes, and she could tell Charlie was making sure she meant what she said.

"Okay," he said at last. "I'll see you at the store. Call me if you need me."

"Get the fuck out of here already," Doug said, and Charlie walked out the door.

Doug slammed it shut with such violence Laurel expected him to put his fist through a wall, as he had done that in his own apartment after the Adam Sandler incident. Instead, he fell back against the door, covered his face with his hands, and started to weep.

"I knew it," he said. "I knew it. I knew you wouldn't be faithful to me."

"For god's sake, Doug. I'm not sleeping with him. I'm not sleeping with *anyone*. I would never."

"I want to die," he said, crying into his hands.

"Please," she said. "You have to stop this. I've never been unfaithful, I swear."

"Honestly, Laurel, I couldn't handle it if you left me."

"I'm not leaving you," she insisted. "And I'm not having an affair."

Doug was so bereft her words couldn't penetrate his sorrow. She began to feel it, and the depth of his anguish was overwhelming.

"Listen to me, Doug. I'm telling the truth." Now, she was crying, too.

"I would kill myself, Laurel. Honest to god, I'll kill myself."

Kill himself? Laurel froze in place. "You…you don't mean that," she stammered.

"Don't you get it?" he said. "You're everything to me. I couldn't live without you."

Laurel took in a hard, halting breath, her gears grinding. Had Doug just offered up the perfect solution to her problems? She imagined all the ways it would be possible. The bottle of prescription sleeping pills he almost never touched. The box of straight edge razor blades in her old craft box. The exhaust pipe on his car.

"I don't know what to say," she muttered.

"Just tell me the truth," he pleaded. "I know Charlie wasn't here to take you out for coffee."

As they locked eyes, Laurel knew she had a decision to make. She certainly wasn't going to tell him about the bags of mice. And that left two choices. She could either stick with the story about going to Starbucks, or she could admit to an affair. Then, he might really do it. He might take his own life. But how could she say such a thing, especially after she spent so much energy denying it?

"The truth is," she said, her mind a confused whirl. "I…"

"Tell me!" he demanded. "I deserve to know."

She looked into his eyes, bloodred from crying, and his pain seared her. It was too much to bear. She closed her eyelids for a moment, and imagined him gone. Laurel saw herself standing in this very spot, a moving truck out front, the house empty and swept clean, her bank account fat with the profits of the sale, not to mention the life insurance money. She could envision walking out the door for the last time, without looking back.

When she opened her eyes again, a strange sensation overtook her. The pain was gone. She was no longer merged with Doug's heart. She took a long, cleansing breath and looked into his blubbering face.

"The truth is," she said, "I'm in love with him."

26

Laurel rushed to Trader Joe's feeling frantic. She had to talk to Charlie right away to tell him what she had done. He was part of her lie now, and needed to know. But by the time she arrived he had already clocked in and gone to work, and their assignments that day put them at opposite ends of the store during their first, second, and third hours. There was nothing for Laurel to do but bide her time, so she focused on her job, giving it everything—on the floor, in the storeroom, at the cash register. She worked quickly and efficiently, hoping it would calm her racing heart, but it was no use. Talking to Charlie was the only thing that would settle her nerves.

During her first break, she found him restocking the frozen vegetables. He glanced at her out of the corner of his eye as he continued his task, his wiry frame engaged in reaching and pushing in a studied rhythm.

"You okay?" he asked.

For a moment, her voice caught in her throat as she felt suddenly embarrassed. She hoped he would understand why she had needed to tell Doug they were in love.

"Are *you?*" she asked.

"That was close."

"Charlie," she whispered. "I need to tell you something."

He shoved two bags of frozen peas into the case. "I'm listening."

"I did something," she said softly. "Something big."

He kept his eyes on his work, but cocked his head toward her.

"It was…a confession," she continued.

Charlie went still, the muscles in his back tensing. "You told him about the mice?"

"No! Of course not." Laurel rubbed her forehead, finding the right words. "He threatened to kill himself if I cheated on him. And he meant it. So I seized the opportunity and I told him you and I… I told him we were seeing each other." She felt her face redden.

"What?" He sounded alarmed.

"It's perfect," she explained. "I won't even have to do anything. I'll just keep telling him I can't bear to break it off with you and eventually he'll…he'll swallow a bottle of pills. He's right on the brink!"

"Oh, Laurel," Charlie said, looking horrified.

"Don't worry," she said. "He doesn't know where you live. And trust me, he's not a stalker."

He gave her a look she couldn't quite read. "I don't give a damn if he comes after me. Let him try. But, Laurel, you shouldn't have done this. It was a *huge* mistake." His gaze was fixed on the frozen food case, but she could tell his brow was tense with worry.

"I don't understand," she said, pierced by his fear. "I thought it was a seamless solution."

Charlie looked left and right, and she knew he was making sure Tammy wasn't close by. Their boss had an uncanny sixth sense about crew members slacking off.

"I'm going to take a bathroom break," he said, as he continued to rearrange the frozen foods. "Meet me there."

Laurel nodded, anxious, and set off, trying to imagine what she had done wrong. Charlie never overreacted, so this felt awful. As she looped around the store heading for the back room, Laurel searched for a phrase to steady her nerves. *Bathroom Break*. BB. *Brigitte Bardot, Benjamin Bratt, Barbara Bush*. It was no use. By the time she met Charlie in the cold, dark vestibule in front of the men's room, she was in a sweat.

He gripped her arm and held tight. "You can't let Doug kill himself." His voice was adamant, and even in the dark his blue eyes seemed to flash alarm.

"Why not?" she asked, unnerved by his suddenly fierce energy. She had never seen him like this.

"Because the life insurance policy might not pay out if it's a suicide."

Laurel gasped. She had never heard such a thing. "What? How do you know?"

"It was at the heart of a true crime exposé when there was a murder staged to look like a suicide. The insurance company didn't pay the claim."

Laurel felt her face grow hot. His alarm was warranted.

"I don't know how I can walk this back," she said, picturing Doug home alone all these hours. For all she knew, he could already be dead. Her legs felt wobbly.

"Do whatever it takes!" Charlie warned.

Laurel put a hand over her mouth, sniffing back tears. What a mess she had made!

* * *

Normally, Laurel left her cell phone in her locker so she wouldn't be tempted to check it while she worked. She liked being one of Tammy's star employees—a solid staffer who put her heart into the job. But after talking to Charlie, Laurel scrambled for her phone even though her break was almost over. She called Doug's cell, and when he didn't answer, she sent a text. Then she put her phone on vibrate, slipped it into her pocket, and hoped for a response.

He's just mad at you, she told herself as she worked. *That's why he's not responding. He's not dead. He's not.*

Still, as she unpacked boxes, stocked shelves, worked the cash register, and helped customers find almond flour, organic chicken broth, sun-dried tomatoes, barbecue sauce, pomegranate juice, and spiced chai, Laurel imagined coming home to find Doug's cold body on the bathroom floor.

Even though she knew she would feel her phone vibrate, she kept checking it to make sure she hadn't missed a text. She was in the middle of restocking the nuts when she pulled it out again. Nothing. As Laurel slipped it back into her pocket, she turned around, and there was Tammy. She'd been caught.

Her boss folded her arms. "Laurel," she said, her face stern, "you know better."

The disappointment in her voice felt like a punch in the gut. "I'm sorry, Tammy. Really. There's…kind of a family emergency."

Tammy shook her head—she wasn't buying it.

Laurel considered defending herself, insisting it was a true emergency. But how would she explain this situation? It was impossible. So she simply promised her boss it wouldn't happen again.

"Okay," Tammy said, then waited a beat to make sure Laurel knew she meant business, and walked off.

By the time Laurel finished her shift, her nerves were more frayed than an old dishrag. She rushed home, and practically tripped up the steps to her front door.

"I'm home!" she called, as she burst inside. She had tried to keep her voice light, but it came out as a screech.

Still, it was met with silence.

"Doug?"

Laurel rushed to the kitchen, which was a mess. Clearly, he'd been eating himself into a frenzy all day. A box of Ritz crackers lay on its side on the table, next to a half-eaten chunk of cheddar cheese and a scraped-clean foil of Boursin. The orange juice had been left out, but at least the cap was on. A two-liter bottle of Coke had suffered a worse fate—left open to go flat. Next to that was a box of Entenmann's chocolate chip cookies, which he hadn't managed to finish. An empty Tostitos bag was on the floor. Also, he had clearly gone out for fast food at some point, as there were Chipotle wrappers on the counter.

Laurel turned from the room and continued calling his name as she went down to the den. At last, she found him. Doug was sprawled out on the couch, and she released a sigh when she saw his mountainous belly rising and falling along with his chest. Just to be safe, she went into the bathroom to check the bottle of sleeping pills. It hadn't been touched. Thank God. She was about to put it back when she stopped herself, and spilled the entire contents into the toilet. One less thing to worry about.

Laurel changed her clothes, and began cooking his favorite dinner—meat loaf and mashed potatoes. She would make them extra buttery, the way he liked them. Over and over, as she put her shoulder into the task of mashing and emulsifying, Laurel rehearsed what she would say when he padded into the kitchen, but she couldn't imagine how she could get him to come around. The food, though. The food could help. She closed her eyes and sniffed at the heady scent of baking meat loaf wafting from the oven.

Everything was almost ready when she heard the sound of Wolf Blitzer's voice drifting up from the den. Doug was awake. She wiped her hands on a dish towel and went downstairs.

"I made dinner," she said.

He ignored her.

"Doug?" she pleaded.

"Leave me alone." His voice was flat. And though he kept his eyes on the TV, they looked dull and unfocused. She had to find a way to break through to make sure he wasn't suicidal.

"Please," she said. "We need to talk."

"Fuck you," he said, without energy or conviction.

Laurel exhaled, regrouping. This was even harder than she expected. If he'd been angry and accusatory, she would have something to respond to. But this... This was like talking to a corpse.

"Honey..." she said, walking into the room. She stood over him, the TV blaring behind her. "I... I'm sorry for what I said earlier. I didn't mean it."

"Go away."

"I was angry. I wanted to hurt you. I'm not really in love with Charlie." She paused. "I'm in love with *you*."

"Ha," he said, mirthlessly.

"Please," she begged. "Can you find it in your heart to forgive me? You're my husband. I love you. I would never cheat on you." She studied his wounded face and felt genuine tenderness toward him then. No one deserved that kind of pain.

"But you want to," he said.

"I don't. I swear."

"Get lost." He looked back at the TV and she squared herself in front of it, reaching out to touch his arm. He swatted her away. "I mean it," he seethed. Now he sounded angry, and Laurel thought that was progress.

"No you don't," she said. "You love me, and I love you. Doug, I—"

"Could you move?" he interrupted, trying to peer around her at the television.

"I'll never leave you," she said. "I promise."

He looked at her, then quickly glanced away, his eyes going moist. His sorrow was deep, black and bottomless. She felt herself tearing in sympathy.

"Never," she repeated.

He gave an exasperated sigh and pointed at the television. She stepped to the side and tried to think of something else to say.

"What do you *want*," he said, his voice now thick with annoyance that she was still in the room.

"I made meat loaf," she said. "And mashed potatoes. With extra butter."

"Fine," he muttered, his eyes on CNN.

"Will you come up and eat?"

"Maybe later."

She stood there for several more minutes, hoping he would engage, but he had checked out. At last, Laurel realized there was nothing more she could do. At least, not tonight. She went back to the kitchen, ate alone, and left out a plate of food for Doug.

In the morning, her bed was empty and Doug's pillow was missing. When she went into the hallway, Laurel saw that the door to Evan's old room—now the guest bedroom—was closed. So that's how it was going to be. There was nothing for her to do, except bake a few of those mini croissants he liked and hope the scent wafted upstairs while they were still warm. Then she retrieved her old craft box with the razor blades inside, stuffed it deep into the trash, and went to work.

27

Sex, she thought, as she went about her day. That was the solution. She would seduce him. It was the only way to prove—once and for all—that she was his.

Laurel thought back to when their sex life was vigorous and new. During the early days of their courtship and marriage—before Evan was born—they were young and hungry, and went at it every chance they got. She remembered Doug as being insatiable. And she, too, was feral and eager. His mouth on her neck…his eyes on her body…and the kissing! It was all enough to make her weak with desire.

Back then, she sometimes came to him in diaphanous negligees—pale and teasing in their ostensible innocence—or in sinful black satin, alluringly wicked. None of it was necessary, though. Not for Doug. She could come home from a run, sweaty and dirty, and he'd beg her not to shower. The intensity of his yearning made Laurel feel beautiful, and that was powerfully seductive. Still, she liked the eroticism of primping and dressing up for him. Sometimes, she even wore high heels in bed. She laughed now, thinking about it, which surprised the customer she was ringing out at the register.

Everything had changed after Evan was born, and they were both so tired from parenthood it was hard to find the energy. And the time. Sex had to be scheduled, which left little room for romance. And she was no longer in love with her own body, so it became almost a chore—one more responsibility on her plate. A wifely duty. Not that she didn't enjoy the sex once they got going. But she rarely felt that burning desire of their early love.

They settled into a pattern, then, of having sex only occasionally. And she had to be the initiator, because he got his feelings hurt by her rejection. So once in a while she would cuddle up next to him in bed and he'd respond. A few years ago, though, he started saying things like, "I've had a long day." And she understood the code. But that was at night. In the morning, he would still be responsive, his erection ready for action. Then, he started pulling away no matter what time she reached for him. And so she simply stopped, and that was it. Sex was in their past, and neither of them had the energy to bring up the subject of Viagra.

Now, though—thanks to her secret omission of the blood pressure medication—his erections were back naturally. At least on some mornings. And though she occasionally felt a small stirring of desire, Laurel's resentment had been too great. Why should she give him sex when he couldn't even bother to get a job?

As she searched for the bar code on a bag of organic brown rice fusilli pasta, Laurel considered how she would go about seducing him. It might not take much more than going into the guest room in the morning and crawling into bed with him. Sure he was still depressed and angry, but she was certain his physical desire would take over once she touched him.

Her own desire would present more of a challenge. It was still there, of course, dormant under the weight of all her responsibilities. But would she be able to summon it at will? She knew one thing for sure—she wasn't going to sleep with him if she didn't feel the pull. As she ran items over the scanner, she thought about going to the mall after work and stopping into Victoria's Secret. Or maybe not—that wasn't her style. Bloomingdales, perhaps. Surely they had a sexy lingerie department. She could imagine looking through the skimpy items, deciding whether she was more moved by the idea of pink and soft or black and sizzling. Virgin or vixen? She tried to recall the feeling of walking into the bedroom in some erotic getup, and a tiny spark of desire came back. Was it enough to catch fire?

Maybe, she thought, as she felt herself growing warm at the idea of Doug's lascivious gaze. She pulled an item from her customer's cart and ran it across the scanner. It didn't beep. She tried it again.

"Uh, I don't think that has a bar code," said a familiar voice.

It was Luke. Laurel looked down at her hand, and realized she was holding an orange. She laughed. "I was a million miles away."

"I could tell," he said.

She blushed, wondering if he sensed she'd been lost in an erotic daydream. But no, that was silly. Laurel breathed into her reality, and tried to remind herself she was a fifty-two-year-old woman in a Trader Joe's unisex T-shirt. Not a sex kitten.

Still, Luke. Seeing him at the moment of sexual reverie was exactly what she needed to fan that spark into a raging blaze.

She decided to go with it and flirt her heart out. After all, she had to make up for her previous behavior.

"I hope you weren't reading my mind," she said, offering him a charming and possibly suggestive smile.

His eyebrows shot up as he caught her drift without fumbling. "And what if I was?" he asked, ready to spike the ball.

She rang up the oranges. "You sure you want me to tell you? In front of Isaac?"

The baby smiled at the mention of his name.

"Sweetie," Luke said to Isaac, "Laurel was just having some very deep thoughts about national politics, foreign affairs, and world peace."

"You read me like a book," she said playfully, as she continued scanning his items.

"It's good to see you happy, Laurel. Last week you seemed a little..." He trailed off with a shrug.

"I was going through a rough patch, but things are starting to look up."

He leaned in. "Would it help to know you're the bright spot of my week?" he said softly.

My god. He was crushing on her. She had opened up the door just the tiniest bit and he had walked right in. Laurel felt a tickle on her neck that traveled right down her flesh, sending her temperature rocketing. They locked eyes and exchanged more passion in one moment than she'd felt in years. She imagined being in his arms, kissing him. Her body pulsed in response.

"Ditto," she whispered, because he was waiting for a reply, and she had to say something.

He smiled then and she smiled back, and they stood there as if in a trance, until another customer sidled over and asked Laurel where she could find the mustard. And that was it. The spell was broken. Her prince took his Trader Joe's packages, his beautiful baby, and walked off.

"See you next week!" he called.

As she watched him leave, Laurel knew exactly how she would work up the passion to seduce her husband. She would think of Luke.

28

Bloomingdales, she decided, was too expensive. And Kohl's didn't have the selection. Then Laurel remembered an ad she'd seen in *Newsday* for Olivia's, a local boutique that specialized in custom bras as well as flattering lingerie. She looked it up on her phone and found a coupon for twenty-five percent off. Score.

"Can I help you?" a woman asked when Laurel entered the lavender-scented shop, which didn't have an inch of wasted space. Everywhere she looked there were panties, bras, teddies, negligees, nightgowns, and various styles of shapewear.

Laurel looked up at the woman, who had a curvy figure and a halo of black curls. Her name badge said Olivia, and it didn't surprise Laurel that the proprietor was also the main saleswoman.

"I'm looking for something...special," Laurel said, feeling suddenly shy.

Olivia nodded, as if she'd seen this kind of reticence before. "Lingerie?" she asked.

"I've been married almost thirty years," Laurel explained. "And my husband is…"

"It's okay, dear," Olivia said. "We all want to feel seductive now and then." She gave Laurel's body a quick glance. "You have a great shape. Are you interested in something naughty?" She pointed to a corner of the store that displayed a sheer red teddy and a black strappy number that had a B & D vibe.

"Not quite that naughty," Laurel said.

Olivia began bringing out a variety of options, and soon enough Laurel was in the fitting room with several different items to try on. She went for the raciest first—a red lace bodysuit with a bustier-style upper half. Olivia had warned that it might be a little skimpy for what she had in mind, but Laurel was eager to give it a shot. As soon as she shimmied into it, she realized Olivia had been right. The garment was tight and uncomfortable, creating a bulge where it cut into her flesh. And the color washed out her skin, making her face look old and naked, in need of lipstick.

"How are we doing in there?" Olivia asked from outside the dressing room.

"The red one is a no-go," she said, almost ready to abandon the whole operation, as this was pummeling her ego. Before putting on that bodysuit, she'd been feeling pretty good about herself. She'd lost more weight, after all, and had expected to feel smoldering in these things.

"Try the white silk babydoll," Olivia said.

Dutifully, Laurel slipped it on and immediately felt better. The satin floated right over her body. She looked soft, appealing, touchable, and could imagine letting the strap fall off her shoulder just before she slowly stepped out of it.

Shyly, she pulled open the curtain so Olivia could get a look.

"Like a beautiful young bride!" the woman gushed, and Laurel did indeed feel young and renewed. She realized, then, that the garment hadn't been designed to turn a woman into eye candy for a man, but to help her feel beautiful. That was the big difference between this silky treasure and the erotic red teddy.

She was ready to tell Olivia to wrap it up for her, but her eye went to the other items in the fitting room—in particular a black negligee with sheer cups and spaghetti straps. It was a little naughtier, but she thought it might be flattering. Olivia caught the object of her gaze.

"You'll love that one, too," she said. "Give a try."

So she did, and the woman she saw staring back at her was...gorgeous. There was no other word for it. She seemed slimmer, with subtle curves and full, round breasts. Even her shoulders looked sexy in this. She adjusted the mirror to get a glimpse of the back. Though Laurel was still wearing her own white panties rather than the black ones that came with the garment, she could imagine exactly how it would look with the revealing G-string highlighting the soft mounds of her buttocks. She had never felt sexier. If she were rich, she'd buy ten of them, and build a special closet with matching satin hangers so they could line up in a perfect row. Like the secret cache of a superhero. She thought of Wonder Woman. No, *Wanton Woman*, able to seduce enemies, conquer armies, and never lose that fresh-as-a-garden scent.

She opened the curtain again and Olivia almost laughed in delight. "Look at you!" she cried.

Laurel looked back at the white satin babydoll, which she absolutely loved, and couldn't decide which one to leave behind. It would be indulgent to get both, but didn't she deserve it? And anyway, maybe she could wear the white one for Doug and save the black one for herself.

Or Luke.

"Do you need help deciding?" Olivia asked.

Laurel smiled. "I'll take both."

On her way home, Laurel stopped to pick up a bottle of wine, and then swung by their favorite Italian restaurant for the take-out meal she had ordered. The seduction would happen before dinner. Afterward, she would heat up the meals and they'd dine by candlelight—relaxed and romantic.

At home, Laurel let herself in the front door and called out for Doug. He didn't answer, but she could hear the TV blaring in the den, so she knew he was there. Leaving the food in the kitchen, she carried the lingerie upstairs, where she took a hot bath, then lotioned and powdered. Once ready, she slipped into the white satin babydoll and shook out her hair. Standing in front of the medicine cabinet, she applied lipstick, mascara, and blush, then stepped back to admire her reflection. So far so good. She left the bathroom to appraise her head-to-toe appearance in a full-body mirror, but stopped. There was one more thing she wanted to do. She grabbed a shoebox from the top of her closet, and pulled out a pair of silver spike-heeled sandals she hadn't worn in ten years.

She put them on, balanced herself, and approached the mirror. Damn, she looked hot for a woman her age. No, she chided herself, any age. Her legs—always slender—looked long and shapely. She turned to look at her behind, and thought the angle of the shoes did wonders for her posterior. Laurel loved the way she looked, and knew Doug would, too. It was showtime.

As she walked down the stairs to the den, holding tight to the banister since she wasn't used to wearing such high heels,

Laurel felt herself growing excited. She hadn't been touched in so long! She decided they wouldn't even bother going up to the bedroom. He'd take one look at her and lose control, and they'd do it right there in the den. It would be heated and passionate. Oh, Laurel, he'd sigh, the way he used to. Laurel, my love, my light, my everything.

"Doug?" she called before she stepped into the room. "Can you do me a favor and turn off the TV for a second?"

"Why?" he said.

"Please. It's important."

"I'm watching the news."

"I know," she said. "Maybe just…pause it?"

He heaved a dramatic sigh at being put-upon, but she heard the television go quiet. Laurel fluffed her hair, smoothed out her lingerie, and arched her back like a porn star.

"Well?" he asked. "What the hell is going on?"

"This," she said, stepping into the room. "This is going on."

His eyes went up and down her body, and she felt more alive than she had in so long. She offered him a seductive grin—encouragement to say whatever came into his mind.

"What the hell, Laurel?"

It wasn't the reaction she had hoped for, but she tried not to feel defeated. After all, he was in shock. She needed to give him time to take it all in.

"Do you like it?" she asked.

His face contorted in confusion. "What are you doing?"

She waited a beat to see if some lust or eagerness would break through, but he couldn't get past his bewilderment.

"I bought it just for you," she said.

"Why?"

"Because I want to show you how much I love you."

He folded his arms. "Was Charlie busy tonight or something?"

And there it was. The great divide. She had to find a way to cross it. "There is no Charlie," she said, into his eyes. "There's only you."

"Yeah, right," he said, oozing sarcasm. He picked up the remote and unpaused the television. CNN was doing a report on toxic waste in Russia.

She turned to shut off the television, bending slightly to make sure he got a glimpse of her mostly bare bottom. "Don't you want to play with me?" she said over her shoulder to him.

He snorted. "This whole act is ridiculous."

"You used to like when I dressed up for you," she said, attempting a sexy pout.

"Yeah, well, that was when you meant it."

"I mean it now," she purred. "I love you. I want you."

He snorted. "Bullshit. This isn't love. This is…" He paused to indicate the entirety of her with his hand. "This is guilt."

"I'm just trying to convince you that you're the one I love."

"Too late," he said, avoiding eye contact.

"Don't you like my outfit?" she pleaded, trying to get him to look at her.

"Waste of money," he said, and snapped the TV back on.

Laurel fought the instinct to argue with him. Counterproductive, she told herself. Stay focused. She rubbed her forehead, thinking. There had to be a way to seduce him.

Laurel approached him and bent over, bringing her breasts close to his face. She put her fingers into his soft curls, which she had always liked. At his age, it was a crowning glory— the rare achievement of a middle-aged man maintaining a full head of hair.

"You're the one I love," she breathed into his ear. "I want you."

When he didn't push her away, Laurel sensed she was close

to arousing him. She took his hand and put it on her breast. His breathing sped up, and so did hers.

"What do you want me to do?" she asked, and placed her warm lips on his neck.

He tensed and pulled his hand from her breast. "No, Laurel," he said sharply. "I'm not doing this."

"Why not?" she said, putting her hand back in his hair. "I know you want it. And I do, too."

"It's a pity fuck," he spat, pulling her hand away.

Laurel sighed. It was, in fact, a pity fuck. Or at least it started that way—as a ploy to pull him out of his depression by proving she wanted him. The irony was that she discovered she actually did want him. And okay, a lot of the heat was generated by Luke's attention. But still. Right now, she wanted to feel her husband's hands on her body, to watch him grow hard with longing, to see his eyes drinking her in with love and lust.

"Doug, please," she said. "Think about how hard I'm trying here. Would I do this if I didn't love you?"

He shook his head. "I don't know," he said, his eyes so mournful she felt a dull ache in her chest. "It just doesn't feel right."

Now, with her lust supplanted by his sorrow, she didn't want it, either.

"I understand," she said, defeated, and went upstairs to change into sweats. First though, Laurel stopped to look at her reflection again, wondering how she could have been so wrong about her appeal. She knew Doug was upset with her, but she had been so sure her allure would override his resentment. Maybe it was her age, and she was simply no longer attractive enough, even for her husband. Perhaps he thought she looked old and spent. But surely some men still found her appealing. Luke. That Marcello guy who was really named Alan. And, if she was honest with herself, Charlie. She mostly blocked out the notion that he had a crush on her, but it was always there, just under the surface.

She snapped a quick selfie of her reflection and sat down to study it. She looked even prettier in the photograph than she had expected, and was tempted to post it on Facebook or Instagram, just for the ego boost of getting a string of compliments. *This is 52!* she might write, as she had seen other women do. But no, it was far too embarrassing. And revealing. So she simply applied a filter to make herself look softer, and saved it for posterity. One day, she might need to look at it again to feel better about herself.

For now, she changed into sweats. Then she wrapped both items in tissue paper, and buried them deep in a drawer, under her flannel pajamas.

29

If seduction wasn't going to do it, Laurel would just have to find another way to pull Doug out of his depression and prevent him from attempting suicide. It would all hinge on convincing him she loved him. She was determined to keep at it, tapping into the part of his heart that wanted to believe he was her one and only. Surely it was there—that spark of hope. If she could penetrate his darkness, she would find it.

He continued spending his nights in the guest bedroom, emerging only after she left for work. Laurel didn't know if he was sleeping late or just avoiding her, but she made sure to knock on the door every morning before work to tell him she loved him. As a bit of insurance, she would promise to make something delicious for dinner, figuring a good meal would make him less likely to take his life on that particular day. His appetite, she had noticed, was as robust as ever. Maybe even more so. In fact, he'd been plowing through the pantry at a rate she could barely keep up with.

His gluttony gave her some peace of mind, and she was able to get through her days at work without too much anxiety. It wasn't until she got home and found herself walking up the steps to her front door that Laurel's apprehension kicked in. Would he still be alive when she crossed the threshold? On some days, she froze, and had to play the initials game just to turn the key in the lock. *Hello, Sweetheart*, she'd think. HS. *Harry Styles. Hilary Swank. Howard Stern.*

But day after day for nearly a month, she entered the house to find him still alive. Relieved, Laurel would tell him again that she loved him, and set about filling the house with enticing aromas.

Still, nothing she said or did affected his mood. He seemed so close to the edge Laurel knew she couldn't let up. Looking for opportunities to pay him compliments, she remarked on his luscious hair, his ability to finish the crossword, the way his butt looked in jeans. She reminisced about his dad jokes, laughing authentically as she played them back to him. He'd always striven for the worst puns, trying to make his wife and son groan in appreciative agony. Then, of course, they'd all laugh. Their little family bonding over silliness.

She reminded him of Evan's know-it-all soccer coach, Rick Piedmont, whom he'd nicknamed Rickypedia, getting the whole team to call him that.

"What about it?" Doug said, without even smiling.

"You know what I was just thinking about?" she said over dinner. In fact, she hadn't just thought of it. She'd spent all day trying to recall a funny anecdote she could regale him with. "I was thinking about that time Evan asked why the flying boy was called Peter Pan. Do you remember what you said?"

Doug ignored her, picking up his knife to cut feebly into the chicken on his plate, as if he barely had the strength.

"You said, 'Because he *never-never-lands!*'"

He chewed and swallowed. "I didn't even make that up."

"But you were so quick with it, who cares?" When he didn't respond she kept chattering. "Anyway, it was funny. And Evan told it to all his friends. He was so proud of you."

They ate in silence as she tried to recall another anecdote. At last, she remembered one he'd been especially delighted with. She was sure this one would make him laugh.

Laurel held up a drumstick to get his attention. "Doug!" she said, her voice chipper.

He sighed, annoyed. "What now?"

"Remember that day my mom was looking in her refrigerator for something to feed you and said, 'Doug, I have a chicken leg'?"

He shrugged and looked back at his plate.

"Do you remember what you said?"

When he didn't respond, she continued. "You said, 'Wear pants and no one will notice.'"

Laurel laughed, but Doug remained impassive.

"Poor Mom thought we were making fun of her," Laurel said. "I had to explain she just had the misfortune of walking right into the perfect setup."

When Doug said nothing, Laurel felt dejected. It had been one of his favorite stories. He'd always beamed with pride when she'd retold it to friends.

She sighed, and they ate in silence for several minutes, the energy slipping away from both of them. When she was about to start clearing the table, Laurel put down her fork and knife.

"Sweetheart," she said, "are you ever going to talk to me again?"

"Why should I?"

"Because this is no way to live." As soon as she said it, Laurel realized it was the wrong thing to tell someone who might be suicidal. "What I mean is, we need to get our marriage back on track. Isn't that what you want?"

He broke off a piece of bread, ran it through the fat left on his plate, popped it into his mouth and chewed as he seemed to consider her question. At last, he pushed himself away from the table.

"I don't know *what* I want," he said, and left the room.

Laurel rested her face in her hands. She was running out of ideas for how to get through to him. It was all so exhausting. Still, she lay in bed awake that night, listening to the silent walls for any evidence of escaped mice, before finally succumbing to sleep.

At Starbucks the next day, Laurel sought Charlie's counsel.

"I've tried everything," she said, shrugging off her coat. The air inside felt warm and steamy compared to the crisp December evening. "I compliment him, I try to make him laugh, I tell him I love him…" She hung her jacket over the back of her chair. "I even tried to seduce him."

Charlie set down a paper tray with their coffees, nearly dropping it. "You tried to *seduce* him?" He sounded incredulous, almost offended.

For the first time, Laurel sensed he was judging her—as if she'd done something promiscuous. She folded her arms defensively. "He *is* my husband."

"I know but…it hasn't exactly been a loving marriage."

Laurel scraped out her chair and sat, releasing a sigh. He wasn't wrong. She had never told Charlie about her sex life— or lack of it—but wasn't surprised he had intuited the truth. "What do you suggest?" she asked.

Charlie sat. He pulled the cups from the tray and opened

the lid on his, peering inside as if searching for the answer in his latte grande. After a moment, it seemed that he found it. He gave a sharp nod and looked back up at her.

"Ride it out," he said. "He's using his depression as a weapon to punish you. Eventually, he'll tire of it."

Laurel considered that. Doug's melancholy seemed real to her—a black hole of bottomless despair. But Charlie had been so perceptive about everything that she doubted her own perceptions. Maybe he was right. Maybe there was some theater in Doug's behavior. All those nights of holding up both ends of the conversation while he just sat there, brooding. Surely he didn't have to make it so hard for her.

Laurel glanced out the window. In the dying light, a couple rushed toward the entrance to the coffee shop, fighting against the wind to keeps their coats close.

"How can you be so sure?" she asked.

"Depressed or not, a man has physical needs, Laurel."

She leaned back, recalling the sound of Doug's breath quickening just before he got so angry. So yes, he'd clearly been aroused.

Charlie went on. "If you tried to seduce him and he turned you down, he was punching back to hurt you. It was retribution. Eventually, he'll decide you've suffered enough, and he'll forgive you."

It sounded so logical she couldn't argue. Still, even if there was anger behind Doug's rebuff, his depression seemed dangerous.

"You don't think I need to worry about suicide?" she asked.

The door swung open and the outside air blew through the overheated interior like an intruder set on reminding everyone what awaited them.

Charlie shook his head. "I didn't say that. I just mean you

don't need to keep trying to seduce him. He'll only use it against you." He picked up his coffee and brought it to his lips.

"But if I could just break his resistance…"

Charlie put his cup back down. "Don't do that," he said emphatically.

"Why not?"

He looked into her face, his narrow eyes earnest and determined. "If you always seem hot to trot, he'll have no incentive to come around. Let him regret turning you down. He'll come begging."

She almost laughed at the expression *hot to trot*, but decided to focus on his wisdom. Would Doug really come begging? He had never done so before. But perhaps that scene in the sexy white negligee was enough to stir him. Perhaps he'd think about it late at night when he was watching porn on his laptop, which she knew he did occasionally. She could almost imagine him appearing at the doorway of the bedroom one night, asking if she would wear it again.

"You always have such good advice," she said. "I don't know what I would do without you."

"Everything's going to be fine," he said, patting her hand. "You'll see."

Laurel didn't understand why people grumbled so much about sleeping alone at night. She had no complaints about having the bed to herself, and if she hadn't been so worried about Doug's mental health, she would actually enjoy it. Slipping under the cool sheets and having full ownership of the space felt luxurious. With Doug next to her, Laurel had always curled onto her side, taking up as little space as possible. Sometimes, he would travel during the night, and Laurel would feel herself poked by a knee or an elbow, forcing her

even nearer to the edge. There were nights she was dangerously close to falling out of bed.

Of course, she had only been living like this for a few
weeks. She tried to imagine a span of months and years in an
empty bed. Still, she couldn't conjure feelings of loneliness,
especially since she would have independence and financial
security to keep her company. With bedmates like that, how
could she feel alone? She'd be the master of her own fate, with
no one to cater to, cook for, clean up after. She would sleep so
soundly on these clean sheets. And in the morning, she would
make the bed, then climb back into it at night, the linens still
crisp and fresh. Her dreams would be as light as air.

And if she did feel lonely, it could be banished easily enough,
as she would have the resources to fly out to California two
or three times a year. Evan and Samara would be thrilled to
see her, and the baby would leap into her arms. So much love!
Then, after a week or so, Laurel would be happy to come back
home, to her own space, her peace. Her life would be filled
with whatever she chose. Hobbies. Book clubs. A wonderful
little dog to cuddle and kiss and take on long walks. If Monica
was gone, Laurel would connect with other old friends. That
wouldn't be so hard. And down the road, when she no longer
had her mom to look after, she might even move out to Los
Angeles herself, getting an apartment just far enough from
the kids so they wouldn't feel put upon. And of course, she'd
make herself available to watch the baby whenever they asked.

In the meantime, there was Luke. She imagined him in this
very bed after a romantic date. Or no, maybe not this bed. A
new one she would buy for herself. One of those special mat-
tresses that kept cool, with memory foam that didn't bounce
and spring, but would cradle her body so tenderly.

I'll be right back, she would tell Luke, and excuse herself
to the bathroom. There, she would peel off her clothes and

change into the diaphanous black teddy that showed her curves so subtly and sensuously. She'd be going to the gym, of course, and her body would look tight and trim. He would gasp at the sight of her, and say something to make her blush.

She would slip out of the nightie and glide into bed with him. Luke would run his hand down the silk of her back as he pulled her toward him, and he would kiss her. He would be so gentle and so passionate, and know exactly how to touch her. Laurel felt herself growing warm and ready. How she yearned for contact!

She put her hands between her legs, aware that it would take only minutes to bring herself to orgasm. She was that close. But of course, it would be hollow and momentary—a bit of friction and release. And that wasn't what Laurel craved. Not really. She needed to be touched, to feel desired.

Laurel stopped herself. It seemed unconscionable to waste this stirring she felt—an opportunity squandered. She wanted Doug in bed with her. She would rub her hand up his thigh, grab his erection, and guide him inside her. They would get back at least a piece of what they'd had, while she imagined it was Luke.

Laurel sat up and reached for her cell phone. She opened it to the picture of herself in the white satin nightie. She texted it to Doug with the message: Miss you.

He didn't respond right away, so she added: I'm waiting for you...

Surely in the dark of night, knowing his wife was in bed, ready for him, Doug would pad into the room. She slipped out of her modest pajamas and waited for him under the covers.

And that's precisely how she found herself when she awoke the next morning, naked and alone.

30

By the time the weekend rolled around, Laurel still hadn't made any progress in breaking through Doug's malaise. If anything, he seemed to be getting worse, staying in bed longer and longer. She tried to tell herself it wasn't as bad as it seemed, that he was being melodramatic for her benefit. But worry tugged at her.

It tugged at her as she ran her Saturday morning errands, stopping by Trio Hardware to see if they had the right size screws for the shower door handle that had fallen off. It tugged at her as she made a trip to the dollar store for a few odds and ends—including those disposable aluminum pans—and then popped into Target for shampoo, laundry detergent and Swiffer refills. It tugged at her as she belted herself into her car, ready to return home for lunch, but instead found herself parked in front of Celia's Café, the organic eatery Luke had gone to with his daughter and her family.

Laurel tried to convince herself she wasn't here to run into Luke. At least, not entirely. She was hungry, after all, and they had healthy choices. In fact, the self-serve café was a very popular place among Trader Joe's customers, as it was the only local restaurant with a selection of organic foods at value prices.

She pulled down the driver's side visor, looking into the mirror as she applied lipstick, then rubbed a bit into her cheeks. Laurel fluffed her hair, put on her sunglasses, and grabbed her purse.

The café was bright and cheery, and smelled of baking bread. But there was no sign of Luke or his family, and Laurel swallowed her disappointment, chiding herself for believing she would run into them. Such childishness.

She ordered the organic chicken salad in a whole wheat pita and a glass of fresh grapefruit juice with mixed berries. She took a seat at a table facing the door, and read the newspaper on her phone as she slowly ate her lunch. The sandwich needed salt, which she was loath to ask for in such a health-conscious place. Still, it wasn't bad.

Laurel left the last two bites on the plate as she stalled, slowly sipping her juice. There was nothing to rush home to except Doug's gloom. And this place had such a happy decor, with its sage and yellow color scheme, and a mural of twisty vines growing from floor to ceiling.

She shifted in her seat. It was still early enough for a family with a baby to pop in for lunch. If she could just see Luke for a few minutes and get the chance to talk to him outside of Trader Joe's, it would give her something to hang on to. But by the time she finished reading *Newsday*, Laurel knew it was futile. She cleared her tray and headed out the door.

The sharp glare of the winter sun sent her rummaging through her purse for her sunglasses. When she finally put them on and glanced up, she was looking straight into Luke's face, about twenty feet away in the parking lot. He was standing next to an SUV as his daughter and son-in-law put Isaac into a stroller.

"Laurel!" he called, sounding delighted.

A trill of nervous excitement buzzed through her and she waved back, grinning. "Hi!" She struggled to take a slow breath to calm herself.

Luke signaled for her to wait as they approached. Laurel turned her collar up against the cold.

"Were you about to go in for lunch?" he asked.

"Just finished."

"We come here every Saturday," he said, marveling at the coincidence.

"I'm surprised we never ran into each other," she responded, as if she were here every weekend, too.

When he introduced her to his daughter, Imani, and his son-in-law, Javier, the young woman exclaimed, "Oh, Laurel!" as if she had heard the name before and was surprised to be meeting her in person.

That single moment gave Laurel more joy than she remembered feeling in years. He had told them about her! It hadn't been her imagination. This crush was mutual, and that was everything.

As Laurel greeted Isaac, touching the silk of his chubby cheek, Luke addressed the young parents, telling them to go on inside—he would catch up with them.

"Got it, Dad," Imani said, pointedly.

After they left, Laurel leaned toward Luke and asked if his daughter was wearing scrubs. It was a silly question, as it was obvious what Imani was wearing under her jacket. But it was a good conversation starter.

"Ob-gyn," he explained. "She did rounds in the hospital this morning."

"God, you must be so proud of her."

"Don't get me started," he said with a laugh.

"Are there other doctors in your family?" Laurel asked, digging for information.

"Just one," he said, and pointed at himself.

"You?" Laurel smiled. "I was wondering what you did before retirement!"

"Thoracic surgery. Unfortunately, I had to throw in the towel." He tapped his leg, to indicate it was the reason.

"Were you hurt?" she asked.

"A semi rammed me on the turnpike, flipping my car. I was lucky to get out alive. And they saved my leg." He held his right hand toward her. "But this is the reason I can't perform surgery anymore." He demonstrated his inability to make a fist.

"Oh, Luke," she said. "That must have been so hard."

He kept his hand out, as if he expected her to slip her own palm into it, but she buried her hands in her pockets, self-conscious. *One day,* she wanted to tell him. *Please, be patient and wait for me.*

"It was. But I try to look on the bright side. I get to help raise my grandson." He paused. "And I got to meet you."

Laurel dug her hands deeper into her coat and pulled it close, as if her heart might otherwise escape. "I'm glad I met you, too."

"This is the part where I ask you out," he said, bringing his face close enough to kiss her. She looked into his dark eyes and felt the world start to spin. She didn't remember ever wanting anything so badly.

"Are you doing anything tonight?" he went on. "I know

it's last-minute, but I've been hoping for an opportunity like this and...why wait?"

Laurel stared at him, confounded. She had assumed he knew she was married and was battling the same push-pull she was. She wore a ring, after all. And yes, her flirtation was over-the-top. But she was so sure they shared an understanding that they were star-crossed...at least for now. Laurel felt her tongue go stiff. How had she been so stupid! She had led him on.

"I... I'm married," she blurted. "I'm sorry. I thought you knew." Her stomach went tight in retreat. This was excruciating.

"Oh," he said, his face falling. "I just assumed..."

"This is my fault," she muttered.

"The way you acted," he said. "I'm not accusing you of anything but I just assumed you were separated or maybe in the process."

"My situation," she said, "is complicated."

He stared at her, waiting for an explanation, but what could she say? *Hey, if you can just wait for a few months, my husband will be dead, and then we can ride off into the sunset. It will be perfect!*

"I don't usually read things so badly," he said.

"It's me," she said. "I gave you mixed messages." Despite herself she started to cry. "I wish..."

"Hey, it's okay."

She opened her purse and found a tissue. "It's not okay." She dabbed at her eyes, her nose.

"Are things that bad at home?"

She nodded, unable to speak.

Luke studied her for a long moment. "Are you unsafe?" he asked.

She shook her head. "No, it's not like that."

He put a hand under her chin and made her look at him. "You sure?"

Oh dear god, he wanted to save her. And she wanted to let him. But this was a mess she had to take care of herself.

"I'm sure," she said.

He put out his hand again—the one that couldn't make a fist. "Give me your phone."

She did as he asked, unlocking it first, as she had a pretty good idea why he wanted it. He began tapping at.

"I'm giving you my number. If you need *anything*... If you have any kind of trouble, you call me."

He extended the phone toward her, and for a moment they both held on to it, unwilling to break the connection.

"I will," she whispered.

He released the phone and she slipped it into her purse. Then she gave him a hug, lingering an extra beat, and left.

31

That moment with Luke had left Laurel with a gorgeous ache. She felt younger and more desirable, with opportunities for a beautiful new life unfurling before her like a carpet straight to a land of dreams.

The next morning, she paid more attention than usual to her appearance, as if she were dressing up for Luke instead of running to the supermarket for her mother. As she assessed her appearance, Laurel decided this would be the day they would go out for lunch. She could envision the two of them at a table with straws and glasses, plates full of bright green salad, as they enjoyed one another's company.

Laurel reached for her more flattering coat—the navy blue with a belt. It was getting pilly and old, but it still looked better than the fake shearling she wore most days. She grabbed her car keys and was ready to dash out the door when she stopped herself. She hadn't seen Doug that morning and needed to check on him. She doubled back and knocked on the door to the guest bedroom.

"I'm going to my mom's," she called.

Nothing.

"Doug?"

"Okay." He sounded wide-awake.

Laurel pushed open the door a crack. "Why don't you come with me?" She didn't really want him there, but was willing to have him along if it meant pulling him from this perilous languor.

He was on his back, hands behind his head as if he'd been engaged in the unassailably important task of contemplating the ceiling before he'd been so rudely interrupted. "To your mom's?" he said, as if he couldn't imagine anything more absurd.

"She'd love to see you."

He rolled away from her. "Too tired."

"I'm going to try to talk her into going out for lunch," Laurel said. "I know it'll help if you're there."

"I just want to sleep."

She paused, wondering if she should give him a chore—like taking out the trash—but doubted it would give him the motivation to get out of bed.

"You need anything?" she asked.

"No."

"You want me to bring something home for you? A bacon cheeseburger? Some dessert?"

Doug shifted, and she knew that got his attention. "Whatever," he said, unwilling or unable to give her the satisfaction of an enthusiastic response.

Laurel walked into the room and kissed his warm cheek, then laid her cool hand on it. "I love you," she said.

He didn't move.

Laurel knelt by the bed so her face was close to his. "You never told me what you thought of that picture I sent," she said softly. The night before, as she lay in bed alone, she had imagined sending it to Luke. Again and again, she played out how he might respond, each scenario stirring her arousal more and more.

There was a long pause, as if Doug was hoping she would give up and leave. Finally, without turning around, he said, "I couldn't look at it."

"Why not?"

"Because it makes me think of you and *him*."

For a moment, she thought he was talking about Luke. But of course not. He held firm to the belief that she was in love with Charlie, no matter how much she denied it.

"I can't take it," he added, his voice cracking. It made her throat swell in sympathy.

Laurel had been getting better and better at shutting out his pain, but sometimes it was like an airborne virus, and she couldn't help inhale it. She closed her eyes for a moment, creating a shield behind which she could find herself. And there she was, the woman who wanted so much, and who had spent so many years with nothing but crumbs. *No more.* She was going to have the whole damned bagel. Toasted. With cream cheese and lox and a juicy red tomato.

She opened her eyes and touched his cheek again, determined to break the shell of his stubborn despair. "I'm going to keep saying this until you believe me. There is no *him*. I've always been faithful to you."

"But not in your heart."

That, at least, was true, even if he didn't know the real object of her affection.

Laurel stood and studied the back of his head, wondering if Doug's subconscious had intuited the truth—not about Luke per se, but about her disappointment the day she discovered the car accident hadn't killed him, and the flood of emotions that followed. She was certain he didn't know about her efforts to hasten his demise. But maybe he sensed her authentic heart.

Maybe her feelings were airborne, too.

"There is no one but you," she lied, knowing how hollow it sounded.

Though Doug remained still, he pulsated like a wound. Laurel gently shut the door, and left.

When she arrived at her mother's house, groceries in arms, Laurel's bright mood returned. Joan was once again dressed for an outing. This time, it wasn't something new, but an outfit she had clearly pulled from the overcrowded, neglected side of the closet. Her cinnamon-colored sweater was gathered at the sleeves and over the bust, and had a row of shiny, multicolored beads embellishing the V neckline. Laurel remembered the style, if not the particular top, and assumed it had been purchased ten or fifteen years earlier. She wore it over camel-colored slacks, with her favorite black patent leather pumps. Her bracelets jangled happily.

"That's a going-out-for-lunch outfit if ever I saw one!" Laurel said. Of course, she wouldn't mention that the effect was dated. Her mother was in a festive mood, and that's what counted.

Joan gave a laugh. "I found it in my closet with the tags on!" she said. "Like I was saving it just for today."

Laurel beamed. Her mother had already decided they would go out for lunch. It was perfect—no cajoling necessary.

"Did you have a restaurant in mind?" she asked.

"Oh, I…" Joan said, surprised. "I'm sorry, I guess I didn't tell you. My friend Beverly invited me to lunch. We're going out for *Japanese*." She punched the last word as if she had never dared dream of anything so wonderful.

Laurel had to contain her surprise. And okay, disappointment. The idea of having a lovely lunch with her mother had been a dream for so long, and she thought today was the day. But never mind, she told herself. This was good news. Her mother now had two friends she could count on, Eleanor the bird lady and Beverly from the doll show. This was exactly what Laurel had wanted for her—real friends and a social life. The courage to leave the confines of this house. Their mother-daughter lunch could wait for another day.

"That's wonderful, Mom. I'm so glad."

"Beverly said she'd pick me up, but I told her not to bother—that I would take a cab and she could drive me home. Unless…" She trailed off, and Laurel caught her drift.

"Oh, Mom, you don't need to take a cab. I'll drive you there."

"Are you sure? I don't want to be a bother."

"It's my pleasure."

They finished putting away the groceries, and Joan excused herself to freshen up. When she returned, she was buttoned up in her blue faux fur winter coat—the one that made her look like a Muppet—holding a doll in her gloved hands like it was a bridal bouquet. Laurel understood that this would be her mother's path to freedom. She could now march through the door of her house, as long as she held one of her collectible friends.

"Ready?" Laurel asked.

Joan nodded and took her elbow as they crossed over the threshold into the outdoors, the two of them squinting into the sharp winter sunlight.

"What I need," Joan said with a girlish giggle as they walked toward the car, "is a boyfriend who drives."

What you really need, Laurel thought, is to get over your fear and get back behind the wheel. But it had been over a decade since Joan had even owned a car, and Laurel doubted it would happen. She wondered, though, if her mother was joking, or if she was really thinking about dating now that she could actually leave the house.

"An Uber app might be a better idea," Laurel offered.

"Isn't that just a fancy way of calling a cab?" Joan asked.

Laurel admitted it was, and considered how hard it might be to teach her mother how to use it. Uber was such a simple thing, really, and would give her so much freedom. But she remembered Doug's resistance to learning the technology, and assumed it would be a useless effort.

"In any case," Laurel said, opening the car door for Joan and her plastic friend, "I'm always happy to drive you."

"I hate to impose."

"It's not an imposition, Mom."

Joan lowered herself into the seat, and swung her legs around, knees together as if she were bound into a tight skirt instead of a pair of slacks.

"I've been meaning to ask you something," Joan said, belting herself in. "Does that charming Charlie Webb fellow have his own car?"

After dropping her mother at the restaurant, Laurel had one more errand to run—stopping by CVS to pick up Doug's prescriptions, which she did once a month.

"Douglas Applebaum," Laurel said when she reached the register.

The crisply efficient young woman typed his name into her computer, and asked Laurel to verify the date of birth. She typed a few more things and then, instead of turning to rifle through the alphabetized bags of prescriptions, she looked back at her.

"They were already picked up."

"For Douglas Applebaum?"

"Yes, ma'am."

"Are you sure?" Laurel pressed, as Doug barely left the house anymore. And besides, filling prescriptions was an errand he left to Laurel, assuming the insurance coverage was complicated business. In truth, the pharmacy had the information on file, and it was rarely more than a five-minute errand.

"About an hour ago."

"The Lipitor *and* the Lopressor?" Laurel asked. She hadn't been giving him the Lopressor, but continued to renew it.

"And the Ambien."

"Ambien?" Laurel repeated. This didn't seem right. Those were the pills she had spilled down the toilet, certain he wouldn't notice they were gone, as he never took them. They were not on automatic refill.

The pharmacy clerk nodded. "Is there anything else I can help you with?"

Laurel froze as a chill of apprehension prickled her flesh. She understood exactly why Doug had taken the initiative to go to the pharmacy. A bottle of Ambien would be just what he needed to commit suicide.

"Ma'am?"

Laurel blinked, broken from her reverie. "I have to go," she said, and flew out the door. She belted herself into her Altima and sped home as fast as she could.

Surely he wouldn't have taken the pills right away, she told herself. He wasn't the type who rushed into any decision. He probably wanted to have them on hand while he weighed his options. A handy solution in case he ever decided to go through with it.

But of course, it was also possible he decided to seize the opportunity while he had the momentum. She replayed what the woman at the pharmacy had said—he picked them up only an hour ago. That wasn't much time, was it? Even if he had swallowed the whole bottle, surely they could pump his stomach and save him. Surely.

When Laurel found herself stuck behind a slow-moving truck that said Mason Transport on the back, she tried to find names to match the initials. *Margaret Thatcher. Mark Twain. Mike Tyson. Marisa Tomei.* Who else? *Mary Tyler Moore.* Did that count? Laurel was so agitated she couldn't remember the rules of her own game. Her heart beat frantically, thumping against her rib cage.

"Move!" she shouted at the 18-wheeler. At last, Laurel found an opening in the right lane and was able to speed around the massive vehicle fast enough to avoid getting caught in his blind spot.

When she arrived home, Laurel burst through the door. "Doug?" she called, out of breath. "Doug!"

No answer. She ran into the kitchen, where she saw the narrow white prescription bags from CVS, the drug information literature stapled to the exterior. She got closer and saw there were only two of them on the table. The Ambien was missing.

"Doug?" she called again—louder this time—and dashed downstairs toward the sound of the TV. She found him on the couch, watching a football game, an open bottle of beer on the coffee table in front of him. Her eyes scanned the room.

"What are you so hysterical about?" he asked.

"Where are they?" she demanded.

He looked confused. "Nobody here but me."

"The sleeping pills!" she said. "Where are they?"

He nodded, looking pleased with himself. "What do you care?"

"Doug, tell me where they are."

"No."

"Did you take any?" she asked.

He gave a mocking shrug, letting her know he wasn't going to make this easy. They stared at each other, and a startling understanding filled her. He was taking charge of his own life and death, daring her to do anything about it. He gave the tiniest smile, as if he found it all terribly entertaining.

Laurel left the room to search for the bottle of pills. She ran straight for the medicine cabinet where the old prescription had been, but it wasn't there. She checked the two other bathrooms, as well as the kitchen cabinet where she kept the rest of his medication. No Ambien. He had hidden it. Laurel was so dizzy with fear she had to prop herself against the wall until she caught her breath.

She thought about how awake he appeared, telling herself it was irrefutable evidence he hadn't already swallowed the whole contents. Just to be sure, she searched every trash can for the empty bottle, digging through with her bare hands to see if he had pushed it to the bottom. Nothing. There was some small relief in that—he was saving them for another day.

She raced back into the den. "You hid them," she said, her eyes filling with tears. It was all just too much. It was torture.

He shrugged again. "I'm keeping them in a safe place."

"Why?" she demanded.

"So you won't throw them out."

She swallowed against a lump in her gullet and approached him. "Sweetie, what are you planning to do?"

"As if you care."

"You're scaring me, Doug."

He turned up the volume on the football game. "I'm watching this."

She crouched next to him. "If you're planning on...on hurting yourself, you have to tell me."

"I don't have to do anything."

"Please, honey," she said, trying to keep her voice even. "This isn't a game."

"Sure it is. The Giants are playing the Eagles."

"That's not funny," she said, disturbed that he was back to making jokes. This was not a good sign. He was feeling his oats again, and she was certain it was because he had taken control and made his decision.

"But you think my dad jokes are so hilarious," he sneered.

"How about if I make an appointment for you to talk to Dr. Sokol tomorrow?" She was the therapist he had seen in the past for a short time, after his mother died.

He made a face. "Forget about it."

"A different therapist, then?"

"I don't need a therapist."

"You do."

"Look at it this way," he said, "once I'm gone, you and Charlie are free to hook up. In fact, you can fuck a different guy every night."

Laurel closed her eyes. Doug's jealousy had always been an ugly beast, with the power to transform him into something irrational and unrecognizable. But this time it was layered with more cruelty than she could have imagined.

"How could you say something like that to me?"

"Don't sweat it, babe. I have a big life insurance policy. You can buy a whole wardrobe of those whorish little getups."

Laurel studied him. He didn't understand that there would be no life insurance claim if he committed suicide. But this was not the right time to educate him on the critical fact that had consumed her life these past weeks.

"You know," she said, "I could have you hospitalized."

"For *what*?" he demanded, rolling his eyes.

"For threatening to…hurt yourself." Again, she found herself unable to say *kill*. It felt too real, too dangerous.

He snorted. "I'll deny it."

Laurel put her hands on her hips. "Tell me where you hid the pills!"

He looked past her at the television, growing excited. Someone scored a touchdown and he whooped, startling her.

Laurel left the den and went into the guest bedroom to search for the bottle. She looked in the drawers, beneath the mattress, under the bed. She opened the closet door, and was confronted with an intimidating sight. Evan had boxed up his old things and stacked them there. She began pulling out cartons and rummaging through them, aware that it was probably a futile effort. There were simply too many places to hide a little bottle of pills. Still, she spent the rest of the day searching the house, determined.

By nightfall, she was exhausted. There were still so many places to look, but she hadn't an ounce of energy left. Laurel put her head on the kitchen table, more tired than she had ever felt. She was out of options.

At last, she lifted her head and did the one thing she promised herself she never would. She called Abby.

32

By the time her sister-in-law arrived, it was after ten thirty, and all Laurel wanted to do was go to sleep. She led her into the kitchen and asked if she'd like a cup of tea.

Abby shook her off. "Not now," she said, an edge of judgment in her voice. "Where is he?"

Laurel exhaled. She had no energy to bristle at her sister-in-law's airs. "Evan's old room. He's been sleeping there."

Abby gave a sharp nod. "You stay here in case I need anything," she said, as if she were about to negotiate with a foreign adversary and might need someone to call in the troops. "I'm going in." She pushed her purse at Laurel—an act of aggression intended to cement Abby's authority. Marching from the room, she was a senior officer leaving her inferior to manage the minor details, like finding a place to put down a handbag.

Laurel's shoulders slumped in surrender. Today, she would

not indulge in her grievances with Abby. She was there to save Doug's life, after all.

Exhausted, she dropped the purse on the table and lowered herself back into the kitchen chair. She could hear Abby walk up the stairs and knock on the door to the guest bedroom.

"Go away," Doug called.

"It's Abby. I'm coming in."

Laurel heard the door open and shut, and then...nothing. She stayed at the table, listening to the sound of her own breath, wondering what they were talking about. Doug's depression was wrapped in Kevlar, and she didn't know if even Abby could penetrate it. But he revered his older sister. He listened to her. At the very least, he was more likely to open his heart to her than to Laurel.

She drummed her fingers to break the oppressive silence and looked at the clock. Twenty minutes had passed. Laurel's eyelids felt weighted and she wanted to climb into bed and sleep—at least for a few minutes. But Abby had instructed her to wait here, and she figured going to bed would make her seem callous.

Another fifteen minutes passed, and Laurel tried to think of something useful to do that might help her stay awake. At last, she had an idea. She made two cups of green tea and put them on a tray. She carried it upstairs, feeling useful if unimportant.

"I made tea," she said, with a gentle knock. "I'm leaving it outside the door."

Laurel set the tray on the floor, then went into the living room and perched herself on the sofa, where she had a vantage point of the landing outside the bedrooms. She watched, waiting to see if the door opened and the tea was brought inside.

Laurel kept her eye on the tray, trying to fight sleep. But she was too weak, and the couch too comfortable. Slumber was a formidable opponent—persistent and persuasive. At last, it pulled her under, deeper and deeper. Even unconscious she fought it, snorting awake several times, only to fall into the blackness again before she could claw her way back.

At last, Laurel heard the door open and forced herself awake. She saw Abby emerge from the room and shut the door behind her. The tray with the tea was gone. Laurel blinked at the realization that she had been in such a deep sleep.

Abby walked down the steps toward Laurel and stood before her. She held out her fisted hand and opened it. There, in her palm, was the bottle of sleeping pills.

Laurel didn't know what Abby had said to Doug during those two hours alone in that room, but she clearly got through to him. In addition to handing over the pills, he had agreed to see a therapist. Then, Abby had made a late-night call to her own psychologist, Dr. Kitman, and managed to get Doug an emergency appointment for the next afternoon.

Insisting Doug shouldn't be alone, Abby showed up again early the next morning to "sit with him" until his appointment. Normally, Laurel would have cringed at the thought of leaving her sister-in-law in her house all those hours to snoop and clean, but on this particular day she was grateful she could go to work without fear of coming home to a suicide note.

Laurel dragged herself through the day, barely speaking to anyone except Charlie, whom she filled in on the drama. He complimented her on having the judgment to call Abby.

"You have good instincts," he assured her.

Laurel shrugged. "It's all so exhausting."

"Listen to me, honey," he said. "This is just a glitch. It'll be okay. I promise. You'll get past all this soon."

"Sometimes it seems impossible, this thing we're trying to do."

"Laurel," he said, "you are going to get everything you

want. You'll have the life you deserve. You have to believe that."

She thought of Luke, then, and her heart filled with light. "Thank you," she said, and for the first time that day, Laurel smiled.

When her work shift was over, she saw a text message from Abby saying the therapy had gone well, and that Dr. Kitman believed the crisis had passed. He wasn't recommending hospitalization at this time, but wanted Laurel to watch for signs of suicidal ideation. In the meantime, Doug would be going to therapy two times a week.

Laurel's relief was palpable, even as she realized the therapy wouldn't be covered by insurance, and this would push them deeper into the hole.

33

The first change Laurel noticed—even before the antidepressants had a chance to kick in—was that Doug answered when she spoke to him. She no longer had to repeat herself again and again, trying to keep her impatience in check while he flaunted his depression like a banner big enough to block out the sun.

Not that he was back to his old self, but at least he was making an effort. He spent more time out of the guest room, and while their conversations weren't scintillating, they were productive. Yes, he would take out the trash. No, he didn't mind if they had chicken again. And sure, he would remember to bring his car in for inspection by the end of the week.

Still, Laurel was uneasy. He hadn't moved back into their bedroom, and she felt a distinct wall between them. There was something about his efforts that felt forced, like he was putting on an act for her benefit, and she worried he still held suicide in his back pocket. Maybe he was thinking he could lull her into complacency so she wouldn't be so quick to stage an intervention if he started acting suspiciously.

Of course, it was more likely he was following his therapist's advice, hoping feelings would follow actions. Laurel knew from experience it often worked that way. But for the time being, she wouldn't take any chances, and decided to suspend her evening coffees with Charlie. It was a hard decision, because she looked forward to those chats, but she had noticed Doug's attitude backsliding every time she came home late, even though she told him she had gone out with "friends from work." No doubt he suspected otherwise.

She decided to break the news to Charlie at the end of their shift. While waiting for him, she pulled her coat from its hanger. And just like that, he was behind her, helping her find her sleeve.

"Ready to go?" he asked.

She turned to face him as he buttoned up his own coat.

"I can't, Charlie," she said, arranging her face into a soft expression. "I'm sorry."

He paused to study her as he drew his cap from his pocket. "Is everything okay?"

"I don't know," she said. "That's the problem. He gets so upset when I come home late. I think we need to cool it for a few weeks."

"A few *weeks*?" he repeated, as if it were a preposterous period of time.

"I hate to do this," she said. "I look forward to our chats more than anything. But I think it's dangerous."

He waved away her concern. "You're overreacting. If you tell him you're having a girls' night out—"

"He's jealous and suspicious," she said. "I need to behave like the perfect wife for a while. It's just temporary."

"This isn't healthy, Laurel. You're subjugating yourself to him. Is that really what you want to do?"

"Of course not," she said, surprised he didn't understand why she needed to do this. "But eventually...eventually it'll all be over. When he's a little better—a little more willing to make an effort—I'll ask him to clean out the basement. And then..." She trailed off, thinking about the mice. Though she hadn't been down there to see for herself, Laurel knew the creatures had been busy breeding, creating a deadly level of toxic fumes. Meanwhile, she continued listening for any skittering in the rest of the house, fearful of the day an escapee might shimmy up a drainpipe.

"I don't like this one bit," he said. "It's a dangerous path for you. Before you know it, you'll be right back where you started from."

"I won't," she said, surprised he had so little faith in her. "I promise."

"Why don't we just head to Starbucks tonight to finish this conversation? Then if you decide you can't do it anymore, I'll understand."

"I'm sorry. I'm not changing my mind."

His brow furrowed. "You're hurting *both* of us. You understand that, don't you?"

"Of course," she said, trying to be sympathetic. "And I hate it. But right now, it's what I need to do."

"You're making a mistake, honey."

"I'm not."

She was so emphatic that Charlie looked startled. They locked eyes, and it unnerved her. She had assumed he would be gentle and compassionate. Laurel waited for him to soften and tell her he understood. Instead, he folded his arms.

"I'm really disappointed in you," he said.

Laurel was so surprised she had to fight the instinct to hang her head in shame. They were, after all, stinging words that brought her right back to childhood. When her parents expressed disappointment in her, Laurel felt her world crumble. It was agonizing.

But Charlie had no right to bully her with guilt. Laurel was doing the right thing. He was being judgmental and selfish. She had expected so much more from him.

"Please don't make this harder than it has to be," she said. "It's really not that big a deal. We'll pick up right where we left off in a few weeks."

He set his teeth, holding tight to his disappointment. "A few weeks will turn into a few months. You realize that, don't you?"

He held her gaze, and Laurel could sense Charlie's hurt turning to anger. She didn't like it one bit. He was the last person she wanted to fight with.

At last, Laurel shook her head. "I'll see you tomorrow," she said, and left.

Laurel awoke the next morning feeling...better. Doug had come back into their bed, a clear indication that his suicidal feelings had passed and he was on his way to recovery. This was just the confirmation she needed. She'd been right to curtail her coffee dates with Charlie.

But there was something else that put Laurel in a good mood. It was Tuesday. Luke would be coming into the store.

Since the conversation outside Celia's, Laurel felt like she'd entered into a covert relationship with Luke, albeit without the romance. But that would come. For now, they had an understanding that there were feelings between the two of them, and if all went well, it would be only a matter of time before they could act on them.

Laurel blow-dried her hair, experimented with some new

makeup, and got dressed for work. She assessed herself in the mirror, and decided it was the best she could look in a Trader Joe's shirt.

"Are you coming straight home after work?" Doug asked, looking up from his breakfast.

She gave him a kiss on the cheek. "I promise," she said, and headed out of the kitchen.

"Laurel?" he called.

She stuck her head back into the room. "Yes?"

"You look nice."

At work, Charlie was conciliatory in his own way.

"I've been thinking about our conversation yesterday," he said, as he punched in. "And I'm sorry if it upset you."

Laurel noted that even as evolved as he was, Charlie apologized like a man. That is, he wasn't sorry for what he did, but for how she felt about it.

"Thank you," she said, because she was really so fond of him, and wanted to get past this speed bump in their friendship. "I accept your apology."

"I know you believe you're doing the right thing, Laurel. And I respect you for that."

"I *am* doing the right thing," she insisted.

He put a hand to his chest to show his sincerity. "If you can get Doug past his suicidal tendencies, it's all for the best."

He was humoring her, as if he didn't expect it to work. So Laurel leaned toward him. "Charlie," she said softly, "he came back into my bed last night."

Charlie's body went still, then he backed up to look at her. "He *did*?"

When Laurel caught his startled expression, she understood he had made a leap of logic she hadn't intended.

"To *sleep*," she clarified. "We didn't get intimate."

"Ah," he said, nodding, then rubbed his chin. "This is very good news, Laurel. It shows that he trusts you again."

"He also told me I look nice today."

"You *always* look nice, honey," he noted, indicating her entirety with a sweep of his hand. "You deserve a man who tells you that every day."

She smiled, thinking of Luke. He would do that. He would pay her compliments every day. Laurel touched her hair, hoping it still looked as good as it had when she left the house.

"Thank you," she said, and then punched in and began her first shift.

To Laurel's delight, she was working the cash register when she noticed Luke making his way down the aisle. Isaac was belted into the shopping cart, playing with a teething toy, while Luke's eyes scanned the store. When they alit on her, Laurel saw his expression go bright and it filled her like a tall glass of sunshine.

He pointed her out to Isaac, and the baby waved. Laurel didn't know if it was the first time he had done it, but Luke beamed. He held up a finger to Laurel, indicating he would need another minute or so to finish shopping, and she went back to her customer.

A short time later, they were face-to-face at her register. She noticed that Isaac was in a new puffy red coat, and so was Luke. Once again, they matched. Laurel let out a spontaneous laugh.

"My favorite twins!"

Luke smiled. "It's not too much?"

"Oh, it's totally too much," she said. "That's what makes it so cute."

"Imani worried people would laugh at us."

"Not *at* you," she corrected. "*Near* you."

"Oh, Laurel," he said with a delighted sigh, "it's so good to see you. Your smile lifts me."

She glanced past him to be sure there was no one else in line at her register. "I was hoping you wouldn't be upset with me after…" She trailed off, unsure what to say.

"Of course not," he said. "I'm concerned about you. You probably don't want to talk about it, but…are things any better at home?"

"A little," she said. "For now." Laurel was careful not to give him the impression that she and her husband were working things out.

He nodded, waiting for her to say more, and in that moment, something crystalized for her. Laurel realized she could tell him the whole truth about Doug's depression—or most of the truth, anyway, and he would fully understand that she was temporarily stuck in this marriage. Of course, he would make the assumption that she was planning to leave him in the traditional way, but that was fine. In fact, in a scenario where money wasn't such a terrible burden, it would be true.

"My husband hasn't been well," she began.

Luke's expression went serious with concern—it was the face of a compassionate doctor—and she understood he was ready to dig into the diagnosis. "He's sick?"

"Depressed," she explained. "We were very concerned for a while. His sister and I."

She could see him connecting the dots, but also wanting to know more.

"He was in crisis," she went on. "You understand?"

"And it was exacerbated by problems in the marriage?" he asked.

Laurel lowered her voice. "It was *caused* by problems in the marriage," she corrected. "He just couldn't handle the issues between us and he was ready to hurt himself."

Luke's face seemed to take in the full anguish of that.

"I was fortunate his sister stepped in," she continued.

"I'm so sorry you're going through this," he said. "You must feel so…stuck."

She nodded. "Luke, when he's better…"

He reached out and touched her hand, and she looked into his large dark eyes, deep enough for her to drown in. "Do you think we can have coffee sometime?" he said. "As friends? Would that be all right? I don't want to complicate things for you."

Remember this feeling, she told herself, as a spark ignited right in the center of her chest, sending warmth everywhere. "Coffee," she repeated, remembering her vow to come home every night and play the perfect wife. But Luke was so dear and so patient she knew he would wait until she felt it was safe. "Of course. I'd love to."

As Luke paid and left, Laurel's heart felt so buoyant she thought she might float right off the floor. But then she looked up to see Charlie standing at the next register, getting ready to relieve another crew member. Laurel didn't know how much he had heard, but it was enough. He had a look on his face that turned her heart heavy. Poor Charlie. He must have felt betrayed that she would have coffee with Luke when she had no time for him.

When there was a lull between customers, she turned to him. "I hope you understand I value our friendship more than anything."

"Well, not *anything*," he said, avoiding eye contact.

"No, I mean it. Charlie, the very minute I feel it's safe, we'll go back to our table at Starbucks. I wouldn't give that up for the world."

"But you told that guy you could meet him."

"I meant later—when I'm back to doing that kind of thing again."

A customer stopped to ask Charlie where she could find pomegranate juice. Since there was no one at his register, he left his post to walk her over. When he returned, Laurel glanced up at him and he said, "You realize you're playing with fire, don't you?"

She shrugged.

"Laurel, don't be foolish."

He wasn't going to say any more, not there in the store where someone might overhear. But she understood his point. She couldn't afford to get even a little sloppy.

"I'm not having an affair," she whispered.

"But you like him," Charlie said, nodding in the direction Luke and Isaac had gone. He had said this to her before, but now it didn't sound like an accusation. His voice was compassionate, open, and Laurel felt so grateful he had accepted her feelings.

She nodded, feeling tears form. "A lot, Charlie."

He shook his head. "Be careful, honey."

"I will," she said. "I promise."

Later, during her final hour of the day, Laurel was restocking the dairy case when she heard a familiar voice. But it was so out of context she was confused. After pushing the last container of milk onto the shelf, she looked up to see Charlie and her boss, Tammy, having a conversation in the middle of the produce section with a woman in a blue faux fur coat, holding a vintage Raggedy Ann doll.

"Mom?" Laurel called, confused. "What are you doing here?"

Joan waved the doll at her, its bright red hair like a beacon. "Laurel!" she sang. "I came to see you!"

Laurel dusted her hands on her pants and approached.

"Are you surprised?" Joan asked, looking delighted by her accomplishment.

"Very," Laurel said. "How did you get here?"

"That's part of the surprise." Joan covered her mouth for a moment, as if the truth were almost too wonderful to reveal. "I took an *Uber!*"

Before Laurel could respond, Tammy interjected. "It was nice meeting you, Mrs. Spector," she said kindly, then turned toward Laurel. "You can take a break now and then punch out early."

Laurel thanked her, and Charlie took it as his cue to excuse himself and get back to work. "I'll see you later, Joan," he said.

"Toodles!" she countered, with a wiggly wave.

Alone with her mother in the middle of the fresh vegetables, Laurel turned to her. "How did you manage to take an Uber?"

"Hmm?" Joan said, and Laurel noted that she had been looking in Charlie's direction.

"I said, how did you manage to take an Uber all by yourself?"

"Oh, Eleanor put it on my phone the other day and showed me how to use it. She's such a wiz at technology. And you know, I don't even need *cash*. It just gets charged to my debit card, like magic."

"That's wonderful, Mom. It'll give you a lot of independence."

"I wanted to try it out, and wondered where I should go. Then I thought, 'I'll go see my daughter at work!'"

Laurel bit back a smile, noting that her mother seemed determined to convince Laurel she came to see her. Or maybe she was trying to convince herself.

"And how nice that you got to see Charlie, too," Laurel said, amused.

"Oh! That man is so charming."

"Yes, he is."

"When I told him that I got the Uber so I wouldn't have to bother you to drive me all the time, he said I could call him for a ride anytime! Isn't that just the most generous thing you ever heard?"

"Charlie offered to be your chauffeur?" Laurel said, surprised.

Joan seemed to twinkle in delight. "I think I have a new friend!" she gushed.

Laurel wondered what Doug would think about this development, and felt a twinge of unease. Surely, he wouldn't be happy with the idea of Charlie insinuating himself into Joan's life, and by extension, theirs.

"You don't really want to bother Charlie, do you? I mean as long as you have the Uber app."

"He said it would be his pleasure and I think he meant it. He's all alone, you know."

Laurel nodded, noting how loneliness could create unlikely friendships. She liked to think it would be good for both of them, but wondered if she would need to keep it a secret from Doug. Even hearing Charlie's name was likely to set him off.

But what if the friendship turned to romance? It was hard to imagine her mother in that kind of relationship, but she seemed schoolgirl giddy over Charlie. The thought of it made Laurel vaguely uneasy, but she let it go. Her mother deserved happiness, after all. She'd been alone so long. And maybe if their friendship turned to romance, Doug would relax, understanding that Charlie didn't pose a threat.

But of course, with any luck, Doug would be gone long before that ever happened. She thought about those mice in her basement, continuing their orgy of eating and pooping and reproducing. She tried to imagine how a bag of bird feed could be processed into waste so noxious it could take down a grown man. It was hard to picture, but Laurel knew that if an oyster could turn a grain of sand into a pearl, a basement full of mice could grant her one simple wish.

Laurel looked at her mother, whose focus was elsewhere. She followed the line of her gaze and spotted Charlie, restocking the salt-free assorted nuts. Joan pulled the Raggedy Ann doll to her chest, and Laurel thought about the unpredictability of love.

34

"I'm so glad you could make it," Monica said, when Laurel pulled out the chair opposite her at the cavernous jukebox-themed Fanfare Diner.

"I'm glad, too," Laurel said.

She had texted Monica only a day earlier, saying she might have to cancel. The problem was Doug. Though a month had passed since he moved back into their bedroom, his jealousy and paranoia always seemed on the brink of emerging. In order to reassure him, she got into the habit of announcing her intentions every time she left the house. *I'm going to Target!* she'd call. Or, *I'm off to the dentist!* Doug would merely nod, but she caught him checking the time, as if monitoring her whereabouts. It was so unnerving Laurel worried what might happen if she was gone all afternoon for a lunch with her friend. But at the last minute, Abby's husband, Gavin, called and asked Doug if he would come over to help him

disassemble the shed in their backyard. Doug was delighted
at being asked a favor, and enthusiastically agreed, without a
single complaint about his weak back. Laurel suspected Abby
had orchestrated the whole thing, cleverly intuiting that the
invitation and the activity would be good for her brother.

Laurel picked up the oversize spiral-bound menu, unwieldy
with its heavy laminated pages, and began to scan the selections.

"What's going on?" Monica prodded. "Are you still worried about Doug?"

"Kind of."

"I thought he was better."

"He is. But you know—depression doesn't have an on/off
switch. He's moving forward bit by bit."

"He's not on suicide watch, though, right?"

Laurel nodded as she pondered how to explain the situation to Monica. Her friend knew about Doug's irrational jealousy, but she didn't know what Laurel had said to him that
day, triggering the spiral of depression. She needed to figure
out how to tell her without revealing why Charlie was there
in the first place.

"That's not what I'm worried about. At least not today. It's
his jealousy."

Monica sipped her water. "But that's *his* problem."

"Mine, too," Laurel said, "until I feel confident he's not
going to backslide."

Monica sighed, as if she didn't care for the explanation.
"What are you having?" she asked, nodding toward the menu.

Laurel put it down. "I know you think I'm being an idiot."

"Yup," she said pointedly, and picked up her own menu.

"You don't know the whole story," Laurel said.

"I know enough."

"That's what *you* think," Laurel muttered.

Monica took off her reading glasses, and Laurel sensed that something big was coming. Her friend had a habit of storing up a speech and waiting for the right opportunity to let loose. This felt like one of those moments. "You always come up with some excuse for letting him walk all over you," she said.

"Not *always*," Laurel said, because this time, it wasn't about feeling Doug's pain more deeply than her own. It was about her agenda—about making sure she got that insurance money. She wished she could tell that to Monica, so her friend would understand that for once, her actions came from strength and not weakness. From looking after herself more than Doug.

"Okay, *usually*," Monica conceded.

"Look, I know I don't always speak up for myself with Doug, but this is different. He was literally suicidal and I can't let that happen."

"Don't you see, Laurel? This was inevitable. You've spent a lifetime acting like his feelings matter and yours don't. So the very second you started acting with some autonomy, he had a meltdown. It was like, 'Wait? What? Laurel has feelings? I thought I was the only one here who mattered.'"

Laurel shook her head, but the truth of her friend's statement hummed through her like the vibration of a running engine. Because even though Monica didn't have the whole story, she was dead right about this. Laurel needed some time to chew on her own role in Doug's self-centeredness. For now, she steadied herself, deciding how to fill Monica in on the missing pieces without revealing the part about Charlie coming over to release mice in the basement.

"It wasn't just my autonomy that set Doug off," she said.

"What, then?"

Laurel drew a long breath and straightened her paper placemat. "That day he came home and thought he caught me with Charlie? His rage was so crazy I snapped and and I did something awful."

Her friend's eyes went wide. "What did you do?"

Laurel felt suddenly parched. She signaled at the waitress. "Can we have a couple of Diet Cokes?" The waitress acknowledged the request without breaking stride.

"Go on," Monica pressed.

Laurel took another deep inhale. "I told him I was in love with Charlie."

Monica almost dropped her water glass. "Are you?"

"No, of course not."

"But you were lashing out at Doug, you wanted to hurt him."

"Yes." And there it was. Laurel had revealed the precise portion of the truth she needed her friend to know.

Monica nodded, taking it in. "Don't you see why this happened? You can't repress your emotions forever. Eventually, it explodes like a volcano and you tell your husband you're in love with an old guy who wears sock garters to Thanksgiving dinner and smells like your grandfather."

Laurel laughed, despite herself. "How do you know he wears sock garters?"

"I just assume."

Laurel covered her face with her hands, thinking about the real reason she had invited Charlie to Thanksgiving. "As long as we're being honest, I have something else to confess."

"Tell me."

"Maybe we should order first."

"Oh, no you don't," Monica said, pulling at Laurel's menu. "Spill."

"Promise you won't be mad?"

"Not till you tell me."

"Okay," Laurel said. "Here's the thing. I invited Charlie

to Thanksgiving for *you*. I thought…you know, maybe you two would hit it off."

"Romantically?" Monica said, so incredulously her Long Island accent sounded like it was still on the Belt Parkway on its way from Brooklyn.

"Stranger things have happened."

"Trust me, stranger things have *not* happened. Not without bursting a hole in the space-time continuum."

"But he's a really lovely man," Laurel said.

"Yeah, I'm sure he's lovely in that I-want-everyone-to-think-I'm-the-world's-greatest-guy kind of way. But romantically he's a zero."

"I thought once you got to know him—"

"Did you actually imagine I might want to sleep with him?"

"You meet so many jerks on those dating sites," Laurel explained. "I thought it might be nice to go out with someone sweet and considerate."

Monica leaned forward. "Be honest," she said. "Would *you* fuck him?"

"I'm married," Laurel said.

"Come on. You know I'm being hypothetical. If Doug died tomorrow, and Charlie was the last man on earth…"

"Oh, stop."

"You know you wouldn't."

The waitress put their Diet Cokes on the table, told them she'd be back for their orders, and hurried off, the floorboards reverberating under her heavy footsteps.

Laurel picked up her soda and took a long sip. "Probably not. But I think my mother's staking her claim."

Monica's jaw went slack. "Joanie wants to shtup Charlie?"

"It would seem so," Laurel said.

"That's never going to happen."

"How do you know?"

Monica sat back in her seat and stared at Laurel. "Isn't it obvious?" she said. "The old guy's in love with you."

It was, in fact, not obvious.

Even after giving it good consideration, Laurel concluded her friend was simply wrong. And on Sunday morning as she backed out of her driveway on her way to the supermarket, she acknowledged that despite having the confidence of a drunk frat boy, Monica didn't know what she was talking about. But Laurel understood exactly why her friend's perspective was skewed on this. Monica was so cynical about men she couldn't accept that there was a genuine friendship between Laurel and Charlie. She just assumed he had some ulterior motive.

Also, there were nuances Monica couldn't be expected to understand. Because it was possible a small part of Charlie still had a crush on Laurel. But the larger picture was that the friendship had blossomed into something deeper, and Laurel was quite certain his feelings for her were more paternal than romantic. It was why he would support her relationship with Luke once the coast was clear. And it was also why it made so much sense that he had responded to Joan's flirting with a generous offer to drive her around town when she needed a lift.

And okay, maybe he had no special feelings for Joan. Maybe he was just being his generous, gentlemanly self. Still, Laurel was quite certain he wouldn't have made the offer to the mother if he were harboring romantic feelings for the daughter.

It was Monica's other comment that plagued Laurel now. Her friend had said, *You've spent a lifetime acting like Doug's feelings matter and yours don't.* She'd said this kind of thing before, of course, telling Laurel she was a cipher. But until that moment, it hadn't occurred to her how deeply she'd been digging

ELLEN MEISTER

her own hole with this subservience. She had always assumed her habit of putting his feelings over her own would smooth the surface for a perfectly happy marriage, free of the bumps and jolts that had derailed her parents' union. But if Monica was correct, her behavior had had the exact opposite effect, convincing Doug nothing mattered but his happiness. And now that she had woken up to the reality that she deserved some, too, their marriage teetered at the edge of a cliff. And it was Laurel who had driven them to this precise destination.

Laurel wondered how different things might have been if she hadn't spent three decades being acquiescent. Would Doug have found a new job by now? Was his complacency her fault? Other husbands were preoccupied with making their wives secure and happy. But Doug never gave Laurel's state of mind a second thought. And why would he? She had spent every day convincing him that his happiness was her happiness. Now, she realized that if she hadn't, he would have been more accommodating about her desire to go to California for the birth of their first grandchild.

Also, if she hadn't been such a doormat, he wouldn't have grumbled this morning when she said she'd be gone most of the day because her mother had finally agreed to go out for lunch with her.

"Didn't you just go out for lunch yesterday?" he'd whined.

This time, Laurel wasn't going to back down. She had been looking forward to this day for years, and wouldn't let him ruin it for her.

"I'll bring home a souvlaki for you," she said, and rushed out the door before he could get in another word.

After stopping at the supermarket, Laurel pulled up in front of her mother's house. She was surprised to see a car in the driveway, as Joan hadn't said anything about expecting company. Laurel parked at the curb and took the bags of groceries from her trunk.

"Hello?" she called, when she let herself in the front door.

"In the kitchen!" Joan sang, and Laurel walked up the steps to see Eleanor at the table, her friend Bob perched politely next to her.

Laurel's hesitated, wondering if her mother had invited the strange couple out to lunch with them. The thought made her throat tighten. She had been counting on alone time with her mother. Also, she doubted the restaurant allowed a bird in the dining room, unless it was served in a pita with tzatziki sauce.

"I didn't know you had company," she said.

"They just stopped by to pick up Thumbelina," Joan explained, holding up a chubby-cheeked baby doll with a soft body. "Eleanor has a buyer for her."

Laurel exhaled in relief as she greeted her mother and Eleanor.

"What am I, chopped liver?" Bob asked, and Laurel laughed.

"Hello, Bob," she said.

"Hello, pretty."

"Laurel is taking me out to lunch today," Joan said, looking from Bob to Eleanor. "We're going to a Greek restaurant!"

"'Ew, David,'" said Bob, and Laurel recognized the line from *Schitt's Creek*.

Eleanor tsked. "That's not polite, dear."

"Sorry, baby," said Bob. "I love you."

"I love you, too," she said, and leaned in for a peck from the bird's curved beak.

Joan looked touched. "You two have such a special bond," she said.

Laurel shook her head, feeling a strange surge of animosity toward the woman-bird couple. It took her a moment to understand where the hostility was coming from, but in a rush, she got it. With the exception of the bird's limited phrases, he had the same relationship with Eleanor as she had with Doug.

"I bet you feel like you couldn't live without him," Laurel said to Eleanor.

She nodded. "I know it's hard for people to understand, but I feel like we're soul mates. Our connection transcends what most human couples have."

"How so?" Laurel pressed.

"Our psyches are enmeshed," she said, weaving her fingers together in illustration. "He always knows my mood. And if I'm depressed, he picks me up. If I'm out of sorts, he soothes me. I don't know what I would do without him." Her eyes went soft and misty.

"And do you do the same for him?"

"Sort of," she said. "I mean, his emotions tend to be driven by mine. Not that he doesn't have his own mind and his own moods, but he's very focused on me, and tends to internalize my feelings."

Laurel's eyes landed on the colorful bird, a beautiful wild creature she could imagine soaring above the Amazon rain forest, living his life as nature had intended. For a crazy moment, Laurel wanted to throw open the window and set him free.

But no, it wasn't Bob who needed to be set free.

All at once, Laurel's head felt strange and dizzy. She put her hand on the wall for support, and closed her eyes to shut out the spinning. It was too much—this realization that she had spent her whole life making herself into Doug's parrot, with the added benefit of cleaning and shopping and cooking and picking out ties.

When she opened her eyes, she had to squint against the light. She knew the room wasn't brighter than it had been a second ago—she was just viewing it with more acuity. It reminded her of the time she went to the doctor to complain about her hearing. She hadn't realized it, but a mass of wax had built up, and once he flushed it out, she was gobsmacked by the clarity of every sound—the nasal buzz in the doctor's voice, the hum of the air conditioner, the keyboard tapping of the staff just outside the exam room. Nothing had really changed, and yet everything seemed different, clearer.

"You okay, sweetheart?" her mother asked.

Laurel shook her head. "No," she said. "But I will be."

35

Laurel had chosen Apollo's Mediterranean Grill for their lunch because of its beautiful decor. It looked like an exotic indoor garden, the delicate greenery vivid against chalk-white stucco walls, and the ceilings draped with vines and billowy swathes of cloud-like gauze. Windows in the back flooded the room with sun-bleached light, inviting patrons to come deeper inside.

"Isn't this lovely!" Joan said as they were seated.

"I've thought about taking you here for so long, Mom."

Joan looked around the room, her doll seated on her lap as if she needed to face the table, too. "It has quite the ambience."

A waiter approached and they each ordered a glass of white wine to keep them occupied while they perused the menu.

"They have salmon!" Joan exclaimed, as if it were the last thing she expected to find on a menu.

"It's delicious," Laurel said. "You'll like it."

She thought back to the first time she came to this restaurant. It had been during the good years, when the store was going strong, and they were socializing regularly with other couples—mostly going out to dinner, but occasionally entertaining. Even back then, when she was happy in her marriage, Laurel felt a covetous pull when witnessing how solicitous other men acted toward their wives. Of course, she tamped down her feelings of jealousy, telling herself the other couples bickered and fought, while her marriage was even and peaceful. Now, Laurel realized the peace came at the price of her autonomy. She simply never made a fuss, giving in to Doug on nearly everything.

"Is that what you're ordering?" her mother asked. "The salmon?"

"Maybe," Laurel said, as she continued to scan the selections.

A few moments later, Joan seemed even more excited. "Oh, the salads!"

"You know, you can order any salad with salmon on top. I do it all the time."

"Well, if you're getting it, I don't want to..."

"Don't worry about me. Order whatever you want."

Joan's face tightened in concentration as she continued reading. "Chicken kebobs," she said, a finger on the menu.

"They're delicious."

"And lamb kebobs! I haven't had lamb in so long."

"Do you even like lamb?" Laurel asked. Her mother was never much of a red meat eater.

"Not very much, no," she admitted, and then added, "I think the Greek salad with salmon sounds so delicious, but I can't decide."

Laurel understood it was what her mother wanted, but was afraid it would look unadventurous if they both ordered the same thing. After all, she so rarely went out, and this was a chance to show that she was free—an uncaged bird able to spread her wings. Laurel considered ordering something else, just to make it easier for her mother. But no, she was done with that. She wanted the salmon, damn it, and wasn't going to compromise just because her mother had some silly idea she was being judged by the waitstaff.

"I'm getting the salmon," Laurel said. "And I think you should, too."

"Really?" Joan asked.

"Really," Laurel said, and her mother's eyes lit up, as if she'd been given permission to chase her own dreams, to hell with the world.

"Okay, I will," Joan said, though she continued reading the menu to make sure she didn't miss anything.

A few minutes later, Joan watched as the couple at the next table got their meals. She leaned in toward Laurel. "What is that?" she whispered, pointing at one of the plates.

Laurel glanced over. "That's moussaka," she said.

Joan nodded in recognition. "Your father liked moussaka."

"He did?" Laurel asked, surprised. "I don't ever remember our family going out for Greek food."

"There was a place in Roslyn he used to take me to. For special occasions."

It was hard for Laurel to recall her parents as a happy couple going out on dates. Mostly, she remembered her father complaining about her mother's attitude, and her mother fretting over his complaints. It was a crazy spiral—the more he complained, the more nervous she got, disappearing into her doll collection for comfort. And the more she obsessed over her dolls, the more he complained. As a child, the solution seemed so logical to Laurel. If her mother were just more cheerful and agreeable, everything would be fine. But it never worked out that way, and when Laurel was fourteen, her father left. Joan always seemed to assume he would come back one day, right up until his death nearly twenty years later.

Now, Laurel understood why she had internalized that a happy marriage depended upon the wife's deference. She also knew that deep down, she considered her own marriage a do-over, the chance to give her child the happy home she had missed out on.

A few minutes later they placed their orders, and Laurel tried to keep the conversation on any topic that wasn't doll centric. She wanted her mother to stay focused on the world outside her collection. She asked about her new friend, Beverly, then she caught her up on the news from Evan and Samara in California, and her plans to fly out there to help them once the baby was born.

"How does Doug feel about that?" Joan asked.

"Not too happy, but I'm doing it anyway."

"You'll work it out, dear. You two have a very solid marriage."

Laurel let it go. There was no reason to burst her mother's bubble about the state of her union. "Have you spoken to Charlie?" she asked, changing the subject.

Joan glanced down and smoothed her doll's hair, looking pleased. "He said that next weekend he would take me to Costco so I could do my own food shopping."

"Costco?" Laurel echoed, surprised. Her mother had never expressed a desire to do her own grocery shopping, and Costco in particular seemed out of character. Even before she was so entrenched in agoraphobia, Joan hated the vastness of big stores. She didn't even like going to a large supermarket.

"I've never been there," Joan said, "so it feels like an adventure."

"You know it's like a great big warehouse, right?"

"It's a little scary, but I'm eager to try."

Laurel couldn't imagine what her mother might purchase in great quantities. She ate like a sparrow, and was frugal in her habits, reusing paper towels and aluminum foil. "I think you'll enjoy Charlie's company," she offered.

"I know I will! We have a lot in common."

"Like what?" Laurel asked, genuinely curious. They seemed so different.

"To start, we're both widowed."

"Mom, you're not a widow." Her mother had engaged in this kind of delusional thinking before, and Laurel believed it was unhealthy.

"Well, my husband *is* dead."

"Ex-husband," Laurel corrected. "You were divorced for a long time before dad died." He had colon cancer and was receiving heavy doses of chemotherapy. Despite the diagnosis, Laurel expected him to be around for a long, long time. So it was a shock when she got the call that he had collapsed in the hospital parking lot after getting a chemo treatment. His heart had simply given out.

"We were talking again," Joan said.

"Talking?"

"Your father and I. Before he perished, we were in touch. I think we could have worked it out."

She was pretty sure her mother was wrong about that. But it was news to Laurel that they'd been in contact. "What did you talk about?"

"This and that. You and Bruce, mostly. What you were up to."

"Did you see him or…"

"We spoke on the phone. I called to ask how he was doing when I heard he was ill. He was very happy to hear from me."

Now it all made sense. Her mother had called her father,

and he was being polite. Laurel wondered if her mother knew he had a girlfriend at the time he died.

"I'm glad you reached out to him, Mom. That was very generous of you."

"He was lovely, really. He'd mellowed. He even asked about my doll collection."

"Ironic," Laurel observed, trying to imagine her father, sick and weak, acting concerned about the dolls. It was strangely touching.

"Ironic?" Joan asked.

"You know, because it was such a big factor in your divorce."

"No, dear. The dolls had nothing to do with my divorce."

"You don't think Dad resented the time you spent with them?"

Joan cocked her head. "Laurel," she said, "I started collecting *after* he moved out."

There was a long pause as Laurel stared at her, trying to understand her mother's revision of history. "You had dolls my whole life."

"I had a tiny inherited collection in the corner of my bedroom. Exactly seven dolls—porcelain antiques from the early nineteen hundreds. I didn't start collecting my midcentury lovelies until after he moved out. They helped keep me company when I was feeling lonely."

"I'm certain you started before that, Mom. And Dad didn't like it."

Joan shook her head, emphatic. "You remember my friend Miriam? She took me to a doll show to cheer me up after your father left. That's where I bought my first Chatty Cathy."

"Are you sure?"

"Trust me on this, dear."

"I remember Dad throwing a fit about all the dolls, insisting you were spending a 'ludicrous' amount of time with them. That was the word he used—*ludicrous.*"

Joan nodded enthusiastically, as if the memory were still fresh. "That was when he came to pick up you and Bruce for the weekend."

Laurel sat back, the specific scene reemerging. Her father was angry that she and Bruce hadn't yet packed up for the weekend, and blamed her mother. *You're spending too much damned time with these dolls,* he'd raged. *It's ludicrous!* Her mother had blinked back tears. *They're teenagers, Norm,* she'd said. *They do their own packing.*

Now, Laurel wondered how she had gotten this so wrong. All these years, she had assumed the doll collection was what broke up the marriage—that her mother had ignored her father's needs to look after her dolls. This was hard to wrap her mind around—that the divorce led to the doll collection, not the other way around.

"So why did he leave?" Laurel asked.

Joan's eyes floated to the distance, as if focused on something beyond the sunlight streaming in from the back. "I think we just never stopped disappointing one another."

36

"I might be home a little late tonight," Laurel announced the next morning, as Doug hunched over the table, spooning cereal into his mouth. "In fact, maybe more than a little."

She had decided to put an end to her moratorium on coffee nights, concluding that it had served its purpose now that Doug was past the worst of his depression. The weekend was proof of that—she had gone out with Monica and with her mother, and here he was happily lapping up his breakfast.

Also, she realized it was important to get back into the old routine as soon as possible, since Doug's expectations were as mutable as a spoiled toddler's. The more she let him have candy before dinner, the more he would demand it as his God-given right.

"Late?" he asked, looking shocked, as if it had never happened before.

And there it was. In a matter of weeks, he internalized the

new routine as normal. This was conditioning in action, and a perfect distillation of their marriage.

"Yup," she said, with conviction. She was the new Laurel. The actual person who asserted her needs. No more parroting back his feelings.

"You have an errand to run?"

"Going out for coffee with friends from work."

His mouth turned down. "I wish you wouldn't."

Laurel took a deep inhale, walling herself off from his sadness. "I know," she said matter-of-factly.

There was a long pause as Doug stared at her, confused. "Don't go," he said. "Please. I'm still not feeling myself."

"I think you're very much yourself," she said.

He thrust his spoon into his cereal, emptied it into his mouth. Laurel noted that he wasn't sad enough to stop eating. *He's playing it up,* she told herself. She waited as he chewed and swallowed.

"But you were out for lunch yesterday with your mom, and on Saturday with Monica," he said.

"That's true."

He gave her a long look, as if waiting for her to say more. She folded her arms.

"It's like I don't even matter to you," he said.

Laurel shook her head. "It's not that you don't matter. It's that I *also* matter. Do you understand that, Doug? *We both matter.*"

He blinked at her. "What are you saying?"

"It's not that complicated."

He chased down the last of the cereal from the bowl and wiped his mouth. "Who are you going out with?"

"Work friends." In truth, she planned to ask Charlie if he wanted to go to Starbucks again, as she missed their chats. She wished, of course, that she could meet up with Luke one day soon. But Charlie was right. For now, it really was too risky.

"Charlie?" he asked, glaring at her.

"Not Charlie," she lied.

He gave her a hard look, as if formulating a challenge, but Laurel didn't flinch. At last his tight shoulders loosened. "You'll be home in time to make dinner, right?"

Victory, Laurel thought. It was easier than she had expected. All it took was standing her ground. "Maybe not," she said. "But we can order in."

At that, Doug's expression brightened. "We haven't had pizza in a long time. I'll call Angelina's."

Laurel fought her instinct to acquiesce. She had gained so much ground—now was not the time to slide back into old habits. She thought back to her lunch with her mother and announced, "I don't want pizza."

"Huh?"

"I said I don't want pizza." There. She had asserted herself and it infused her with energy.

Doug looked confused. "What are you talking about, Laurel? You *like* pizza."

She did, but not the way he liked it. Not with passion. It was one of those things she could easily give in to because he was so enthusiastic about it. Then, of course, she felt compelled to eat very little, since it was so fattening. Occasionally, she cajoled him into ordering her favorite pizza—the kind New Yorkers called Grandma Pie, which was garlicky, with fresh, chunky sauce. Then she would overindulge, and feel guilty. Her relationship with pizza was complicated.

"I don't like it that much," she said.

"I can order you a hero. Or a salad. They have salads, don't they?"

Laurel folded her arms. "I don't want pizzeria salad for dinner."

"How about a Grandma Pie?" he said.

"No pizza!" she repeated.

"But you're the one going out," he said, sounding petulant. "I should get to decide where we order from."

"Who made *that* rule?"

"You're being unreasonable," he said.

Laurel stared out the kitchen window, trying to decide on a tasty alternative. "Thai food," she announced. "We'll order Thai food."

"I have to be in the mood for Thai food," he said.

"And I have to be in the mood for pizza."

"Why are you being so difficult?" he asked. "What's gotten into you?"

"Sometimes, Doug, we need to do what *I* want. And tonight I want Thai."

He pushed his bowl away. "We can talk about it when you get home."

Out of habit, she grabbed his bowl, ready to put it in the dishwasher. "If I get home and there's a pizza in this kitchen," she said, waving the bowl at him, and let the threat trail off.

"If I want pizza, I'm going to order pizza!"

"Fine, then I'll ask a friend to go out for Thai food with me tonight." It wasn't really what she wanted. She'd be tired and grungy after work, ready to relax at home with takeout. But she refused to give in to his childish demands.

"Who?" he demanded, folding his arms. "Who would you go out to dinner with? A female friend?"

This was the tipping point—the place where she could backtrack and cool down this argument. But her anger was already out of the gate and racing toward the finish.

"Maybe," she said, keeping her face as still and cold as she could, "and maybe not."

His eyes went wide with anger. "You've lost your mind!"

"I've *found* it."

"Great! I'll just swallow some pills then!"

This was untenable—this posturing. There was no way she would be held hostage by his empty threat. "Seriously, Doug? You're going to kill yourself because I don't want pizza?"

"Maybe, maybe not," he mocked.

Laurel fumed at the playacting. "Well, the pills are gone, and so are the razor blades. So you'll need to be creative."

"I'll do it in the garage," he said. "With the car exhaust."

"Good luck with that," she countered. "The door doesn't close all the way."

"I'll stuff it with towels."

"Use the green ones in the back of the linen closet. I don't want the new towels getting ruined."

His jaw unhinged. "Don't you care about my feelings anymore?"

"I've cared about your feelings for thirty years, Doug. Maybe it's time for my feelings to come first."

He shook his head in distress. "I can't believe you could be so cruel."

Cruel, she thought. All because she admitted she didn't want to have pizza and knew he was making fake suicide threats. This was the marriage she had created for herself.

Laurel pushed the bowl at Doug. "Put this in the dishwasher," she said, and left.

Charlie beamed when Laurel told him she was ending the moratorium and wanted to go to Starbucks for coffee that very night. And she beamed right back. They had both missed their special chats.

The sky was already painted a dusky palette of slate and pink when they got out of work at five and headed to Starbucks. They continued chatting after darkness fell, ignoring the clock. But at last Laurel knew it was time to go home, even if it meant another fight with Doug. So she texted to let him know she was almost on her way. And then, wired up on caffeine, she drove home, wondering what she might expect. Would Doug be sitting in the kitchen, defiantly eating pizza out of a box? Would he be on the couch in the den, drinking a beer and waiting for her to order dinner?

Either way, he'd be geared up for an argument. Or worse, he would be blubbering and carrying on for her sympathy. Whatever happened, she was determined to hold her ground. All the way home, she fortified herself. No matter how weepy or furious Doug acted, she would not internalize his feelings.

"I'm home!" she called, when she walked in the door.

"In the kitchen!" he yelled.

As Laurel approached, she smelled something savory and delicious, and it definitely wasn't pizza. When she got to the door of the kitchen, she saw what it was. The table was set for two, and right in the middle were take-out containers from her favorite Thai restaurant.

For a moment, she couldn't speak.

"I ordered that chicken dish you like," Doug said. "And pad thai."

Laurel closed her eyes and inhaled. It smelled so good her stomach rumbled.

"You okay?" he asked.

"You ordered Thai food," she said, trying to wrap her mind around it. She had expected so much pushback, assuming Doug would never give in to her preferences. Was this really all it took? Her eyes teared at the thought of all those years she spent subjugating herself. She could have had such a different life if only she had spoken up.

"There's something else," Doug said.

She studied his face. He looked so proud and happy. It was an expression she hadn't seen on him in years.

"Yes?" she asked.

"It's big news," he said. "Should I wait until you're ready for dinner?" Doug knew she liked to change out of her Trader Joe's shirt before sitting down to eat, and he was giving her the chance to do it.

"Tell me now," she said.

His mouth turned up in a shy smile while his eyes sparkled with joy. "I did it, Laurel," he said. "I got a job."

37

It was a part-time job at a ladies' shoe store. Earlier in the day he'd gone to the mall for frozen yogurt, and noticed a *We're Hiring* sign in a shop window. On a whim he went in and applied. Apparently, they were short-staffed, and made him an offer on the spot. The way he told it, the manager thought Doug was the luckiest thing that had ever happened to her. He would be working Tuesday and Thursday nights, as well as weekends.

Laurel was astounded. For nearly two years, she'd been cajoling and pushing and begging him to take a job like this, always tiptoeing around his wounded ego. Now, it was clear that all it took was a big dollop of enmity. If she'd only known, she would have fought with him over pizza a long time ago.

Doug, of course, seemed to have no self-awareness about his motivation. He thought it was dumb luck, being at the right place at the right time, conveniently forgetting that he had spent the past two years claiming his back was too weak for this kind of work.

Regardless of his self-delusion, the job was a relief to Laurel in so many ways. First, there was the money. It wasn't much, of course—and due to their second mortgage they still couldn't cover their monthly expenses without digging into savings—but it would slow the bleeding. Also, getting a job represented a huge leap out of depression. She wouldn't have to worry about suicide anymore.

As Laurel stared at him that night in the kitchen, she realized how much rage she'd been containing over his lazy refusal to find work. Because now that it was released, her body felt strange and dangerous—released from constriction, like a person rescued from beneath the rubble of a collapse.

As she changed out of her Trader Joe's shirt, Laurel tried to ground herself. She gazed into the mirror and it was almost like looking at a stranger. She realized, then, that she was so unaccustomed to getting good news it was a literal shock to her system. She needed time to adjust. Or maybe a glass of wine.

"Great idea," Doug said when she mentioned it, and he went to the garage, where there was a bottle of prosecco in their second fridge.

"As good a time as any for a celebration," he said when he popped the cork.

The bubbly was just what Laurel needed, and over dinner, her nerves calmed and her focus returned. As they finished their meal, savoring the last tasty morsels of basil chicken, they chatted about his schedule, and the kind of adjustment it would mean for them. At last, Laurel put down her fork and dabbed at her mouth. It was time. She was ready to claim her future.

"I've been waiting to ask you something," she said. "And now that you're feeling better…"

Doug put down his glass. "Yes?"

"Remember when you offered to clean out the basement?"

"You wanted me to do the gutters instead." He paused to laugh. "Abby had a fit." This seemed to fill him with pride, and he leaned back in his chair, pleased.

She smiled at him, sharing the pleasure. It was pretty sweet seeing Abby blow a gasket.

"Well, this wouldn't piss Abby off, unfortunately, but it would definitely make me happy if you got around to cleaning the basement one of these days," she said.

He picked up her hand and kissed it. "Of course, babe."

As she leaned in for a hug, Laurel listened carefully for the sound of mice skittering in the walls, but it was blessedly silent. For now at least, the critters were containing their breeding orgy to the area directly beneath where they sat.

Doug got busy in the coming weeks, though not with the basement. Instead, he decided it was time to clean out ten years' worth of old files in the junk room, sorting and shredding and reorganizing. It was the kind of work Doug loved, and he insisted he was clearing out space for some of the items in the basement, which he promised he would get to soon.

He seemed genuine, so Laurel decided to let it go for a couple of weeks, counting on that big bag of feed to last until Doug made his way down there.

Besides, things were more peaceful than they had been in a long while. Having time apart was good for both of them, and they even found things to chat about on the evenings they were together. But also, Laurel loved being alone in the house for hours at a stretch, even if she had nothing to do. Or maybe *especially* if she had nothing to do. Having time to herself just felt so damned good, and she was able to fill the space with fantasies of Luke. It finally felt within her grasp.

So when he approached her in the store one Tuesday and

asked if that weekend might be a good time for them to finally grab a coffee together, Laurel had to dig down to search for the strength to say no. And then tunnel even deeper. With Doug out of the house, it would have been so easy to meet him for a coffee or a bite or even a drink. Hell, she could rendezvous with him in a hotel room and Doug would never find out. And dear god how she wanted to! The very thought of his desire made Laurel burn and melt. She imagined the look on his face when she emerged in that black teddy. And then, being in his arms…feeling his warm breath on her neck…letting her negligee fall to the floor. He'd be so passionate yet so tender.

But of course, she wasn't going to have an affair. It just wasn't in her nature. And at this point, she couldn't risk even the slightest hint at impropriety—not with those dangerous mice in the basement so close to changing everything for her.

She looked into Luke's dark eyes. "I really want to be alone with you," she whispered in the cereal aisle. "But I need to ask you to have just a little more patience."

He held her gaze for a long time, a message passing between them. And she knew he understood that her marriage would be over soon. Of course, he presumed she would be leaving Doug, not hastening his demise. But as long as he waited for her, everything would be okay.

"You have my number," he said.

Laurel looked up and down the aisle, to make sure they weren't in anyone's sight. Then she slipped her hand into his and gave it a gentle squeeze.

Late Saturday morning, Laurel got a text from Evan asking if she had a few minutes to talk.

"Everything okay?" she asked when she called him. The baby was due soon, and she worried about early labor.

"I was going to ask you that same question," he said.

"What do you mean?"

"I got a call from Aunt Abby," he said. "She told me that Dad was suicidal. Is that true?"

Abby. What a meddlesome pain in the ass. This information was not hers to share. In fact, Laurel and Doug had discussed whether to tell Evan and Samara about his crisis, and Doug said he would do it when he was ready.

"It's not," she assured him. "I don't know why she would tell you that. He went through a rough patch a few months ago, but he's much better now. He's working, he's happy…"

"Aunt Abby says he's seeing a therapist and he's on antidepressants."

The nerve of her! Abby didn't give a damn about her brother's privacy, as long as she got to be in the middle of things, exerting control. But now that Evan knew, there was no taking it back. Laurel could do nothing but try to clarify.

"That's a good thing, hon," she said rubbing her forehead. "He's getting the help he needs, and he's feeling better than he has in years."

"Are you sure?"

"Positive."

"Because Aunt Abby said it would be disastrous if you left him for a week to come stay with us. That's the word she used—*disastrous*."

"What?" Laurel felt her fury rising. "Evan, no! It's not true. Why would she say such a thing?"

"She said I need to intervene and tell you not to leave him. She even offered to pay for a baby nurse to come stay with us so we wouldn't need you."

Laurel felt ready to explode. A baby nurse? Instead of *her*? Abby could go straight to hell. How dare she!

Laurel tried to imagine how her sister-in-law had convinced herself it would be okay to make such a phone call to Evan.

Then, the light came on with blinding force. Abby hadn't made the decision unilaterally. She and Doug had discussed it. In fact, the whole thing must have been his idea—a way of keeping her from making the trip. Of all the duplicitous, backstabbing things he could have done, this was the worst— going behind her back to have his sister do his dirty work. And laying a guilt trip on Evan! It was all so unforgivable.

At that moment, Laurel didn't even want to wait for Doug's lungs to fill with hantavirus toxins. She wanted to strangle him right then and there.

"Don't hire a baby nurse," Laurel said. "I've got my bags packed. I promise."

"Are you sure?" Evan said. "Because if we're going to hire someone, I need to make arrangements soon. In LA, all the good nurses get—"

"Don't," she said. "I've got the money, and I'm going to be there. Aunt Abby doesn't know what she's talking about— sticking her nose in to make herself important. Trust me, your dad is fine. And I can't wait to see you!"

There was a long pause. "Okay," Evan said. "That's a relief. Because we're going to need help, especially if Samara winds up with a C-section."

Laurel sensed there was hesitation in his voice, as if he wanted to have a nurse on call just in case. She could envision the whole scenario—flying out there only to discover a nurse had already moved into the baby's room, and that she was superfluous.

"Trust me, Evan. Before Samara even has her second labor pain, I'm going to be on a plane."

"I love you, Mom," he said, and she could tell he meant it. He always did. He had such a generous heart, her sweet boy.

"I love you, too," she replied, and ended the call.

Even her love for Evan couldn't quench the fire that now

raged in her. Doug and Abby. How could they! How could they do this! It was vicious. Heartless. She wished Doug were home so she could have it out with him. But he was at work and wouldn't be back for hours.

Laurel paced the kitchen, contemplating her next move. She considered driving to the mall to confront Doug, or visiting her sister-in-law and having it out. But no. She wanted to get them in the same room, and drop the evidence of their betrayal like a bomb. It would have to wait until tonight.

In the meantime, Laurel wanted to do something selfish and indulgent. Something to reward herself for all her years of sacrifice. She deserved it.

She picked up her phone, scrolled through the contacts, and found the name she was looking for. Then she did it. She called Luke.

38

Despite her agitated state, Laurel remembered the risk. If she came under any suspicion for Doug's murder and some neighbor reported seeing her out with a handsome stranger, it could be trouble. So she told him that meeting for lunch at Cecilia's or the local diner wasn't a good idea. Instead, Laurel's suggested a seafood restaurant on the South Shore of Long Island. It was a popular spot in the summer, but a remote destination on a February afternoon, and she knew they would be safe there. Besides, Luke was new to Long Island, and she thought he might appreciate the waterside view. Laurel had been there for dinner on a long-ago midsummer night, and it had been lovely.

After getting off the phone, she rushed to her room to dress. Laurel knew exactly what she wanted to wear—a sexy, low-cut sweater she hadn't fit into in years, and the designer jeans she bought for a steal at Marshall's last year. But when she put the items on and stood back to look in the mirror, her heart sank. It was awful. The pants were baggy and the tight sweater looked desperate and inappropriate. Laurel pulled one thing after another from her closet to try on, until she was almost out of time. She finally settled on a V-neck microfiber top in jewel red, and a pair of skinny jeans that were passable. Studying herself, Laurel remembered how washed out she had looked in the red teddy at Olivia's, and wondered if this shirt would do the same to her complexion under different lights. But she was out of options and out of time, so she put on her black boots, her navy jacket, and was out the door.

When she arrived at the restaurant, it looked shabby in the afternoon light, the damp air smelling dank and mushroomy beneath a mask of aggressive cleansers. She felt a pull of regret over her choice, but when she looked up and saw him waiting at the hostess desk for her, everything refreshed. He wore a joyful smile and an olive green cotton sweater that clung to his large muscular frame. They gave each other a chaste hug and she inhaled his sweet and spicy cologne, wishing she didn't have to let go.

The hostess walked them through the nearly empty dining room until they reached a table by the window. Laurel looked out at the view—a rustic dock with a few brave boats rocking in the gentle blue bay, which stretched out to meet the sky. She sighed, relieved that the vista was even better than she had remembered. The hostess handed them their menus and promised their server would be with them shortly.

"What do you think?" Laurel asked him when they'd settled.

"Quite a view," he said. "And the water isn't bad, either."

She smiled. Maybe the red top was the right choice, after all. "Thank you."

He gave her a lingering look that made Laurel feel like

nothing in the world existed but the sea, the sky, and the two of them. It made her so happy she had to close her eyes to keep from crying. Was it really possible she could have a future with this man? It was almost too splendid to imagine.

"I'm glad you called," he said.

"Me, too."

He leaned forward. "What changed your mind?"

Laurel put down the menu the hostess had handed to her. "It was Doug," she told him. "He pulled the rug out from under me and I just... I didn't see it coming."

"What happened?"

She told him about the phone call with Evan that morning, explaining that there was no truth to Abby's assertion that Doug was still suicidal.

"He put her up to it," she said. "I'm sure of it. He just doesn't want me to leave. He's that petty and possessive."

Luke shook his head with a sympathetic cluck. "I don't know how you bear this."

"I don't, either."

"Do you even know if his earlier suicide threats were genuine? I mean, a man like that... It sounds like he'd do anything to manipulate you."

Laurel nodded. She knew exactly how it sounded. "He was serious at the time," she explained. "He bought a bottle of pills and hid them. It was a true crisis. But now..."

"He's better?"

"Better than he's been in a long time. But you're right—he still uses it to manipulate me. The other day he threatened to kill himself when I said I didn't want to order pizza."

Luke frowned, his doe eyes soft with worry. "Oh, Laurel. You need to extricate yourself. This isn't healthy."

"I'm trying," she said. "I really am."

"I know it's easier said than done, but you can find the

strength. You just have to remember that you deserve so much more."

She nodded. "It took me a long time to realize that."

"Do you have a plan?" he asked.

She did indeed. But it wasn't something she could share with him...or anyone besides Charlie. "Sort of," she said. "I'm waiting until after the baby is born."

"And then you'll ask him to leave?"

"Or I'll leave," she said, playing along with the fiction.

He reached across the table to lay a warm hand on her cheek. "Don't martyr yourself," he said. "Make *him* leave."

She turned her face to smell his palm before he pulled it away. "Yes. Okay. That's good advice."

A waitress came by to take their drink order. Laurel asked for a glass of Riesling, and Luke requested club soda with a twist. He resumed the conversation.

"And you'll be going to California for the baby?" he asked. "Regardless of his pressure?"

"Nothing could stop me," she said. "I have to be there. I *need* to be there. I just... It's almost all I think about—holding that little bundle in my arms." Even now, right here in this restaurant, she could imagine it so vividly it was almost as if she already knew this baby.

"That's how I felt when Isaac was born."

"I knew you'd understand."

"Laurel," he said, and turned his hand up on the table—an invitation for her to take it. She did.

"I think you know how I feel about you," he continued. "But understand, I would never rush you or pressure you. Just let me know what I can do to make your life easier." He released her hand.

"You're an angel," she said.

He chuckled ironically. "No, I'm definitely not."

She could tell he was hinting as something he wanted to confess about his life, his history. "To me you are," she said. "But…it's okay. We all have things in our past."

"Somehow I don't think you have a dark side, Laurel," he said.

She waved away the comment, even as she pictured those mice in her basement, the balled-up paper bags Charlie carried out of her house. "And you do?" she asked.

He stared past her out the window and then looked back at her. "I don't want to keep secrets from you," he said.

She studied his face. "Is this about your ex?" He had mentioned something about an acrimonious divorce, but hadn't given any details.

He exhaled, as if preparing for a long story. "That's part of it," he said. "We split up when Imani was two and her older brother five. It was brutal, breaking up my family. And it was completely my fault."

"Completely?" she said, ready to protest. Because there were always two sides to any story.

He held up a hand to stop her. "I said no secrets so here goes. I'm an alcoholic. I'm in recovery now, but I was a drunk for a long time. It ended my marriage, and very nearly ended my career."

Laurel looked into his eyes. She had never suspected anything like this, although maybe she should have. Maybe all those invitations to go out for coffee, rather than drinks, should have tipped her off. It didn't matter, though. She liked knowing he was complicated, imperfect…it gave her the opportunity to be understanding. He had been so kind and generous toward her, and now she had the chance to do the same for him.

"You said you're in recovery?" she asked.

"Fifteen years sober."

"Is it still hard?"

"Some days."

The waitress brought their drinks and set them on the table atop cocktail napkins. Laurel bit her lip.

"I'm sorry," she whispered, when the waitress walked away. "I wouldn't have ordered wine if I—"

"It's fine, please."

"I'll send it back."

"Don't," he said. "It doesn't bother me."

He looked sincere, but she knew that couldn't be completely true, and promised herself she would never again order a drink while with him.

"Do you want to talk about it?" she asked. "The divorce and everything?"

"Another time," he said. "I just didn't want to keep such a big secret from you."

"I'm glad you told me," she said, and the moment felt so intimate, like they were moving closer and closer.

"And you're okay with it?"

"Of course."

He smiled. "Good. I don't know how I would have dealt with rejection from you. I think about you so much." This time, his hand went under the table and landed on her knee.

Laurel closed her eyes, imagining his hand snaking higher. "I think about you, too," she breathed. She would have been happy to stay in that precise moment for the rest of the day, or the week, or the year. But minutes later, a waitress approached, and so they ordered their lunch, and ate, chatting and even laughing. They talked about their kids and their histories, their favorite foods and tolerance for spiciness. He told her how he used to love white water rafting. She told him about the one time she'd done it, when she was in her twenties. He explained that his sister had taken him in after his divorce, and had seen him through rehab, and that she was there for him again after the accident that ended his career as a surgeon. Laurel told him about her brother, Bruce, and her mother's doll collection, as well as her odd new friends, Eleanor and Bob.

By the end of the lunch, Laurel felt sure this was more than a crush. She was falling in love.

So when they finished eating and went for a walk down the dock in the frigid February air, and he asked if he could kiss her, Laurel said yes. And just before she closed her eyes, she saw the vapor of their breath mingle and join and float away. And then, she did, too.

39

The glow of her date with Luke stayed with Laurel as she drove home, and even as she changed into a T-shirt, folded and put away the clothes in the dryer, paid four bills online, sewed a popped button back onto Doug's gray chinos, and replaced the light bulb in the bathroom fixture. But as she swept the kitchen floor, finding crumbs in every crook and corner, her mood began to shift. She imagined Doug coming home from work at the shoe store, acting stupid and cheerful, as if he hadn't colluded with his sister to try to destroy his wife's one chance to live the dream of holding her newborn grandchild.

It was an unfathomable betrayal, and Laurel wasn't going to let either of them get away with it. By the time he arrived home, she was ready.

"Hey, babe!" he called, when he walked in the door.

"In the kitchen," she said, her voice even.

He appeared in the doorway and Laurel knew everything

looked orderly and normal to him. The room was clean, his dinner was in the microwave, and she sat at the kitchen table, calmly drinking a cup of tea. He had no idea she knew exactly what he had done.

He rubbed his stomach. "I'm starved."

Laurel rose and turned on the microwave to heat his dinner. "You'll want to eat quickly," she said. "Abby is on her way over."

"Abby?" he echoed, looking at his watch. "It's after nine."

"I asked her to come."

"Why?"

She stared at the microwave's display counting down. "We need to have a chat."

Doug poured himself a glass of water and sat down at the table. "Is everything okay?"

"It will be," Laurel said. The microwave beeped and she extracted his plate of leftover chicken fricassee over noodles, putting it on the table in front of him.

"Smells good," he said.

Laurel went into the living room and sat reading a new Vanessa Erickson romance as she waited for Abby to arrive. But she was too distracted to pay attention, scanning the same paragraph over and over. When the doorbell rang at last, Laurel let Abby in and brought her to the living room. Doug emerged from the kitchen.

"What's the emergency?" Abby asked, loosening her scarf.

Laurel lowered herself into the wingback chair and held on to the armrests. "I spoke to Evan this morning," she said.

Abby blanched, and Laurel almost laughed. Had she really expected Evan to keep their conversation a secret? Her sister-in-law didn't understand her sweet boy at all. He was as empathetic as his mother, and never would have lied to her.

"Is everything okay?" Doug asked. He took the chair across

from her, while Abby remained standing, her purse over the bend of her arm.

"I guess you two think you're very clever," Laurel said.

Doug cocked his head. "What do you mean?"

Abby, who had regained her composure, stayed silent.

"Nothing to confess?" Laurel asked her.

"Is this what you brought me over here for?" Abby asked. "In the freezing cold?"

Doug looked from one to the other. "What are you two talking about?"

Laurel turned to him. "Oh, please. Don't pretend you weren't part of this."

"He had nothing to do with it," Abby spat.

"Nothing to do with *what*?" Doug said. "Somebody tell me what's going on."

"Did you or did you not tell Abby to call Evan and say I couldn't go out to California for the baby's birth?"

He stood. "What? No! This is the first I'm hearing of it." He turned to Abby. "What is this? What did you do?"

Laurel studied his face, which looked sincere, but she need to be one hundred percent sure. "Are you telling me the truth?" she demanded.

Abby opened the top button of her coat and pulled it from her neck. "Like I said, he had nothing to do with it."

Laurel leaned back in the chair and stared at her sister-in-law. "So that was all you? Without even consulting Doug, you told our son about his suicide crisis?"

Doug's head whipped toward his sister. "You did *what*?"

"I was protecting you!" she said.

"You had no right!" His complexion burned red in fury.

"Your son deserves the truth."

"I was going to tell him when I was ready," Doug said. "This is none of your business."

Abby shook her hair out of her face. "Your wife intends to go to California and leave you all alone," she said. "I had to do *something*. For everyone's good."

"Why? Why did you have to 'do something'?" He was angry enough to mock her voice.

"Because you're suicidal."

"Not anymore!"

"How do I know that?"

Exasperated, Doug held a finger in his sister's face. "You had no right to interfere. Who do you think you are?"

"I'm the person who saved you," she said through her teeth. "Or did you forget that?"

"That justifies nothing!"

"It gets worse," Laurel said to him, fully aware she was stoking this argument. "She told Evan she would pay for him to hire a baby nurse so they wouldn't need me."

Doug's eyes went wide as he looked from his wife to his sister. "Abby! What the hell?"

Abby grabbed her heart indignantly. "I do something this generous for your whole family and that's the thanks I get?"

"It's not your place!" Doug shouted.

Abby sneered. "She really has you wrapped around her finger, doesn't she?"

At that, Laurel leapt from her chair, unsure what she might do. Knock Abby down? Yank her hair out? Because this was too much. To be accused of pushing her husband around when she'd been subjugating herself to him for a lifetime, was more than she could bear. Doug inserted his body between the two women.

"I think you've said enough, Abby," he seethed.

She rebuttoned her coat. "Well, I'm not going to get between the two of you," she said, magnanimously. "You can work this out on your own."

She hesitated, as if waiting for Doug to stop her. But he simply shook his head, disgusted.

"Namaste," she said with a small bow, and left.

40

"Laurel," Doug said, after the door closed, "I hope you believe me. I had no idea she was going to do that."

"I do believe you," Laurel said. "But when Evan told me, I assumed you were in on it. I just didn't think Abby would—"

"Come here," he said, holding out his arms for a hug.

She approached and let him wrap her in the soft familiar embrace of his arms, so different from Luke's hard, broad shoulders. He put a tender hand on the back of her head and she leaned into his warmth.

"It really means a lot to you, doesn't it?" he said.

She knew he was talking about her trip to Los Angeles. "It means everything."

"We'll find the money," he said.

"You mean it?" Laurel asked. She had, of course, intended to go whether she had his approval or not. But this was better, more peaceful. She exhaled, relieved.

He kissed the top of her head. "I'll miss you," he said.

Laurel rested her head on his chest and listened to the steady *th-thump, th-thump, th-thump* of his heart.

"I'll miss you, too," she said, and in a strange way, she meant it.

The call from Evan came less than two weeks later.

"Samara's water broke," he said. "We're heading to the hospital."

This was it! The baby was coming and Laurel would be there. Even after anticipating it for all these months, it was hard to believe it was actually happening.

Laurel harnessed her galloping heart and leapt into action, amazing even herself at how much she was able to accomplish within a single day. And by the next morning, she was on an early flight from JFK to LAX, with Doug's blessing, her boss's approval, Charlie's good wishes, her mother's doll-shaped wrapped present, and Monica's advice to enjoy every minute.

Laurel had an aisle seat next to a heavily pierced young woman who plugged in a pair of earbuds and gently rocked to her private concert. Just as well. Laurel wasn't in the mood for idle chitchat—she was simply too excited.

Since she was able to receive texts on this flight, Evan had promised he would message her with any developments, and Laurel held tight to her phone even as she tried to nap. She took out her paperback and managed to pay attention to two whole pages in a row.

And then it happened. Her phone vibrated with a text from her son. Grace Mikaela Yaris Applebaum was born via Caesarean section at 5:15 a.m. Pacific time, weighing eight pounds, one ounce. Mother and daughter were both doing well. Laurel wept so hard the flight attendant asked if she was okay.

"I'm a grandma," she choked out, pulling a tissue from her purse, and everyone within earshot congratulated her, including the pierced young woman, who said it was like, so dope.

When her flight landed, Laurel was so agitated she wanted to beam herself from the plane. Why did it take so long for everyone to file out? But she just gripped her purse and waited while her fellow travelers crowded the aisle, snapping open the overhead bins and pulling out bags and coats, wrestling them out amidst elbows and heads and cumbersome torsos. When at last the cabin door opened, Laurel rose and joined the throng shuffling toward the door.

"Ma'am?" the flight attendant said, as Laurel was passing the cockpit.

She looked up, and there was the pilot, holding up a JetBlue teddy bear, dressed, she presumed, as a flight attendant, in a red shirt with a blue polka-dot scarf tied into a jaunty knot.

"For the baby, Grandma," he said, and Laurel wept again.

After making her way through the hectic terminal to baggage claim, Laurel texted Evan's friend Davis, as she had been instructed. He wrote back to say she should go outside and look for a silver Mazda and a very hairy driver.

He wasn't lying. Davis's features were barely visible beneath a bushy black beard and a mass of wild curls that encircled his head. He wore thick-framed purple glasses, obscuring the one visible strip of his tawny complexion. Laurel understood that he worked at the same advertising agency as Evan, as a copywriter.

She waved, pulling her suitcase behind her, taking a moment to appreciate the Southern California weather. It had been a rainy forty-one degrees when she left New York—the last little jagged mountains of a dirty snow washing away.

Here, it was a perfect, breezeless seventy-two. Like a movie set, she thought.

"Mrs. Applebaum, I presume?" Davis said, taking her bag.

"So nice of you to pick me up," she said. "And please, call me Laurel. Or Grandma."

"And who's this?" he asked, pointing to the teddy bear.

Laurel studied the bear's face, waiting for inspiration. "I don't know," she finally said. "Maybe I'll let you pick a name—you're the creative one."

He hoisted her bag into the trunk. "We'll brainstorm."

"Are we going straight to the hospital?" she asked.

"Evan thought you'd want me to let you into their apartment so you could settle in, maybe get some rest."

"No, no!" she said. "I want to see the baby."

He laughed. "Yeah, I kind of figured. I can drop you off at the hospital and take your bag to their apartment."

Laurel thought he was a darling young man and told him so.

She was ebullient as they chatted in the car, making their way through heavy Los Angeles traffic. He was a talkative guy, and she was happy to let him prattle on. She asked him about his job, his boss, his fiancée. He told her about his grandmother Ruthie who passed away over the winter.

"Were you close to her?" Laurel asked.

"She was my best friend," he said. "Nobody believed in me like Grandma Ruthie."

Laurel nodded, fighting back tears, and was comforted to know that Evan had made such a good life for himself, with friends like Davis.

Less than an hour later, they pulled up in front of the UCLA Medical Center and Laurel opened the car door.

"Hey, we didn't name the teddy bear," he said.

Laurel looked at the bear and then back at Davis. "I think I'll call her Ruthie."

★ ★ ★

Laurel's breath caught in her throat when she entered the hospital room. Samara was in bed, propped at an angle, looking pale but happy, and Evan sat on the vinyl chair next to her, holding a tiny wrapped bundle in his arms.

"Hi, Mom," he said gently.

Tears spilled down Laurel's face, and she couldn't find her voice. The baby. It was all so real.

"You okay?" Samara said.

Laurel laughed at her own foolishness, and waved her hand until the crying was at least a little controlled. "I'm supposed to be asking *you* that."

Samara gave a small smile. "I'm in pain, but I'll be all right. Thank you for coming."

"Do you want to hold your granddaughter?" Evan asked.

"Give me a sec," Laurel said, and turned away from him toward the sink in the corner of the room. She wet a paper towel to dab at her face, which she knew was a mess. Then she gave her hands a good, soapy washing, dried them off, and turned back to him.

"Please," she said.

Evan pointed to the other chair in the room and Laurel sat. He stood and lowered the baby into her arms.

"Meet Grace," he said.

Laurel held the newborn, who was swaddled in a well-washed pastel-striped flannel blanket that still smelled like the heat of a dryer. She stared, awestruck, at her little pink face, marveling at the perfection of her tiny nose, her translucent eyelids, her delicate black lashes, her button chin, her puckered bow lips. Laurel pulled at the blanket covering the baby's head, revealing a perfectly rounded shape and a dusting of dark hair.

As she studied this small miracle, a memory came rushing

back. When she was pregnant with Evan and didn't know the gender of the baby she carried, she dreamed she was in a hospital room like this one, with her own mother next to her. She had given birth to a girl, and as she held the pink-wrapped bundle in her arms, Laurel stared, awestruck, at the baby's perfect face and said, *I know all mothers think their babies are the most beautiful, but she really is.* The words felt so profoundly true it was like a revelation.

Her mother leaned over to see. *Prettier than any doll could ever be,* she'd responded.

Now, Laurel looked at the very real baby in her arms, a dream come true.

"Grace Mikaela," she said. "I'm your grandma, and I've been waiting my whole life to meet you."

The decision to extend her stay by a week was easy. Samara needed time to recuperate from her C-section, and Laurel wasn't ready to go. She was perfectly comfortable on the air mattress they had set up on the floor of the baby's room. Okay, maybe not perfectly, but she napped on the sofa every afternoon, and made it work. Doug was surprisingly stoic about her decision, and her boss at Trader Joe's was agreeable, since it was unpaid leave.

Laurel quickly learned Grace's cries, understanding exactly when the newborn needed to be lowered into her mother's arms to be nursed. She gave the new parents pointers on dressing, changing, and bathing the baby, but only when they asked. Otherwise, she stood back, and let them figure it out while she did something else that needed attention, like running a mop over the kitchen floor or breaking down the boxes of the many gifts that arrived from friends and relatives.

And at least once a day, Laurel sat in the glider Evan had set up in the nursery, and just held her sleeping granddaughter in her arms as she stared at her face and whispered private messages of love.

When the day came for her to leave, Laurel hugged her son and daughter-in-law, and told them to call for any reason at any hour.

"I mean it," she insisted.

"I know you do," Evan said with a laugh.

Laurel picked Grace up one last time, told her she loved her, and left, making no effort to stop the tide of tears.

Flying home, the whole trip felt like a dream that had ended too soon. But the glow of her connection to Grace clung to Laurel like a medicinal patch, curing so much of the resentment and malaise that had infected her life.

The plane touched down on the tarmac at JFK, its engines roaring in reverse to fight the thrust of forward momentum. They taxied to the gate, and Laurel exited the plane with the slow shuffle of travelers, ready to resume her routine with a new kind of peace. Perhaps it was just exhaustion, but her anxiety about controlling the next phase of her life had dissipated into the ether. It might, she knew, come roaring back once her jet lag abated, but for now, she felt almost Zen-like in her acceptance of what the future might hold.

She laughed when she saw Doug waiting for her in the baggage claim area, holding a mixed bouquet of lilies, mums, and other flowers right in front of his face. His mouth opened comically just before he caught a sneeze on his sleeve. He recovered and opened his arms toward her.

"I missed you so much," he said, wrapping Laurel in a warm, clinging hug.

"I missed you, too," she said. She hadn't. But she hadn't thought much about Luke, either, as her whole focus had been centered on the baby. Now, she was nothing but tired and fuzzy, dedicated to living in the moment and seeing what happened.

As they walked out the sliding doors, Laurel noted that the New York weather was exercising its March madness, greeting her with a day so mild it was closer to what she had experienced in Los Angeles than the freezing rain she had left behind. Doug put her suitcase in the trunk and Laurel held the flowers in her lap as they drove toward the airport exit, following the signs to the Belt Parkway East.

Doug sneezed four times in a row and Laurel laughed, putting the bouquet in the back seat.

"I don't think your allergies love the flowers as much as I do."

"It'll pass," he said, and then sneezed again.

Not right away, she thought, as they were heading into spring and she knew he'd be miserable for at least another month or two. But she just said, "God bless you," and handed him a tissue from her purse.

When they got home, Laurel unpacked, threw her dirty clothes into the laundry, and got into bed for a nap. It was a thick, dreamless sleep, and she awoke hungry and disoriented to the sound of a doorbell. It took her a moment to realize she wasn't on the air mattress in the baby's room. She padded downstairs to see Doug at the front door, paying the pizza delivery guy.

"Hey," he said, looking up at Laurel as he shut the door. "I thought you might be hungry."

"You ordered pizza?" she said from the top of the stairs, blinking. A thread of resentment began to snake its way into her consciousness. She was still groggy, trying to rouse herself back to life, and for a moment wasn't even sure why she was supposed to be angry at this development. Then it came back to her. Pizza. It was Doug's default choice, and the last thing they'd had a big fight about. He'd been so selfish and childish.

He looked up, and Laurel expected him to say something churlish and defensive. Instead, a huge grin broke out across his face.

"It's a *Grandma* Pie!" he announced, as proudly as a child producing a straight-A report card.

And in that moment, looking down at her goofy, joyous, dad-joking husband—who had more love in his eyes than anyone could ever hope for—Laurel made a decision. She would try to make this marriage work.

41

That night, Doug woke her twice with his allergic sneezing and coughing. But instead of taking her pillow and storming out into the guest room, she simply rolled over and went back to sleep. In the morning, she awoke to find him on his side, looking at her, as if waiting for her eyes to open.

"Everything okay?" she asked.

He touched the skin on her shoulder with the back of his hand, and it made her shiver.

"I really missed you," he said.

She gave him a sleepy smile, and he kissed her. Gently at first, then with growing passion. Her body responded with urgency. Had his kisses always roused her like this? Before she had a chance to think about it, they were both breathing heavily and kicking off their pajamas. It felt so good to be touched, to be desired. She wanted to feel his hands everywhere on her naked flesh, and then they were, as his mouth went to her neck and she could barely stand to wait. Hard as he was, he slowed it down, making sure she was so ready she emitted desperate cries of need. Then he was inside of her, both of them locked in a storm of impatient hunger, getting closer and closer and closer to what they once had.

"Oh, Laurel," he breathed, the tender tip of his finger helping her along. "My love, my light…" He watched her face, even as she closed her eyes and arched her back, crying out as she climaxed. He let himself go then, as she still bucked and shuddered.

"I love you," he said. "I love you. I love you."

The next day, before he left for work, Doug asked Laurel if she had seen his old high school yearbook. He'd been feeling nostalgic when she was in California and wanted to thumb through the memories, but he couldn't find the book anywhere. She promised she'd look for it, though in truth, she knew exactly where it was. The basement. She would have to find an exterminator sooner rather than later.

But not today. It was her lone day off before going back to work, and she needed the time to relax and readjust. Laurel was glad it was a lazy rainy day, which suited her mood. She glanced out the window and noted that it wasn't the kind of fierce downpour she'd left, but a gentle and intermittent spring shower, coaxing the sleeping grass awake, reminding the trees to sprout their early leaves.

She spent the day nursing her jet lag by alternating between catnaps and coffee while Doug was at work. By late in the day she was feeling more energetic, so she finished the laundry and made pot roast for dinner.

She awoke the next morning to sunshine, and left Doug sleeping soundly while she headed out to work. Laurel belted herself into her Altima and put on the classic rock station.

They were playing an old Eagles hit, "Take It to the Limit," and Laurel sang along all the way to the store, her hands tapping the steering wheel as she anticipated the joy of showing pictures of Grace to her co-workers.

They didn't disappoint, cooing over the baby and complimenting the new grandmother.

"Nice to see you so happy, honey," Charlie said to her. "Time for coffee after work today?"

Laurel nodded, as she was eager to share her other big news—that she had made a decision to back off on the plans about Doug.

"Maybe we can go for a walk instead?" she asked, knowing it would be easier to have the conversation in private. "I'm in the mood to be outdoors."

He studied her face and nodded, as if he understood. "Sounds like you want to do some catching up," he said, smiling.

She returned the grin. "You read me like a book."

As she worked, Laurel's mind went to the baby, and she felt washed in joy every time she thought of holding sweet Grace in her arms. She also thought about Doug, and how they would be able to manage financially. She was so sick of worrying about money, and knew there had to be a way for them to dig themselves out and line up their income with their expenses. Maybe if they sold the house and moved to an apartment they'd have enough to meet their expenses on their limited salaries. Maybe Doug could get more hours, or trade up for a better-paying job. She had always pictured being in an apartment alone, and it was hard to imagine finding room to breathe if she were sharing such a small space with Doug. But perhaps it wouldn't be so bad if they could find a sunny little place with a second bedroom, and maybe a balcony.

After punching out, Laurel and Charlie put on their light

jackets and exited the store. As they walked through the parking lot and turned left onto the main street, and left again into the neighborhood behind the strip mall, they caught up on her trip to California and the latest Trader Joe's gossip.

"So what's your big news?" he asked, once they were on a quiet street.

She laughed, because he had so astutely intuited that there was something important she wanted to tell him. They stopped at the foot of a driveway as a woman backed her minivan out.

"Well," she said, "I've come to a decision." She waited for the vehicle to pass and they continued walking. "I want to make my marriage work."

Charlie stopped. "What?" He pulled on her shoulder so she'd face him.

He looked so disturbed it confused her. Perhaps he hadn't heard right, because surely he would be happy about this good news.

"Things with Doug are so much better now," she explained. "I'm voicing my opinions more and he's respecting me. I'm happier than I've been in a long time."

"What are you saying?"

"I'm saying I changed my mind about the plan. I'm not going through with it."

His eyes went dark and angry. "What do you mean you're not going through with it?"

"This is a good thing, Charlie," she said, certain that if she could explain it right he'd respond with one of his wise, paternal smiles. "Doug is being kinder, more considerate. And I'm feeling more grounded now."

"And just like that everything is different?" He seemed furious, as if he'd been fully invested in Laurel's unhappiness. It was unnerving.

"I've been married nearly thirty years," she said. "That's not nothing. I think we can gain solid footing again."

"I think you've lost your mind," he snapped.

"Why aren't you happy for me? If I can have a truly fulfilling marriage—"

"What about us?" he said, grabbing the top of her arm.

She stared at him, confused. "Us?"

"For god's sake, woman!" he said, squeezing her arm so hard it hurt. "What did you think this was about?"

"I don't understand," she said, yanking her arm from his grip.

"This," he said, pointing between the two of them. "What did you think *this* was about?"

Laurel blinked at him. "Friendship?"

"No," he said, shaking his head sadly, and she saw that his anger had been replaced by an expression she'd never seen on him before. He looked...mournful, bereft.

"Charlie, what's the matter?"

He took both her hands in his and studied them for a moment before looking into her face. "I love you, Laurel."

"What?"

"I've always loved you. You're everything to me. Don't you know that?"

"No," she said, pulling her hands away. "We're friends, Charlie." Laurel felt so stupid. Monica had seen it as clear as sunshine. Hell, even Doug saw it. But she had been completely blind to this.

"Don't do this to yourself," he said. "Don't settle like this. You deserve so much more. A beautiful woman like you! You deserve a man who appreciates you and treats you like a queen. And a comfortable life, Laurel. You deserve that. And we need that insurance money."

We? A chill swept under her hair and ran down her back.

She shook her head hard, because suddenly, it all crystallized in a way it hadn't until just this minute. All those plans to take Doug's life. It was wrong. So very wrong. She was not a killer.

"I can't do it, Charlie. I can't!"

"Of course you can. I'll help."

"No," she said. "I'm not that kind of a person. And I don't think you are, either. Not deep down."

"But I am," he said.

At that, Laurel put a gentle hand on his shoulder. "You're not," she assured him.

"You aren't getting it, honey."

"What do mean?" she asked, and looked up to see a man come out of the house across the street, staring curiously at them.

Charlie followed the line of her gaze and then grabbed Laurel's wrist, pulling her around the next corner onto a dead-end street. He tried to usher her past the last house, but she stopped.

"What is it?" she said. "What am I not getting?"

Charlie's clear blue eyes matched the sky behind him as he looked straight into her face. "Marie," he whispered.

His wife. His dead wife. An eddy of wind whipped around them and Laurel held her jacket close as she understood exactly what he meant.

"You killed her?" she said against a knot in her throat. She knew the answer, but wanted to be wrong, wanted to hear him deny it, to assure her it wasn't true.

"And her policy was only a hundred grand. Just enough to pay off the mortgage."

Time seemed to halt as she stared at him, trying to find her voice. "Why, Charlie?" she finally said. "Why did you do it?"

"Do you know how hard it is for an older man to find work? I'd been laid off and we had nothing. *Nothing!*"

Laurel gasped as hot tears spilled down her face.

"I did her a favor," he continued, "believe me. She was so miserable. And she was losing her memory. There was nothing left for us."

"Oh, Charlie," she choked out.

"And Doug has that huge policy. Think of it, Laurel. We could be so happy. We could buy an RV and tour the country—just you and me. We could have everything!"

42

Laurel drove home in a daze, feeling as if she were still awakening from a confusing nightmare. How had she been so blind to the truth about Charlie? And how had she let herself get so swept up in such a dark and terrible plan? *She was not that person.*

A car honked and Laurel realized she had veered from her lane. She held tight to the steering wheel to keep her hands from shaking. God, she had come so close to killing her husband! How had she gone so far astray?

Searching for an answer, she ran smack into that terrible word again. Cipher. A person with no thoughts or feelings of their own. A nonentity.

No no no! she thought, and searched for a phrase to calm herself. She was behind a FedEx truck, but that wouldn't do. To her right there was a white van with a decal on the door that said *Blackman Stillwell Plumbing.* BS. *Bernie Sanders. Ben Stiller. Becky Sharp. Bull Shit.*

Bullshit was right. She wasn't a cipher. She had opinions, emotions, passions. She had just spent so much energy making others more important than herself that she washed away her own good sense. Not anymore, though. She was determined. From now on, she would think for herself. Judge right from wrong. She would take the path that was righteous and true.

And that included making up for the evil thing she had very nearly done. Not that she would prostrate herself to Doug. Just the opposite. She would be honest from this point on. And that meant telling him how she truly felt—good or bad.

Well, except for one last lie. She wouldn't tell him about these past few months and what she tried to do. It would just be too cruel. She would take this secret to her grave. It wouldn't even be that hard, once she got rid of those mice in the basement. Laurel reminded herself it would have to be the very next thing on her to-do list—calling an exterminator.

By the time she pulled into her driveway, Laurel felt stronger and more determined, but when she checked her face in the mirror on the back of the visor, she realized how hard she had been bawling. What a mess. She took a few deep breaths to compose herself. Then she cleaned the mascara streaks from under her eyes and put on a fresh coat of her new lipstick. It was a little bolder and plummier than what she usually wore, but she thought it suited her.

"I'm home!" Laurel said, when she walked in the door. There was no answer, and she cocked her head toward the den, straining to hear if the television was on. "Sweetie?"

She heard a noise coming from the bedroom and went upstairs to see what was happening. Doug was seated on the side of the bed, looking out of breath.

"You okay?" she asked.

He held up a finger and then bent over, coughing. He always suffered allergies in the beginning of spring, but this seemed worse than usual. Much worse. For a vivid and frightening moment, her guilt rose up like a beast. She flashed back to the shock of Charlie's confession, and wondered if she was about to follow that same dark path, despite her change of heart.

Oh, for god's sake, Laurel told herself. *Your husband has allergies. And besides, he never went into the basement. This is nothing. Get ahold of yourself.*

She took a long, slow breath and realized how ridiculous her train of thought had been. Of course Doug was fine. The guilt was playing tricks with her mind. She laid a hand on his shoulder.

"That sounds pretty nasty, babe," she said.

"Man," he said, sitting up again, "those early trees are killing me this year."

"You need some antihistamine?"

"I just took two Benadryls—waiting for them to kick in."

His eyes looked glassy from the coughing fit, but she couldn't trust her own judgment on what that might mean. "You sure this is your allergies?" she asked, trying to sound casual. "It kind of sounds like that bronchitis cough you had."

He waved her off. "I'm fine, see?" He stood up and flexed an arm. "What's for dinner?"

Laurel laughed, relieved. If he was hungry, it meant he was okay. Feeling lighter, she went downstairs to make a salad and heat up the pot roast she had made the day before.

When the table was set and the food was ready, she called him down but he didn't respond. She went upstairs to find him asleep in bed, breathing through his mouth. The Benadryl had knocked him right out. As long as he wasn't coughing, she figured he was all right, and thought the best thing to do was let him sleep for a bit.

She went downstairs and ate dinner while reading her book,

a Regency romance so compelling she could hardly turn the pages fast enough. She was just getting to the passionate crescendo when she heard Doug hacking upstairs. It sounded raspy, dangerous. Laurel dropped her book and ran to him. He was on the side of the bed again, coughing from deep in his throat, unable to stop.

"My god," she said, and felt his face with the back of her hand. "You're burning up."

He looked at her, his eyes bloodshot and watery. Before he coughed again, he croaked out one word. "Bronchitis?"

"Maybe," she said, fearing it could be pneumonia. Or worse, hantavirus. But no, it couldn't be. She tamped down her guilt and stayed focused. This had nothing to do with those breeding mice. "Let's get you to the ER, just in case."

Doug didn't argue, and let her help him into his jacket and out the door. As she locked it behind them, she thought about God. Laurel's religious leanings usually hovered somewhere between secular and agnostic, but at that moment, she couldn't help wondering if this was the Creator's idea of a cosmic joke—felling her husband with a grave illness right after she decided she no longer wished for his death.

She fought back against the guilt. *This isn't about the mice,* she told herself again. *It isn't.*

Laurel paused, wondering how she had been so certain he had never ventured into the basement. Then she remembered he had asked about his yearbook. Surely he would have seen it if he'd gone down there...wouldn't he?

"Hon," she said, as she opened the car door for him, "did you go into the basement at all while I was in California?"

He nodded but couldn't speak, as he was locked in another coughing fit, wheezing for air. She waited, pounding his back. When he finally stood upright again he said, "That's why... that's why..." He stopped to cough again, and then looked back at her. "That's why I asked you about my yearbook. It was a ruse." He coughed into his hand. "I wanted to surprise you. I thought you'd go down there and see. I cleaned it so perfectly, Laurel. I cleaned it for you."

"You cleaned the basement?" she said, feeling like she might faint.

"It took days. It was gross." He got in the car and buckled his seat belt. "Did you know we have mice down there?"

As Doug was whisked past triage into a curtained-off area of the ER, Laurel stayed at his side. And though she tried to keep out of the way, she stayed as every doctor, nurse, and aide rushed to and from his bedside. She stayed as they listened to his heart and took his pulse. She stayed as they drew blood, ran an EKG, checked and re-checked his blood pressure. Then they wheeled him out for a chest X-ray and back in again, hooked up an IV, put him on oxygen. They were still trying to diagnose his illness, and Laurel knew she had to find a way to tell them it was hantavirus before it was too late. But she needed to do it without arousing suspicion.

Finally, she waylaid a young resident who was interviewing the two of them about Doug's symptoms and medical history.

"Could it be…hantavirus?" she asked him, as she glanced at her husband on the bed, struggling for air.

"Hantavirus?" The young doctor wore a mask, and Laurel tried to read his expression. She wiped her sweaty palms on her jeans.

"I read about it in *Newsday*," she said.

"It's very rare." He clicked the top of his pen. "And not transmissible. Unless he worked on a farm or something…"

"We have mice!" she blurted. "In the basement. He just told me."

The resident looked at Doug. "Do you spend a lot of time down there?"

Doug held up five fingers and tried to speak, nodding.

"He's saying five days," Laurel interpreted. "He spent five days down there cleaning it out."

"Were there a lot of droppings?" the resident asked.

Doug gave a big nod and a thumbs-up to indicate that there were, indeed, mountains of rodent waste.

The young doctor froze, dumbfounded. "I'll be right back," he said, and rushed out.

After that, everything happened in a frantic blur. There was more bloodwork, a CT scan, an infectious disease specialist, a pulmonologist. The doctors conferred at his bedside, discussing his pulse-ox level, and going over the complications of his preexisting conditions.

And then, Doug was admitted and moved from the ER to the ICU. Laurel felt as invisible as a speck in a vast sea of activity as everyone rushed around her, ministering to her husband.

Then the pulmonologist—a slender dark-haired woman named Dr. Dalvi—called Laurel into the hallway and explained that her husband's oxygen was very low, and that if they didn't see an improvement soon, they would need to put him on a ventilator to breathe for him.

Laurel put her hand to her mouth to hold back a small shriek. She understood how grave this was. "But what about the diagnosis?" she asked.

"We'll know in a few days if it's hantavirus," said the doctor. "We sent out his blood."

"Shouldn't you be treating him for that in the meantime, just to be safe?" Laurel asked.

"There is no treatment for hantavirus."

"No treatment?" She leaned against the wall for support.

"We just have to make sure he's getting enough oxygen and let his body fight it off."

Tears spilled down Laurel's face. Her husband was on the precipice of death and it was all her fault. She shook her head, refusing to believe it. He couldn't die. Not now. Not after she realized how very wrong she had been. She wanted to tell his doctor they needed to do more. They needed to save him.

"Please," she said into the doctor's kind eyes. "Please, there has to be more you can do besides putting him on a ventilator. Isn't there *anything*?"

Dr. Dalvi put a gentle hand on Laurel's shoulder. "Do you believe in prayer?"

43

Please, God, Laurel prayed as she sat by his bedside. *This isn't fair. Punish me, but not him. He doesn't deserve this.*

It didn't work, and she nearly choked on fear as Doug's oxygen level continued to drop, and the respiratory specialist called for an anesthesiologist to help put him on a ventilator. Laurel froze. It meant they would be sedating and paralyzing him. And if he didn't survive, this could be the very last moment she saw him awake. It didn't seem possible that almost thirty years of marriage could crystallize into this single, banal moment in a hospital room, amidst machines and strangers. *Wait!* she wanted to scream. *We need more time! Let me call our son. Let him kiss his granddaughter!*

But they escorted her out the door unceremoniously. And there was nothing Laurel could do but turn back and call, "It'll be okay!" into his terrified eyes. At that moment, she thought it was a more important message than *I love you*, and she hoped she was right.

"He's in good hands," she told Evan, when she called him from the waiting room. "He's in good hands," she repeated to her sister-in-law, Abby. *He's in good hands,* she said over and over in her head as she paced. It was a plea. It was a prayer. It was all she had.

When she was allowed back in, Doug barely looked like her husband. He was unconscious, with his eyes taped shut and his mouth wide-open to accommodate the tube down his throat. His coloring looked paler, waxier. For a full hour she wept, holding on to his hand, pleading with him to fight, and alternating between begging God to help, and cursing Him for His cruel vengeance.

Laurel stayed through the night, dozing for only a few minutes in the uncomfortable chair. The kind nurse who monitored him through the late hours told Laurel to go home and get some rest, but she couldn't. If she stayed, she reasoned, maybe God would understand she was truly remorseful and offer some mercy, helping Doug's oxygen levels to rise so they would take him off the ventilator.

A few hours after the sun rose, as Laurel sat sweaty and headachy at Doug's side, Abby came into the room. Despite wanting to be angry with her sister-in-law for her interference with Evan, Laurel had told her over the phone that yes, of course she could visit. And now, here she was. Laurel collapsed into her arms, weeping.

"I'm sorry," Laurel said, sniffing.

Abby patted her back. "You don't need to be sorry."

"I do… I really do," she wept. Laurel wasn't going to explain why, but her soul seemed to push the confession from her.

Abby backed up and looked at her. "You need some rest.

Why don't you go home and take a nap? I'll stay with him in the meantime."

Laurel shook her head. "I can't," she said, then realized that the painful, hollow feeling in her stomach—normal hunger exacerbated by the acid of worry and exhaustion—might actually benefit from some food. "But maybe I'll go down to the cafeteria and get a bite."

"Take your time," Abby said.

As Laurel walked through the hospital hallways, she felt so disconnected it was as if she was using someone else's legs. And then she found herself in the cafeteria, where she bypassed the hot food, as the smell made her sick. She was pretty sure it was breakfast time, but she stared at an array of wrapped sandwiches, reading the labels over and over, trying to make sense of the words. At last, she grabbed a turkey sandwich on soft bread, as it seemed like something she might be able to swallow. She poured a cup of hot tea and carried her selections to the register.

Laurel took the cardboard tray with her meal and drink to a little round table in the corner. Sitting alone, she pulled off the plastic wrapping and bit into the flavorless sandwich, masticating until it went down her throat. Some bites got stuck, and she had to chase them down with the tea. The cashier had given her little packets of mayonnaise and mustard. Laurel studied and poked them, knowing either one would make the sandwich more palatable. But she couldn't imagine that she deserved anything even remotely pleasurable. Not now, when her husband lay unconscious, unable to breathe on his own, and it was almost certainly her fault.

When she got back up to the room, Abby had her head bowed at Doug's bedside and didn't hear Laurel come up behind her.

"He's my baby brother and I love him so much," she was

saying. "I'm not ready to let him go. And his wife isn't, either. Please, God, give him strength. Make him well. Make him well. Make him well."

When the hantavirus test came back positive, Laurel wasn't surprised, but she wept and wept, knowing she had done this. By then, she was on a first-name basis with his two ICU nurses, Amy and Rosa.

"Don't give up hope," said Rosa, the older nurse. "I've seen patients sicker than him rally. Just keep talking to him so he knows you're here."

And she did, alternating between whispering to Doug and praying to God. As the days went on—and she got into a routine of going home for a few hours every night to sleep and shower—it was sometimes hard to tell the difference.

"You have to fight, Doug, please. We have so much to look forward to. You haven't even met your granddaughter yet."

She watched Amy and Rosa come into and out of the room all day and all night, checking his vitals on the monitor, taking blood gas, making notes on the chart. And Laurel would study them, searching for any sign of hope that he was improving. Twice, the respiratory specialist came in and increased the oxygen Doug was receiving. Laurel knew that was a bad sign. He was getting worse. There were times Laurel found herself holding her own breath, and she understood what she was doing. She was trying to stop time. Because as the days ticked on, it seemed they were steering toward a tragic and inevitable conclusion.

"Please, Doug," she continued to whisper. "You have to fight."

In between, there were conversations with her mother, her son, and Monica. She tried to sound brave as she kept them apprised, letting them try to talk her into holding on to hope. *He'll beat this,* they said. *Stay positive.*

Mornings were the hardest, after she had gone home to sleep and drove back to the hospital, wondering if he would still be alive when she got there. *He's fine,* she told herself again and again. *They would have called you if there was a problem.*

Then, early in the morning on day eleven, when Laurel came back into the ICU freshly showered with her hair still wet, Amy was at the foot of the bed copying numbers from the monitor into his chart.

"The pulmonologist was just here," she said.

"And?" Laurel asked, hoping this was good news, bracing for bad.

"And she's going to talk to the respiratory specialist about lowering the oxygen to see how he does."

"That sounds positive," Laurel said, biting her lip.

Amy smiled. "He had a good night, Mrs. Applebaum. I think he's turning the corner."

44

Amy was right. And a few days later, Doug was released from the hospital, though not to Laurel's care. First, he would be spending two to three weeks in a rehab facility, where he would get almost round-the-clock help to regain his strength and lung capacity. It was just as well, since the exterminator was still clearing traps from the basement.

"I can't believe I don't get to go home," Doug said, as Laurel helped him dress. An orderly waited outside the room with a wheelchair.

"Can you pick up your arm?" Laurel asked, as she helped him thread it through the sleeve of his shirt. He was so weak it was almost like dressing an oversize newborn.

"It feels like I'm going to prison," he said.

"It's one of the best facilities," she insisted. "You'll probably like it so much you won't want to come home...all those pretty nurses waiting on you hand and foot."

"I'll be thinking about you every minute," he said, and Laurel kissed his forehead.

"Before you leave," she said, lowering herself into the chair facing his bed, "we need to catch up on a few things." She actually had a pretty big bomb to drop on him regarding the house, but she figured she'd ease in with her other news.

"I take *catch-up* on a lot of things," he quipped. "Hamburgers, French fries…"

Laurel smiled at the dad joke. It was a sure sign he was getting his normal oxygen. "How about some organic Whole Foods brand *catch-up*?" she said. "Because starting tomorrow I'll be working there."

"You quit Trader Joe's?" He looked shocked.

"They changed my hours," she explained, which was true enough, but she was obfuscating. She had, in fact, asked for her hours to be changed so she wouldn't need to work with Charlie anymore. But once she found out Whole Foods was hiring, she put in a quick application, and got the job offer within days.

Of course, that also meant she wouldn't be running into Luke anymore, which was more painful than she wanted to admit. But if she was going to commit to this marriage, she had to make a clean cut. One day soon she would give Luke an explanation—she owed him that much, especially since she had texted him when Doug got gravely ill and hadn't followed up. No doubt he was wondering what was going on, perhaps even waiting for a call that her husband had perished.

"More opportunities for advancement?" Doug asked.

"I think so," she said. "And a fresh start just feels right."

The words *fresh start* hung between the two of them, and he gave a thoughtful nod. She knew what he was thinking— that she had done it as an act of love, separating herself from

Charlie Webb to prove she was committed to the marriage. That was truer than he could possibly imagine.

"I guess I don't have to tell you how relieved I am," he said.

Laurel let out a long sigh, hoping they could let this topic rest once and for all. She didn't want to think about Charlie...or Luke.

Doug reached out to give her hand a squeeze. "Thank you, babe."

"There's something else," she said, taking her hand back. "But I don't want you to get upset."

He cocked his head. "As long as it's not about Charlie."

"This is bigger than Charlie," she said, and cleared her throat. It was time to make the announcement. "Yesterday I spoke to a Realtor about putting the house on the market."

His eyes went wide. "You did *what?*"

"Honey, it's the only way," she said. "But we'll be fine. We'll find an apartment. Maybe one of those lovely—"

"I don't *want* an apartment."

"I understand," she said gently. "But we're underwater as it is. And with the hospital bills, the rehab...our insurance won't come close to paying for all this. It's going to be astronomical."

Doug shook his head emphatically. "Don't, Laurel! Don't sell the house!" He sounded almost hysterical.

"If there was any other way..."

"Of course there's another way."

"I don't think—"

"Call Phil Ebner," he said, referring to their accountant. "Tell him you want to cash in my life insurance policy. I'd much rather lose the policy than the house."

Laurel studied him, confused. "What do mean 'cash in'?"

"It's a whole life policy," he explained. "It has cash value."

This was news to Laurel. Doug had always managed their finances, and she had assiduously avoided getting involved in it, as it made her too tense. All she knew was that a number of years ago he bought a very expensive policy. She had begged him not to, saying they couldn't afford it, but he had insisted it was a smart investment. She thought he was talking about her widowhood, since they both assumed she would outlive him.

"How much cash value?" she asked.

"A lot. I don't know. Ask Phil. It'll be at least enough to cover the hospital bills."

Phil Ebner and Laurel played phone tag for two days. When they finally connected, she was kicking off her shoes after a long shift at Whole Foods, the landline handset tucked between her chin and shoulder.

Phil had heard about Doug's illness, so she had to chitchat for several minutes, catching him up on the news and the prognosis, which was excellent.

"I'm so glad to hear it," Phil said. "But I can guess you're pretty concerned about your financial picture now."

"Doug wanted me to call you about cashing in his life insurance policy."

"Under the circumstances, I think that makes a lot of sense."

Laurel hesitated, concerned about sounding mercenary. "He didn't know the cash value," she began.

"I can get that for you," he said, more casually than she had expected. "Hold on a minute."

While she listened to the vague instrumental hold music, Laurel opened the refrigerator to see what she might be able to rustle up for dinner. She pulled out a jar of tomato sauce, just to see what was behind it. And then, Phil was back on the line. She braced herself for disappointing news.

"Right now," he said, "the cash value of the policy is four hundred and twenty thousand."

"Excuse me?" Laurel said, sure she must have misunderstood. But she didn't hear his response, because the tomato sauce jar had fallen to the floor and shattered. And then she dropped the phone.

45

A week later, Laurel sat on a bench in the Eisenhower Park Rose Garden, waiting for Luke. It was a clear morning after three solid days of spring rain, and she was struck by how green everything looked. The roses weren't yet in bloom, but she could imagine the riot of reds and pinks and yellows, the sweet scent beckoning bees, enticing busy humans to slow down, if only for a moment.

Today, Laurel was the one who needed to stop and reflect. She was relieved Doug was better and would be coming home from rehab soon. It felt like more than a gift. It felt like a miracle. And now that a massive pile of cash was coming in to wipe out all their debt, she realized how much of her behavior had been influenced by stress. It had snaked itself so deep into her psyche she had almost forgotten what it felt like to breathe freely. How astonishing to have this burden lifted so suddenly! The whole world seemed lighter and brighter, as if Laurel was the one who had received oxygen.

Now, she was open to a feeling she hadn't experienced in so very long. Gratitude. Laurel knew she was lucky to have a husband like Doug. She thought about her father, who had treated her mother with such disdain. And men like Monica's husband, Andrew, who couldn't keep it in his pants. Doug would never do that to her. He wasn't perfect, of course. He could be jealous, self-centered, inconsiderate, gluttonous. But some of that was merely a reflection of her own behavior. Anyone would be susceptible to the kind of programming she had engaged in over the decades, convincing him his feelings mattered and hers didn't. If she changed, he would change. She just had to speak up, assert herself, be more demanding. Soon enough, he would become the kind of husband who would take her feelings into account. Maybe he would bring home flowers once in a while, for no reason at all. Perhaps he'd even start paying her compliments again.

Unfortunately, there wasn't much she could do about the jealousy. But she supposed that would mellow as they aged.

In the end, though, the most important thing was that his love was unconditional. It meant he would hang in there while she grew and changed, committed to making their marriage a more equitable union. There might be some pains of adjustment along the way, but they could handle it. They were that solid, rooted in love.

And oh, to be grandparents together! What a singular joy. It laid out their whole future as a starlit path they could walk together, basking in the glory of their precious Grace.

She took out her phone to scroll through the pictures of her infant granddaughter. She had looked at them hundreds of times already, but simply couldn't get enough.

Admiring the baby now—her sweet face changing almost

daily—Laurel fantasized about a future where they could spend more time together. Perhaps Evan would get a job in New York, where there were more ad agency opportunities. Or maybe, when they were ready, she and Doug would finally sell the house and take their nest egg to California. Either way, there was so much to look forward to.

But Luke. He remained a problem for her. The passion she had felt had not diminished. In fact, there were still random moments when she would remember his kiss with a shiver, and feel the pull of desire. She didn't know if it would ever leave her. All she could do was separate herself from him, and hope the feelings faded over time.

Laurel sensed him nearby, and looked up to see his striking broad-shouldered figure moving toward her, past the white trellises that marked the perimeter of the garden. She couldn't exactly see what he was holding in his hand, but somehow, he moved gracefully despite his limp, and she felt compelled to throw herself into his arms again.

No, no, no, she told herself. *Do not.* But when he approached and held out his strong arms, she found herself falling into them. He smelled like a mixture of the outdoors and that spicy cologne he always wore. She inhaled him, pulling his scent as deep inside as she could. *Do you love me?* she wondered. *It feels like you do.* He seemed to sense the question, and pulled her closer, as if to tell her to have no doubts about his heart— she could have every bit of it, if that was what she wanted. It took all her strength to break the spell and pull them apart.

He searched her face. "You look good, Laurel," he said, his voice was so warm and deep it rumbled through her.

She nodded her thanks. "I have a lot to tell you."

"This is for you," he said, and handed her a long-stemmed red rose.

She paused to appreciate the pure romance of this moment,

so she could store it inside her heart in case she ever needed to revisit it. Her eyes watered as she looked into his face and then back at the blossom. She put her nose into it and sniffed.

Laurel looked into his eyes, smiling. "Do you realize this is the only rose in the Rose Garden right now?"

"Not the *only* one," he said, putting a knuckle under her chin.

She smiled, digging deep for strength to resist this impossible pull.

"Do you want to walk?" he asked.

Yes, she thought. Because it would be so much easier to have this conversation if she didn't have to look directly into his eyes.

They strolled down the walkway toward the reservoir, which had a level path around it. It was just the two of them and a man jogging several yards ahead, his yellow T-shirt damp against this body as he pulled farther and farther away. A soft breeze blew a brackish scent off the water, light and fleeting.

"Doug is in rehab now," she began. "Getting PT and respiratory therapy. He'll be home in a week."

"I'm glad he's recovering," Luke said, and she knew he had layers of understanding about Doug's condition that she wouldn't even be able to grasp. But he was so gentle and unassuming he didn't flaunt his knowledge.

"So am I," she said.

"And things between the two of you?"

The wind had died down and the water went still. Laurel glanced out across it, and her eye was caught by some nearby movement. She looked down and saw a turtle about the size of a saucer poke its head over the surface, then dive down and back up again.

"Look!" she said, and they paused to watch the creature

enjoy his swim, almost as if he were performing for them. Finally, he disappeared under the murky green surface and they continued their walk.

"Evan had a turtle when he was little," Laurel recalled.

"So did Imani and Raymond," Luke said, referring to his daughter and son—the one who still lived in New Jersey. "What happened to yours?"

"His name was Dash," she said with a laugh, recalling Evan's fascination with the slow-moving creature. "One day he got out of his aquarium—we don't know how—but we never found him. I hope to god he got out of the house. Otherwise, I expect to discover a rotted turtle corpse one day—probably when I'm getting ready to sell the place."

The runner had managed to loop around and came up behind them. "On your right," he called as he passed.

"Did your kids beg for the turtle?" Laurel asked.

"It was my idea," he said. "Typical divorced dad move— I bought the kids a pet so they'd be eager to spend time at my place."

"Did it work?"

"For a while. But a year later I found him dead in his tank. Then I kept him in the freezer until my next weekend with the kids, so we could bury him together." He crossed his hands over his heart. "It was a lovely service."

She laughed softly. "You're a good dad."

They walked quietly for a few minutes and he tried to take her hand.

"I'm sorry," she said, pulling it away. "I can't."

"Talk to me."

Laurel took a deep breath. This wasn't going to be easy. "Doug's close call changed things," she said. "And I really want to…" She stopped to swallow. It would be so easy to change course now, to turn around and walk this path in the other direction. Laurel looked up and watched the runner pounding forward, his yellow shirt a flag, beckoning her to the finish line. She looked up at Luke. "I'm sorry. I need to make this marriage work."

"Is that what you really want?" he asked.

"When I'm next to you I feel less sure," she admitted. "But yes. I still love him."

"A marriage needs more than love."

"I know."

They walked on in silence for a few moments.

"I'm not trying to talk you out of your decision," he said. "But have you asked yourself if you're happy?"

"The thing is," she said, "I think I *can* be, now that I understand I have some responsibility in what went wrong."

"What *did* go wrong?"

She thought about that for a long minute. "The marriage stopped being about *us*, and started being about *him*. It was... inequitable. But that didn't happen overnight. I've spent almost thirty years convincing Doug his feelings mattered and mine didn't. I was modeling my marriage on some nonexistent old-fashioned ideal. And when it didn't happen, I kept telling myself I just needed to try a little harder, make him a little happier. Along the way, I stopped mattering completely."

His gait slowed as he considered it. Then he paused and gazed into her eyes, taking her face in his strong, tender hands. It looked like he was going to kiss her, and Laurel's heart thudded against her ribs.

"You matter," he said.

She could barely respond, but managed to whisper, "I know."

"I have to let you go?" he asked.

Warm tears spilled from her eyes, but he held on, using his thumbs to wipe her face. It was such a tender gesture she considered how easy it would be to take it all back and leave Doug for this beautiful, compassionate man. With Luke, she'd never have to work at reminding him she deserved consideration. He would always be giving. Always loving. Always eager to make her happy.

Laurel closed her eyes, recalling those days at Doug's bedside, her heart breaking as she pleaded with God to save him. At those moments, she understood exactly how much she loved him.

She opened her eyes and looked up at Luke. "Yes," she said. "You have to let me go."

46

As a new employee, Laurel wasn't in a position to ask for time off. So on the afternoon of Doug's release from the Nassau Health & Wellness Palmer Family Center for Rehabilitation, she had worked all morning, with no time to freshen up or even plan something special for his homecoming. After clocking out, she took off her store apron and drove straight from work, her aging Altima tick-ticking in effort.

When she arrived, the glass doors slid open before her in efficient silence, and Laurel stepped inside the highly air-conditioned lobby. She scanned the space, as Doug had texted he would be waiting near the entrance. Glancing past an over-size floral arrangement, she saw him in a comfortable wing-back armchair, looking handsome and relaxed. He had lost weight since falling ill, and was dressed in the robin's egg–blue button-down shirt she had bought several days ago, specifically for his homecoming. It was a flattering color on him, and his complexion looked rosy, his hair freshly cut.

Across from him was a stick-thin woman going over some paperwork. She wore a lavender lab coat, and they were absorbed in conversation.

Laurel paused to study the tableau. There was something about Doug's demeanor that seemed so different. He didn't just look happier, but more confident, more comfortable in his own body. Perhaps it was his brush with death that gave him a new outlook, washing away any lingering depression, bathing him in his own newfound gratitude. Or maybe it was all Laurel. Maybe she was looking at him through more loving eyes than she had in a long time.

Doug seemed to sense her presence and looked up. "There she is!" he said, as if they'd been talking about her.

He rose slowly and carefully, grabbing the cane next to his chair. Only a few days ago he had needed a walker, and soon, the cane would be history, too.

The woman also stood, and as Laurel approached she felt self-conscious and grimy. Doug looked so freshly showered, emitting a clean, soapy scent. And the woman had a dancer's posture, with a long neck and sharp cheekbones accentuated by a taut face-lift. She was attractive, but wore too much makeup, and Laurel thought her straight and shiny bottle-black hair was unnecessarily severe, adding years to her face.

Doug put his arms out and wrapped Laurel in a welcoming hug. His body felt different, smaller. She would need to get used to it. She tucked her hair behind her ear as he introduced her to KathyAnn, his nutritionist.

"She wants me to keep losing weight," he said.

"I'd like you to keep making healthy choices," KathyAnn corrected.

Laurel smiled at her husband. "You look great, honey."

"He does," the nutritionist agreed. "But we don't want him to get off track."

"We have to get rid of all that crap in the house," Doug said. "The chips, the cookies—all those carbs."

"Exactly," KathyAnn said. "High protein, low carbs, controlled portions. He'll do great."

Laurel looked from one to the other, and got the impression that this was an intervention aimed at her, as if they'd been discussing Doug's biggest obstacle—a wife who was an enabler. The worst part was that she couldn't defend herself. She had, in fact, been loading his diet with the worst possible choices.

"Fine," Laurel said. "I'll stop bringing home the terrible stuff you beg for, but you have to stop sneaking off to Chipotle." She offered a playful grin, but KathyAnn responded with a condescending smile.

"Actually, Chipotle really isn't that bad...in moderation, of course."

Got it, Laurel wanted to say. *I'm the bad guy here.* She turned to Doug. "Ready to go?"

He looked at KathyAnn. "Are we finished?"

She tucked the pages they had been reviewing into a folder, and handed it to him. "It's all in here, but call if you have questions. We're very proud of you, Douglas."

He beamed. "I can't believe I'm actually going *home!*"

The woman crossed her arms with an approving smile. "I'm sure your wife has something very special planned."

In fact, she didn't, though she supposed she could make a fuss over the fact that she had invited Abby and Gavin over. That was something, at least. They said goodbye to Kathy-Ann and walked slowly to the car, as Doug took cautious, deliberate steps.

Driving home, Laurel convinced herself it was lucky she hadn't had time to plan anything. Otherwise, there would be a big sugary frosted sheet cake, with *Welcome Home Doug* written across the center in curly script. And he'd feel guilty having even a bite of it.

Still, she wished she'd planned ahead and put up a welcome home sign. That would have been such a thoughtful touch. She wanted to kick herself for not thinking of it until this minute.

"How do you feel?" she asked.

He rubbed his hands together. "Energetic!"

"Good," Laurel said. "Because I invited Abby and Gavin over. They're dying to see you."

"I hope they didn't bring a cake. You think they brought a cake?"

Almost definitely, Laurel thought. And felt a small sense of satisfaction that it would be Abby, and not her, who would be sabotaging Doug's diet.

"Probably," she said.

"I hope it's not that chocolate ganache." He was referring to his favorite—the one his sister often bought for special celebrations. Laurel glanced over and saw a familiar gleam in his eye. Despite himself, he was already imagining the first bite.

"I'm sure it would be okay if you had one little sliver," she said.

"KathyAnn says once you start making excuses it's hard to stop."

Laurel nodded, impressed by his commitment. She'd never seen him like this. "You're really serious about your new diet."

"And I want to keep exercising," he added. "My physical therapist said its important. Maybe I'll join a gym."

"How about if I join with you?" she said, smiling at him. A gym membership! It had been so long that it felt bold. Extravagant. And okay, she knew that a monthly gym membership wasn't exactly reckless, but after years of privations, it seemed almost criminal. Laurel was having a hard time adjusting to the idea of not being strapped, even though the insurance money had cleared, and their bank account was now bulging with so much cash they needed to make plans for where they could park it to earn at least a little interest while they planned for the future.

Just this morning, Laurel had to remind herself it was okay to loosen the purse strings a bit. She'd been struggling to blow-dry her hair with her broken-handled round brush, and felt a surge of joy when she realized she could afford to buy a new one without feeling guilty. She'd made a mental note to visit the beauty supply store, and maybe even replace the rusty nail clippers she'd been using.

Now, as she drove, Laurel let her imagination run even wilder, and considered scheduling a mani-pedi for herself. Perhaps she'd even treat her mom. The idea made her heart even lighter.

Doug seemed to sense her buoyant mood and reached over to pet her hand on the steering wheel. "I love you, Laurel," he said.

"I love you, too."

There was joy in the car, and it sent her imagination into overdrive. She knew just what she could do to make his homecoming special. She thought about that sexy black nightie buried in her drawer—the one she had been saving for Luke. Tonight, she would wear it for Doug. Her flesh tingled in anticipation.

Then she got another idea, and it was like a bolt from the beautiful blue sky. It was so thrilling she could barely believe she hadn't thought of it before. She ran it through in her mind, examining it from several angles, and couldn't find any reason why it wasn't exactly as wonderful as it felt.

"Hey," she said, "our anniversary is coming up." She glanced over at him and then back at the highway.

"Thirty years," he agreed. "A biggie."

"Why don't we do a vow renewal?" Saying it out loud made it so real she almost cried. It was perfect. A true chance to start fresh. To reconnect with her husband. To begin down a new and wondrous road. She imagined them writing romantic vows and reading them aloud. There would be tears of joy. She saw herself shopping for a sophisticated and slinky gown in white or silver. Maybe blush pink. They could put up a tent in their backyard and hire a caterer. And a professional photographer.

"Vow renewal?" he asked, as if the very words were absurd.

"Please, Doug," she said. "It'll be so romantic! We can have a beautiful ceremony…invite all our friends…maybe the kids will come in from California." Immediately, Laurel had a vision of her mother dressed up, sitting on a white-draped chair in the front row, holding baby Grace in her lap instead of a doll.

"Can I think about it?" Doug asked.

"Sure. But just so you know, I'm not going to let this go. I really want to do it." Laurel was puffed with pride. Here was something she desired with her whole heart, and she was going to insist on it.

Doug accepted her pronouncement without argument, and to Laurel, even that felt like a victory.

When they rounded the corner toward their house, she saw that Abby and Gavin had already arrived, their silver Lexus parked in front. Laurel gave a quick toot-toot of the horn to announce their arrival, and prepared to make a big fuss over their presence so that Doug would feel that she had done something special for him. He'd been so sick, and had been gone so very long. She wanted to make sure he knew how much he'd been missed.

Abby and Gavin emerged from the vehicle, and Laurel saw that her sister-in-law was holding a cake box.

Laurel wondered if Doug would appreciate it as a gesture of love. But when she glanced at his face, he wasn't looking at his sister. He was staring at the house, his expression as bright as a fireworks display.

She followed the line of his gaze, and once again, Laurel felt grateful for her meddlesome sister-in-law. Because there—draped across the garage door—hung a massive, custom-made banner, with three words spelled out in colorful capital letters.

WELCOME HOME DOUG

47

It was a happy homecoming, with a long and laugh-filled conversation about Doug's new dedication to health and fitness.

"Who are you and what have you done with my brother?" asked Abby, as she waved a forkful of cake in his face.

Laurel thought it bordered on cruel, but Doug took it in good humor. A short while later, her mother made a surprise visit, arriving by Uber with a small plastic doll and a tray full of brownies.

"The only one here not trying to kill me is Laurel!" Doug joked, and she nearly choked on her Diet Coke.

Joan spent a long while complaining that Charlie hadn't been answering her calls. This eased Laurel's heart, as she was glad to have him cut out of her life completely. She didn't know what she would have done if her mother and Charlie had suddenly become BFFs. Still, she worried about the effect the conversation might have on Doug, who was never happy to hear Charlie's name mentioned. But he was distracted and cheerful, and the whole thing seemed to roll off him like rain down a windshield.

Later that night, when the guests had gone, Laurel took a shower as Doug got ready for bed. She knew he might be too tired for sex, as it had been a long day and he was still getting his strength back, but she was determined to shimmy into that sheer black nightie and present herself to him.

As Laurel inspected herself in the medicine cabinet mirror, she was flooded with images of Luke. Until today, every time she thought of herself in this filmy garment, she had pictured Luke's eyes on her, feeling the powerful tug of his desire for her body. Even now, the thought heated her, and she wrestled with the notion of using her longing for Luke to excite her passion for her husband. *It's okay,* she told herself. *You're being faithful.* Laurel decided that her desperate attraction for Luke only further proved her devotion to her marriage. Why else would she have sent him away? It was the surest sign of her commitment.

When she emerged from the bathroom, she left thoughts of Luke behind, though her body was already reacting to the stimulus with an insistent pulsing between her legs. *Doug,* she reminded herself. *This is about Doug.*

She stood in the doorway, waiting to be noticed, but he was in bed reading a paperback, a pair of reading glasses perched low on his nose.

"Babe?" she breathed, and he looked up.

After a single second of hesitation, he tossed the book against the wall with comic alacrity.

"Hellooo!" he called, with lascivious exaggeration, and Laurel laughed. Yes, yes, and yes. This was the man she loved.

"You like this?" Laurel asked, giving a twirl.

"It's the sexiest thing I've ever seen," he said. "How fast can you take it off?"

But she didn't take it off. At least not right away. She approached the bed and straddled him, putting her face into his warm neck.

She could feel him getting hard, and moved against his erection as his breath sped up. Now, she was fully there, and it was all about Doug. She traveled down his body, kissing his chest, his stomach, that teasing trail of dark hair that had always turned her on. Then she held him in her mouth and he moaned in pleasure, getting even harder.

"Should I take this off now?" she asked, coming up for air.

"Did you think I'd say no?"

She pulled it off over her head, and the way he looked at her made Laurel so excited she was ready, too. But she didn't object when he flipped her over onto her back, making sure she was desperate with need before he entered her.

And then, she let herself go, arching and gasping and pleading and releasing for the man she had vowed to love for the rest of her life.

When they were done, and she lay in his arms relaxed and sated, she ran a finger up his chest and said, "I want to talk about the vow renewal."

Doug never explicitly approved the idea of renewing their vows, but he didn't reject it, either. So the plans and decisions became a part of their daily lives. As Laurel taught Doug how to manage his own medications, patiently explaining that no, she would not be scheduling his physical therapy appointments—he would have to do that himself—she would seek his input. Did he want to invite his cousin Richard from Connecticut? How about Lawrence, who had been his stock boy in the store for so many years? Did he have an opinion on the photographer's portfolio? On the caterer?

"I'd like to invite Emira," he said one day, referring to the pretty young physical therapist who had been coming to the house three times a week. "And maybe KathyAnn."

"Of course!" Laurel said. "That would be great." In truth, she liked Emira, but found KathyAnn officious and judgmental. One day she had come home from work to find KathyAnn in her kitchen, pulling items from the pantry and dumping them in the trash as Doug sat by and watched, nodding at her lessons on proper nutrition. Laurel had gritted her teeth and said nothing, but later took the items from the trash and put them back. Who did that woman think she was?

She was relieved when Doug stopped carrying on about the nutritionist and turned his focus to Emira, who was younger and prettier, but also less intrusive. It seemed he would always be smitten with any woman in the role of caretaker. Laurel was okay with that, certain her husband had no romantic attraction for these women. He just liked being tended to.

In any case, if inviting Emira and KathyAnn made him more enthusiastic about the vow renewal, Laurel was on board.

When it came time to shop for a dress, she told Doug she would keep him out of the decision, as she wanted to find something spectacular and surprise him. "Like a bride," she explained.

"I can't wait," he said, eyeing her with appreciation, and to Laurel, it was all she needed to hear.

"Just keep it under a thousand dollars," he had added, and she felt deflated, even though she agreed on the expense. Despite their financial cushion, Laurel was conscious of sticking to a budget for this party and for life in general, in order to make the nest egg last. Besides, she felt certain she could find something pretty spectacular for a thousand bucks.

Still, she had hoped Doug would be more focused on her happiness than their bottom line. But this new beginning would have its bumps and ruts, as they were both learning how to traverse it.

On hearing about Laurel's quest for a knockout dress, Monica insisted on taking her to Zarina's of Great Neck, her favorite boutique for formal wear.

"I was thinking of Stella's," Laurel said, referring to the discount dress store where she had purchased her gown for Evan's wedding. The idea of Great Neck made her nervous—it was one of Long Island's most affluent communities, and she was sure the selections would be out of her price range.

"Oh, honey, no," Monica said.

"Maybe Kleinfeld's?" Laurel suggested, imagining a nearly endless sale rack.

"No way," Monica said. "I won't let you subject yourself to a store full of gaggling young brides with their ten-thousand-dollar budgets and cute little squads of influencers and cell phones. We'll shop like grown-ups. Responsible. Sophisticated. Zarina is going to take good care of you."

It was the word *responsible* that convinced her, so she agreed. But when they walked into the fancy shop and a striking silver-haired woman emerged from the back, so lanky and exotically beautiful she looked like she had just stepped out of a *Vogue* spread about aging gracefully, Laurel panicked. Would there be anything here she could afford?

"Darling!" Zarina said to Monica, kissing her on both cheeks. "Did you bring me a mother of the bride? She's lovely!"

"More like a bride herself," Monica said.

"It's my thirtieth anniversary," Laurel clarified.

Monica fingered the hem of a short gold cocktail dress that looked like it came from Tina Turner's closet. "They're renewing their vows, and she needs to look spectacular."

"But not in a minidress," Laurel said, giving Monica's hand a playful slap.

"Of course not, darling," Zarina said. "Let's talk."

She took them to a seating area with a velvet sofa facing two plush chairs. After pouring them each a glass of champagne, she sat down to ask Laurel what kind of dress she was looking for.

"I hope I'm not wasting your time," Laurel blurted. "I'm on a tight budget."

"I'll let you in on a secret, darling," Zarina said. "That's my specialty. My ladies come in here with a thousand dollars to spend, and leave looking like a million. Now, let's talk about color."

Monica gave Laurel a huge grin, raising her eyebrows as if to say, *Didn't I tell you?* And sure enough, Zarina was the dress whisperer. She brought Laurel six different gowns, each so spectacular they could have turned heads on the red carpet.

"Which one do you want to try on first?" Zarina asked.

Laurel pointed to a pale silvery blue sequined gown with a boat neck and cap sleeves. At $1200 it was the most expensive, but there was something about it that seemed magical. Besides, she knew that Doug wouldn't make a fuss over breaking the budget when it was something that meant so much to her.

"That's my favorite, too," Zarina said, as she pulled it off the hanger and helped Laurel slide into it.

The fabric poured over Laurel's body like liquid satin, hugging her curves all the way to her hips, then draping to the floor. It looked like a dream. Laurel admired her front and back, then stepped out of the dressing room to show it to Monica, who gasped.

"That's it!" Monica said. "That's the one."

"It's a little over budget," Laurel said, wondering if Monica would try to talk her out of buying it.

"I'm not letting you walk out of here without that dress," Monica said.

Laurel was pretty sure she wouldn't, but it was hard to say yes without trying on at least a few more, to see if there was something under budget she liked nearly as much.

Zarina helped her decide which dresses to try next, and they were all lovely. One of them even had a high slit up the thigh to show off her legs. But none matched the magic of the first one. So Laurel got back into the dress she decided was the most beautiful gown ever made, and the elderly seamstress was trotted out to pin up the hem—the only alteration the dress needed.

As the two friends left for lunch, Laurel's joy nearly brought her to tears.

"I owe you one," she said to her friend.

Monica laughed. "Hell yeah, you do!"

They walked to the corner diner, and were led to a booth in the back of the narrow restaurant. As they passed two octogenarian gentlemen having lunch, one of them smiled up at Laurel, and she smiled back.

"Are you single, beautiful lady?" he asked.

"I'm the least single person I know," she responded.

"I think you blew it back there," Monica whispered, as they settled into the booth. "You could've gotten lucky."

"I've been getting lucky regularly since Doug's been home."

"No wonder you're all aglow."

A busboy deposited two sweating glasses of ice water on their table and hurried off.

Monica leaned forward. "I'm glad you're in a good mood," she said, "because I have to tell you something."

Uh-oh, Laurel thought, as she had a pretty good idea of where this was heading. For a while, it had seemed as if Monica had abandoned the idea of moving to Texas. But lately, she had been poring over a brochure from a retirement community just outside of Austin.

"I'm listening," she said.

Monica licked her lips. "You know that condo I was showing you?"

Laurel nodded. It was a stunning duplex, flooded with light. The kitchen had white cabinets and a crystal chandelier.

"I'm about to go to contract." Monica sipped her ice water and studied her friend's face.

Laurel knew she shouldn't have been surprised, but this was hard to hear. She took a moment to process the news as she swallowed against a Texas-sized knot in her throat. "When?" she managed to choke out.

"The papers are sitting on my kitchen table, waiting for my signature."

"I mean, when are you moving?" Laurel grabbed a paper napkin to blot the tears now spilling down her cheeks.

Monica began to cry in sympathy. She pulled a tissue from her purse and handed it to Laurel, then took one for herself. "Probably September," she said.

"I'm going to miss the hell out of you," Laurel said, blowing her nose.

"You'll visit," Monica said. "I'll have a beautiful spare bedroom with a view of the golf course."

"Of course I will."

"But call first."

Laurel laughed. "Frida's going to love it," she said, trying to be supportive. "So many new doggy butts to smell."

"Well, actually, I wanted to talk to you about that, too." She took a jagged breath, then wept softly into her tissue.

"What's wrong?" Laurel asked.

"No dogs," Monica said, sniffing. "I can't take her with me."

"Oh, honey," Laurel said, and reached out to grab her friend's hand.

"I struggled with it for a long time. At first I thought, no way. I'm not leaving her. And I looked at private houses and apartments that took dogs and couldn't find anything I liked. Then Dani said, 'Mom, Frida is *thirteen years old*,' and I realized she's right. I'm basing a life decision on a dog who might not even be with me a year from now. Still, I feel like such a shit."

"I'm sure you made the right decision."

"Thing is, I haven't signed yet. I wanted to talk to you first, to ask if—"

"Yes!" Laurel blurted, anticipating the question. "Yes! Of course I'll take her! She's my buddy." Even as she said it, though, she realized her offer to take the dog meant she would lose her best friend. It was the right thing to do, but it was as painful as it was joyous.

Laurel sat back and tried to be philosophical. She had wanted a dog like Frida for so long, and now it was actually happening. A dream come true. She had also wanted to be there for the birth of her grandchild, and that dream had unfolded in a reality that exceeded her imagination. In a way, she was getting nearly everything she wanted. But of course, she'd had to let go of Luke, and now she would be losing Monica. It seemed that with each dream realized, she lost something precious.

"I can't thank you enough," Monica said, reaching out to grab Laurel's hand. And then, just like that, she let it go.

48

When Laurel got home, there was a shiny black sedan in front of the house, and she assumed it belonged to one of Emira's colleagues, as the agency occasionally sent a substitute physical therapist. But when she walked in the door, Laurel heard voices in the kitchen, not the den, where Doug usually had his sessions.

"I'm home!" she announced.

She heard Doug say, "She's here," before calling out his return greeting. Laurel dropped her purse and keys by the door, and walked into the kitchen to see him at the table, sitting across from KathyAnn, the nutritionist.

"Oh, hello," Laurel said to the woman, her voice tight. "I didn't know you were making another house call today."

Laurel had assumed she'd seen the last of KathyAnn, even though she knew Doug spoke to her over Zoom every so often. Home visits, she believed, began and ended with that single plunder of the kitchen cabinets.

"I got some new low-sugar protein shake samples," Kathy-Ann explained. "So I thought I'd drop them by." She nodded toward the six-pack on the counter, as if Laurel required proof.

"That was nice of you," Laurel said, straining to be polite. In reality, she wanted this intrusive woman gone.

Then she noticed that the kitchen trash can—which had been taken out from beneath the sink and placed under the pantry—was filled with the products Laurel had put back on the shelves after KathyAnn's last visit. "What the hell?" she asked, pointing at it.

Doug followed her eyes and reddened, as if caught with his hand in the gluten-free cookie jar. "KathyAnn doesn't think it's a good idea for me to have that kind of temptation around."

Laurel folded her arms. It wasn't like she still had a pantry full of garbage-like chips and Mallomars and Frosted Flakes, as she had before she changed her mind about sabotaging Doug's health. Now, she merely kept some innocuous carbs around, as she was entitled to have a cracker now and then, or to make pasta for dinner. But she could see that all of it had been emptied. Even the bread crumbs were in the trash can.

"I don't care what KathyAnn thinks. This isn't her house. She has no right to come here and throw away my food."

"I asked for her help," Doug said. "You have no idea how hard this is for me."

"Then talk to *me*!" Laurel said. "Don't bring this stranger into my house to go through our things. It's offensive!"

"Laurel," KathyAnn said, eyeing her, "sometimes we *all* need a little tough love when we're trying to break bad habits."

Now the woman was calling her overweight? Laurel might not have been as close to zero-percent body fat as the boyishly shaped nutritionist, but she had been eating like a bird for months, and was proud of how slender she'd become.

"News flash," Laurel said, pointing to her own torso. "I

don't have bad habits. And even if I did, you'd have no right to come into my house and put your hands through my things."

"Well, this isn't just about you," KathyAnn said so gently Laurel wanted to smack her. "It's about Douglas."

Laurel gritted her teeth. "I've been cooking low-calorie dinners since the day he came back from rehab."

"But I'm home all day," Doug complained. "It's hard not to snack."

Laurel glanced at KathyAnn, wondering if she would gently suggest it was almost time for him to go back to work. Instead, the woman addressed her directly.

"If you would leave some cut-up carrots and celery in the fridge—"

"Me?" Laurel shrieked.

"I didn't mean—"

"I spend all day breaking my back at a job suited to twenty-year-olds while he reads the paper and watches *Judge Judy*, and you're telling *me* to cut up carrots? How about you ask him to—"

"Laurel, calm down," Doug said.

But she couldn't. This woman—with her condescension and her glossy hair and her skinny neck and her shiny black car—could go to hell.

"Do you have any idea how hard I work?" she asked Kathy-Ann. Then she turned to Doug. "Do *you*?"

"I don't think you need to take this personally," Kathy-Ann said.

But it *was* personal. It was very personal. Doug had invited this woman over so they could sit around and complain about his terrible, unsupportive wife. She could feel it. The air was thick with judgment. She looked from Doug to KathyAnn, then took all her fury and compressed it, until it was like the energy of the sun squeezed to the size of a marble.

"I think you should go now," she said to KathyAnn, so slowly and quietly it cast a darkness over the room.

Doug looked shaken by her tone of voice. "Babe," he pleaded.

But Laurel wasn't going to tame her anger. Not this time. There would be no seeking of initials to steady her nerves. She held tight to that marble, harnessing the energy of her fury.

"I'll be in the bedroom," she said, in the same icy tone. "Let me know when she's gone."

With that, Laurel went upstairs and slammed the door.

In the bedroom, Laurel paced, her eyes on the red numerals of her nightstand clock. She was timing how long they stayed in the kitchen, speaking in hushed tones. One minute. Two minutes. Three minutes. Laurel could imagine their conversation. KathyAnn wouldn't be giving Doug advice on nutrition, but on how to *handle* his difficult wife. Four minutes. Five minutes. Laurel listened to the sound of her own breath going in and out as she stared at the illuminated red numbers. At last, after nearly twelve minutes, she heard the front door open and close, followed by Doug's footsteps coming up the stairs.

He gave two soft knocks on the door before opening it. Laurel faced him, prepared for anything—whining, excuses, accusations.

He stood in the doorway looking forlorn. Laurel was surprised. Apparently, her fury had broken through. He looked like he wanted to speak, and was struggling to find the words. She waited.

At last, he sighed and looked down at the carpet. "I'm sorry," he said. "Very, very sorry."

Sorry? Laurel was so surprised it took her a moment to process the message. She couldn't remember ever hearing those words from him. Coming out of his mouth, they were powerful indeed. The tension in her body began to release.

"I'm sorry, too," she said. "That woman pushed all my buttons."

"I understand." He stepped into the room. "I mean, at first I thought you were being unreasonable. Then I remembered how angry I'd been about Charlie."

Laurel nearly laughed. He thought this was about jealousy? But she stayed quiet and he continued.

"So I sent her away," he said, his eyes watering. "I told her I thought it would be best if I found another nutritionist."

His earnestness touched the tenderest part of her raw heart. "Come here," she said, her arms out.

He approached and hugged her. "I love you," he said into her hair.

"I love you, too."

She held tight, feeling grateful and relieved. She had lost her temper, spoken her mind, and it was all okay. The fight was over. The love remained.

She took a step back and looked at him, appreciating all he'd been through with this terrible virus she'd inflicted on him. And now here he was, prostrating himself, even as she changed the rules of their relationship.

"We're going to be fine, you know," she said, touching his face as a tear rolled down her own.

"Of course," he said, and sat down on the bed. He patted the spot next to him.

Laurel wiped the moisture from her cheeks as she sat. Now that the marble of fury had dissolved into the stream of their marriage, all she wanted to do was float.

Doug took her hand. "I didn't even get to ask about your day."

"My day," she said with a shy smile, "was sublime."

He looked delighted by this news. "You found a dress?"

"Very possibly the most beautiful dress in the world."

"And it was under a thousand?" he asked, his eyes filled with love and admiration for his remarkable bride—the one who could accomplish almost anything, and bring it in under budget.

"Actually," she began, but stopped. It felt almost cruel to disabuse him of this vision of wifely perfection. And as her brain wrestled with whether she should tell the truth, her mouth blurted, "Yes. It was!"

She regretted it almost immediately, and tried to think of a way to take it back. Before she could say anything, though, he pulled her into his arms and held her so tightly for so long she thought he might be getting sexually aroused. But he released her, and looked deeply and tenderly into her eyes.

"Babe?" he said.

"Yes?"

"What's for dinner?"

49

The lie troubled Laurel so much she had difficulty sleeping that night. After all, she had promised herself she was done with subterfuge. Going forward, she wanted her marriage to be open and loving. No more secrets. Doug deserved that. She resolved to tell him the truth the very next day, and fell back asleep.

But when she woke up, there was little time to do anything but get ready for her early shift at Whole Foods. So she showered and dressed and slipped out the door while Doug slept.

She didn't tell him that night, either, as she was tired and cranky, and Doug was so solicitous—still trying to make up for angering her with KathyAnn's visit—that she couldn't find the words. But the next day, for sure. It was Sunday, and they would have breakfast together. It was perfect. She'd apologize and he'd laugh, and all would be well.

As usual, she awoke before him and went into the kitchen

to make coffee. She yawned and went through the motions of counting out scoops, then pouring water into the coffee maker and flicking it on. Minutes later she heard Doug get up and use the bathroom, then shuffle outside in his slippers to get the newspapers.

"What's for breakfast?" he said, arriving at the kitchen door. He rubbed his flattening belly.

"I was thinking of egg white omelets."

"Can I help?"

Laurel glanced over at him, surprised. But she realized this was all a continuation of his solicitude following the Kathy-Ann episode. He was giving everything he had to making amends. She almost wanted to tell him it was history, and he didn't need to feel guilty. But she just said, "Sure, thanks."

So they worked together in the kitchen, beating eggs, making turkey bacon, toasting two thin slices of nine grain bread. This, she thought, is what they call domestic bliss. Plus, it was a beautiful morning—the birds were full-throated in song and the dogwood was in bloom, its delicate pink flowers shading the patio. She suggested they eat outside, and they brought their plates to the small round table on the deck just beyond the kitchen door.

Laurel wanted to ease into the conversation, so she started by chatting about the plans for the party, pointing out where she wanted to put the tent, and also the perfect placement for the ceremonial canopy where they would say their vows.

"There?" he asked, trying to follow the line of her pointed finger.

"No, there."

"Oh, I see!" he said. "It's right where that butterfly is hovering. It must be a sign!"

Her eyes scanned the area until she finally saw the butterfly, but it wasn't in the spot where she wanted to put the canopy—

it was in the unshaded part of the yard, where it could be blazing hot for the seated guests if it were a sunny day. She didn't want to diminish Doug's enthusiasm, so she just said, "How do you like that?" and went on discussing her plans.

Doug was agreeable to every suggestion—almost as if he were afraid to get her riled by challenging her. She brought up the DJ then, hoping to get some input from him, as she knew how opinionated he was about music.

"We should probably give him a playlist," Laurel suggested.

"Good idea."

"He's a pretty young guy," she explained. "And his idea of classic rock might not be the same as ours."

"You want me to make the list?" he asked.

"That would be great."

Laurel exhaled. This was harder than she thought, as Doug was being so…amiable. And for once, she wished he was pushing back. But she knew it was time to confess, so she put down her fork and dabbed at her mouth with the napkin.

"Listen," she said, "there's something I need to tell you."

He took a bite of his toast, and finished chewing. "What's up?"

"The dress," she said. "I don't know why I told you it was under budget. It was actually twelve hundred dollars, plus tax and alterations."

"What?"

"But you should have seen it, Doug. It was like… I don't know…a magic dress. Monica gasped when she saw it."

"You lied to me?"

"I didn't mean to. But you seemed so…impressed. And I didn't want to disappoint you. In that moment I—"

"You lied," he spat, his brow tight. "And now you're trying to tell me it's my fault?"

"That's not what I'm saying."

"This is fucked-up, Laurel."

"When you see the dress you'll understand. It's spectacular. Like something you'd see on the red carpet."

"This isn't about the dress," he said. "It's about the lie."

"I know. I know. I'm so sorry, Doug. I shouldn't have done that."

He stood, so angry it was clear he hadn't even heard her apology. "How could you do this? Don't you realize how hard I've been trying to make you happy?"

"Yes, of course. And I appreciate that."

"You were so rude to KathyAnn!"

Laurel stared, confused by the non sequitur. "What does that have to do with anything?" she asked.

"But I forgave you. And I apologized to her, made excuses for you."

"Look, babe," she said. "I'm very, very sorry. I know I shouldn't have done that."

He threw down his napkin. "I'm going for a walk," he said, and tramped down the steps of the deck and off into the suburban morning.

"I'm sorry," she said again, when he returned. "Really and truly."

He shrugged. "Whatever."

"Come on, Doug, please," she said. "I want to get past this."

"Okay, okay," he said, as if she were annoying him with her apologies. "I forgive you."

After that, there was nothing for her to say, despite how obvious it was that he didn't forgive her. He had absorbed his indignation too deeply to purge it that easily.

But Laurel remembered that hug in the bedroom, and knew they would be okay. Eventually, he would release his resentment, just as she had done for so many years.

The next day he was still cold toward her, and the day after that, as well. But then, slowly, he came around, and Laurel was relieved. Still, she couldn't shake the feeling that there had been a shift in their relationship. Most days they were fine, but on others, she felt like they weren't quite connecting. Again and again, Laurel told herself this was normal—the kind of thing that almost had to happen when a relationship tried to break thirty years of ingrained habits. To be safe, though, she mentioned it to Monica, the most cynical person in her life. If it didn't send up any red flags to her testy bestie, she knew she was okay.

"It's hard to describe," Laurel said, as they power marched down the boardwalk at Jones Beach. "We just can't seem to get in sync these days."

It was a sticky June day, and Laurel was grateful for a soft breeze blowing off the ocean.

"It's your schedule," Monica said, pumping her arms. "You're working crazy hours now."

It was true. Laurel's Whole Foods schedule kept her at the store through most dinner hours, which was when she and Doug had normally connected. Her mornings were usually free, but that was when he met with his personal trainer, or took his long walks.

"I'm sure you're right," Laurel said. "I think we're both having growing pains."

"I wouldn't worry about Doug," Monica assured her. "That boy is crazy about you."

Laurel decided she was absolutely right. Doug was happier and healthier than he'd been in a long time, and becoming more independent. He had started shopping for his own clothes, buying updated styles suited to his new physique. He even purchased new cologne without asking for her input. And wasn't that what she had always wanted? Laurel just needed to get used to the fact that he didn't need her as much as he had for so many years.

"I know he's been working hard on writing his vows for the ceremony," Laurel said, as they closed in on a group of elderly women walking slowly. She veered left to prepare for passing them.

"See?" Monica said. "Nothing to worry about. You guys will be fine."

What Laurel didn't tell Monica was that Doug had started having Zoom meetings again with KathyAnn, insisting she was the only nutritionist who really understood his cravings. Talking about it, Laurel believed, would only give oxygen to her own silly stirrings of jealousy. And she wanted that to dissipate into the atmosphere, like it didn't exist at all.

She breathed in the briny breeze off the ocean—a scent she adored—so she could store it up and find it later, settled deep in her sinuses.

"How's the sex lately?" Monica asked, loudly enough for two of the elderly women in front of them to turn around.

Laurel led her friend around the slow walkers and waited until they were out of earshot before responding.

"That's partly what I mean about being out of sync," she explained. "He's been going for walks most mornings, and that's when I'm home. In the evenings, I'm too sore and tired to even think about it."

"You'll work it out," Monica said. "As long as he's writing those vows, he's thinking about romance."

Just after they reached the end of the boardwalk and turned around to begin the two-mile trek back, Laurel's cell phone vibrated in her pocket. It was Doug.

"I'm at your mom's!" he shouted over a noise so loud it sounded as if he were calling from the engine of a 747.

"What's wrong?" she said. "What's that noise?"

"What?"

"That noise!"

"Hang on," he said, and called out to someone. Then the engine went silent.

"Is everything okay?" she asked.

"That downstairs toilet flooded," he said. "And she didn't know how to shut off the water. So I came over. Eleanor came, too. She brought a shop vac."

"Wait," Laurel said. "The den flooded? Where her doll collection is?"

"We're cleaning it up now."

"Oh, shit," Laurel muttered. "I'll be there as soon as I can."

By the time Laurel got there—which entailed power walking the two miles back to the parking lot under the beating sun, finding her car, dropping off Monica, and then getting back on the highway toward her mother's house—she was twisted in knots, imagining the worst. Poor Mom! That doll collection was everything to her.

She pulled up in front of her mother's house just in time to see the plumber's truck back out of the driveway and leave. She hoped that wasn't a bad sign.

"Hello!" she called, when she walked in.

"Down here!" Doug yelled.

Laurel walked down the steps, worried about what she would see. But when she entered the room, everything looked...fine. That is, except for the three living occupants—Joan, Doug, and Eleanor—who appeared disheveled and exhausted. Bob was nowhere in sight.

"There was a flood in here?" Laurel asked, confused. But as soon as she stepped onto the carpeting, she understood, as it squished with water under her feet.

"We did the best we could with the shop vac," Eleanor said. "But we'll need to remove the carpeting as soon as possible."

"Thank God all the dolls are up on shelves," Joan said.

Thank God, indeed, Laurel thought. It was close to a miracle that the collection was intact.

"What did the plumber say?" she asked.

Doug told her that the toilet was fixed and it was all a matter of cleanup now. Eleanor explained that her handyman was on his way over with a crew, and that the plan was to take all the shelving units outside, and then pull up the carpeting and bring it to the curb.

"That's so much work!" Laurel said. "Does it need to be done right now?"

Doug nodded. "We don't want the place to get moldy."

She studied her husband, sweaty and rumpled, looking like he was about to drop. But he had such a good heart that he didn't want to leave her mother in the lurch. At that moment, Laurel was so filled with love for him her eyes burned. He was so kind, so decent. What more could any woman want from a partner?

"You look exhausted," she said.

Doug used his own shirt to blot his forehead. "I've had three of your mother's Ensures, but I'm starting to crash."

"I've been trying to tell him he can go and leave the rest to the crew," Eleanor said, "but he won't listen."

"I wanted to wait for you to get here," Doug said to Laurel.

She told him to go on home and get some rest, promising she would meet him back there soon.

"You look pretty tired, too," he said.

"I'm fine." In truth, she was ready for a shower and a nap herself, but she wanted to help her mother through a few things, starting with a massive pile of wet towels she spied in the bathroom. They would need to go into the washer and dryer.

After Doug left, and Laurel had managed to get all the sopping towels into the laundry room to start the first wash, she ordered Eleanor and her mother into the kitchen so she could make them something to eat.

She poured them each a tall glass of water from the Brita pitcher, and set about inspecting the contents of the fridge and pantry, looking for something she could rustle up quickly. She settled on scrambled eggs and toast.

"This was so generous of you," she said to Eleanor, as she put a plate in front of her. "You must be exhausted."

"I don't mind," she said. "I have a solid constitution."

"Eleanor was on her way out to kickboxing lessons when I called," Joan explained. "But she came right over. She's such a dear."

"Kickboxing lessons?" Laurel repeated, surprised.

"She's very strong," Joan said, her eyes wide in awe.

"Mario is making me stronger," Eleanor said.

"He's an ex-boxer," Joan added. "In the seventies, he was famous. A local champ."

"I take private lessons," Eleanor explained. "He's taught me how important it is to build muscle mass as we age."

Joan tittered behind her hand. "We think he might be interested."

Laurel's first instinct was to ask, *Interested in what?* But the giggle was a giveaway.

"Do you like him, too?" she asked Eleanor, and wondered how that would work vis-à-vis Bob. If she went out on a date, would she leave the bird home in a cage? Despite herself, Laurel felt almost sorry for the talkative creature. She put the pan into the sink and ran water on it.

"He's a little rough around the edges," Eleanor said, "but he's very thoughtful."

Laurel went to work on cleaning the pan. "I hope that works out for you," she said over her shoulder. When she finished, she poured herself a glass of water and guzzled it down.

Joan nibbled at her eggs. "I understand Doug is working out these days," she said.

Laurel sat at the table, realizing how tired she was. "But I'm not worried about him running off with his personal trainer. I don't think Frank is his type."

"Are you worried about KathyAnn?" Joan asked.

"What?" Laurel said, wondering what Doug might have said to prompt this question.

"His nutritionist," Joan clarified.

"He talked about her all day," Eleanor added.

"I… I'm not worried about it," Laurel said, but a thread of doubt snaked its way into her gut. Was she being naive?

"I'm sure it's just a harmless crush," her mother said. "You two have such a strong marriage."

Harmless crush. Driving home, Laurel was so troubled by the words she had to resist the urge to form them into initials. Was it true? Was Doug carrying a torch for KathyAnn? She thought about the new cologne he had bought and wondered if it was a sign.

Probably not, she told herself. She was letting her imagination run away with her. But Laurel knew she would never be able to let this go without talking to Doug about it. She needed to hear him say it was nothing, and that her mother had misinterpreted his enthusiasm.

He was already asleep when she got home, so there wasn't much for Laurel to do but take a shower and get into bed. She expected to pass out instantly, as it had been such a very long and tiring day, but she tossed and turned, more concerned about her mother's observation than she wanted to admit. Finally, she padded into the kitchen and made herself a cup of herbal tea, splashing in a little milk to help her sleep. She sat in the shadowy room, illuminated only by a single dim light under the counter, and sipped, hoping for drowsiness to overtake her.

She was about halfway finished when she heard Doug get up and go to the bathroom. After another minute or so, the stairs creaked under his footsteps, and he appeared at the kitchen door in his pajama bottoms and undershirt.

"You okay?" he asked.

"Couldn't sleep."

"Worried about your mom?"

Laurel shook her head. "Something else."

Doug pulled a glass from the cabinet and pushed it into the water dispenser on the refrigerator door. He took a long gulp, then scraped out the chair opposite her and sat. "Want to talk about it?"

Laurel nodded in the silence of the deep night, considering how to ask her question. Doug waited, sipping his water, and she listened to the hum of the refrigerator, the delicate buzz of the small fluorescent light.

She looked into his shadowy face and down at her tea. "My mother thinks you have a crush on KathyAnn."

Laurel hoped he would laugh and say something like, *That's ridiculous.* But he went quiet for a long moment and then simply said, "Ah."

She tried to study his expression in the darkness, but couldn't make out much beyond the light reflecting off his irises.

"Is it true?" she pressed, studying a ray of moonlight hitting the table.

"Well," he said, releasing a long breath. "Kind of."

Laurel felt the back of her neck go cold, but tried to tell herself they'd been through this kind of thing before and it was nothing. Early in their marriage, when they lived in an apartment in Queens, they'd been friends with their neighbors, the Radfords. Cindy Radford was flirty, petite, and overtly sexual, with a Goth edge that made her exotic. She acted as if everything was an innuendo, and Laurel could tell it turned Doug on. When Laurel said she felt tame and boring by comparison, Doug insisted Cindy wasn't his type, swearing he had no kind of crush on her. And she appreciated that he was sparing her feelings. Now, though, he was owning up to his infatuation.

"Should I be worried?" Laurel asked.

He reached across the table and took her hand. "No, of course not."

"But you said you have a crush on her."

"I said *kind of.*"

"What's the difference?"

"The difference is that I would never cheat on you. It doesn't matter how I feel about her. You're the one I love, Laurel."

"What do you like about her?" she pressed, unable to resist dangerously picking at the wound.

He shrugged. "She's very smart and caring. And she really understands me."

Laurel put her head down on the table and started to weep, gently at first, and then harder. She felt broken, bereft, robbed of the one constant in her life—Doug's devotion.

"Hey, hey," he said, rising. He came around from behind and hugged her. "I told you, it's nothing. We're just friends."

"It doesn't feel like nothing."

"We're renewing our vows, aren't we? Laurel, you're my one and only."

50

Laurel got through the next two weeks by reminding herself that she, too, had weathered a crush and come out the other side. This, she thought, had a certain symmetry. A poetic justice. An evening of the score. Now, when they took their vows, it would be truly meaningful. They would both be scrubbed clean and absolved. Their marriage would truly be renewed.

But of course, Laurel's sins were far darker than her crush on Luke. When she thought about it now—about what she had nearly done to Doug—she thought of that phrase *slippery slope*, where a single step could send you sliding into the abyss.

She only partially blamed Charlie. Sure, he had manipulated her. But she had gone willingly, even enthusiastically, into the darkness. By the time she came to her senses and saw the light, it was very nearly too late to change course.

Now, she thanked God that Doug had pulled through, and that they could start fresh.

The day of the vow renewal, Laurel wore a silver satin cocktail dress to greet her guests, the exquisite gown hanging from the door frame in her bedroom so she could change into it for the ceremony. Doug dressed in a vivid blue suit—more fitted than the boxy cut he normally wore—with a silver tie and a white boutonniere. She thought he looked dashing... and ten years younger.

"Please, please, help yourself to hors d'oeuvres," she said to all the guests, directing them to the catering stations, where there were mimosas and Bloody Marys and canapé-sized brunch foods. Everyone remarked on the perfect weather with some version of the same joke about who they had contacted to order such a beautiful day.

Laurel kept glancing at the gate to the backyard, eager to see her most important guests emerge. Evan, Samara, and the baby had come in from California the day before, and were staying in New Jersey with her parents. Laurel wasn't sure whether she was more excited about the party or about seeing her granddaughter again.

She greeted some of her new co-workers from Whole Foods, old employees of Doug's store, neighbors, friends, and a dozen or so nieces, nephews, and cousins of hers and Doug's, as well as her brother and his wife, and Abby and Gavin. Most of the folks were milling about, but her mother had already snagged a seat for the ceremony, sitting in the aisle of the front row. Eleanor and her date, Mario the kickboxing instructor, kept her company. The man was stocky, with a thick neck and broad shoulders, his head shaved clean. Eleanor, who appeared to be taller than him, was beaming.

Laurel approached the officiate—a bohemian woman cantor who was a friend of Abby's—to be sure she had whatever she needed.

"What time do you want to get started?" the cantor said.

"Let me ask Doug," Laurel replied, looking around. In truth, she was stalling, as she wanted to make sure her son's family arrived before they began. Then the gate opened and there they were—her beloved threesome followed by Samara's parents. Natalie, still recovering from her injury, walked with a cane.

"Excuse me," Laurel said to the cantor, and ran to greet them.

She kissed all the adults, then looked down at the baby, beaming.

"She got so big!" Laurel said, trying not to cry. Her makeup had been professionally applied, and she didn't want to mess it up.

"Do you want to hold her?" Samara asked.

"Always!"

Her daughter-in-law laid a cotton burp cloth over Laurel's shoulder to protect her dress from a leaky baby, and laid Grace in her arms.

"Hello my sweet, my Grace," she said into the tiny and increasingly beautiful face. The baby's skin looked like poured cream, her dark eyes wide and curious. When she grinned at Laurel, the tears were impossible to hold back.

Laurel sniffed, and looked up at Evan and Samara. "I want to introduce her to her great-grandma."

"Of course," Samara said.

"Hey, where's Dad?" Evan asked.

"He's around here somewhere," Laurel said, and led the group toward her mother.

Joan remained seated, clearly enjoying her role as matriarch, as everyone bent to kiss her. And then, at last, Laurel lowered the baby into her arms.

"I'm your great-grandma," Joan said, staring into the baby's face. "Your daddy calls me Grandma Joan, and you can call me that, too." She looked back at Evan. "Is that okay?"

"Of course, Grandma Joan."

"She's perfect. And I think she looks just like you."

Evan and Samara exchanged a look, and Laurel was pretty sure they had already shared a private joke about how everyone on his side thought the baby looked like him, while everyone on her side insisted she was a clone of her mother.

The cantor approached and told Laurel they should probably get started soon.

"Of course," Laurel said, and looked around. "Has anyone seen Doug?"

She excused herself and went to search for him, weaving in and out of the clots of guests.

"Everything okay?" Monica asked, when she saw Laurel wandering around.

"We're ready to start but I can't find Doug."

"You go change and I'll find him," Monica said.

Laurel thanked her and went into the house and up to her bedroom, which had the window air conditioner blasting, as she had anticipated needing to cool off before slipping into her gown.

She took off her silver dress and put it on the hanger, then sat on her bed, letting her flesh dry and chill. She listened to the sounds of the caterers tromping around in her kitchen, as well as the voices of the guests in the backyard, as the DJ played soft jazz. Laurel closed her eyes and went over her vows, which she already had well memorized. She murmured them out loud now, just to be sure she wouldn't freeze in front of the crowd. Or choke with emotion. She had no idea what Doug planned to say, as they agreed to keep their vows a secret until the ceremony, but she anticipated a mix of jokes and sentimentality. She was comforted to know that if she couldn't hold back tears, the guests would weep right along with her.

She went to the bathroom to touch up her makeup, and then, at last, stepped into the beautiful gown. It looked just as sublime as it had in the Great Neck boutique. She had made the right choice.

Laurel was on the edge of the bed, strapping on her new pewter sandals, when there was a knock on the door.

"Laurel?" Monica's voice called.

"Come in."

The door swung open and Monica looked flushed. "I can't find him," she said.

"What?"

"I can't find Doug," Monica repeated. "I looked every-where."

"Did you check the bathroom?"

"Every room in the house. And I called his cell, but there was no answer."

"Well, he has to be *somewhere*," Laurel insisted. "Did you check the basement? The garage?"

"Honey," Monica said, and the look on her face was so sad and sorrowful and sympathetic, Laurel wanted to scream.

"Don't even," Laurel said. "He's here. Did you look out front?"

"No, but—"

"Well, then, that's where he is." She stood and hitched up her gown, determined to find him herself. She went down the stairs, through the living room and out the front door, with Monica following behind as she received quizzical stares from the catering staff.

Laurel stood at the top of the front steps looking left and right at all the parked cars up and down the block, like beads on a chain.

Holding up her gown to keep the hem clean, she walked down the stairs in her high heels. Monica supported her elbow to steady her. At the end of the driveway, Laurel peered into the parked cars to see if there was any sign of movement inside.

At last, she noticed a shiny black sedan across the street. Behind the wheel sat a woman with glossy hair. Laurel recognized the profile—it was KathyAnn. And there, in the passenger seat, was Doug.

"Stay here. Please," Laurel said to Monica, and crossed the street.

Doug and KathyAnn were so engrossed in conversation, they didn't notice her approaching. When she knocked on the passenger side window, Doug startled before rolling it down.

"Laurel!" he said, as if she were the last person he expected to see.

"What's going on?" she asked, shooting a glance at KathyAnn before looking back at Doug. "You have to come into the backyard. We're ready to begin."

Doug shook his head, tears rolling down his face. "I can't," he said.

"What do you mean you can't?" She looked back at the woman, who glanced away, avoiding eye contact.

"I can't do it," Doug said. "I can't go through with the vow renewal."

"What are you saying?" she demanded.

"I'm sorry, Laurel," Doug said, and covered his face with his hands. Then he looked back at her, his eyes bloodshot from crying. "I'm in love with KathyAnn."

51

After Doug and KathyAnn drove off, there was nothing left for Laurel to do but explain to the guests that there would be no ceremony. Or rather, nothing left for Monica to do, as Laurel hid in her bedroom, weeping, while Evan and Samara tried to comfort her.

Doug moved in with KathyAnn that very day. And for the first time in her life, Laurel was alone.

Three months later, she opened her front door to another life-altering event, though this one had been expected and carefully planned. It was Monica, coming by to leave Frida in her care. The movers had come to Monica's condo the day before, and now her car was packed for her own journey all the way from Nassau County, New York, to Austin, Texas, where she would begin her next chapter.

"I promise I'll take good care of her," Laurel said, accept-

ing the dog from her friend's arms. She nearly choked on the
bitter sweetness of the moment, joyful to be holding Frida,
but bereft over losing her best friend only months after her
husband moved out.

They had all warned her about the loneliness—Monica,
her mother, even Eleanor. But no one had explained the pain
of feeling hollowed, as if everything that mattered had been
scooped from her core. It was a confusing emotion, and Laurel tried to make sense of it. She felt like she was missing more
than Doug, but she could never quite put her finger on what
else she had lost.

"I bet you're glad to have a roommate," Monica said.

Laurel kissed the dog's soft head. "Of course." She studied
her friend's sad face. "Are you all right?"

Monica nodded. "Are *you?*"

Laurel gave a soft laugh, shaking her head. "Not even a
little."

"I know this is hard to hear, but I think you're doing great."

Laurel thanked her, but she wasn't convinced. After Doug
left—trading her in for a woman as willing to dote on him
as she had once been—Laurel had spent a full week in tears.
She called him no less than four times, begging him to come
home. It was pitiful. When at last it was clear she was wasting
her time, Laurel finally moved on. Or at least, went through
the motions of moving on.

Because even as she put the house on the market, Laurel
felt sure, deep in her gut, that Doug would come back to her.
She just had to make it through this period of atonement—
her penance for what she'd nearly done to him. Laurel wasn't
particularly religious, and had certainly never believed in a
vengeful God, but this felt like punishment, and she would
suffer through.

But it was okay, because she was certain the thing with

KathyAnn wasn't real. It was a flirtation. A late midlife crisis triggered by a brush with death. A reaction to an evolving marriage. One day he would awaken, just as Laurel had, and realize their bond was inseparable.

Meanwhile, she had kept herself busy, trying to hold on to hope and keep the grief at bay. Getting the house ready to go on the market was an enormous job, as every corner needed to be scrubbed, and decades' worth of clothes, files, books, kitchenware, toiletries, knickknacks, appliances, linens, keepsakes, tools, craft supplies, and thousands of other things sorted through and, for the most part, discarded. Once in a while, something triggered a memory. A photo of five-year-old Evan in his soccer uniform, Doug standing behind him with a paternal hand on his shoulder. The box of cards Laurel and Doug had saved from their wedding day thirty years ago—all those people wishing them a lifetime of happiness. The packets of wildflower seeds Doug never got around to planting but wouldn't let her throw away. Any one of these memory triggers could pummel her so hard she would slither to the floor in tears. *He's coming back,* she repeated like a mantra. *He's coming back.*

Now, nearly everything she owned was in boxes, as the house had been sold to a young couple eager to move in quickly, as the new school year had already begun. Laurel would soon be closing on a condo a lot like the one Monica was moving out of, but farther east and sunnier, with a southern exposure. The timing wasn't perfect, as there was a gap of a month before she would be able to take possession of it. So all her things would be going into storage, while she spent the intervening weeks at her mother's house.

She didn't believe the divorce would actually happen, but if it did, they would be splitting everything fifty-fifty, leaving her with a decent little nest egg once they closed on the house.

Naturally, she'd thought about Luke a lot these past several weeks. A few times she had nearly called him. But it didn't feel right, or fair. In her heart, her marriage was not over.

"I'm going to miss you so much," Monica said.

"Are you talking to me?" Laurel asked. "Or Frida?"

"Both." She smiled, then, and Laurel noted that the Invisalign braces were gone. She really was ready to turn the page of her life.

When they hugged goodbye for the last time, Laurel wept and wept, though she sensed she wasn't yet feeling the full force of her grief. She knew from experience that it would come in discrete waves, when she least expected it.

Laurel decorated her condo as she had always dreamed she would, in shades of aquamarine and sand. It was airy and bright, with an open floor plan and a white kitchen. Even though she had the master bedroom to herself, she had bought a king-size bed—comfortable and expensive—an extravagance she had justified by telling herself nothing was more important than a good night's sleep. Here, in her private space, she added splashes of pink, and she especially loved the shell-colored velvet side chair, tufted and proud.

There were moments when it occurred to her that Doug would never come back, and these filled her with a panic. How could she possibly live like this, alone, for the rest of her life? Then she would hug Frida, and tell herself it wasn't true. Of course he would come back. After all, they had become friends over these past few months, texting with news and updates. Sometimes, he even wrote to ask Laurel for advice. Once, he called to find out where the farmer's market was—the one where she had found those crisp apples and softball-sized bell peppers. And they had stayed on the phone for nearly forty minutes, reminiscing about that vacation in the Berkshires where Evan had run smack into a fence, somehow managing to get such a large gash on his chin they had to find an emergency room where he could get stitches. Laurel asked if he knew the kids were planning a trip to New York at the end of January, as Samara's best friend was getting married in Manhattan. He hadn't heard, but was delighted.

"I didn't get to meet the baby last time," he said.

"I know," she responded, dropping the conversation like a rock. She did not want to revisit that memory.

Laurel continued working at Whole Foods, impressing the manager with her skills and diligence. Eventually, she'd be promoted to manager herself. It was, she felt, inevitable. Meanwhile, she was happy there, enjoying most of her co-workers, and even some of the regular customers. Sometimes she thought she saw Luke wandering the aisles, but it was always another tall Black man with elegant posture.

He was in her thoughts more and more these days, as she continued wrestling with the idea of contacting him. Some days, she convinced herself she deserved the happiness of a relationship with him, especially when she remembered that kiss, down on the dock by that seafood restaurant. The problem was that it felt like admitting defeat with Doug. It was almost a superstition, this reluctance to reach out to Luke. It was as if that one call would seal her fate, assuring that Doug would never return. She couldn't let that happen.

52

On a bright and cold January morning, Evan, Samara, and Grace arrived for a visit, blowing in like a blizzard to fill Laurel's condo with noise and movement, and a shocking quantity of jackets and suitcases and bags and totes and equipment. There was a stroller, a car seat, a bouncy seat, a pack-and-play, a diaper bag and, it seemed, a thousand other essentials.

"Sorry about all this," Evan said with a laugh. "We're like an invading army."

Laurel laughed, too, recalling what it was like to travel with a baby. There was always so much to pack, so much to remember.

"Well, I'm happy to surrender," she said, holding her hands out for her granddaughter.

Grace was almost twenty pounds now, with chubby legs and a head full of soft dark curls. Laurel was quite certain a more beautiful baby had never been born. She parked the child on her hip and introduced her to Frida. Grace was enthused, Frida not so much. The poor little dog was terrified, yet curious, backing up and yipping, then stepping forward and backing up again.

"Shh, it's okay, girl," Laurel said gently, and waited for the dog to stop barking. When she did, Laurel pulled a treat from her pocket as a reward. Eventually, Frida calmed down, and they settled into the living room, to await the other lunch guests—Doug and KathyAnn.

It had taken all of Laurel's strength to invite them, and she was braced for a stormy afternoon. Or maybe not, she told herself. Maybe the joy of passing Grace from one to the other would supersede everything, filling the space with warmth and love.

She had invited her mother, as well, but Joan had plans with a group of women she now played mah-jongg with every Wednesday. "I'll come by afterward," she promised.

The change in Laurel's mother over the past year had been significant. Independent now, Joan did her own marketing, getting around via Uber. Her obsessive need to have a doll with her when she left the house hadn't completely abated, but it had been tamed to a manageable little keychain in the shape of a naked Wishnik troll with bright yellow hair.

For Laurel, it had been a painful adjustment, knowing her mother no longer needed her. But they had settled into an easy friendship—with a weekly lunch date and even occasional dinners. It gave them a chance to get to know one another in a way they hadn't in so many years. In fact, her mother had even offered a bit of wisdom that finally helped Laurel understand why she had felt so hollowed out after Doug left.

"Sweetheart," Joan had said, "the hardest thing about being alone is knowing you're no longer needed. But you get used to it, you know. And after a while, you don't even miss it."

Laurel nodded, amazed that her mother had zeroed in on why she had felt so very gutted. She wasn't sure she would ever exactly get used to it, but she was glad to at least understand the cause of the brittle pain.

When the baby got hungry, Laurel handed her to Samara, who made herself comfortable on the sofa. She deftly lifted her blouse and nursed as if she'd been doing it for a lifetime. Watching the baby suckle, Laurel recalled that distinct feeling in her own breasts, when her milk let down. Now, the memory was like a sweet ghost.

She set about getting lunch ready, pulling items from the refrigerator. When the doorbell rang, she looked at the clock—they were right on time.

"Can you get that?" she said to Evan, as she wiped her hands on a dish towel. Laurel smoothed out her sweater and followed him toward the door. There was Doug, looking handsome, though not quite as trim as he had the day he left her. Laurel glanced past him into the hallway, but KathyAnn was nowhere in sight.

"She couldn't make it," he explained, and left it at that.

Laurel was relieved. The day would be so much easier without her presence.

She set up the lunch as a buffet on her kitchen counter—a large salad as well as sandwiches and a plate of lean sliced turkey breast she had bought specifically for KathyAnn, to keep her from making any judgmental comments.

They brought their full plates to the table, and Grace was inserted into a portable high chair that attached to it. The adults talked and laughed, while the baby made a mess of herself, the table, and the floor. Samara apologized repeatedly and Laurel told her not to worry about it.

"Frida thinks Grace is the best thing that ever happened to

her," Evan observed, and Laurel looked down to see the dog greedily inhaling everything that had been dropped.

Doug bent to look under the table, as well. "If you like turkey this much," he said to the dog, "wait till you try pastrami."

Several times during the meal, Laurel looked up to catch Doug's eye. He would smile at her then, and she would smile back. They were being such adults about this whole thing.

After lunch, as Evan and Samara set up the pack-and-play in the spare bedroom to put Grace down for a nap, Laurel began clearing the table. Doug helped, following her into the kitchen. She set down a stack of plates next to the sink, and turned to see Doug loading glasses carefully into the dishwasher.

"Your place is beautiful," he said as he worked.

Laurel blinked at the miracle before her. Doug was cleaning up...without being asked.

"Thank you," she blurted, then added, "You don't have to do that."

"I don't mind."

She'd noticed he'd eaten a carb-free lunch, bypassing the sandwiches for salad and turkey. But now he grabbed a chocolate chip cookie from a platter she planned to put out later.

"I need to tell you something," he said, biting the cookie over the counter so the crumbs wouldn't fall on the floor. Laurel was impressed. KathyAnn might not have been able to completely break his carb addiction, but she had taught him not to make a mess.

"What is it?" Laurel asked.

Doug popped the last bite of the cookie into his mouth, and dusted his hands as he chewed and swallowed. "KathyAnn and I aren't together anymore."

Laurel stared at him, startled by the announcement. Her pulse quickened as she braced herself for what might come next. Was this the conversation she had been waiting for? She wiped her own hands.

"I had no idea," she said. "Are you okay?"

He nodded. "The whole thing was such a mistake."

Yes! she wanted to say. *Of course it was! We belong together. You and me!* But she waited, practically holding her breath.

"I've been staying with Abby the past two weeks," he went on. "Trying to figure out what I want to do."

"I'm sorry," she offered. "I know you must feel—"

"No, don't," he said. "I'm the one who's sorry. I never should have left you, Laurel. Looking back... I don't know. It seems like momentary madness. Do you think you could ever forgive me for that?"

Laurel considered her own temporary madness. All those months she had colluded with Charlie to hasten Doug's death. Now, it seemed like a disease she had contracted and recovered from.

Ironically, it was Charlie who had died. Laurel got the news from her old Trader Joe's boss, Tammy. Just about a month ago—in the middle of the Christmas rush—they had run into each other at the mall. Tammy said that Charlie had come in one day looking pale and tired. She told him to take the day off, and the next thing she knew he collapsed in the break room of an apparent heart attack.

"Everybody loved that dear old guy," Tammy had said, clucking.

The dear old guy, Laurel thought, who murdered his wife and tried to get Laurel to murder her husband. But she just said, "They sure did."

Now, thinking about how close she had come to achieving her goal, Laurel could hardly believe Doug was the one begging forgiveness.

"I know I have some nerve asking this," he continued.

"But do you think you might ever take me back? I miss you so much. And I need you." He paused, his eyes going moist. "I never realized how much I need you. I'm sorry it took me all this time to understand that."

Need. There was that word again. She looked out over the open floor plan of her apartment—this space of her own she had dreamed about for so long. She thought about that conversation with her mother, even as she tried to picture Doug moving in, sharing her bed, taking up half the closet. And somehow, it seemed wrong. This was her place, not his. There was no room for him here, was there?

She searched for that hollow ache inside of her, and discovered the pain was gone. It had happened so slowly she hadn't noticed. And now, she realized she actually liked being alone. And more importantly, she liked knowing that no one needed her. She was unburdened. She was...free.

"Babe," Doug pleaded, "look at me."

She complied, and saw so much regret in his face. He really was sorry, and so very desperate to have her back. It would be easy, of course, to say yes, to extinguish this glow of freedom and absorb his pain. And she could spend the rest of her life taking care of him, trying to make up for what she had meant to do. And maybe she deserved that.

"What do you think?" he pressed. "Should we give this another shot?"

Laurel closed her eyes, imagining growing old with Doug. Maybe not here, in this condo, but elsewhere. It wasn't hard to conjure. She knew every beat of that song. Envisioning life without him was more difficult, because it could play out in so many different ways. She might be with Luke, happy and fulfilled. Or she might be alone. When she opened her eyes, she realized she would be okay either way.

And so would Doug. In fact, he would probably find another woman who would take care of him just as she had for all those years. Someone who didn't mind if he had a chocolate chip cookie now and then. Someone who could put herself last without feeling oppressed.

"You don't have to answer right now," Doug said.

Laurel glanced through the living room at the glass door leading to the terrace. The afternoon sun flooded the space, and Frida slept in a heap where the light created an intense rectangle of warmth. Soon, the old dog would be gone, and Laurel would once again wrestle with the grief of loss. But whether she did it alone or with a man at her side, she would get past it. The revelation filled her. Or rather, it emptied her, erasing the nagging anxiety that had been her companion for as long as she could remember. In its place was a blank space she could fill with her very own colors. There was, she realized, a word for this clean expanse in her psyche. Peace.

Laurel took a deep breath and told Doug she loved him, but she would not be taking him back.

Then she picked up the sponge, and wiped away his crumbs.

★ ★ ★ ★ ★

Acknowledgments

When I first got the idea for a dark comedy about a woman who pines for her husband's death, I was excited but also scared. Could I really pull it off? Would anyone want to read it?

And what would my husband think?

I'll be forever grateful to my wise and wonderful agent, Annelise Robey, for her enthusiasm and encouragement. She was certain I could do it and assured me the story would be relatable to nearly anyone who lived through the pandemic in close quarters with a significant other.

I'm also grateful to my editor, the sagacious Kathy Sagan, who courageously championed the book and gave such excellent editorial direction. She knew exactly how to make this novel stronger, and her guidance has been invaluable. I'm lucky to have such a smart and patient editor.

Extra thanks to all the incredible folks at MIRA Books and

Jane Rotrosen for working so tirelessly to keep everything humming through such difficult times.

Of course, I would be nowhere without my beta readers. To my dear and funny friend Saralee Rosenberg, who gave the book a careful read and, as always, offered such insightful advice, I am so thankful. And to my incredibly generous friends who offered their valuable time and expertise to make the book richer and more authentic, a million thanks. Where would I be without Charlie and Barb (aka Dr. Charles Goldberg and Dr. Barbara Drye) and the astute Myka Hanson? Whoosh, I am a lucky gal!

To all the other writer friends whose light shined like the North Star, I give profound thanks. These include Susan Henderson, Alix Strauss, David Henry Sterry, Arielle Eckstut, Amy Ferris, Caroline Leavitt, and many others.

I also want to acknowledge my kids, Max, Ethan, and Rook, for grounding me with humor, love, and rock-solid goodness. And to the rock himself, who never once complained about the subject of this book, the greatest thanks of all. Mike, I love you.